CHOSEN BY THE VAMPIRE

OMNIBUS

ATLAS ROSE

"You do want to be chosen by us, don't you?" The faint scent of blood wafted in the air.

The frigid touch of his finger trailed down my arm before he leaned in and pressed those lips to my shoulder. I could almost feel the tips of his fangs on my skin, almost feel the commanding touch of his fingers delving under my skirt.

Almost *feel his body trapping mine.*

I wanted him. I *hated* him.

Hated myself because of it.

They're sinful.

Beautiful.

Deadly.

And more dangerous than the wolves who hunt us in the woods.

Three Vampires rule our world.

And now I find myself in their clutches.

BOOK ONE

PROLOGUE

"Y ou understand what you have to do?" the Vampire whispered from the shadows.

I closed my eyes, refusing to answer...*refusing to see*.

Sinful.

Deadly.

The words raced through my mind as his icy breath spilled down the hollow of my neck, making me tremble.

He was close...*too close.*

I couldn't turn my head, couldn't look into the shadows.

I already knew what I'd find.

Cold, stony, moonlight-kissed skin, and intense eyes that seemed to stare into my soul. But it was his mouth that captivated me. White fangs peeking from blood-red lips as he whispered commands like the devil on my shoulder.

But there was no angel on the other side ready to save me. There was just the darkness...just the *need*. I clamped my legs tighter, stilling the flare of heat that bloomed like a deadly rose between my thighs.

"Open your eyes, Asena. Look at him."

I was helpless to defy him, *drowning in a sea of desire.* But hate swirled around me, *and inside me,* like a tornado filled with the terror of my past. I allowed that hate to consume me, battling the flames of unwanted desire that both disgusted me and intrigued me in equal parts.

Still, I obeyed...and opened my eyes.

My victim stepped through the open doors from a marble patio outside and into the ballroom, following three of his friends into the masquerade ball. Shy, quiet, his brown eyes glittered as he scanned the room and our gazes connected. A hint of a smile as he stared at me, and then a slow tilt of his head, an acknowledgement of my presence.

He stilled, and electricity charged through me like a live wire.

"He looks as awkward as you do," Cassian murmured in my ear. "Tell me how you'll seduce him."

Music swirled all around me, soft music, seductive music. The beat mirroring the panicked thudding of my heart.

Seduce him.

That was the game. *Their game.* I swallowed the urge to tremble. I would not let Cassian scare me, not let him win. The mortal male broke my gaze and searched for his companions. He was good looking, with a ramrod-straight spine and relaxed shoulders. Wealthy. That's what he looked like, kind, careful and well to do.

"Tell me how you'll walk toward him. How you'll give him a hint of a smile," the monster in the dark murmured. "How you'll brush past him just enough for him to be ensnared by the scent of your perfume...and how, when he turns toward you, you'll do the same and smile, that sweet, *innocent,* seductive smile. How you'll step backwards, drawing him closer and closer and you'll angle your body so his gaze will be drawn by the swell of your breasts. How you'll lead him into the darkness and press your spine against the wall, pretending he's the one who trapped you, when it'll be the other way around. How you'll lean close and whisper into his ear, just so he can look into the plunging neckline of your gown. How you'll make the poor sap blush with the whisper of your desire, how his body will harden and quake and that look of hunger will consume him."

I swallowed the bitter tang of acid in the back of my throat. "I won't. I won't do it. I *can't*."

"Oh, you'll do it," the beast growled. "Or I'll puncture his vein in the middle of the dance floor. I'll spray your perfect sky blue dress with the warmth of his life, and I'll make you watch while I drain him dry. You *will* do this, Asena. You will if you want to save him...*and if you want to be chosen*."

He moved closer, just an inch--but it was enough.

Enough to snatch my attention and trigger my fear.

"You do want to be chosen by us, don't you?" The faint scent of blood wafted in the air.

Blood and death...*and sex.*

The frigid touch of his finger trailed down my arm before he leaned in and pressed those lips to my shoulder. I never flinched, never moved. I was frozen with fear, *and excitement.*

My body betrayed me, trembling, *wanting.* I could almost feel the tips of his fangs on my skin, almost feel the commanding touch of his fingers delving under my skirt.

Almost *feel his body trapping mine.* I wanted him. I *hated* him. *Hated myself* because of it.

I wanted to be used by him. I wanted to be taken by them all, every savage thrust, every brutal bite.

They were beasts...*monsters.* They were cruel and uncaring, and promised eternity in the slide of their tongue and the hardness of their desire.

"I will make you mine, Asena," Cassian whispered. "I will lash those wrists to the headboard of my bed and ride that sweet body until you quake with fever, and beg for release. I will show you all the sins of this mortal world and all the rapture of mine, and you will know what it's like to be *chosen*. You will know what it's like to be *owned by us.*"

My breath caught, and my pulse raced. To be owned by all of them. I glanced toward the others, knowing where they were by instinct alone...*or was it need?* Lorcan stood in the shadows near the entrance, watching the men as they stepped inside--like a moth to a flame.

We were that flame.

I skimmed the darkness to the right, where the glow of the fire didn't reach, and felt a flicker of fear. Arkyn was back there, watching everything, deciding which one of us passed the test. He was the one I was truly afraid of. He was savage and calculated. He was the one Lorcan and Cassian obeyed.

Vampire.

They were almost as dangerous as the Wolves.

Cassian would kill this mortal if I didn't seduce him. He'd make good on his promise to this mortal man...*and to me.* He'd make me stand there and watch while the spark ebbed in the man's eyes, he'd tear my dress from my body and bathe me in the man's blood. He didn't care who watched...only about making me bend to his will.

"I'm waiting," he whispered. "The dance is almost over...and his time in this world is almost done."

Ten other women were imprisoned in this castle in the middle of the woods, they moved around me now. Some meek and terrified, casting careful glances my way, and others stalking the mortal men who came here tonight like prey. They never looked at me, or cared.

They were beautiful. Long, stunning dresses and plunging necklines. Lorcan liked them in bold colors, daring midnight blue, shimmering black, and drenched, blood red. But I wasn't dressed like them. No, I was different.

I skimmed my hand along the pale blue chiffon skirt and

lifted my hand. My fingers trembled, dancing in the air as I touched my lips.

"I can't do this," I whispered.

"Can and *will*," he commanded. "You know what happens if you don't. Pass this test, Asena. Pass it *or else.*"

I shuddered at the words. I'd been forced here just like all the others, but there was one difference between us. *I knew who these fanged monsters were.*

Please....

Cassian's voice filled my mind. With a surge of desperation and terror, I clenched my fist around the perfect blue chiffon, lifted my gaze to the mortal man standing all alone and took a step. He lifted his head at the movement, and his eyes widened with surprise.

My lips curled on their own, the smile yearning and playful as Cassian had urged.

That's the way, Asena...

I'll make you mine yet.

wo Weeks before

"Are you ready for this?" Jacob grabbed my hand. "You can back out, it's not too late. You can take longer to think about this. Make a better plan."

Make a better plan?

I stilled, sucked in an icy breath, and slid my hand from his. "*Revenge* has always been the plan, Jacob. You've known this for the last eleven years."

It's been your plan. Not mine.

The words raged in his eyes. He was hurt. Betrayed. Already pining in my absence. I licked my lips and tried again, this time making my voice a little less cutting. "I've waited a long time for a chance like this, and there won't be another..."

He turned from me, his fists clenched by his side, corded muscles in his arms trembling. He took a step away, as though to leave me behind, his voice a growl. "You know what they do to girls like you, don't you? You know they bite them...they seduce them...they...*fuck* them."

My breath caught with the word.

He'd never spoken like that to me before, never used *those* kinds of words.

"In case you haven't noticed, I'm not a little girl anymore."

He turned toward me. Hate raged in his eyes, still, he lowered his gaze in a slow slide along my body. "I *have* noticed, that's why I don't want you to go. They'll ruin you...they'll change you. They'll take your innocence and turn it into something sick and depraved. I've heard the stories, and I've seen the girls when those Vampires are done with them. I've seen how they crave them, like a drug they can't get enough of. They'll do the same to you."

"No, they won't. I'm going for one reason, and one reason only...to drive a stake through their hearts."

The words sank deep, stilling the shake in my hands. The sky was brighter in the distance. Midnight blue blended to amber with the fires already blazing in the middle of town. They'd burned earlier tonight, hungry licks of fire warding off the beasts in the dark.

A lone howl cut through the night, sending goosebumps racing across my skin. The townspeople were scared tonight, and they had good reason to worry.

Wolves flanked the streets, and stole our children. Two were taken last night...one the night before. So we pledged our loyalty to the Vampires. Three infernal beasts who invaded our towns with their guards. We pledged with our honor to the Sinful...still, it wasn't enough.

I'd waited eleven years for this plan. I smoothed down my dress and watched Jacob take a step until he towered over me.

There was a second when I thought he'd say something, where he'd beg and plead. Instead, he leaned close and brushed his lips across my cheek and slid his hands to my waist. "Please,

Asena. You trust too easily, and they'll hurt you. Don't go," he murmured, and yanked me closer.

His lips were on mine in an instant, bruising my mouth as he bowed my spine. I couldn't think, couldn't react. My thoughts were a flurry as he drew me harder against his body.

Then he broke away. I sucked in hard breaths, trying to understand what just happened. "Jacob."

Sparks of hope flared in his eyes.

"I have to," I answered.

I tried to swallow the lump in my throat and stepped away from him. My pulse was pounding inside my head. Panicked thoughts moved in, threatening to derail the entire thing. The flare of hope in his eyes hardened to stone. "You're leaving me...for what? Hate and bloodshed, or maybe you just want to leave? Is that it, Asena? Are you that blinded by your own need to get away from this town...or is it me you're running from?"

"Jacob." I murmured his name once more, only this time, a heaviness consumed me.

Is it worth it? All the heartache and the terror. Is it worth leaving all of this behind?

I stepped away from the stony wall of my home and felt the ache move deep. I had a life here, had a home here, one that came with so many memories. But the only ones I could remember were the ones where I built this person...carefully constructed, immaculately created to be everything these monsters wanted.

Now was my chance.

I left Jacob behind, just like I left everything behind. Guilt weighed down my steps as I walked along the footpath of my family home and out through the open gate, taking one last look at the pathetic garden surrounding the front of the house.

The Vampires killed my family, leaving a nine-year-old girl alone in the world.

I'd done my best after losing them, as much as a young girl

could. I'd tended the leaking roof and fixed the windows when they swelled with the rains and became stuck.

I scrubbed and cleaned my home until it was spotless, and then went to work in Mrs. Orion's haberdashery to afford food and protection. Protection everyone paid for. Everyone but me. I held onto the money, shaking my head when the Sinful guards came.

I knew not paying them was dangerous, a debt with the Vampires was not a debt you wanted. Still, I played the poor orphan, answering the door with fake tears and desperation time and time again.

I knew what was coming.

A chance to reclaim their debt...

They'd come for me, I'd always known they would. The Sinful guards were sending men into the towns, mercenaries who stole young women as payment for a debt their families could never repay and take them to a place where the Sinful were waiting. I lifted my gaze to the full moon in the sky. I could feel them close. Don't ask me how, I just did.

A howl came once more, this time further in the distance. The Wolves were growing restless, hunting in packs. So the fires burned a little higher.

This world was ruled by beasts, one just as cruel and ruthless as the other.

Vampires and Lycans.

Memories flashed inside my head. Bodies lying in the darkness. My mother...and father, blood cooling under them. Terror rose in the back of my throat, just as it had that night.

I cut across our street to the main road leading into the town. Fires burned all around us, the pyres stacked high. Every day the woodsmen would carve and chop enough to carry us through the night.

But that wasn't the protection we paid for...protection that barely kept the other beasts at bay, and paid for in money and flesh. I hated the Sinful more than I hated anything in my life.

They said it was better the devil you knew.

No one knew them better than me.

Windows were alight in the houses that lined both sides of the streets. Families busy with their dinner and children. I risked a glance over my shoulder to the darkened front yard of my home.

Jacob was gone, not that I expected him to stand there to watch me forever. But the darkened front yard speared an ache through my chest. He'd been my best friend, my rock. The one I turned to when I first came up with a plan to get revenge.

I knew what this was doing to him...*what I was doing to him.* Still, there was no other way. He had to see that.

The roar of the fires grew louder the closer I came to the town. I'd been careful, *very* careful. No one suspected I was hunting the beast paid to protect us. Not with the careful questions to the old woman in the hills. The one who knew the Sinful best of all.

I'd sat with her for hours, listening to who the Sinful really were and what they wanted. She'd been their housekeeper for a time, tending to their house...a castle in the middle of nowhere. She said they'd been cold, and detached, and merciless. She told me of the many parties they hosted. The endless wine...and the endless mortal women...an unrelenting parade of degradation and filth.

I shuddered as her words filled me, and dragged the cloak higher around my shoulders. The sound of my boots echoed behind me as I walked into the heart of the town. I had a plan...this might be my last chance...*my only chance.*

The red ribbon of my cloak flapped against my throat with a gust of wind. I fought the need to watch the shadows. Instead, I kept my head down, grabbed the crimson tie, and kept walking.

Footsteps sounded behind me, faint at first. I slowed and

risked a glance over my shoulder at the sound, before I hurried toward Mrs. Orion's. But the sound came once more, this time closer…

My pulse sped, mirroring my steps.

Shadows blurred at my right as I passed Olden's Grocery and lifted my gaze to the darkened doors in the distance. The haberdashery's windows glinted orange with the fire. I reached into my pocket, fingers skimming the cold metal keys, before a hand grasped my arm from behind.

"Nice night for a walk," a man growled against my ear.

I spun, panic rising, and met savage brown eyes. The male met my stare and then dropped his gaze to the crimson ribbon around my neck. There was a flicker of something in his eyes…*regret?*

"*No!*" I shook my head, clenching my jaw, and tried to yank free. "Get away from me."

Those brown eyes darkened, muscles flared along his jaw. "You're young," he growled. "I have a daughter your age."

Fear spiked, ramming through my chest. I sucked in a breath and spun. Movement came from the street in the distance, a couple strolled arm in arm. They turned at the last minute as I lunged, driving my hand into the air.

But there was no scream, nothing but a muffled moan as he slammed his hand over my mouth and dragged me backwards. The couple watched it all with resignation in their eyes as I thrashed and fought. I saw it all…*it's the will of the Vampires* their wide eyes screamed. The woman clutched her partner, and held on for dear life as I dragged my heels in the dirt, tearing my head from side to side.

"For Christ's sake," my attacker snarled. "Stop it…stop fighting."

I kicked harder, swinging my hand through the air to beat his head. His head snapped to the side with a *slap*. The flare of anger replaced guilt. The shift was sudden in his eyes as he shoved a hand into his pocket and dragged a folded piece of fabric free.

"Didn't want to do it this way..." he snapped, wrestling me into the shadows. "But you've left me no choice."

The slosh of liquid in the bottle came before he shoved the cloth against my face. The sharp stench of something foul invaded my nose. I shoved and thrashed, punching his hand as I tried to scream.

But there was nothing but the muffled sound of my screams, nothing but the bitterness in my nose invading my lungs, and suddenly, the world around me grayed.

Darkness moved in.

Darkness and panic.

And I knew no more.

2

Frigid air slid over my skin, leaving me trembling.

I curled my legs to my chest and dared to open my eyes. Darkness surrounded me. I sucked in an icy breath and unfurled my fingers, inching them higher until I reached my temples.

A dull throb cut through my head as I opened my eyes. I tried to remember...tried to think. Only the past was slow to come, smothered in a dark fog.

Hinges howled as the carriage door swung back and forth from the icy breeze. Dread locked my jaw tight as the unknown covered me in shivers. What in the world? I shoved myself upright in the seat of the old carriage sitting still in a forest ruled by Lycans. Faint trickles of whatever foul liquid the man had used to knock me out lingered at the back of my throat.

Had he left me out here alone? That wasn't part of the plan. He had to kidnap and deliver me to the ceremony.

I stared outside, my heart thumping. Trees swayed in the breeze, their leaves rustling, and the heavy stench of moldy, decomposing leaves stung my nostrils each time I inhaled.

A single howl pierced the night, and I flinched forward to

reach for the door, when the sound of breaking twigs and crunching leaves came from up ahead.

My hand fell to my boot for my blade, my mind conjuring images of a bloodthirsty beast lunging at the carriage.

A shadow slipped out of the woods, and I caught my breath.

The man emerged from the shadows, fiddling with the buttons of his pants, when he glanced up, meeting my gaze. He looked less savage in the moonlight, less hard and brutal...now he looked like any other man. "Thank heaven, you're finally awake."

He rushed over, his gaze swinging left and right, watching for predators, as he should in these woods. No one was safe out here, where monsters lived and hunted us humans.

"Is this the place?" I pushed the door wider and stepped outside, my boots cushioned by the softened soil. The red ribbon around my neck flapped in my face, and I tucked it under my coat as I pulled the collar tighter around me.

"You sure you want to do this?" Concern pinched his features, but he didn't know me, didn't know I'd been ready to do this for the past eleven years. All he saw was a young girl who reminded him of his daughter.

I nodded and glanced to the orange glow amid the trees up ahead. "We need to hurry," I whispered. He gripped my arm and we moved faster, him taking charge.

Smart thinking, in case guards noticed we weren't playing this stupid kidnapping game correctly.

The old woman in the hills had told me the Sinful loved games to keep their boredom at bay. Her words terrified me, because it meant the Sinful had nothing to lose. A man with a purpose could be negotiated with, could have compassion. Not these vile monsters who played their wicked games for nothing more than pleasure.

We passed horse drawn carriages, left unattended, the beautiful animals snorting, hot steam rising from their nostrils.

We stepped off the main road, leaving the carriages behind, and reached a narrow trail in the forest, knotted by tree roots and low-hanging branches. Only the burning flames ahead guided our path.

Fear weighed me down with each step we took. I carried no doubts about my mission… none at all, but I couldn't push the worry away.

Whispers and soft cries reached us as we emerged from the dense woods into a small clearing. My heart thumped hard at seeing families huddled close in small pockets across the grounds. Their cries and terrified voices locked my legs in place.

Families were invited to say farewell to their daughters, knowing very well they'd likely never see them again. Not even the old woman in the hills knew what became of them. They disappeared, she explained. Gone from this world in a heartbeat. And I was about to walk into that devil's den on purpose. That reality sat like a noose around my neck.

Guards circled the perimeter, giants compared to normal men, dressed in black coats that fell to their knees, with more black underneath. Faces were stoic, but they watched everyone and everything. Step out of line, and they'd drag you somewhere in these dark, dark woods, never to be seen again. But they served a purpose beyond threatening us into submission…they kept us safe from the Lycans.

Beyond the huddles stood two fire torches, an entry to the ceremony grounds.

A drumbeat started, so loud it echoed through my soul.

One of the girls pulled from her parents' arms, squared her shoulders, and walked slowly forward. Shattered cries erupted behind her, the mother falling to her knees, devastated. The pain of her cries hurt deep inside me, and I wanted nothing more than to insist I'd take her daughter's place, but that wasn't how this worked. Every family had a debt to pay to the Sinful, and *we* were the price.

My heart sank as more girls left their families and walked forward. The steady beat of the drums grew faster, faster.

"This is it," I mumbled to myself and took a deep breath before pushing one foot in front of the other, needing to do this before my bravery buckled.

The man grasped my wrist, strong fingers holding me still. "Wait," he muttered, his voice soft and worried. "Don't trust anyone, and--"

I turned toward those heartfelt eyes that glistened with tears. His words were waiting to come out, needing to come out, but a shadow fell over us. A guard, ensuring no one stopped the girls. And I wanted to tell the man everything would be all right, but I couldn't.

Show no weakness, everyone knew. I'd play the role, appear as the perfect girl who listened to the rules, who didn't fight back. They needed to believe me.

His grasp tightened, fingers digging into my flesh, his fear painted over his face. I gave him a small smile, something reassuring to help him, then I pulled my arm free from his grip and turned away.

The sentinel stood tall, and silent, but his gaze weighed heavy on my back. I walked with pride, but on the inside, I crumbled and cried to run away, my mind insisting I'd made a terrible mistake.

But it was already too late. I wouldn't blow my cover. Not when I'd come this far for revenge for my parents.

For them, I walked tall and would play every game in this damned world until I uncovered the Sinful's weakness. Then I'd show them…. I'd show them who the real monster was.

Cries and sorrow flooded the woods as I approached the blazing torches, and further ahead, shadows swallowed the ceremony area.

A brunette walked ahead of me, her posture hunched forward. When she glanced over her shoulder to her family, tears streamed down her cheeks. She was young, so damn young. Maybe fourteen.

"D-daddy!" she sobbed uncontrollably, her shoulders shaking, and she looked ready to collapse. But in a heartbeat, she burst out of the line and made a run for the woods, her legs and arms pumping hard.

Someone screamed, and I flinched.

Two guards darted into the woods after her, so fast they were a blur, the wind shifting past me from their speed.

My feet froze on the spot, but someone nudged me in the back to keep moving.... always keep moving.

I couldn't take my eyes off the woods where the girl had vanished, panic strangling me.

Moments later, a bloodcurdling scream shattered the night.

I stumbled forward, hugging myself, my vision blurred from tears. *What had they done to her? This was my fate.. This was* my *fucking fate...*

It wasn't long before the guards returned, minus the girl. They made no sound when they returned, but one of them slipped a set of iron shackles onto his belt. My heart stuttered. I glanced at the others, scanning their belts until, I stopped. A set was missing on one of the guards' belts. Words pressed on the back of my throat to ask them where she was, what they'd done.

Her parents wailed, the sound shredding my heart. They ran into the woods to search for their little girl.

My heart collapsed, and I burned on the inside for that girl, for her family, for all of us.

I couldn't breathe, but I'd hold it together and be what the Sinful expected.

In control.

Obedient.

Quiet.

I wiped my cheeks dry with the back of my hand. Leaves crunched under my steps as I blended into the shadows, becoming one with them. My eyes squinted to make sense of what was around me, barely adjusting to the dark.

Shapes came into view--ten girls. I moved deeper, stepping into the lineup. I recognized one of the girls. Tiam shook her head, tears shining against her cheeks. Her parents owned Mrs. Orion's haberdashery where I worked, but she'd never looked my way, though I'd seen her often arguing with her parents. She once stole money from her mother's bag, but I kept my mouth shut, said nothing. I didn't want to lose my job.

A thinner girl in a flowing dress glanced over her shoulder, another sobbed, and one constantly pushed lose strands of hair from her face. The girl to my right stood with her chest sticking out, revealing so much cleavage, she might drown a small town. But she knew that to survive in this new world, she had to use any trick at her disposal.

Anything to survive the new world.

Lifting my head, my gaze landed on three silhouettes under the arch of two branches.

The night stole their features, their clothes, their eyes... giving us nothing but dark shapes who watched us. Admiring. Determining who they'd break first.

The young girl in the woods meant nothing to them. Place one foot wrong, and no mercy was shown.

My rushed breaths came out in misted form in front of my face, my arms trembled. The old woman in the hills said when I came face to face with the devil, I'd never sleep peacefully in the dark again. She was right, and this knowing crept along my spine.

These three weren't sentinels sent to keep us in check, but something darker, something menacing. Something that devoured girls like us.

They were the Sinful.

3

"Take them," the command cut through the night.

Out of the darkness they came, tall, regal...*deadly.* Moving without a sound as they stepped from the trees and out in the open. My crimson ribbon lashed the air like a whip, drawing their gaze. One broke away from the others and strode toward me, with hungry strides like a predator. His long, midnight hair lashed the air as he walked.

He was beautiful as he moved, graceful and carnal, drawing my gaze along his body. But I knew he was ugly on the inside, cold, *undead,* his heart as hollow as the rotting trunk beside us on the ground. I shifted my gaze as he neared.

"No!" one of the fathers begged, and fell to his knees in the middle of the clearing. "I beg you, let my daughter go. I'll pay...I have the money...*I'll pay.*"

"Are you not going to whimper?" the Sinful murmured as he stopped in front of me.

I never shifted my gaze toward him. Just clenched my jaw and let hate roll through me like a summer storm. I could kill him...just reach into my boot for my blade and plunge it into his chest. I'd not even blink, not even breathe.

Not even exist.

"Beg, even?" He moved closer and I caught the heady scent of him on the wind. Sweet, and pungent, like ripe cherries...*or like blood.* He smiled, and the tips of white fangs peeked out from his deep red lips. My pulse spiked in response before he turned and made his way toward the others.

Long strides consumed the distance between him and the two other bloodsuckers as they headed toward the pleading man. I was captured by the sight as the Vampire stepped into the beam of moonlight. The Vampire looked almost human, if 'human' meant he looked detached and cruel. He stopped in front of the pleading man and stared down at him.

"We provide you with protection, do we not?" Stony words rang through the night. "Have you felt safe from the Wolves? Have you been afforded the safety of my guards?"

The two other Vampires came to a stop behind him. He was the leader, that was plain to see. Shorter, mousy brown hair. A hard, strong jaw. Perfect red lips.

"They...they take from us, My Lord. They come in and help themselves to our food, to our livestock."

"And yet your heart still beats."

I shook my head, feeling the bitter breeze change direction. *Stop talking. Stop talking and get up.* White fangs shone under the moonlight as the leader of the Sinful curled his lip. "You should thank me. You should open your homes *and* your pockets whenever I demand." He leaned closer to the blubbering mortal man. "You want to be free of my rule? Go, be free. Harmond, see that this man and his family are left outside the protection line."

"What?" the fool stammered.

His eyes widened as a young woman screamed in the distance. "No! *Not my family.*"

"No, please, no!" The man shoved to his feet and swayed. "I didn't mean to offend. I didn't!"

But the Vampire was done. He just turned, giving the mortal father his back.

"You'll kill us!"

The Vampire walked away, as did the two who followed him.

"The Wolves will come and kill us all!"

I closed my eyes and felt the night sway around me. Twigs snapped under heavy boots. I wrenched open my eyes to see darkness stride forward as the Sinful guards moved, grabbing the mortal man by the arms and dragging him away.

He thrashed and yanked, but it was useless. There was no amount of fighting, or begging, or pleading that would change their minds. I held back the ache piercing through my chest at hearing his agony.

Save your energy. You'll need it.

"You *heartless animal!*" the daughter screamed as they dragged her father away.

The Vampire just stood there, staring at her and then answered, "Yes, yes, I am."

They looked almost human, perfect skin, blood-red lips. They moved like a mortal, and yet they weren't. This was why I'd come; to see these beasts as they really were.

"If anyone else would like to change their mind?" The second of the Sinful stepped closer to the line of young women and their families. "Now would be the time to speak up."

The clearing was silent as the grave.

"That's what I thought," the fanged beast growled. He jerked his gaze to the guard. "Into the carriages, *now.*"

The guards surged toward us like the tide, moving to either side of us. One grabbed my arm, his hold cruel, fingers digging into my flesh. I wrenched my gaze over my shoulder, to the mercenary I'd paid to bring me here. He stood further back, his focus locked to mine. Fear welled in his eyes. But there was no going back now. No undoing all the things that'd brought me here to this moment.

My feet were numb as the guard yanked me forward. Sticks and twigs snapped as I stumbled. The sound mingled with the cries of the others as we were hauled between towering trees toward a worn dirt trail.

Four carriages waited. Four drivers stepped to the side and opened the doors.

"In," the guard beside me snapped and pushed me forward.

I had no time to think, just to grab the railing and climb. Sobs and wails filled the air, making the horses whinny and paw the ground with their hooves.

"They'll kill us," one girl whimpered behind me as I sat on the bench seat.

She sat opposite me, shaking and shivering, while I just felt...*numb.*

Slick tears shone under the moonlight as she clutched her old, worn dress. Two more climbed into the carriage, making the space tight and confined. One girl, with deep red hair, sat opposite, while a blonde took the seat beside me. The redhead whispered prayers and wrapped her arms around herself. Her vibrant hair darkened to the color of blood as she lowered her head to the shadows and prayed.

"Don't bother," the blonde beside me spoke. She stared straight ahead, her eyes as emotionless as those who'd dragged us here. "Not even God can help us now."

"There has to be a way out of this," the redhead whimpered. "There *has* to be a way."

"This is a game to them," the words slipped from my lips. "It's *enjoyment, a chase.*"

The blonde glanced my way and nodded. "My thoughts exactly. I'm Nilsine."

"Asena," I answered.

"I'm Willa," the redhead murmured.

"Aislinn," the last captive added.

The carriage jolted, tearing a whimper from her lips. Aislinn grasped the handle, and held on while the horses settled.

"Where do you think they're taking us?" Willa stared out of the carriage into the forest.

"Nowhere good," Nilsine answered.

The door was closed and latched to the carriage, with the windows covered by black curtains throwing us into darkness. And the air seemed to smother me, the space squeezing around me.

I felt trapped.

Tight.

My breaths wouldn't come, and I pulled at the curtain, gasping for air.

Nilsine said, "You don't like small spaces, do you?"

"No." I held the curtain partially open, while Willa pulled them all open to let in the moonlight.

"Thank you." I could hear the scuff of boots outside. There'd be no escaping now. No matter how fast we ran, they'd hunt us down. We were owned by these monsters now, payment for a debt. They could kill us. They could keep us.

We were at their mercy.

The carriage surged forward once more, but this time momentum took us. Wheels crunched against rocks as the horses neighed and stamped hooves against the dirt.

The crack of the whip was followed with the urgent calls of the drivers as we pulled into the night. Fear filled the cabin, white-knuckled terror in every gaze, even Nilsine beside me let out a whimper as the carriage lurched.

I'd spent every day since I found my parents dead waiting for this moment. I'd planned and pleaded. I'd tried to find a way into their clutches. Now I was here. Trapped, just like how I'd planned. Only I'd never expected it to happen like this. I wasn't sure what to expect, but not piled into carriages and guarded from escape.

"What do you think they'll do with us?" Aislinn searched my eyes, and then Nilsine's.

You know what they do to girls like you, don't you? They bite them...they seduce them...they...fuck them.

Jacob's words rose to the surface of my mind.

I came here for revenge. Not to be anyone's victim.

Still, words failed me now. I'd heard the stories. I'd seen what they did in the woods back there, we all did. They were barbarians, without a care for human life.

And we were disposable.

The knife was in my boot. All I had to do was to get close enough. One stab of a silver blade and we'd all be free. One slice and it'd be all over. But if I failed? If the tip of my knife missed its mark...

What will they do with us?

That was a question no one wanted an answer to.

A howl cut through the night air. Shivers followed, racing along my spine. I turned my head as a blur of black raced the carriage. The thunder of paws filled my ears, or it could've been my heartbeat.

Eyes flashed silver in the night as a cry of alarm came from the driver up ahead, and was followed by the terrified whinnies of the horses.

"What is it?" Nilsine pressed against me.

I reached down, fingers trembling as I delved into my boot and yanked the silver blade free. "Wolves."

Willa whimpered and grabbed the handle as a terrifying howl of rage followed. But this was no Wolf, this was male and savage...*that was Vampire.* I leaned close to the door as something streaked past the carriage. Dark hair flowed out behind him as the Vampire lowered his head and charged. He was savage and unmerciful, hitting the Wolf head on as it lunged toward us.

But the Vampire was ready. Thrusting his boots into the

ground, he lunged, hitting the Wolf mid-flight. The beasts slammed against us, rocking the carriage off one wheel.

Willa and Aislinn cried out and clawed the seat. But I was riveted as the Vampire picked up the Wolf, threw the beast over his shoulder, and slammed him to the ground.

Rage and desperation flared in his eyes as the Vampire lifted his gaze, meeting mine as the carriage raced past, leaving them behind.

"Oh my God," Aislinn cried. "Did you see that?"

I clenched my grip around the knife and looked out the window behind us. My hair flew across my face, blurring the sight. But I was stunned. He saved us...the pounding inside my head smothered the words. "He saved me," I whispered.

"A silver knife?" Nilsine murmured, her gaze on the needle-tipped blade.

I swallowed hard and lifted my foot, sliding it back into the crease made especially for the weapon. "For protection," I answered.

"Sure it is." She slid back on the seat.

I thought about that while listening to the sound of hooves and the roar of the drivers as they cracked their whips, and the panicked thunder of my heart filled my head. Aislinn hugged herself, Willa prayed. But Nilsine was silent, staring at her feet as though she tried to figure out what she'd do with the information I'd given her.

Would she betray me?

Would she offer to help?

I didn't know. All I could do was wait and hope.

Memories drifted to the surface, happier times with Mom and Dad, and Jacob. But I didn't linger in the warmth of their love. Instead, I pulled away into the cold and the dark. I was hollow now, my chest as empty of love and life as these beasts who claimed us tonight. I stared into the darkness as we rushed past and listened to the thunder of hooves...and *waited*.

Trees whipped past us. I inched closer to the window and watched the moon rise in the sky, and then disappear across to the other side, when I was jolted forward and the thundering cry of *"Whoa there!"* came from the first carriage up ahead.

The roar carried, tearing along each of the hurtling coaches before I slammed backwards, and we slowed.

Aislinn and Willa cried out, gripping the bar as they slid out of their seats. But Nilsine gripped the door, staring out the window before she turned her head. "Look."

I knew where the moon had gone now, and it wasn't to trail behind us somewhere overhead. It was to forsake us and instead, linger above an expansive castle that appeared from the belly of a forest.

"Where the fuck are we?" Nilsine glanced my way.

We were a long way from anything, that's where we were.

The carriage veered around a sweeping drive and slowed once more. Two towering sconces burned at the entrance of the castle grounds, tall amber flames stretching up into the night as though somehow these lifeless creatures could turn night into day.

"Oh my Lord," Willa whispered.

The dark stone castle stretched out behind perfectly manicured lawns. It was majestic and magnificent. Towering windows captured the glint of the fires like beady eyes watching us as the carriages pulled up to the front stairs and stopped.

The doors opened, and a line of male servants rushed forward. Behind them strode the three Vampires we'd watched hours ago in the clearing.

"How," Willa whispered, "how did they get here?"

"They're Vampires," Nilsine growled as a servant neared the carriage door. "How do they do anything?"

The door swung open. "Ma'am. May I assist you?" The male servant reached upwards.

Willa and Nilsine were closest, and yet neither of them could move. They were frozen with fear, about to step into a Vampire's den. I stepped forward, grasped my skirt with one hand, and reached out with the other.

My hand grasped around another's. Warm, strong. I lowered my gaze to the soft brown eyes of a human male and stilled for a second. *How...how could you work for these beasts?*

His stare never answered. His smile was frozen, locked into place as he lowered his gaze and helped me step from the carriage to the ground. I lifted my gaze, watching as the three Sinful stood in silence above us at the top of a long set of stairs.

One by one, the rest of us climbed out and stood near the carriages, waiting for the death and depravity to begin. But it never did. Instead, one of the Sinful stepped forward, his long dark hair flowing out behind him, captured by the wind.

"Welcome," he started. "My name is Cassian, behind me the two other Lords of Nightingale Manor, Lorcan and Arkyn. We are your hosts for the duration of your stay, and these men are under our employ. You'll be shown to your lodgings and a place to freshen up. You'll be locked in your rooms until you're called on. This is for your own protection. Please don't try to run...I guarantee you won't get far. There are far more dangerous creatures than us who hunt in these forests."

One nod was all he gave, and the line of male servants herded us like cattle for the slaughter. I jerked my gaze back to where the Sinful stood only seconds before. But they were gone, just like before, in the woods.

The blade in my boot rubbed as I walked. The sensation threw me into panic as I climbed the stairs to the top and stared at the Sinful castle.

Nightingale Manor, that's what these beasts called it. I lifted my gaze to the full moon as it hung heavy in the sky above us, the pale silver glow swallowed by the darkness of this place. I reached out and trailed the tips of my fingers along the granite railing.

"They're going to kill us inside, aren't they?" someone called behind me.

"No," another answered. "Not tonight, at least. If they wanted us dead, then they would've killed us before bringing us all the way here...*to their home.* They want one of us, that's what they want. One woman to share their beds and sit beside them on the thrones."

The words gripped me. *Their beds and their thrones?*

You know what they do to girls like you, don't you? You know they bite them...they seduce them...they...fuck them. Jacobs words came back to haunt me.

"How do you know?" one of the other girls whimpered. "They might just want to bite us and then send us home."

"Don't be stupid." The one who seemed to know everything muttered. "They are three males living in a castle, what do you think they want to do with us?"

I tried to remember to breathe and pressed my fist against my side. The old woman in the hills had said nothing about a crown.

"Please follow me," one of the servants called to us, before turning and making his way toward the towering castle.

We followed like good little women, but instead of taking us to the front doors, we descended the stairs, and were led along a path down the side. Guards waited in the darkness, some close enough so that we could see them.

A scream shattered the silence from somewhere in the distance. At first, it sounded like a woman's scream, only it grew deeper and more guttural, sending shivers along my spine. My steps stuttered as I passed a guard.

He watched me with unflinching eyes until I moved with the others through a doorway and inside. The black granite walls and amber flames of the corridor were like stepping into the cold, dark earth.

We slowed to a crawl, the front ones barely moving, until we bunched up.

"Please, this way." The servant in front of us urged us on with a wave of his hand.

One glance over my shoulder and there was no turning back. A guard stepped inside behind the last of us, driving us forward. Willa was behind me and followed my stare. Instinct drove her forward until she smacked into me.

"Sorry," she whispered and reached out.

I took her hand, turning back to head along the corridor.

"There are three ladies to a room," the servant called.

Someone burst into tears behind me, and another snarled, *"Shut up!"*

Bedroom doors were opened along the hall, and three at a time stepped inside. Panic filled me as the door was thrown open, and a woman in front was ushered inside, then it was me...and Willa surged alongside me.

The door was closed as soon as we entered, and the *snap* of a lock sounded. Willa's hand trembled in mine. Still, we never moved, staring at an opulent midnight-blue bedroom with one large bed. A black chandelier filled with lit candles illuminated the room, tossing shadows over the stone walls and floor. A wooden closet pressed up against one wall and a small table stood nearby. A desk was in the corner, and two large chairs, and on the other side was a cracked-open door to what could only be a bathroom.

"We're going to die here," the woman in front of me said, turning.

Even in the faded light, I was struck by her beauty. Her dark hair and wide eyes were accentuated by the splattering of dark brown freckles across her face, like stars across a pale sky.

"No, we're not," I answered. "We're going to survive this...whatever *this* is."

She just stood there, stunned, and closed her eyes. I let Willa's hand fall and stepped deeper into the room. The faint sound of voices carried under the door. Doors were closed and locked, the others cried out, some even beating their fists on the doors.

I headed for the window above the bed, hiked my skirt up, and climbed upwards.

"What are you doing?" Willa hissed.

I gripped the bottom of the frame and yanked until my back strained. There was no give. Locked. I searched along the top of the pane for the latch. But there was no latch. *Strange.* I tried again, only this time, there was a faint charge of energy that zapped the tips of my fingers. I pulled away.

"What is it?" Willa whispered.

I just shook my head, confused. "Nothing."

There were no other ways to escape that I could see, just one immovable window...and a bathroom. I climbed down from the bed and made my way inside it. There was a flickering candle on the shelf, a pitcher and a basin with neatly stacked fresh towels, and a toilet.

I turned back, to see them watching me. "I'm going to close the door for just a minute and freshen up." Neither of them answered. So I peed, and washed my hands, lathering a cloth to wash under my armpits and between my legs, and then stepped out.

They were still standing in the same spot, still staring at nothing.

I crossed the room, grabbed Willa by the hand, and reached for the other companion. "My name's Asena."

"Chaska," the brunette murmured.

Her lips trembled, she was close to tears, but she was holding on.

We were all just holding on.

The knock on the door was soft and gentle, still we all flinched like it was a banshee's scream of fate. The door opened and one of the male servants, dressed all in black, entered. Careful eyes missed nothing as he glanced around the room and then met our gazes. "You have been summoned."

4

———————

*S*ummoned.

The word coiled tight in my mind. I'd never get used to being summoned like we were less than a human. Less than anything but a pet, a slave at their beckoning... it was exactly the Sinfuls' intention. They planned to suppress us, break us, and it burned me up with hatred. I'd planned this moment for years, practiced controlling my emotions, memorized the rules.

Never escape.

Never say no.

Never look ungrateful.

I was theirs and I'd better like it or they'd know. Didn't matter that we were the payment to cover our family debt to the Sinful. None of that was important anymore. Just survival.

That brunette in the woods had run for her life... her terrified scream still rang in my ears. The devastation twisting her parents' faces would haunt me for eternity. No one should go through such horrific loss, no one... my heart clenched at the memory I wished I'd never witnessed.

The shuffle of shoes on the stone floor had me raising my

head toward the servant, who retreated from our room, leaving the door ajar. No locking us in, and I exchanged puzzled looks with the two girls who shared my room.

Willa pushed loose strands of red hair out of her face, green eyes watery and fearful, her chin quivering. "Y-you t-think it's a trick?"

I stared at the door. "I wouldn't put anything past them."

"They summoned us," Chaska's words trembled as she pushed toward the door, shoulders stiff, arms swinging by her sides.

Instinct tore through me. I lunged after her, snatching her arm. "I wouldn't do that."

I shouldn't have bothered, but I couldn't get the brunette's scream out of my head, couldn't stop picturing the old man being dragged away. The Sinful showed no mercy, no second chances, and I'd had enough of death for one day.

Chaska ripped her arm away. Her breaths came hard and fast as she turned toward me, her wide eyes filled with fear. "You're going against their command if you stop me."

I was shaking my head. "No, we don't leave our rooms until we're called on. The servant never gave an order. He simply said we were summoned."

She stared at me with those black-rimmed almond eyes, long lashes, and arched brows like I was losing my mind, but everything I'd discovered about the Sinful showed them as ruthless, taking joy in playing games. Nothing would be simple with them. Nothing.

"It could have been an order?" Willa asked.

"See, even she agrees," Chaska answered, not bothering to spare a glance at Willa.

"And what if you're wrong?" I murmured, my arms trembling with the need to make her understand. "You're willing to risk everything?"

"What if *you're* wrong?" she insisted. "Have you forgotten

what they did to that girl in the woods?" The color drained from her face, and Willa winced, turning toward the window, where the wind shook the trees in the distance. We were so far high up on the mountain, so far from our homes.

I dragged in a harsh, raspy breath, unable to stop remembering the girl's scream, wanting it wiped from my mind, but it clung to my thoughts like cobwebs.

"Eira was scared," Willa muttered and turned to us, swiping at her eyes. "I knew her from Windtorn, you know? Her family's had bad luck since she was born. She broke her arm three times, caught the pox twice. The flooded river took out their house completely and didn't touch another. Some say she was cursed as a baby."

Chaska rolled her eyes. "Superstitious nonsense. This has nothing to do with being unlucky and *everything* to do with our families not paying their debts. Now we're the ones to pay that price. That's what we are to them, currency. At least Eira did what all of us were thinking of doing."

Unlucky, because I'd lost my family to someone who shouldn't be underestimated.

Deep down, I knew this had nothing to do with luck.

This all came down to survival.

I marched across the room and grabbed the door knob to shut the door, but instead, I stood there, staring out into the dark hall, my ears pricked for sounds.

Footfalls. Whispers. Muffled cries from the other rooms.

A shiver ran down my spine. *Was* I mistaken? Had the servant summoning been an order?

"Should we run?" Willa whispered in my ear, and I jerked around so fast from her unexpected closeness, I lost my breath.

"Give me some space, please." My heart pounded. Fear gripped me.

Chaska narrowed her gaze on me, while Willa's flipped between us like she expected us to break into an argument.

I stared out into the hall once again, past the ostentatiously detailed pillars painted in black. No shadows or other doorways in view. The hall curved out of sight on either side.

My muscles flexed, and I stood there, toying with the idea of listening to Chaska and going out. The more I let those thoughts into my head, the more I feared getting caught. Once I had laid eyes on the Sinful back in the woods, I'd felt their brutality, seen it in their eyes, along with the curiosity belonging to a predator who'd trapped his victim, taking pleasure in taunting and terrifying the prey. Goosebumps prickled over my arms and I turned to the girls, stilling my racing heart.

"They locked us in here initially," I began. "So we wait. Maybe the servant just made a mistake by leaving the door open."

"I don't remember anyone putting you in charge." Chaska pushed toward us, mumbling something else under her voice about backwater townsfolk.

Fire burned through me, and I kicked my foot backward into the door. It shut with a thud.

She shot a glare at me. "Why do you care if I stay or go?" she waited, searching my gaze before she spoke once more. "You're scared, aren't you? You want us to stay in case you make the wrong decision. Those monsters won't spare you because there are three of us breaking the rules. They'll kill all of us."

I swallowed hard. She thought she was being strong, preparing herself to meet the Sinful head on. But this wasn't how they played. *I knew that.* They didn't leave doors open. They didn't allow servants to give a statement and not a command. I stared into her gaze and searched the freckles on her face. She had to watch for the smaller details, to realize we weren't dealing with just any beast who wanted to rip us apart. Everything was a game for them.

"I'm trying to save both of you," I lowered my voice.

"Never asked for your help," she said, pushing her face closer to mine, but I didn't flinch, wouldn't back away. "I'll follow my instinct. It's gotten me this far in life with just me and my dad." Pain shook her voice when she mentioned her father and she lowered her gaze, looking away from me like I'd made her reveal something personal about herself.

So, I stepped aside from the door and let her choose her own fate. She wouldn't listen to me, and I'd promised myself to not get close to anyone, not to care. Just focus on the Sinful and deliver the retribution owed to them.

I crossed the room, my boots thudding on the stone floor, and flopped down onto the huge bed. "If we survive the night," I said, "I'm sleeping on the left." Perfect vantage point to see anyone coming into the room, and the furthest to reach.

Chaska's words were stolen by Willa's hitched breath as someone pushed open the door to our room. I jolted to my feet as Chaska recoiled.

A woman with pale gray skin entered the room, carrying what looked like a gown the color of midnight draped over an arm. Short blond hair pushed off her face, she could be a few years older than us, except her eyes gave away her real age. Exhaustion spun behind them, like she'd seen so many things, experienced unspeakable things.

Dressed in a body-fitting black dress that fell to her ankles, buttons running from her throat to her feet, she marched inside, focused on Willa, who backed away, her eyes bulging with terror.

Two more maids entered our room. The one coming for me wore a cruel grin like she'd enjoy whatever she had planned. Trepidation wormed through my veins, but I stilled and waited.

Show no fear.

"What's going on?" Chaska asked, her voice suddenly soft and vulnerable.

"Look at yourself. You're disgusting. You can't look like that in front of our Lords," her maid barked, her voice barren of emotion.

The woman in front of me laid a dress the color of violet lilies on the bed, then turned on me, hands grabbing my shirt, pulling and ripping buttons in an instant like I was nothing.

Jostled on the spot, I clenched my hands, blinking back the tears as she stripped me with no decency. The three of us were nothing more than objects.

Obedience.

My stomach cramped as she ripped the clothes from my body, pulling hair in the process. But she never marked my skin. She barely even touched me. Was it because she didn't want to upset the Lords? We were their property after all, weren't we?

Willa was crying, standing naked, hugging herself. She was a waif of a girl, beauty marks dotting her arms.

"Keep it down," her maid remarked, grabbing the gown to dress her.

Chaska held her head high, lips tight, eyes on the ceiling, as the maid dragged down her pants and underwear. Bruises the size of my fist marred her ribs, the marks of a whip crossed her legs.

Her maid tsked. "You're ruined. And they call us the monsters." She poked a finger into a blue and yellow marbled bruise right on her hip bone.

Chaska held tight, didn't blink or move. She knew we looked at her, and my insides turned to jagged glass at seeing her pain. Who beat her that way? Her dad?

"Come, we'll get you dressed, and I'll arrange for liquid supplements for you to take for four days," the maid said, the caring nature behind her words surprising me. "You want those ugly bruises gone before the Lords lay eyes on your body." She grabbed the dress for Chaska, who glared my way, and I dropped my gaze.

The maid in front of me snapped my underwear off at my

hips with the flick of a blade and yanked the fabric from between my legs, leaving me feeling vulnerable and raw. She tossed the material on the rest of the pile behind her. My head was hammering with fury, with dread, with the desperation to shove this woman off me.

But I swallowed the emotions drowning me, the ache, the humiliation.

She pulled the dress over my head, the softest of fabrics sliding over my skin, and I raised my hands as she tugged the dress down my body. It was tight across my chest, cinching in at my waist, then falling to my feet in soft waves of silky fabric. The maid pulled the sleeves down to my elbows and shuffled the dress around my chest before stuffing a hand down the front and adjusting my breasts to sit upright more.

I gritted my teeth, Willa's constant whimpers flooded my ears, and it took every ounce of strength to not scream to have my breasts handled.

The maid stepped back and eyed me head to toes. "You will do. Now, shoes off."

And the command reminded me of the blade in my boot, sending my pulse into a frenzy.

I spun and hurried to the side of the bed, bending over to slip the boot off, while swifty sliding the knife out and pushing it under the bed.

When I looked up, the servants were gone, as were our torn clothes, and the three of us stood there in gowns I'd never wear at home or be able to afford. But if I did, I'd wear underwear.

I glanced over to the door, left ajar.

"Thank god, we didn't leave the room before," Willa murmured, running a hand down her blue dress that glinted in the candlelight. Long, loose sleeves reached her knuckles, the gown falling to her ankles, and a thick black belt around her waist accentuated her chest. She'd look cute, if it wasn't in preparation for pleasing a Sinful.

Chaska never said a word, just pushed her dark hair off her face, wiped her cheeks, and marched across the room.

She grabbed the door knob, and I rushed after her, now convinced without a doubt that we weren't meant to leave the room. With the door wide open, she stared out into the hall, and I moved to her side, Willa joining us.

Darkness. Silence.

"What do you think they want?" Willa whispered when shadows shifted from within the darkened corner of the hall.

My heart dropped.

I couldn't breathe, couldn't think straight for those few moments. Not when a figure stepped out into the chandalier's candlelight.

Tall. All shoulders. Deliciously wicked.

Fear spiked through my chest, and at first, I didn't move a muscle as I processed who I stared at.

Cassian. A Sinful. Messy dark hair falling to his shoulders, piercing, pale green eyes, and full lips that called to me. A shadow of growth covered his jawline, and I couldn't have looked away if I tried. God, he was so tempting, so beautiful. So deadly.

He strode closer, black pants pulled tight across strong legs, hanging low on his hip bones, his bare chest exposed--smooth and rippling with muscles. His long coat hung open as he strode closer, his gaze locked on Chaska. Those full lips twisted, the bridge of his nose wrinkled with disdain. Had he heard about her bruises?

"Chaska," I uttered her name in a whisper, "get back into the room."

I must have hit my head on the way to Nightingale Manor that I even contemplated this, but as he crossed the hall in a few long strides, I stepped in between him and Chaska.

"She did nothing wrong." I explained, holding myself stiff, refusing to buckle under his gaze.

"She intended to leave her room." His voice slid over my skin like raw silk. He paused a few inches away, staring down at me, his shadow swallowing me.

Was I making a huge mistake? I drew in a ragged breath. "She didn't leave. None of us did."

"She wanted to." He dragged the back of his hand across his mouth, staring at me with such hunger, a surge of fire ignited in the pit of my gut, roaring to life. I couldn't remember the last time a man affected me so strongly.

But were these Vampires any different from wild animals?

Dark. Untamed. Vicious.

"Wanting to and doing are completely different. She didn't leave." I stood my ground. Even if shaken, I couldn't sit back as they hurt someone else.

"Bravery will get you killed." I watched those full lips move as he threatened me. He lifted a hand and touched my cheek, his fingers cool against me, like he'd just come out of a cold river. "Don't you know that?"

I tilted my head back and stared intently at the Vampire, those predatory eyes wild and intoxicating. He was incredibly beautiful, more than any man should be, but on him... on the Sinful, they made me question my own sanity when I burned beneath his stare. His fingers slid to my neck, and a gasp fell past my lips as he leaned closer.

My mind screamed to be cautious, that I shouldn't encourage him to come so close.

His words were cool against the tender skin just below my ear lobe. "I can hear your heartbeat...I can feel it."

A jolt of electricity raced through me, and I clenched my thighs. *No...no goddamn way.* Hate. Rage. Retribution. That's what I forced myself to focus on as I waited for him to lower his hand, to do *something...* instead, he just watched me.

Games, that's all this was to him, yet I shivered in his presence.

"What do want with us?" I finally found my voice.

His hand fell to mine, cold fingers wrapped around my wrist. "It's all a bit tragic, isn't it?" He pivoted and hauled me after him down the hall.

Panic dug its claws into my chest, and I fought against him. "Tell me...tell me what you want with me."

"You stood in the way of my enjoyment, Asena. I was quite looking forward to watching Chaska end her own life with one small step. But you saved her, even when she refused to listen...when she wasn't *worthy*. Why was that?"

He knew my name? Dread locked me in place.

"I didn't know." I pushed against his cruel grip on my arm, my feet sliding on the stone floor as I resisted. "I won't do it again."

Don't fight them.

The words surfaced through the panic.

Control.

Nothing but fear. All I saw was Eira running into the woods. All I heard was her screams in my head.

Obedience.

"Yes," he whispered and lifted his hand, "you will."

The tips of his fingers were like ice against my skin. But heat moved inside me.

He grabbed me by the shoulders and spun me to face him. Need shimmered in his eyes.

Terrible, *unfathomable* need.

I lifted my head, trapped in the devil's gaze. I'd made a mistake thinking I was ready to come here, that I was prepared for whatever darkness revenge had held for me.

I was wrong...

5

Cassian's eyes were a blend of teals and greens, changing like a raging storm. His unflinching stare never left me, fingers digging into my shoulders with desperation, like he might say something... do something, and I was frozen, caught in his gaze.

I watched his full lips, imagining him kissing me roughly, forcefully pushing me up against the wall, hands sliding over every inch of me. I swallowed hard, my heart racing. This raw desire... it was so wrong... and I hated myself for thinking anything but death for these monsters. For eleven years, I'd thought of nothing but this moment, when I'd reach their home, years filled with resentment for what they'd taken from me. Not years of planning to let myself just fall for their charm and make my parents' deaths a cruel joke.

He'd destroy me if I let him, all the Sinful would.

You stood in the way of my enjoyment, Asena.

Cassian's words rang through me. We were nothing more than entertainment for these savages. I had to remind myself of my mission, not fall for their lure, not let their looks deceive me. I burned up with embarrassment that I'd reacted so intensely to his touch, and I looked away, needing him to see he didn't affect me.

Hard footfalls hit the stone floor. I glanced over at an approaching Sinful guard, dressed in black pants and a tight-fitting jacket, gold buttons down the front, pale skin like the others, hair slicked off his determined face.

Cassian's grip loosened, and I pulled free, stumbling out of his reach.

"My Lord." The man bowed his head at Cassian.

Silence fell between us, as though they exchanged unspoken words, before the guard nodded and reached for me, his hand icy against my flesh, eyes dragging over my body, watching, studying, leering. Was he picturing what he'd do to me if Cassian wasn't there?

Vampire... I could tell it from his cold, stony eyes, his porcelain skin, his icy touch.

"This way," he commanded and pulled me down the hall. Cassian never said a word or made a move to stop him, and when I glanced over my shoulder, the hall where he'd been standing seconds earlier was now empty. How did they keep vanishing like that?

"Where are we going?" I stumbled after the guard.

He didn't respond, but we moved with haste. Around the next dark corner, we entered an open hall with black pillars. A statue of a naked woman stood in the middle of the enclosed area, arms crossed over her breasts, hair blowing in the wind, her mouth half open in a silent scream.

Was that how they pictured us humans? Vulnerable and always scared?

Clenching my teeth, I planned to change that perception soon enough.

The guard hauled me toward a set of doors, black and studded with gold. The double doors opened as if they had a mind of their own, and the guard's hand gave me a shove on my back. My feet flew forward and I stumbled into a grand room.

Elaborate candle chandeliers dripping in crystals lit up the study. Two walls held floor-to-ceiling shelves packed with books, and my insides swelled with excitement to explore every inch of this room, run my hands over the leather spines, discover their secrets. Books weren't easy to come by back home, and when they were available at the weekend market, I bought as many as I could afford, reading them several times over. But then my attention shifted from the books to the black rug that ran the length of the room and the grandeur of the rest of it.

I stared at the Sinful sitting at the rear of the room on dark thrones. Chairs carved of wood, crested with jagged diamonds around the edges of the seats. While the thrones were impressive, they were nothing compared to the Vampires.

I stepped forward, my bare feet cushioned on the rug, warmer than the flagstone flooring. My attention moved to Cassian. Dark hair falling over an eye as his focus remained on something on a bookshelf, he ignored me completely.

A soft panic rose through me that I faced the three of them alone, that they'd punish me, throw me to the Wolves. But as much as I hated standing there in front of them, I'd be lying if I said I wouldn't stand up to Cassian again.

Lorcan lounged in his seat, legs stretched out and crossed at the ankles, hands interlaced and laid over his stomach. Golden eyes watched me. Elegant hair, dark as midnight, draped over his shoulders and down to his chest in soft waves. Chiseled cheekbones, square jaw, he looked suave and debonair in his high-collared shirt with gold embroidery on his cuffs. That striking face left me wobbling on my feet.

Oh, hell no.

I quickly lowered my gaze, hating how my body heated up

just looking at them, how they were my enemy but I stared at them with such admiration.

Arkyn cleared his throat, and my gaze lifted to him.

He sat in the middle, on the tallest throne, and didn't speak a word, his perfect red lips parted and the tips of his white fangs press down on them.

"So, this is Asena," Lorcan declared, like I ought to believe he didn't know who I was all this time. His mouth twitched, resisting a grin. "The brave, foolish girl who stepped in to protect another. Very valiant of you." He leaned forward in his throne. "Come closer, don't be afraid." That time his greedy smile spread, the look of the devil in his gaze, ready to do unspeakable things.

I stepped forward, my throat feeling like it had closed. "And I'd do it again. Chaska was scared, we're all scared."

"You don't look frightened to me," Arkyn finally spoke, his voice leaving me in shivers. He terrified me the most. "But you're foolish and naive if you think those fighting words will protect you here."

"I never--"

"*I didn't say you could speak!*" he barked.

I should have lowered my head, but I held Arkyn's stare as my stomach churned.

"You're right about her," Lorcan murmured, looking over at Cassian.

I bristled, curious what they'd said, but with Arkyn looking me dead in the eyes, I wasn't brave enough to tempt fate and ask. I'd studied the rules for years, learned them off by heart, yet things kept going wrong.

"I'm sorry," I murmured, forcing my gaze to the ground by sheer will alone. "Exhaustion made me forget my place," I forced through gritted teeth, praying they'd grant forgiveness.

Silence.

I had nowhere to escape.

Nowhere to run.

I clenched my fists until my muscles trembled. A sting tore through my palm. The pain forcing me to focus. There was a sharp draw of breath. Arkyn shoved from his seat on the throne, striding forward...until our bodies touched.

The tips of my breasts pressed against his chest. But the rise and fall of the Vampire's breaths never came, only mine. Not until he summoned it. He drew the air deep into his body, and a low growl sounded in the back of his throat. One that made my own clench with fear.

"Who are you?" he murmured, that low growl sending shivers along my spine.

Danger mingled with the pounding in my chest. I became acutely aware of him...aware of them all. Their cold, unmovable presence, their fangs hidden behind perfect teeth. I fought the need to lift my head, my gaze boring into the stony floor at his feet. But heat soon followed, licking between my thighs, sending a surge of desire through my core.

"I can smell your need," Arkyn murmured. "I could take you here and you'd barely put up a fight, would you? Tear that pretty dress from your body, expose those beautiful breasts for all to see. I think Cassian would like to see you like that, all meek and hungry, trembling as I spread those creamy thighs and plunge in deep...yes, I think he'd like that very much."

Heat filled my cheeks. It wasn't anger now that kept my gaze to the floor as the sound of voices drifted near. The other women drew closer, their chatter from the hall stronger until, with a breath, the sound silenced.

They all watched me from the doorway, with my cheeks burning and Arkyn pressed against my chest until, in an instant, the Vampire turned and was sitting back on his throne. His unflinching eyes met mine as I lifted my head, and then he looked away...no longer interested.

He'd had his fun.

Leaving me with the torturous image of him looming over me, his cock sheathed in my body, his fangs scraping along my neck. Slowly, the chatter started up again, but no one moved to my side.

Instead, I forced myself to stare at the enormous painting on the wall behind them. A stunning, towering male with fire encasing him, burning red eyes, and one shoulder covered with blazing armor that ran over his bare chest. I'd heard tales of Vampires once fighting in battles on the side of humans against Wolves, Dragons, and the Dark Ones. Once they were our heroes, but that was a long time ago. So long ago, they seemed to have forgotten and had become the monsters they'd once protected us from.

The shuffle of feet came from behind me. I turned my head to see the other women rushing inside the room, heads low, terror twisting their faces. They lined up on either side of me. The doors shut behind them, closing us all in together.

Eleven women.

Three savage beasts.

The silence was deafening. Alongside me, the others wore terrified expressions. Willa stood at the end of the line, lips pressed tight, head low like she fought her tears.

Nilsine flicked blonde hair over a shoulder, her chin high, lips pink and pouty, just like Chaska and a couple other women who knew how to play the games. They understood these Sinful wanted our flesh for more than just feeding, while the rest of the girls just wanted to crawl under a rock. Me... I stood in the middle somewhere. Not wanting to be noticed, which I'd failed miserably so far, and watching until the right moment came to strike. I had three adversaries to take out, three times the risk of getting caught.

Cassian eyed the lineup in front of him, never looking at me.

Arkyn rose from his throne, drawing all our attention. Tight black pants, matching button-up shirt, open at his throat, he dressed simply compared to the others, but he carried power within him. I saw it in his eyes, the color of the darkest sea, in the tightness of his mouth. He was used to getting his way and showed no mercy, and right now he was in his element, staring down at us.

"Welcome. Nightingale Manor will be your home while you're with us and pay off your families' debts. We hope your rooms are to your satisfaction."

No one responded, not that they would look the devil in the eyes and complain. Nilsine and another woman with a low neckline and the palest eyes smiled widely, giving hurried nods. Maybe their rooms were less cramped than mine, because I wouldn't call sharing one bed with two others a satisfying experience.

"For the duration of your stay, remain in your rooms at all times." His gaze passed over every girl, meeting our eyes. "There will be tests held," he instructed. "Pass them and you'll go on. Don't pass them and, well... there'll be no need for you to be here."

Tests? Was that what they called these games, their reasons for bringing us here, watching us to see if we'd leave the bedroom without permission? None of the girls responded at first, but the tension in the room choked in my throat.

"What kind of tests, My Lord?" Chaska meekly asked, and I glanced over to see the fear on her face.

Arkyn flicked his gaze my way, searching for some kind of reaction. I waited for him to lash out at Chaska, to reprimand her the way he'd done to me. But the sharp sting of his words never came. Maybe I'd pissed them off more than I thought? They'd take every opportunity to hurt me, to make me heel.

"These are just tests until we find the one we'll select. It's simple, you pass or you don't." He strode toward us, confidence in how he held himself tall. We were toys for them, something to keep them occupied and pass the time.

Tests. The one we'll select.

What would happen to those not selected? Various punishments came to mind. Taken out to the Wolves? Sacrificed to the demonic Dragons? Killed or made to work in servitude for life? The scream we heard when we arrived… was it a Wolf waiting to be fed? The Vampires said there were more dangerous creatures here.

I gritted my teeth. *The mission.* I chose to come here. Hatred burned through me, but I swallowed back the bile in my throat. They owned us, and we obeyed them… for now.

Arkyn took long, slow strides in front of us, and my heart beat unsteadily. He towered over us, staring at each intently. A quick lick of his lips, and his fangs appeared, long pointy things.

Stopping in front of Nilsine, he gripped her chin and tilted her head back to better inspect her face, her neck. Would he sink his fangs into her flesh now, drain her until she fell to the floor?

We all watched, but I knew the answer already, it lingered in my thoughts, dove deep to the pit of my gut each time one of the Sinful came close to me. They wanted more than our blood.

They were savages and took what they wanted from women like us.

"Have you been touched before?" he questioned.

Nilsine trembled, her words barely a whisper. "No, My Lord. I've never been with a man."

The brunette next to me smiled widely, almost bouncing on her toes, her curls bopping over her shoulders. She was loving this, and I disliked her for taking enjoyment from everyone's misery.

Arkyn released his hold and strode along the line, studying every one of us like we were cattle at auction. The brunette smiled, the dark makeup around her eyes and three dots down the bridge of her nose told me she was from the west plains, where Dragons ruled the lands. The village there was made up mostly of warriors. It surprised me the Sinful's reach went that far.

Her smug expression slipped as Arkyn approached, and revealed the fear she hid. We were all the same in the end.

In front of me, he paused. "And you?"

I held my breath, his question taking me off guard, and I stood there, shuddering with dread. His gaze swallowed me. I couldn't look away, captivated by his beauty. Should a man look this striking and alluring? In that moment, my thoughts faded, drowning with images of Arkyn's hand on my neck, moving down my body in harsh strokes, sliding under my skirt, finding the fire the Sinful ignited within me.

Something shifted behind his gaze, the corners of his mouth twitching.

Gods, could he read my mind? Would he think I craved him and take me here, in front of everyone? My breaths raced. *Focus.* I had to focus and remember to breathe.

The brunette elbowed me in the ribs, and panic spread through my veins.

And you?

"No, My Lord." I'd kissed boys before, but no one had ever touched me that way. A blistering blush seared my cheeks that he'd made me announce that in front of everyone.

Obedience. It was what they wanted from us. So that's what I had to give them. I swallowed the bitter taste of acid. Even if that's all they saw, someone falling into line...someone willing to complete their *tests.*

I held my head low. Shiny black boots remained in my vision, then he stepped further down the line, but I didn't move, didn't dare. It was what he expected.

The sound of the door opening froze me. Heavy footfalls, and I chanced a side glance at the guard who approached Arkyn and whispered something into his ear. The Lord never looked at him, but his top lip curled, his long fangs on show, and it scared me to think he'd pierce my flesh with them. In moments, the guard marched back to the door.

"You can go now." Arkyn dismissed us with those few words and returned to his throne. The girls shuffled around me to leave.

I swallowed the boulder in my throat and walked away.

My legs felt heavier with each step I took out of the room. I eyed the shelves of books on the way. *Dragon Anatomy. Hunting With Wolves. History of the Dark Ones.*

Five races lived in our world, four that fought and took without mercy. Humans were the weakest, the one the others used, killed, or toyed with.

The sense of being watched raked down my back and I peeked back quickly to find Cassian staring at me with intensity.

I had to focus, remind myself these weren't men, no matter how beautiful they were. They were monsters. Family...killing...*monsters.*

Following the other girls out, my bare feet were silent against the stone floor. Another glance over my shoulder at Cassian, who was staring at the books I'd eyed moments earlier, and I walked straight into the girl in front of me, stumbling.

"So sorry." I recoiled to catch myself as the brunette who stood next to me in the line turned to give me a death glare.

She shoved a hand into my chest, sending me backward. "Watch it."

"Come on, Polaris, don't do this here," Aislinn, the girl I'd shared a carriage with on the way to the manor, said. She yawned as she took her friend's arm, and they headed down the dark hall. What did she mean by not doing this here? Exhaustion dragged through me, as we'd been up most of the night since arriving, but I took a last look back into the study as the doors shut, stealing Cassian from my view.

6

Cassian haunted my dreams through the snatches of sleep I was able to get. So I forced myself awake, testing the locks throughout the early hours of the morning. But no one came to set us free...or sneak into our room. Willa and Chaska slept fitfully, snoring and muttering.

At one point, Willa woke with a start, panicked, with a scream trapped in her throat.

"It's okay, you're safe," I murmured from the end of the bed and glanced toward her. "I'm right here."

She said something I couldn't understand, and then lowered her head to the pillow once more, snoring a heartbeat later.

But we weren't safe at all. We were in a castle in the middle of nowhere. Our hosts were Vampires that wanted to test us. *They play with their food.* The old woman in the hills had told me months ago. Now I knew what she meant.

But we were more than just food to them. We were a source of enjoyment, a *purpose.* A game. *Selected.*

The word resounded as the shadows blurred. Selected for what? To be free? To be one of them? *To be bitten...*

Cold crept along my spine with the thought. I'd never let

that happen. I'd stab, and cut...*and kill* before I let them sink their fangs into me.

"Just you fucking try," I whispered as the room slowly spun.

I closed my eyes and tried to force sleep away. But the emptiness surrounded me. The corridor was silent. Soft whimpers and sobs from the other girls had faded, and through the window behind me, the sky started to brighten.

The rising sun gave us some protection from the Vampires at least. The Sinful and the guards would've gone to ground, leaving us locked in here. But there were other beasts out there...beasts that hunted through the day just as well as they did at night. Chaska mumbled and then turned, throwing her arm across my middle. I closed my eyes and shifted higher on the bed, until I lowered my head to the pillow and let sleep drag me under.

Darkness moved in like a predator, taking me past the fear, to where my best friend waited. Jacob smiled and held out his hand to me.

Hurry up, he urged. *Figure it all out so you can come back to me.*

I tried to understand what he meant, tried to reach out to him, until a deep, threatening snarl slipped from the shadows to surround us. I turned my head toward him as the Vampire, Cassian, stepped out of the shadows.

Tall, powerful...I couldn't look away.

His pale skin shimmered through the open neckline of his shirt. I was captivated by the hard swell of his chest and the predatory way he moved.

Don't look at him, Asena. Jacob urged. *He's a monster...a beast.*

Cassian smiled at the words, revealing the tips of his pointed white fangs. He lifted his hand to me as he neared. I swallowed hard, fear rooting me to the spot. But a quake raced through my body, one that almost broke the spell...one that urged me to go to him, and do all the things the glint in his eyes promised.

I jolted awake with the panicked *boom...boom...boom* of my heart filling my head.

"There you are," Willa muttered from across the room. "Thought for a while you'd turned into one of them...you know, an *undead.*"

I ran my tongue along my teeth, trying to find enough moisture to speak. Still, my voice came out raspy and raw. "What time is it?"

"Late," Willa said with a sigh. "And we're bored."

I shoved against the mattress and felt the faint throb at the back of my head grow claws. A moan rose in the back of my throat. I swallowed, winced, and slid my feet from the bed.

"You look like hell," Willa murmured, watching me.

"Thanks." I felt the world sway. It was the dream...something about the dream.

"You were panting in your sleep and moaning...*a lot,*" Chaska commented from a seat in the corner. "What were you dreaming about?"

Heat traveled along my cheeks. "Nothing." I broke her stare, finding the sunlight softening in the window behind me. It had to be two or three in the afternoon. I'd almost slept the entire day away.

I may as well be a damn Vampire.

The thought caught my breath. I lifted my gaze to the door. I had moved the dresser, and it was now in its usual place. "Who's been in here?"

"No one," Willa muttered. "Just us."

I took a step. But it hadn't been *just us.* I lowered my gaze to the floor and searched for scuff marks on the stone. I'd moved the dresser across the door as a barrier. I was sure I had. I clenched my hands and felt the dull ache in my muscles. *No...I knew I had.*

The sinking feeling weighed like a stone in my gut. I crossed the room, sleep long gone from my grasp, and knelt at the doorway. There were scratches in the stone, faint ones that ran all the way to where the dresser stood.

I lifted my gaze to the doorway. Someone had been in here without making a sound while all three of us slept in the bed. A shiver crept up my back at the thought of being watched while we slept.

Was it the Sinful?

Cassian's cruel, seductive smile filled my mind. My heart thundered as I remembered my dream, and the commanding way he seemed to call me. *Like somehow he knew me.*

"There's clothes in the bathroom," Willa announced. "Apparently, last night while we were getting the rundown on this selection game, someone put out fresh towels and laid out a clean set of clothes for each of us. There were twelve of us, right?" she muttered. "Twelve women, twenty-four dresses. That's a lot of dresses."

"Eleven," I answered and pushed to stand, meeting her gaze. "There's eleven of us now. Don't tell me you forgot what they did to your friend already?"

She flinched as though I'd slapped her, and her cheeks burned with the same color as her hair. "She wasn't my friend." Her nose wrinkled like the idea disturbed her, but I saw the truth from the hurt on her face. She didn't want to be Eira's friend because that meant admitting she'd lost someone close and it made everything here too real. Too terrifying.

I turned from her, went into the bathroom, and closed the door.

I had to think. I had to figure this all out and not be caught up in the fairytale of dresses and Dragons. Still, despite my intention, the Vampires' study from last night drifted into my thoughts. That painting on the wall of that warrior. He was bigger than anyone I'd seen before. I imagined the three Sinful dressed ready for war, deadly and terrifying.

I poured water into the basin, glanced at the door once

more, and peeled the dress from my body. There'd been so many books along the shelves, more than I'd ever seen in my life. More than I could possibly read.

But they weren't just written about Vampires.

But about the Dragon hunters...the Wolves...and the Dark Ones. The ones they called Fae.

Were they the creatures the Sinful spoke about? The ones who hunt in the forest through the day...

I dipped the washcloth into the water and lathered with soap, taking my time to scrub my body. My nipples tingled. My thoughts raced with memories from last night, with my dream. My eyelids fluttered closed. I could almost feel Cassian's breath on my skin as the droplets cooled.

My fingers crested my nipples, touching lightly. Heat raced between my thighs. An image reared, Cassian with his head lowered, midnight hair falling across the peaks of my breasts as he licked and sucked, drawing me deeper into his mouth.

I tried to shove the image from my mind, but the harder I tried, the stronger it grew.

Don't fight me, Asena. The words whispered through my mind. *I take what I want.*

I closed my eyes and felt the bathroom sway. The tips of my fingers skimmed my breasts, finding the softer parts of me. The parts I'd never touched before.

A moan tore free, low and bestial...not like me at all.

"You okay in there?" Chaska whispered against the door.

I wrenched from the moment and snapped open my eyes. "Yes...*yes*. Thank you, I'm fine." Coming back to reality in a rush, I shook my head, wrenching my hand as far away from my breasts as I could.

"It's pretty, isn't it?"

My focus narrowed as I turned to the voice from the other side of the door. "Pretty?"

"The dress they laid out for you. It has your name on it."

I turned my head to the dark splash draped over the dresser in the corner of the room and saw my name. *Asena.* I was frozen, my hand cupping my breast, and I felt the tiny shudder as I caught my breath.

It was beautiful, long, flowing, shimmering. I eyed the cloth and moved closer as moisture beaded on the tips of my fingers. I brushed them across my stomach and then reached out.

I'd seen this fabric in the haberdashery, velvet they called it. Soft and lovely, flowing around curves, as it was heavier than cotton. Excitement overtook me. I took the dress, returned to the bathroom, and rubbed lotion onto my skin, then found a small nest of perfume bottles on a shelf.

I plucked the glass stoppers from the bottled and lifted them one by one.

Look at yourself...look at what you're doing.

Dressing for them.

Putting on perfume for them.

My heart lunged with the thought. I put the bottle back down and turned to the dress. What was happening to me? Was it this place? These people? Hate welled like acid in my belly as I snatched the dress from the dresser and held it in my hands.

So soft. My fingers sank into the fabric. It was a dress...just a dress. Nothing more, or less. I glanced to the discarded dress on the floor. It was wet now, and creased. I lowered my gaze to my hands and felt a surge of anger.

They thought I'd put on the dress and become what? Pliable...*weak and pathetic.* I swallowed and lifted the hem, slipping it over my head, and let it fall to the floor. It hugged my body in just the right places and, as I lifted my gaze to the mirror, I knew even without the blade, I had a weapon.

These *beasts* played seduction like it was a game. I wanted to do the same. Even if I'd never kissed a man, I was good at pretending. It'd carried me this far, hadn't it?

"Asena?" Chaska called from the other side of the door.

I left the perfume bottles behind and went to the door. Her eyes widened after I twisted the knob and yanked it open.

"Wow," Willa whispered, staring. "You look...stunning."

"You do," Chaska murmured. "Truly stunning."

I lowered my gaze, looking at their pale blue and yellow dresses. They looked pretty and perfect. But frills stood no chance against the sheen of midnight blue.

What were these Vampires playing at?

And why me?

The thought lingered as Chaska turned and flopped back into the chair, picking up a book from the small desk in the corner of the room. I scanned the spine, *The Hunter,* and moved closer. "Are there more books like that?"

She gave a shrug, not bothering to lift her gaze. The temperature in the room suddenly grew chilly. I glanced from Chaska to Willa. Both refused to meet my gaze. That was fine. I crossed the room to the desk and looked along the spines until I grabbed a book called *Kingdoms and Creatures.* Maybe it had information about the Sinful?

I made my way back to the bed and climbed up, pushing the pillow hard against the headboard, and settled back. The gold filigree etching on the leather cover was smooth under my fingers. I ran my touch along the spine and then slowly opened the cover.

May you find the one you search for.

The writing was stunning, loops and swirls so seamless it could only have been made by the author, or someone special. Someone who gave it as a gift. "May you find the one you search for." The words danced in my mouth.

"What did you say?" Willa muttered and lifted her head.

I shook my head, glanced at her, then returned to the book.

"Nothing." I was already entranced, opening the pages to the contents, and then to the first words.

Beasts walk among us. Heavenly beasts. Hell-bound beasts. Beasts who wear a mortal skin...and beasts who breathe fire. But not all these creatures are dangerous...some are as tormented by their own purpose as we are by their presence.

I kept reading, drawing my feet higher on the bed and pressing my spine into the pillow. Page after page, I read about those creatures who suffered. I hated them. Cursed them. But the more I read about them, the more I felt a flicker of compassion.

These beasts weren't the reason I'd come here.

They were *not* the Sinful.

Not murderers….

A heavy *boom* came from the doorway, making me flinch. I blinked, waiting for my eyes to adjust as Willa rose from her seat and turned to look at me with a strange expression I couldn't quite understand. Darkness had slipped into the room while I wasn't watching.

I glanced over my shoulder to the window, finding the sky already deepening to match the color of my dress. Night had come, and I wasn't prepared.

"Please open the door." Came a courteous male voice.

I slipped from the bed, leaving the open book behind, and crossed the room.

"Wait," Chaska whispered as she stepped closer.

"I'd prefer not to knock the door down." The tone wasn't as pleasant now.

I gripped the door and turned the knob.

There was a *click* but there was no key and no lock. I stared at the unimpressed look on the servant's face as I swung the door wide.

"The ladies of the manor have been requested to attend the

Night Room. If you'd like to find your shoes, you may follow me."

Nervous chatter filled the corridor. I stepped toward the servant and glanced into the hall toward the others. There were other servants, one for every room. Ours cleared his throat and shifted his gaze to those behind me. "Time is of the essence," he insisted.

"Of course it is," I answered and forced a smile. "The nights aren't ever long enough for a Vampire, are they?"

"I wouldn't know," he answered coldly. "If you'd like to accompany me, I'll take you to the Night Room."

Night Room. That was the second time he said the name. Chatter filled the corridor, some urgent and filled with fear, but some breathless with excitement. I gave the servant a slow nod and turned. "I'll just get my boots."

Chaska and Willa moved when I turned, sitting to pull on their heels. They may not have asked me to stand up for them...but they were sure good at following my every move. I yanked on my boots and laced them along the middle of my leg before dropping the midnight gown.

The chatter was fading, drifting along the hall, leaving us behind. I strode toward the doorway as Willa and Chaska came along. We all followed, leaving the bedroom door open behind us.

This was the second time we'd been escorted through the corridors. But this time, he led us a different way. Instead of turning back the way we'd entered the castle, we turned right. Darkness hugged the corridors, faint flames flickered, but the torches smoldered more than burned, leaving us to find our way in the blood-red hue.

I followed the servant, sneaking glances into rooms as we passed. But there were no fires alight to illuminate the spaces. There was only the growing darkness...and the cold.

The air grew colder the further we went. Willa tripped and pitched forward, grasping my arm as she stumbled.

"Careful," the servant called. "The floor is uneven."

The toes of my boots slammed against the floor. The floor wasn't uneven, it was angled...*downwards.* I slowed and glanced over my shoulder, finding the faint red glow of the torches higher than they should be. "Where are we going?"

I slowed my steps, leaving Willa to walk into the back of my heel.

"I told you, the Night Room," the servant said carefully.

Voices drifted from the darkness. I didn't like this one bit. Still, where could I run to? I was trapped between darkness and death. I gripped my dress and kept moving.

That's it, Asena. The words whispered in my ear. I whipped my gaze around, catching the servant's shadow and Willa behind me. "Did you say something?"

"No," she muttered. "Just keep walking. On second thought, just let me past."

She pushed me to the side and stepped around me. Chaska brushed her hand along my arm and followed her. I swallowed the beating of my heart and pressed on, following them deeper into the earth, until the voices grew louder and the darkness had an amber glow.

Three fires blazed, casting soft light through a room. It was big, with towering walls. I looked up to the ceiling, and froze.

I forgot how to breathe, forgot to move, leaving Willa and Chaska to join the others. The ceiling glittered like stars across the night sky. "The Night Room," I whispered.

"Yes," our servant answered, close to me. "It's actually the reflection of the granite ceiling. I'll leave you to enjoy it."

He disappeared without a sound, leaving me to stare up at the ceiling in amazement.

"It's beautiful, isn't it?"

I turned to see Nilsine. "Yes."

Her voice turned cold. "Don't let it fool you, the most dangerous are skilled in the art of illusion."

"Oh, wine," one of the others called.

I turned, my gaze adjusting to the light. There was a table along one side of the expansive room. Places were set in a splash of blood red and gold utensils.

But not silver. *Pity.*

"What are you doing?" Willa hissed as one of the girls with tight blonde curls grabbed a gold goblet from the middle of the table and lifted it to her lips.

"I wouldn't." Chaska shook her head and turned, finding me.

There was fear in her eyes, gripping, choking fear. She knew more than to drink from a cup that wasn't hers...or walk through an open door without being invited.

"She's right," I affirmed.

All heads turned my way, they all scanned the dress, some of the women widening their eyes at the sight, others curling their lips in a sneer. I focused on the one with the cup of wine. "We have to be careful here, everything we *touch*, everything we *do*, they are watching."

"Why would they put a glass of wine here if they didn't want us to drink it?" the one holding the goblet snarled. She moved toward me, her pale pink dress flowing out behind her.

"Devika, maybe she's right," one of the others whispered. and the sound carried through the underground room.

The woman holding the goblet jerked a savage glare her way. "And what would you fucking know."

Drink it.

The deep masculine whisper cut through the room. It was a test...it was all a test. Everything we did here, and everything we wore. I sucked in a hard breath and felt the room still.

"Did you hear that?" someone whimpered.

Still, Devika held my stare. Hate flared as she lowered her gaze to the midnight velvet dress and then lifted the rim of the goblet to her lips. Red slipped down her lips, like blood. Her throat moved, the gulping sound of her defiance filling the air until she lowered it to the table.

The goblet was empty. She didn't even know what it was and still she drank it. The room was captivated, staring at her as she slowly swayed. Her lips curled, the smugness all over her face. But it didn't last long...the wicked smirk died in a heartbeat.

There was a flash of worry...and then she lifted her hand, curled her fingers, and pressed her fist into her middle. "I don't feel so good."

"That's because you're an idiot," Nilsine muttered, earning her a glare from three others. "What? Don't you know it's rude to drink someone else's drink and help yourself to their food?"

Devika gave a cry and lurched forward as liquid shot from her lips to splash against the floor. The room was filled with a moan of disgust. Some of the others turned away, a couple lifted their hands to their mouths and retched.

But Devika wasn't finished. She stumbled forward and grasped the edge of the table as the agonized moans turned into something else...something *savage.* Devika whipped her head upwards and scanned the room, stilling on one of the other women. The sickening sound of hunger that ripped from Devika's lips made the other woman quake with fear.

Devika's blonde ringlets bounced as she stalked forward, her perfect voice now tainted with need. "I can smell it on you...and in you."

"Smell what?" The terrified woman jerked her gaze to us and stepped backwards.

"Your blood," Devika answered and rocked back on her heels.

She moved faster than I could track, lunging across the room to slam into the other woman. While the rest of the group scrambled away, I raced forward, grasping Devika by the arm and dragging her away.

"Get the fuck off me!" Devika howled and wrenched her arm from my grasp.

But I was used to fighting. I was trained. I was angry and filled with rage. I shoved, making her topple sideways. Before she had a chance to find her footing, I wrenched my hand backwards and lashed out, slapping her across the face. "Get *off her.*"

Devika reached upwards and pressed her hand to the burning red imprint of my palm. A moan slipped from her lips as she rocked forwards, until the sound turned into a sickening chuckle that sounded inhuman.

"You think you can hurt me?" Her pretty lips moved, but it wasn't Devika who spoke. It was whatever foul thing she'd drunk. "You can't hurt me. I *like it.*"

I flinched as she reached upwards, gripped the neckline of her pale pink dress, and yanked.

The sound of tearing fabric caught my breath. Milky skin shimmered in the dark. The amber glow of the fire licked the hardened tips of her nipples as she shrugged the ruined dress down.

I couldn't look away. She skimmed her hands down the curve of her breasts, the tip of her fingers lingered at her puckered flesh. "I like it," she whispered and shoved to stand.

"Devika...*no,*" someone whispered.

There was no stopping her as she shoved the rest of her dress down and stepped free, every inch of her body bare for all to see.

I was captured by the flare of her hips, the shadows slipping a hand between her legs to the thick dark bush that glistened in the fire's glow.

The air turned ravenous. Heavy pants of breaths mingled until it was all I heard. This wasn't right...this wasn't...*human.*

Movement came in the corner of my eye. I stiffened as Arkyn stepped closer, his gaze fixed on Devika.

"You drank the wine." It was not a question.

She swayed before him, all blush-pink nipples and quivering knees. "I'm sorry."

"You're sorry? Beg for forgiveness."

Her eyes widened even more. Tight blonde curls bounced as she shook her head. "I don't know how."

"Get. On. Your. Knees. We'll start there."

She stared into his eyes, her own widening in terror as she sank to the floor and knelt at his feet. My chest rose and fell hard with panting breaths. She obeyed him.

Just like that.

7

*D*evika trembled on her knees, her eyes lowered to the floor.

The Vampire, Arkyn, just stood there, not making a sound, and the silence turned as sharp as a blade.

"I-I didn't expect you here, My Lord," she whispered.

Arkyn's head cocked to the side, a wicked grin spreading his lips. "Don't sound too disappointed, I might think you don't like me."

His sarcasm wasn't lost on me. It was exactly what he wanted to see... just a matter of which one of us fell for the Sinful's trap first.

My heart banged so loudly in my chest, I was convinced everyone in the Night Room heard it. Except all eyes were on the Sinful and Devika.

Tears tracked down her cheeks. Blonde curls fell over shoulders that shook with her cries.

I should have looked away from her humiliation, but I couldn't rip my gaze away, needing to see, needing to understand how the Sinful delivered their punishment, what triggered their behavior.

Cassian and Lorcan stood back, their gazes tracing Devika's naked body with hunger in their eyes. Arkyn circled the girl like a predator would, taking her in, searching for the weakness in his prey, the best way to attack. Except, he had the poor girl exactly where he wanted her. This wasn't about the attack... no, he wanted to lengthen the game, see her suffer, humiliate her, remind us all of the consequences if we didn't play along.

"Do you know what I want?" Arkyn asked, glancing down at Devika.

She sniffled and tilted her head back. "Obedience," she choked out.

He exchanged a knowing look with the two other Sinful, conveying their unspoken words, then looked back to the girl. "That's all I ask for, all we want." He paused in front of her, then crouched down to face her, his large hand on her cheek, wiping her tears with a thumb. "You are beautiful and tenacious, but you don't think before you act. That makes you a risk."

"I didn't know the rules," she murmured.

I winced inwardly. *Shut up, just damn shut up.* Several others gasped, knowing speaking back wasn't going to win her any favors. We all saw it from a mile away, except for Devika, who seemed to forget we were in the home of monsters who owned us.

"Silly girl." His hand slid to her milky white shoulder, his thumb taking a slow path across her collarbone, and he leaned closer, his mouth dangerously close to the pulse in the side of her neck.

I held my breath, expecting him to bite into her, pierce her flesh... holding her with such dominance. I swallowed the lump in my throat, imagining his breath on *my* neck. Those lips so close that a tremble shot down my spine.

Heat engulfed me and I shoved it down. And I hated myself for reacting this way.

Loathed the Sinful.

Despised my life for ending up here.

But when the right moment came, I'd kill them... all three of them.

Arkyn smelled Devika's neck, his nostrils flaring.

One bite, one drop of blood on his tongue, and he'd have a taste of her. Rumors spoke of that single taste bringing her closer to becoming one of them. To drink their blood in return stole her soul and made her an undead, a Sinful.

His fingers feathered down Devika's chest, and I watched, captivated.

Her hand lashed out, grabbing his wrist to stop him.

"You're playing a dangerous game." His features darkened, his words loud and punchy.

I choked on the silence in the room, the intensity of everyone's stares on them.

Without a pause, she lowered her hand, her shoulders dropping, but her gaze held onto his like she needed him to see the fear in her eyes.

But she was wrong. This wasn't a man with a limit, with mercy, with understanding. He was a monster, who took what he wanted. He owned everything about her, about us. There was no choice, or question, or anything we could do.

His hand lowered, curved over her small breast, fingers tweaking the hardened pink nipple.

She whimpered but didn't fight back or say a word.

All rational thoughts fled as my jaw dropped, not in dread but excitement. My breaths grew ragged and harsh, and I craved his touch more than I ever should.

"I smell your arousal," Arkyn whispered, loud enough for everyone to hear, his blue eyes lifting to me for a sliver of a moment... but it might as well have been an eternity, because everyone saw the gesture. There was a light gasp from someone to my right, and my cheeks blazed with fire. My desire evaporated as my heart threatened to burst out of my chest, beating in a chaotic rhythm.

Devika's mouth opened, but he placed a finger to her lips. "We'll continue this conversation later." Lifting himself to his feet, he brought Devika to stand by her elbow and walked her backward to join the lineup with all of us.

Her gaze shot to the dress she'd tossed on the floor earlier, then to Arkyn, but with a quick shake of his head, she remained in the line, hugging her naked body.

Silence flooded the Night Room, and despite the beauty of the overhead stars, the long dining table with candelabras, gold jugs and plates, and bowls overspilling with fruit, no one moved.

Arkyn's lips twitched as he glanced over to Lorcan, who stepped forward. Black was his color of choice in clothing. He wore pants and a leather belted waistcoat the color of midnight, no shirt underneath, leaving his strong arms bare. He scanned the line of women, his sight lingering longer on Devika, before he paced in front of us.

"It's come to our attention you might not be who you seem to be. We thought we might get to know you a little better. Tell us something about yourselves, a secret. We will know if you're lying. Consider this a *real* test."

We bowed our heads in a sign of acceptance... but panic clawed at my chest on the inside. Only Jacob knew the reason for me being here. He wouldn't have told a soul. Not my Jacob.

One of the girls broke into cries, burying her face into her hands. I peered down the line to find Polaris sobbing, her body wracked with agony.

"Let's begin with you then." Lorcan stepped toward her, and she lifted her head from her hands, her black makeup smeared under her eyes.

Polaris licked her lips and dried her cheeks with her fingers. "A man three times my age paid my father very well to marry my younger sister." Her breath hitched, but she continued. "The night before their wedding, he tried to rape me, so I stabbed him in the eye with a knife and I left him in the woods to die." She lowered her head, tears streaking her face. "No one knew it was me or I'd be killed by the elders." Lifting her head, she half snorted a laugh, half sniffled. "Guess it doesn't matter now if they found out, and my sister didn't end up marrying that pig." She stood tall, and something about her pain struck a cord. We all did what was needed to survive, and in her shoes, I would have done the same.

I'd come to the manor with the need for vengeance… and nothing would stand in my way.

Lorcan didn't respond, but turned to the next girl, a girl with short chestnut hair and a deep cleavage. "And you, Nascha."

She ran her hand down her burnt orange gown over and over. "I stole two chickens from our local store when Father came down sick and couldn't work."

Lorcan studied her with narrowed eyes before moving to the next girl. My stomach dropped the closer he got. Was this a ruse to get me to confess I came here to find a way to get revenge for my parents' deaths? What if they knew and just waited for me to confess? Either way, I'd be dead.

More secrets revealed from the women, but I couldn't focus, not when sweat poured down my back, when I felt Arkyn's stare from across the room.

Chaska's strong voice reached me, and I glanced up.

"I ran away to escape from my father and lived in a barnyard for two weeks." She closed her eyes, taking deep breaths, calming herself. "He thought I ran away to escape going with the Sinful, and when I did leave, I never said goodbye to him." Her shoulders lowered as if in relief that was over, but an ache tugged in my heart when all I pictured were the bruises on her body, the whip marks on her legs.

A girl at the end of the line mumbled something to herself

and broke down, collapsed to the floor, crying uncontrollably. No one moved to console her. No one dared. We all carried darkness within us, and revealing them was like sticking a hot poker to our flesh. We'd lived with our secrets for too long, guarding them so no one found out.

Willa was next, and she stood tall, methodically interlacing her fingers and pulling them apart. My brain was shuddering, and despite listening to her words, nothing registered. I froze and considered disobeying the order, making something up. But they'd know I lied, and I'd never keep a straight face.

"Asena," Lorcan's velvety voice glided into my mind, and my first thought was that I didn't want to die. In this place, step one foot wrong, and my time would have been wasted coming in. He stared at me, expectantly, as did Cassian and Arkyn. My arms trembled by my sides, and the words tumbled from my lips in a blind panic.

"I paid someone to abduct me and bring me to you."

The sobs and shuffling sounds died, everyone staring at me, the insane person admitting I chose to come to the Sinful on purpose.

"Why?" Lorcan asked, tilting his head, studying me like I somehow looked different, like that wasn't what he'd expected to hear.

I gave a shrug. "Nothing to go home to, nothing to lose."

"Your life was that mundane?" the Vampire's whisper seemed to hypnotize me, forcing me to lift my gaze until our eyes locked.

"Yes." I answered, and it echoed with the truth.

"And you did that, knowing you might never return to your home," Cassian interjected with a curious expression.

"What's wrong with her," a female's voice murmured from somewhere in the lineup, drawing my attention to a girl twisting a lock of gleaming white hair around a finger.

"I certainly hope that's the case and nothing else." Arkyn

frowned, his suspicions, knowing I hid something, causing my breaths to shorten.

"I don't have much to aspire for in my mundane life," I answered.

"So, it's an adventure you seek," Lorcan stated, and I nodded, wanting them to move on. But he didn't right away, and his gaze traveled over me, while the other two studied me with amused expressions.

Finally, Lorcan turned away from me, and my stomach unclenched. I could barely hold myself straight, convinced they'd call me a liar and ask for the real secret. I stood upright, frozen in time, as the rest of the women spoke about their secrets when Lorcan finally gave a loud clap, and I flinched, hating that my body feared them and reacted that way.

"Thank you, ladies, now please take a seat and enjoy your dinner." He turned to the perfectly laid out table and, as if on cue, servants rushed out with filled plates. We all moved to take a seat, Devika joining us, still naked, holding her middle, walking with shoulders curled forward.

Anger vibrated under my skin at their cruel punishment, at the humiliation they made her feel so she'd never forget.

Everyone rushed to take a chair, Willa suddenly nudging against me to get a seat first, Nilsine on my other side. No one said a word, we waited for the servants to lay fabric napkins over our laps, to place food in front of us. Roast meat in red gravy filled my plate. Vegetables, steaming fresh bread, pumpkin smeared with butter, smoked sausages, cheeses, and a whole suckling pig were in the center of the table. Everything I could think of filled the table. Fowls stuffed with nuts and herbs sat in front of me, and I eyed the crispy drumstick, my mouth watering.

At home, I'd be lucky to eat meat once a fortnight after I'd sneak into the woods to catch a wild goose without drawing the Wolves' attention. But this feast was incredible. Servants poured white wine into our goblets, fussing about to ensure we all had food in front of us.

We all stared at the meals, and not one person moved to touch a morsel.

"Eat," Arkyl announced. "Don't waste this food. Enjoy."

He stepped back and took a seat alongside Cassian and Lorcan across the room from us, studying us. Fear choked inside me to not touch the food, but my stomach hurt with hunger.

The clink of metal drew my attention to Nascha, who cut a slice of the roast and placed it into her mouth, her eyes closing like it was the best dish she'd ever eaten.

When the Vampires didn't react with a punishment, the rest of us ate. The clatter of utensils, sipping of wine, and some light chatter ensued. Shadows from the flicker of candlelight danced over the table, and we devoured the meal like it might be our last chance to eat.

I had no way of knowing what the Sinful thought, but each time I looked up, their gazes were either on Devika or me... staring at me like I might be naked, like they barely contained themselves to keep their distance. I washed down a mouthful of roasted potato with the sweet, fruity wine, catching Cassian running a thumb over his lower lip while eyeing me. Was he picturing me naked? My thoughts swept me away...

Come to me, he'd whisper.

I'd go to him and let him strip me, the fabric sliding off my shoulders, his greedy fingers pressing into my flesh, dragging down my body.

He'd play with me, tease me, and I'd melt under his desire. *Snap out of it.* The words were a roar through my head, and the blinding light of reality cut through. Panic closed in, pressing me against the shadowed walls inside my mind. This was all a trick to them...*all a game.* I had to stay focused. I had to force myself to remember who they were.

Shifting in my seat, I lowered my attention to my plate, pushing those thoughts aside, keeping my focus on anything but the three Sinful who put dirty thoughts into my mind.

Arkyn rose from his seat, and everyone's heads lifted, no longer eating, frozen at the table. Had we done something wrong?

"We have something exciting planned for you in the next few days. Something that will test each and every one of you. Something thrilling and exciting. Nightingale Manor will do something it's never done before. It will open its doors for a masquerade ball, and you, my beautiful conquests, will be the ultimate prize."

Willa gasped, and the food churned in my gut.

Ultimate prize. What did that mean?

I finished my meal, feeling the Vampires' eyes on me. The other women glared, but I didn't care. I wasn't here to please these women or make friends.

"If you are finished, the guards will walk you back to your rooms."

Standing from the table, I couldn't stomach another bite. The others followed me, and we made our way to the door, the air thick and heavy.

"Devika," Arkyn murmured, his voice dangerously low, like he hid a secret. "Please stay back for a moment."

Her brow furrowed and she hugged herself. My fingers buzzed with an urgency to reach out for her, somehow steal her from their clutches, because the terror on her face scared me. Was this another test?

We all moved out into the hall as a group, the guards breaking us into small groups.

I stretched a hand to Polaris' shoulder during the shuffle. She looked back, her features twisting into a wry frown at seeing me. "What?"

Her reaction took me off guard, but I wanted to give her the benefit of the doubt. These were terrifying times for all of us. "Just wanted to say you did a brave thing to protect yourself and your sister."

Her face didn't flinch or soften, the dark makeup around her eyes smudged like she'd cried black tears. "What makes you think I need pity?" she murmured softly. "I've seen what beasts like these three can do, so I did what I had to."

I startled, rocking on my feet. "You lied?" I whispered.

"I have a sister but--" Her mouth hung open, her words never coming as she shifted her gaze to someone over my shoulder, then she just turned and walked away.

I spun, finding Cassian watching us from inside the room. Devika stood in front of the three Vampires, and I gritted my teeth, hating that we left her behind. There was a moment when her eyes widened in terror, a scream trapped in her throat, before the doors slammed shut.

"Move!" The guard drove his palm in the middle of my back, shoving me forward.

I stumbled forward through the dim hall with everyone else, and a sick feeling rose through me. We'd left her alone...with a coven of Vampires.

8

There was movement in the corridor outside our room. I pressed my hand against the door and eased my ear to the wood. Scrapes and steps, a grunt of effort.

"What is it?" Willa muttered behind me.

I ignored her, pressing harder, focusing on the sound as it slipped away. It wasn't the first scrape I'd heard...something was happening out there. I needed to know what that was. Was Devika all right?

"Nothing," I finally muttered and glanced to the window above the bed. The sky was brightening at the edges, daylight was almost here. Would the moving and the scraping stop then, when all the Vampires went to bed?

I turned back to the door. Clinking of glasses echoed, making my pulse race. What were they doing?

"Asena?" Chaska murmured from the bed.

"Go to sleep," I whispered over my shoulder.

We'd become just like the beasts who imprisoned us, sleeping when the sunlight beamed through the window and awake as the sky darkened. I hated that we were changing, hated that we were at their mercy. I shoved back from the door and paced the bedroom.

Chaska's breaths evened out, soon she'd be snoring, leaving this hell behind. But Willa battled the darkness, fighting sleep as she watched me. But she wasn't a fighter, not like I was. Her head tilted, falling forward until she jerked upright.

A scrape outside the door pulled me closer. I splayed my palms against the wood and leaned closer. Grunts and heaves were punctured with the grating, splintering sound of something heavy being dragged along the floor. It sounded woody...*like a coffin?*

Maybe it was for the masquerade ball?

Snores echoed behind me...deep growling gasps were followed by a grunt. I glanced behind me, both my roommates were dead to the world. Tiredness closed in, stinging my eyes. I swallowed a yawn. I had no time to be tired, not yet...I turned back to the faint sounds. I needed to know what was happening.

I headed for the bed, stilling at the side, and stared down at Willa. I didn't trust her, didn't trust any of them, not really. Willa had a temper, and, I suspected, a mean streak, but there was one part of her personality that drew me here in this moment. She loved to look her best, and pinning those unruly fiery curls was something she was good at.

I held my breath, watching her eyes for a hint she was awake and reached out. My fingers snapped toward a hairpin and yanked it free. A strand of hair broke. She muttered and turned her head, sighing softly before she settled once more.

I didn't dare breathe and was too afraid to move. I waited, while my chest filled with fire, until her snores started once more and then gently stepped backwards away from the bed.

My heart was thundering, breath came in a rush. I sucked in gulps, waited for the room to stop spinning, and then knelt on the floor. I'd picked a lock three times before, and each time it was different. I yanked open the pin and gently inserted it into the opening in the door.

Please let this work.

I wiggled the damn thing, twisting the ends until they hit something in the chamber. *If I could just get it...*something inside went *click.* I jerked my gaze to the knob and reached for it. My fingers curled as I twisted, and, with a *snap,* the door opened. Surprise consumed me. I sank back on my heels, staring for a second, until the faint scrape of something further along the hallway pulled my focus.

I shoved upwards and held onto the knob as the door cracked further open. Daylight was coming hard and fast, brightening the corridor outside the rooms. I waited, listening for any kind of sound, and gripped the open door.

There was a faint *click,* and then a muffled whisper. But it wasn't coming from the hall. I glance to Willa and Chaska once more, then opened the door. My footsteps were too loud. I winced, and made an effort to roll my steps as I stepped outside into the hallway.

I had to close the door, so I prayed whoever checked the rooms didn't test the locks. My roommates would sleep for hours yet, still, there was no time to waste. I eased the door closed behind me and took a step.

Cold clung to the air in the hallway. There were no sun rays to warm my skin, just a growing lightness that reached along the corridor. I stepped, making my way along the closed doors of the other girls' rooms, and tried to remember the ways we'd traveled through the castle. I wanted to stay, to search every room of this place, to uncover every sinister secret.

Footsteps sounded faintly in the distance. I froze, craned my head, and listened. Nothing. Like it'd been a trick of my imagination. Or maybe it wasn't? Curiosity pulled me deeper, leaving the rooms behind. I had no idea where I was going, just that I needed to know what was happening...and to plan a way out of here.

My escape.

The words resounded in my mind as I reached out, trailing the tips of my fingers along the wooden walls. Familiar rooms came closer, the open doors of what looked like a sitting room, dressers and sofas covered with canvas shrouds. I lingered in the hallway, looking into the dimly lit room as it slowly brightened.

I wanted to spend more time looking, more time searching, uncovering every dresser and secret in this place. But I didn't have time...not today. A noise swept my focus along the hallway, the sound of a giggle.

The hairs on the back of my neck stood on end. But the sound wasn't deep enough to be masculine. A scrape followed, like something heavy dragging on the stony floor. I left the sitting room behind and edged closer.

My calf muscles tensed as I rolled my steps. But there was no sound of my boots. I tried to steady my breaths, closing my mouth and breathing through my nose. There was someone in the room up ahead, someone that cast a shadow across the floor before they moved. I pressed my side against the wall and crept closer.

The flutter of a bird smacked a window as I neared the doorway. This room was different, expansive, so big I couldn't see the end. The covers had been removed from the furniture and the hearth had been stocked with wood. There was a table on the other side of the room that ran under the window sills. Black table cloths and crystal glasses. It looked like they were getting ready for a party...*or a masquerade ball.*

Nightingale Manor will do something it's never done before. It will open its doors for a masquerade ball, and you, my beautiful conquests, will be the ultimate prize.

Panic filled me, and the Vampire's voice slipped through the cracks.

I stepped inside and passed the open door, before someone grabbed my arm, and another slapped a hand across my mouth.

No! Not again.

Fear punched to the surface as I spun. Faces rose out of the darkness behind the door. Familiar faces of the other girl, in a cruel twisted sneer. One grabbed me by the throat as they all dragged me back into the shadows behind the door.

"Scream and we'll cut you."

I stiffened at the words, my heart thundering in my head.

"Careful, she has a knife."

I jerked my gaze to the familiar voice as Nilsine stepped out from behind them. Her cold focus fixed on me. "What? Did you think you're the only one smart enough to find a way out of your room?"

There were at least five here. Nisline, Polaris, three others. I didn't know their names. Two of them moved away, and the faint scraping sound I'd heard followed as they inspected every book and object in the room.

I shook my head and waited for them to let me go.

But they didn't, instead they drove me backwards, slamming me against the wall.

"I don't like you," Nilsine murmured. "I sure as hell don't trust you. You're hiding something, and more than a damn knife in your boot. Some of us want to be chosen by these Vampires, and we don't need Miss Velvet Dress fucking that up. We want this party. We *want* this chance to sit on the throne and be their Vampire Queen."

I shook my head, glanced from her to the others. They couldn't be serious? Polaris stood behind them, her arms crossed over her chest. There was a flicker of fear in her eyes, but it wasn't because of me.

She didn't want to be here.

"You scream and bring the whole castle running, and we'll stick you with your own knife. You understand me?"

The hand over my mouth pressed harder, smashing my lips against my teeth. Jacob's kiss pushed to the surface of my mind. The ache and the terror the same. I nodded my head, searching their eyes, and stilled.

Nilsine watched me like a hawk, then gave a nod. The hand eased against my mouth, releasing me from the crush against the wall.

"Stay out of our way," Nilsine warned. "Or suffer the consequences."

I waited for them to make a move toward my knife. But they didn't, just stepped backwards behind Nilsine.

"We'll be watching you," she said as she cast her gaze around the others.

They all nodded...except for Polaris.

And in a heartbeat, they turned and, without a sound, stepped out of the room and headed along the hallway back to the rooms once more.

I sucked in hard breaths, my mind racing. They wanted to stay here...*they* wanted *to be chosen by these monsters? They wanted to be a...a...Vampire Queen?*

The image bloomed inside my head. Four stony thrones, three behind and a smaller one at the front, and the monsters who sat there. Only it wasn't Nilsine who occupied the seat in that image...*it was me.*

The idea sickened me. I lifted a shaking hand and braced against the wall. That couldn't happen...*that wouldn't happen.* I'd stick myself with a knife before I let that happen. I waited until the faint scuff of their steps faded and my legs stopped shaking before I found the strength to move. But I wasn't giving up. I wasn't serving myself up as a prize for anyone...especially those beasts who lived in the dark.

I pushed away from the wall and made my way through the

mammoth room. Glass doors opened onto a granite patio. The doors were locked and bolted, the blinds drawn halfway. Still, it was stunning outside, green manicured lawns and towering red bramble bushes closed in the grounds. In the distance, towering pine trees blocked out part of the sun.

So where were they?

I spun and looked around me, there was no sign of anything but pretense and lies here. My legs were shaking, but I made my way out of the room and further along the hall. Room after empty room I searched. There wasn't even a maid, or a servant in sight.

It's like they all went to ground.

I found the kitchen, cold stone and stainless steel that looked like it hadn't been used in centuries. A doorway sat in one wall, like some kind of locked pantry. I stepped closer, hearing a low moan.

A shudder raced down my back. I wrenched my gaze over my shoulder, but there was no one hiding in the shadows this time. So I turned back, pressing my hand against the door. "Is anyone in there?"

The moan came again, low and feminine. My stomach tightened. I leaned closer. "Hello? Are you hurt?"

"Yes." The whisper came from inside, followed by the clink of metal on metal.

Shackles. That's what it sounded like. I reached into my pocket, yanked the hairpin free, and knelt. I worked faster this time, finding the catch quickly before the door swung open.

I blinked into the darkness, my eyes adjusting to the light. There was a woman huddled in the corner, her arms raised above her head.

It took me a second to recognize her, and when I did, I froze. It was Eira, the woman who'd run from the Sinful and charged through the trees. I glanced at the shackles around her wrists and saw the puncture marks in her wrist. *"You?* I thought you were dead."

"They're coming for you," Eira whispered and shifted her feet. Her thin, pale dress slipped between her thighs. She'd been bitten, and more than once. "They'll tear you from the light and leave you craving the dark. You won't be able to escape them, Asena."

I flinched, my heart lunging against the confines of my chest. "How do you know my name?'

She smiled an unhinged, manic smile and closed her eyes, swaying where she sat.

Fear was in the driver's seat, punching me forward until I grasped her hand, making her wince. "I said, *how do you know my name?"*

"They know everything," she chuckled. "The dance...the seduction. You think it'll be you doing the seducing. But you're all wrong...you're all so very wrong. He wants you, did you know that, Asena? *They all want you."*

9

Silence dragged over my skin like jagged edges of glass, while my hurried steps rushed me down the hall.

They know everything.

I gulped down the sickening sensation rising through me. Eira's words stayed with me, her voice ringing in my ears. What did the Sinful know? I stopped dead outside my bedroom, my hand resting on the metal knob. How would they know my real mission? Had my mistake been saying too much during the secret test… admitting I came here on purpose?

Stupid.

Stupid.

Stupid.

What was I thinking? Except my admittance just happened tonight, so it couldn't be that, right?

He wants you, did you know that, Asena? They all want you.

The only way she knew my name was if she'd heard someone else talking about me.

I was shaking my head, staring over my shoulder. The hall stood silent, dimly lit, and I watched the shadows, expecting a Sinful to step out, but they never did. I sucked in a ragged breath. Shivers raced up my legs as I remembered poor Devika's humiliation, her punishment.

Arkyn's fingers on her nipple, and I fought the pure pleasure coursing through me so fast at the mere memory, at the heat pooling between my thighs, picturing myself under their attention, their touch, their desire.

But I shook my head, pushing away the fire swelling through me. My body shouldn't respond that way to these monsters, shouldn't want them when they'd hurt so many people. I lied to myself thinking my reaction had anything to do with shock… I'd never been with a man in the ways they promised, and these Sinful, they were unlike any man I'd encountered before. They did things to my insides that left me confused and longing. It was safe to say my body was betraying me when it came to these Vampires.

It was wrong, all of it a game, and I hated myself for letting them affect me this way.

Instinct had me pushing open the door and darting into my dark bedroom, shutting myself in without making a sound.

Breaths raging, I tugged my dress up and over my head and drew on the nightdress the servants had left in our room earlier in the day. I pushed the wild strands of russet-colored hair out of my face, letting them fall against my back before I climbed into bed next to Willa. The soft snores from her and Chaska were comforting in knowing they wouldn't ask me questions about where I'd been. I slid under the blanket, laid my head on the pillow, and shut my eyes, trying to sleep while my brain replayed the night's events over and over.

They settled on Eira… she was still alive, but she was no longer free. The fact that she was chained up and being used as food by the Sinful terrified me… Was that how we'd all end up?

The next evening the three of us woke early, washed and dressed, then waited to be called for breakfast. I spent those few early hours with my nose in a book. Willa and Chaska kept to themselves, withdrawn, barely saying two words to me or each other.

Shock.

Reality punched into us last night, and now... now we dealt with the repercussions of what we were really dealing with.

Danger.

Imprisonment.

Seduction.

I lowered my gaze to the book in my hands, filling my thoughts with how Wolves hunt their prey rather than thinking about the monsters at my doorstep.

When Wolves make a successful kill, they don't eat in moderation. They can eat up to twenty-two pounds from one kill. The Alpha always eats first, and what remains can be scavenged by the rest of the pack.

Several people from our village had gone missing over the past year... Wolf hunts, many said, but we'd never found their bodies. This explained a lot. Regardless of what the Sinful said about protecting the townsfolk, the Wolves still took what they wanted.

The shuffle of feet on the stone floor drew my attention to Willa, who paced in front of the door, sunlight brightening her auburn hair, her brow furrowed.

"Is everything all right?" I asked.

"One of the girls said she thinks the dance is tomorrow night," she blurted, her hands rubbing the red material of her dress cinched in at the waist in a nervous twitch. The skirt dragged on the floor around her feet, since the dress was made for someone taller than five-foot-three. "I'm not ready," she mumbled, her eyes wild and crazy. "I need more time to... I don't know. Be ready. What if they ask me to strip? What if…" her breath hitched.

Chaska hopped up from where she lounged on the bed and made her way across the room toward the bathroom. "Who cares when it's on. It's going to happen, regardless. And then, we just do what we're told," she tossed the words over her shoulder before shutting herself in the bathroom.

"It's not that," Willa called out, her jaw clenched. "Last night I thought I'd pass out when they asked us to reveal a secret." She flopped onto the end of the bed, her huge eyes watery and looking at me. "These tests aren't about finding out who we are, it's about pushing us until we break. Did you see what they did to Devika? I'd die if it was me." Speaking quickly, her chest heaved up and down. "I don't think I can be here. This isn't for me." She was shaking her head, her body trembling, and I leaned forward, reaching out to place my hand on hers.

"You're not alone."

She pushed to stand up, pulling from my touch. "What difference does that make? They are going to target each one of us, one at a time until we're nothing more than slaves. Until we become one of them." Hugging her middle, she paced again. "They scared Devika into submission. They killed Eira in the woods when she ran. We have no way out. We're just waiting to die!" Her voice squeaked like she might burst out crying.

"Eira isn't dead," I said. "I saw her last night." But as the words left my mouth, I regretted saying them. I didn't want to admit to having snuck out of the room, and could I really trust anyone here? The encounter with Nilsine still thrummed through my veins, her threat, the other girls who followed her.

Willa froze mid-step and stared at me, her mouth dropping open. "Where? I didn't see her at the dinner?"

The bathroom door opened and Chaska stuck her head out. "Are you lying?"

"Why would I lie about that?" A sliver of manic laughter

escaped from my mouth that I kept encouraging this, then glanced down at my book, but I couldn't read a single word. Maybe they'd let it go.

Willa scrambled over to the bed again, sitting close to me. "Was she alive? God, had they turned her into one of them? Where did you see her?"

"Just let her speak," Chaska groaned and rolled her eyes as she stepped out, wrapped in a towel.

"I honestly don't remember much. It was dark, but she was alive." If being imprisoned and fed on was called living.

"And? What did she say?" Willa asked hungrily.

I shook my head, remembering her words. *They know everything.* I trembled, regretting saying anything.

Willa and Chaska stared at me with bated breaths, desperation in their eyes to understand what would become of us when we crossed the Sinful. "Nothing. I rushed past a room and caught a glimpse of her before a door shut. I think she was chained."

Lips pulled into a crooked grin, "What else?" Chaska asked. "Was she alone? Wearing clothes? Did she look like a Vampire?"

I shook my head. "It happened too fast. But the point is, she was alive."

Both girls looked at me, unamused. "Why are you holding out on us?" Willa asked. "Sure, she's alive, but why isn't she with the rest of us?"

Gripping my book tightly, I was shaking my head. "That's all I saw." Why had I opened up my big mouth?

I couldn't tell them what Eira said. Her words were like thorns, scraping through my insides. And I'd seen the sliver of jealousy already in the other girls' eyes. How much they wanted to become the Vampires' Queen, how they'd step over anyone to get there.

No, I couldn't trust anyone with this, couldn't dare let them know what Eira had told me.

Chaska shrugged, her expression taut, and marched back into the bathroom, slamming the door shut.

Willa just stared at me... through me.

I swallowed hard and licked my suddenly dry lips. "What do you think they'll make us wear for the masquerade ball?"

With her disappointment crossing her features, she shot to her feet and crossed the room to stand near the window, staring outside.

"That's all I saw," I murmured.

Her head snapped around to face me, fire in her gaze. "You think we don't know you snuck out of the room last night."

My stomach dropped through me, and I winced. Would they tell the Sinful?

Silence fell between us and she turned her back to me.

Priority was surviving. As much as I contemplated trying to smooth this over, I kept quiet. I sighed and lowered my attention to the book, having learned my lesson about what I shared. Better to be quiet than draw attention to myself.

"What are those?" Willa leaned over my shoulder, peering at the small stack of books in my hand. *The Lore of Vampyre and My Immortal Soul.*

"Nothing," I answered with a rush and palmed the small note with my name in elegant scrawl.

"Doesn't look like nothing. Did the servants bring them to you?" She pouted when she spoke.

"Yes," I whispered.

Liar...

Cassian's whispered inside my head, followed by a low, chuckle filled with wicked delights.

Tsk. Tsk, Asena.

I whirled around, grabbed the books and raced for the

bathroom. Two days I'd had this...two days of him inside my head. I closed the bathroom door harder behind me and strode for the mirror.

Bloodshot eyes and a mess of hair.

You look tired, he whispered his voice heavy with savage hunger.

"If I'm tired it's because you wait for me in my dreams." I hissed quietly. "Just leave me alone."

Never.

I dropped the books to the edge of the basin and swayed under exhaustion. The first dream he came to me, whispering things I never remembered when I woke. But last nights...I lifted my gaze to the mirror and stared at the tiny red spidered veins in my eyes. Last night he did things to me...I woke moaning...with my hand speared between my legs.

"Asena?" Willa's concerned voice cut through the doorway. "Are you okay?"

"Yes." I lied.

This was what *they* made me into; a liar, someone not to be trusted. I looked down to the note in my hand...

Asena, Soon now.

There was no place I could hide from him...and I felt the oncoming masquerade ball like building storm. Something was going to happen. I lowered my gaze to the stack of books and lifted my hand.

My Immortal Soul.

The words were etched into the spine.

Soon, Cassian whispered inside my head. *Soon you will be mine.*

A knock came on our door. We exchanged worried looks, and Chaska padded over to open the door. A female servant wearing a black dress, her sleeves pushed up to her elbows, and her dark hair pulled tightly off her face, stood in the doorway.

"Tonight is the masquerade ball, and it's time to get you ready. Follow me." She turned, her footsteps fading down the hall.

Panic squeezed my lungs, and Willa was on her feet, making a strange whimpering sound. Chaska had already lifted her chin and marched out of the room without a glance our way.

I climbed off the bed and moved after her, Willa suddenly glued to my side. "She scares me sometimes," she whispered.

"The servant?" I asked, glancing over at Willa.

She was shaking her head. "Chaska."

I eyed Chaska marching alongside the servant with determination, shoulders squared, but I remembered the agony in her voice when she told the story of how she hid in her barn before taken by the Sinful. "I don't think she'll hurt any of us."

Willa eyed me suspiciously. "You trust too easily, you know that?"

Jacob had said something similar when I last saw him, but that wasn't true. I cared about others, kept quiet when I saw things to avoid causing trouble. Maybe that made me look trusting, but I wasn't naive.

We followed the servant into a room, and I froze in the doorway, my gut clenching.

Four wooden bathtubs were scattered around the room, a girl in one of them, while the servants washed and scrubbed her like they bathed a pet dog. Other girls were dried off, then laid on a table in the back corner, completely naked. A maid ripped strips of fabric off their legs and even from the small mound between their thighs. The girls whimpered, eyes shut tight.

Willa gasped loudly, her eyes on Nascha on the nearest table, wincing each time the woman pulled back a strip of sticky fabric from her legs. "We only wax on the night before our wedding," Willa murmured. "What are they going to do to us at the dance? Gods, what if we have to strip?" Her breaths rushed, a hand to her throat like she might pass out.

Well, I'd never shaved anything on my body in my life, so this should be fun.

Someone nudged me in the back. "Hurry, get undressed."

Chaska was already climbing into a tub while Willa and I removed our clothes. I couldn't stop shaking, not sure where to look with most of us naked and being pulled and pushed and plucked. My heart stuttered, but this was nothing more than getting us ready for how the Sinful wanted. What worried me more were the Sinful's intentions for us tonight.

A servant with iron fingers and wiry gray hair snatched my wrist and hauled me to a tub I could easily sit crouched in, so I climbed in to get this over with. Her black dress was drenched down the front, clinging to her thin frame, covering small breasts, hip bones poking out. Was she being fed?

"Remain standing." With a bar of black soap in hand, she dragged the thing down my arms, feeling like jagged stones tearing my flesh. I grimaced through the pain ripping over my skin. Hands reached everywhere, over my breasts, down my stomach, up my thighs and even between them. I flinched, but she gripped my arm, nails digging into me. "Sit still. It's no fun for me either."

Willa's cries flooded the room, while Nilsine was laughing, enjoying herself as she followed a servant across the room. She eyed me with the threat from our encounter in the hall in her eyes. I held her stare until the servant scolded her with words I couldn't hear.

By the time I'd been finished and climbed out, I was raw and red all over, then I was dragged by the arm to the table, and I cringed on the inside. But I followed their instructions, dried myself, and lay on the table on my back, eyes shut, thinking about being back home, the creek behind my home where I sometimes caught fish, the jokes Jacob would tell me. When the first strip was ripped off my leg, I cried out, and several girls laughed.

My cheeks heated, and I lay there, beyond embarrassed.

Holding still, I rode through the excruciating pain that felt like someone skinned me alive. When she ripped the hair from the apex between my legs, I died on the inside, tears sliding out of the corners of my eyes at the piercing pain swallowing me. Why in the world would anyone ever do this to themselves on purpose?

Up on wobbly legs, I stared down at myself once they finished, feeling more exposed, more vulnerable with no hair. Was this what men preferred?

Grabbing my hand, the servant dragged me across the room, and I stumbled after her, lashing an arm across my chest to cover myself. Which made no sense, considering I was running naked, but it made me feel somehow less exposed.

The woman snorted a mocking laugh at seeing me. "The Lords of this manor don't subscribe to the same prudish rules about being naked like the townsfolk. You'll soon learn to accept that."

Before I'd caught my breath, two servants tossed a pale blue dress over my head, yanking the gown down my body, pinching my skin, tugging my hair. I winced, riding through the pain. My head and arms pushed out the top of the dress and the women hastened to tighten the laces at my back. The dress sat off one shoulder, chiffon fabric embracing my body in a tight-fitting style like it'd been designed specifically to hug my body like a second skin. A scooping neckline skimmed low over my chest, making my breasts look incredible. The fabric cascaded down from my hips like a stunning waterfall, falling to my feet.

I laughed a little and then gasped at seeing myself wearing such a gown.

This was unlike anything I'd worn before. The woman at my

back pulled the bodice part tighter, the material following every single curve, and taking a deep breath was close to impossible.

Someone was brushing my hair off my face, another woman coating my arms in a vanilla oil, bringing a natural shine to my skin.

The servant held a black lace butterfly-style eye mask. She placed it over my eyes, and pulled the silk ribbons behind me to tie it up at the back of my head.

"Wow," Willa started, and I turned to see her staring at me with a gaping mouth. She wore a golden gown that glinted like jewelry, cinched in tight at her waist, with a plunging neckline at the front, and flared out a bit at mid-thigh before falling down. "You look insanely gorgeous."

"You think?" I looked down, still unable to believe I fit into this dress or looked like this. "You look so beautiful," I said.

She nodded, but couldn't stop eyeing me head to toe, and I caught that slight twitch at the corner of her mouth, the envy in her eyes. "We better head off, most of the others have left." Her voice hardened and she pulled her eye mask down over her eyes, two yellow feathers sticking out on either side. She really was beautiful.

The servant placed a set of heels with diamonds across the front before me, the color matching my dress, , while another woman painted my lips ruby red.

"The Lords are going to..." she gasped and smiled so wildly, it scared me.

I was torn between excitement at seeing their expressions, and repulsion with myself that such a thing should have me tingling all over.

Willa walked out of the room, and I stepped into my shoes and wobbled after her. If I walked slowly, I'd be fine.

Nerves twisted my insides, but there was no reason I ought to feel anything but disgust at being paraded like this... even if secretly I loved this dress with every ounce of my being.

A guard waited farther down the hall and escorted us, walking outside through a courtyard where stars blinked in the dark sky, then more hallways until we reached two open ornate doors.

Breaths choked in my lungs, but I raised my chin and held myself steady.

I could do this. Just walk in and smile. Nothing else.

Despite the beautiful dress, for being tricked into feeling special, I was still a prisoner like everyone else. I'd still lost my parents. The Vampires were to blame, and I had to remind myself of that in this place, recall who I dealt with. No dress or flashy mask could change the cold hard facts that any time they chose, they could end my life.

I stepped into the elaborate hall with its crystal chandeliers and black wallpaper with ornate golden swirls. Statues of beautiful women adored the corners and oversized vases with flowers brought color to the room, while waiters in black suits walked around with gold trays filled with glasses of drinks.

Close to fifty people mingled in the room, mostly men, all wearing masks, and I recognized none of them. Unease crept through me. What were we getting ourselves into?

Several of the girls I knew stood around, close to each other, whispering, all dressed in gowns of every color, plunging necklines, high-cut splits in their skirts. This was a party for showing us off, and that terrified me. Who were they showing us off to?

Polaris stood at the side of the group of girls when Nilsine turned to me, followed by them all. Ugly stares raked down my body, their lips pulled into sneers. I trembled and turned away, following a servant to take a glass of water... anything to wet my dry throat, to escape the glares. I didn't want to be here, under scrutiny. That was when my gaze found Lorcan, standing near two older men, his eyes heating as they trailed lazily down my body, a captivating grin spreading his lips.

Others looked, too, and suddenly I felt like I no longer belonged in my skin... or here. My heart beat too fast, too loudly in my ears, my body shook. Too many eyes on me, their starved looks weighing heavily on my shoulders. My feet slipped backward, taking me to the side wall, where the shadows festered. Sweat rolled down my back, and more than anything, I wanted to be invisible and disappear, needing to get away before I fainted or something, because I couldn't take this attention. This wasn't me... this wasn't who I was.

10

The dance...*the seduction*, Eira's words raced through my mind. *You think it'll be you doing the seducing. But you're all wrong...you're all so very wrong.*

A low, terrifying growl came from the shadows at my right. I closed my eyes as my heart slammed against my ribs. Movement followed, so subtle you could miss it.

But I didn't. I knew the inches between us...and instinctively who it was. "Cassian," I whispered and opened my eyes.

"You understand what you have to do?" the Vampire whispered from the shadows.

I closed my eyes, refusing to answer...*refusing to see.*

Sinful.

Deadly.

The words raced through my mind as his icy breath spilled down the hollow of my neck, making me tremble.

He was close...*too close.*

I couldn't turn my head, couldn't look into the shadows.

I already knew what I'd find.

Cold, stony, moonlight-kissed skin, and intense eyes that seemed to stare into my soul. But it was his mouth that captivated me, white fangs peeking from blood-red lips, which curled back from his teeth as he snarled. The sight didn't scare me like it used to.

More young men strolled through the door and looked around. But it was an awkward-looking guy who held my attention. It wasn't because I was attracted to him...I looked at him the same way as the fanged beasts looked at me, like a conquest, something to be claimed.

The thought hit me like a slap.

"I can't do this," I whispered.

"Can and *will*," Cassian commanded. "You know what happens if you don't. Pass this test, Asena. Pass it *or else*."

The Vampire's voice seemed to echo through my head, like he spoke directly to me. I flinched at the sound. My heart pounded.

"Open your eyes, Asena. Look at him."

I was helpless to defy him, *drowning in a sea of desire.* But hate swirled around me, *and inside me,* like a tornado filled with the terror of my past. I allowed that hate to consume me, battling the flames of unwanted desire that both disgusted me and intrigued me in equal parts.

Still, I obeyed...and opened my eyes.

"Tell me how you'll walk toward him. How you'll give him a hint of a smile," the monster in the dark murmured. "How you'll brush past him just enough for him to be ensnared by the scent of your perfume...and how when he turns toward you, you'll do the same and smile, that sweet, *innocent,* seductive smile. How you'll step backwards, drawing him closer and closer and you'll angle your body so his gaze will be drawn by the swell of your breasts. How you'll lead him into the darkness and press your spine against the wall, pretending he's the one who trapped you, when it'll be the other way around. How you'll lean close and whisper into his ear, just so he can look into the low neckline of your gown. How you'll make the poor sap blush with the whisper of your desire, how his body will harden and quake and that look of hunger will consume him."

I turned toward the darkness, where the monsters of my nightmares watched me from the shadows. "Please don't make me do this. I can't."

"You will if you want to be chosen. That is what you want, don't you? The alternative…"

I knew what the alternative was. I'd found her shackled like an animal, with fang marks all over her body.

Eira came back to me. The way she'd licked her lips and arched her back. The way she'd been terrorized by these beasts and yet she craved more.

"I will kill him," Cassian warned. "I will tear his throat from his body and bathe you in a sea of his blood."

My victim stepped through the open doors from the marble patio outside and into the ballroom, following three of his friends into the masquerade ball. Shy, quiet, his brown eyes glittered as he scanned the room and our gazes connected. A hint of a smile as he stared at me, and then a slow tilt of his head, an acknowledgement of my presence.

He stilled, and electricity surged through me like a live wire.

"He looks as awkward as you do," Lorcan murmured in my ear. "Tell me how you'll seduce him. Tell me how you'll take such a timid little mouse and make him roar."

I didn't know. I didn't know anything. I stared at him, fighting the urge to scream *RUN! ALL OF YOU RUN, NOW!*

My fingers curled, clenching the pale blue chiffon in my grasp. I focused on my prey and took a step forward, fighting back the horror of what I was about to do.

That's the way, Asena…

I'll make you mine yet.

That same echo boomed inside my head. Panic flared, smothering the sound of his voice with the thunder of my heart. *Get out,* I growled. *Get out of my head.*

A low, unbridled chuckle slipped through my mind like a promise.

They were in my thoughts now, rifling through my emotions like I was their personal plaything.

In the ballroom, the man lifted his head at my movement, stars igniting in his eyes as they widened in surprise. *Seduce him...or else.* I forced a smile and closed the distance. But an ache tore through my chest as I left the darkness behind. I fought the need to turn...to stare into those bestial eyes and give into the need roaring inside me.

I was tortured, haunted, and terrorized, and all within my own mind. My body betrayed me, heating with the Vampire's words, envisioning all the wicked things he could do.

Instead, I climbed the stairs from the dance floor and lifted my hand, meeting those soft, *mortal,* brown eyes and whispered, "Hi there, I'm Asena."

He glanced at my hovering hand and then gripped it with his own. "Trevor."

My knuckles crushed together under his grip. I smiled, smothering the wince of pain. A shudder coursed through me. *What are you doing? This isn't you.* I fought the urge to glance at the shadows, to the monster I knew watched me, and instead whispered, "Would you like to dance?"

Panic flared in his eyes. He swallowed hard and glanced at the others swirling around and shook his head. "No... if that's okay. I don't tend to move that well, especially when other people are in close proximity."

The music deepened with the treble of the cello. A long, drawn-out tone was punctured with sharp, frantic notes. It triggered something inside me, something desperate, something *hungry.*

Like a spell. The words raced through my mind, and this time they were my own. I glanced across the dance floor to the heavy, half-lidded gazes from all the women held by their will. That's exactly what they looked like...hypnotized, *entranced.*

"Are you thirsty?" my date murmured, his focus fixed on my mouth.

His gaze seemed captivated by my mouth, and I stilled, my tongue poised midway along my lower lip in a slow slide. "No," I whispered and stepped closer. "I'm actually cold."

There was a flinch in him, like the words were some kind of trigger. This was his moment to draw me closer...if he was interested. *Was he interested?*

I didn't have to turn my head to feel the pressure of this challenge, all I had to do was shift my gaze. Willa leaned closer to a male standing against the wall. She smiled and picked up her dress, twirling seductively.

She was a natural, flashing perfect white teeth, bending low enough so the tops of her creamy breasts showed, and the male she was with was enthralled.

*I'm not like that...*the thought stuck like glue. My breasts weren't spilling, not enough to draw his focus. I shifted my gaze to my newfound date. Not that he'd notice. So what *did* he notice?

I lifted my hand, fingers twirling a strand of my hair. He glanced at my fingers and then back to my mouth. I parted my lips and dragged my teeth across the flesh. "Did you know Vampires live here?"

He jumped with the words. "Have you seen any?" His eyes widened. "I mean, is there anything about them you can show me?"

Something niggled at the back of my mind. He was acting strange, not at all like someone who was terrified of running into an Immortal...more like he was *intrigued.*

"No," I lied. "The place was empty when we came."

"Mother said this place had new owners, that is was a place

for women like you. It's the only reason why we all came tonight."

"Like me?" I stepped closer.

"You know…" he glanced around. "Looking for a husband."

That kick in my stomach almost fought its way to my face. "Tell me, Trevor. Are you looking for a wife?"

He jerked his gaze back to me. "Mother says I…"

I licked at the edges of my mouth, my tongue darting. "Have you ever kissed a woman?" I whispered as the ravenous tone of the music swirled and swept right through me, stealing the edge of fear and caution. I tried to search for the panic and terror, but all I felt was soft, pliable…*yielding.*

"No." The answer was a rush of breath.

Seduce him…or he dies.

Cassian's words tore through my head. Urgent *and dangerous,* tearing me from the moment. My knees shook, my pulse sped. I stuttered, sounding like a damn fool, drawing on the only fumbling, petrified moment of romance I'd ever had. "I've kissed someone before, you want me to tell you what it felt like?"

I scrambled to find the right words. The poor idiot should be running. Some of the women were already kissing their victims…passing the test, while I floundered.

Tick…tick…tick…

A lump formed in my throat. I swallowed, trying to force the panic down.

"Yes," he answered. "Tell me."

The words tumbled out of my mouth. "It was angry and urgent, teeth gnashing. Panicked, not at all like I thought it'd be my first time."

Trevor's eyes sparked. "How did you envision it'd be?"

I took the bait and prayed not to mess this up, and held onto his gaze as I whispered, "Soft, quiet, demanding, but not too much. I envisioned a hand at the small of my back. The fingers of his other hand tangled in my hair." *Fangs sliding down my neck.*

The image roared to the surface and the seductive male chuckle filled my mind.

Is that what you want, Asena? You want me to bite you? To...claim you? But it wasn't Cassian's voice inside me now. It was Arkyn's. I quaked with fear.

I will take you right here in the middle of this ball... just say the word. I'll tear that pretty dress from your body and part your thighs. You'll look up at me while I claim you...and all you'll see is fangs.

Terror claimed me. It was a trick, just a trick, but heat pooled low in my belly, making me slick with need. They were trying to derail me. I glanced at Willa, who was pressed against the wall, her conquest's hand over her breast.

Others were kissing. I could feel them, their ravenous hunger. It swirled around me like a storm, whipping my own aching need into a frenzy.

Movement came from the darkness. Arkyn stepped out into the light and passed between them, slipping amongst the throng like he was invisible. I closed my eyes to the rhythm of the music and felt the beat move deeper through me.

Sex.

Seduction.

It was all around me. I stole a deep breath and focused on the man in front of me.

"No," I whispered.

"No?" Trevor murmured. "No, what?"

I jerked my gaze to his. "No, it wasn't like that at all. Not slow and seductive, not teasing with his tongue against mine." I stepped closer under the guise of lowering my voice to a whisper. Heat flared in my cheeks, and I let it claim me. "I want..."

He swallowed hard, his voice deep and husky. "Yes? What do you want?"

"I want a do-over," I answered. "I want the perfect kiss. My heart is racing with the thought. Is yours?"

"Yes," he admitted quickly.

"I want to bite." The music claimed me, taking me, stealing my last resolve. I gave into it, falling head first into the abyss of hunger and desire, and in a voice that was not my own I finished. "I want to be like the beasts that lived in these walls. I want to hunt, and fuck, and be *unafraid.*"

11

My bravery buckled, the words I'd said out loud felt like stones lodged in my throat, and I couldn't swallow past them, could barely draw a breath into my lungs.

This wasn't me... this wasn't who I was.

But I had to become whatever *they* wanted, including a temptress, to save Trevor's life. My insides seethed that the Sinful put me in this position in the first place, made me quiver with fear, and worst of all, had me desiring them when they were the enemy.

My gaze shifted to the luxurious ballroom, polished floorboards, the extravagant paintings of animal battle scenes in thick golden frames, and lush velvet chaise lounges at one end of the room. They looked expensive, one of them most likely costing more than I'd make in a year at the haberdashery. Fiery sconces adorned the walls, adding to the expensive feel of the ballroom.

People danced or milled around in gowns and suits, the men gravitating toward the women. They looked so comfortable with each other, like they might be enjoying themselves. That heavy seduction tethered me here, running hands all over my body and my mind.

I gave into it, feeling the throb echo through me.

There was no sign of the Sinful anywhere. Just shadows crowding the corners, and the thumping of my heart in my ears, telling me I'd fail.

A brunette dragged her date by a hand across the hall, her gaze swinging left and right, but she was a fool to think no one saw her. They fell into the shadows behind the stairs, while my gaze settled on the double doors they'd walked past. A way out of the manor. Escape.

The fleeting longing to run away vanished as fast as it hit me. I had to be careful now. Three Sinful spoke to me through my mind like they'd always had the ability. They read my thoughts… including why I'd come to Nightingale Manor. I knew this now. No secret lay unturned from them. I just hadn't known it until now.

I felt my heart sink to my stomach and the knowledge made me sick. It could only lead to terrible things.

They know everything.

Tension pulled through my body like a knotted rope unraveling. Eira's words made sense now… the Sinful had known all along. But they'd done nothing about it. I was a game for them, a challenge to see what I'd do.

I turned to Trevor, who stared down at Nascha amid the dancers, pressing herself against a broad-shouldered man with short black hair. She drew her skirt to her tanned thighs and hooked a leg around his, her lips lifting toward his. The move looked awkward to me, but her date embraced her tightly. Was that what Trevor wanted? A dominating woman, someone else to take control?

I wiped sweaty hands down my gown and reached out for him, forcing a smile, my fingers curling around his wrist.

You're disappointing me. Cassian's voice slid into my thoughts, leaving me trembling.

Trevor turned back toward me, the corners of his mouth creasing into a half grin. "You mentioned beasts living in these walls, in this castle."

I nodded, and his eyes lit up.

His hand swiveled over mine and grasped me tightly, drawing me closer.

I splayed a hand against his strong chest. "I can tell you so many of the manor's secrets." I batted my eyes, which felt wrong, considering my topic of conversation, but Trevor responded, his honeyed brown eyes smiling.

He traced a finger across the edges of my eye mask. "Do you ever worry the Sinful might one day return to this mansion?" He guided me up a few more steps by my hand, and we stood near the black railing, overlooking the dancing.

I stepped closer to him, brushing my breasts against his chest, and whispered, "They might still be here, watching us. Anything is possible in such an old mansion."

I caught my lower lip between my teeth, and Trevor's gaze fell to my mouth. His lips were thin, red from constantly licking them. He was just as nervous as I was.

His hand slid around my lower back and pressed himself against me, his cock hard through his pants, and I gasped. The thrill of danger aroused him more than anything else, it seemed.

Though he carried none of the poise I'd witnessed with the Sinful, the grace and fierceness in their movements. Unlike the three Vampires, I felt nothing near Trevor, no impossible attraction or my body burning up from a single touch. This man did nothing for me.

That isn't what the test is about, Asena. Lorcan's voice whipped across my mind, bringing with it shivers. Having my own fear tangled with seducing Trevor was hard enough without having Vampires in my head, constantly pushing and pushing.

"What's it like, living in a place where beasts once walked these halls? Where they slaughtered innocents?" Trevor's ravenous eyes stilled on mine.

Sucking in a deep inhale, I pressed a hand to my chest to slow my racing heart, to calm my thoughts, to remember my mission and focus. Except Trevor took that as my fear and leaned closer, his lips a mere brush on my lips. "Will you show me around?"

I stiffened, his kiss feeling wrong, but I raised my gaze to his. "Leaving the ballroom is not a good idea."

He drew away from me quickly, his eagerness already fading. Fear spiked through me. So I reached my hand out and snatched his in mine, interlacing our fingers together.

"Come, let me tell you about the things I've seen in this manor."

A hungry smile pulled his lips apart, and we strolled in a slow walk around the curved balcony overlooking the ballroom.

I curled myself against his side, just as I'd seen the other girls do. I spent the next few minutes telling him stories I made up about ghosts in the manor, tales of a coffin in the basement, walls that still ran fresh with blood. The lies came so easily, and he devoured them, while I couldn't stop my eyes from darting around the room. Barely anyone was dancing anymore. Most had paired up, lips on the women's necks, hands sliding under their skirts. Before I could avert my eyes, feeling like I ought to give them privacy, Trevor's fingers slid up my arm.

"Are you ever scared?" he asked, a hand cupping the side of my face, and I leaned into his touch, looking into those deep brown eyes as if I knew his desires, holding his stare. Men liked attention, to feel like the world revolved around them, to have women stare at them as though mesmerized.

Good girl, Cassian whispered.

"Sometimes." I circled my thumb across the back of his hand. "The sounds in this manor at night are terrifying."

Hands on my shoulders, he walked me backward, my breaths racing. I reminded myself this was my test, to get him so aroused he couldn't resist. My heart gave a wobble at the thought of Trevor pushing himself onto me... his presence did nothing for me. Not like the Sinful. Yet they were blood-thirsty monsters, vile things that had killed my parents, evil, and yet I still craved them...

Nerves churned in my gut as I let Trevor pin me to the wall, his body shoved so close, I winced. His hands fell to my hips, and he fisted handfuls of my skirt, lifting and find the warm flesh of my thighs. Greedy fingers slid over my skin, and I stood there, letting him touch me. I gritted my teeth, hating his hands on me, but I did nothing except play that ridiculous game.

"Is that wincing sound the noise you make when you're scared?"

Our chests mashed together, my heart drumming so loudly now, and I looked around, waiting to see if Cassian or one of them would step in. Rip this man off me. But no one came.

"Have you ever dreamt of the Sinful?" He tenderly placed a finger under my chin and tilted my head back, forcing me to face him.

Repulsion seared me, but I could have him if I wanted. He was eager, I saw the hunger in his eyes, felt his arousal nestled against my stomach.

"Come with me," he whispered. "Leave this place. It's just a house for women who want to find a husband, anyway. You can be with me and I can show you so much."

His words sounded clumsy and wrong. Fingers crept to the apex between my thighs and terror consumed me, drowning me. I didn't want this and rebelled against his move in my head, but my hand lashed out when his fingers slid between my legs, and I shoved his hand away.

This wasn't me.

Asena, Arykyn's voice growled in my mind, and I froze, instantly regretting my action, swallowed by the dread of what the Sinful would do to me. *I need to show you, need to teach you until you understand,* he threatened.

Trevor's gaze darted back and forth from me to the dance with fury, and he grabbed my arm, wrenching me toward him with such force, I tripped over my feet.

He snatched my shoulders, fingernails digging into my flesh, and shook me aggressively, before dragging me against him, his disgusting mouth crushing against mine. But it was wrong, everything felt wrong and revolting.

I shoved my fists into his chest. "Don't," I cried.

Rage rippled across his face as his hand jutted toward me, seizing me before I could react.

My blood boiled, and I drove my knee into his groin, then shoved my hands against his chest. I stumbled backward, while he crumbled to his knees, cupping himself, groaning like a wounded boar.

"Try that again and see what happens," I goaded him, wishing I had my blade with me.

A groan fell from his lips when his hateful eyes met mine. "Bitch, you'll pay for this."

I would, I knew that, but it wasn't coming from this asshole.

"You'll never lay another hand on me," I warned, shaking violently, tears already pricking my eyes.

He looked up to me with hatred in his gaze, his mouth twisted into a filthy promise of pain. This man hurt women, I saw that now. "I was fucking promised--"

The lights went out.

Stealing his words.

I flinched and stepped back.

Darkness stretched out, swallowing everything from view.

I needed to get the hell out of this place, the heavy doors to escape flashing in my mind. There was no way I'd beat this test, not with this man. The Sinful had put me into an impossible scenario.

From the deepest of symphonies, the music morphed into an upbeat tune, a crescendo coming out of the violin, a seduction that curled around me and sped up. An explosion of voices rose from down in the ballroom. Moans and exhilarated cries followed, like we'd suddenly fallen into a dance of arousal, an orgy.

I didn't belong here.

The double doors swung open with a loud crack, gusts of wind rushing inside like a deadly storm coming to collect its victims. Silvery moonlight spilled inside, illuminating the silhouettes of so many frozen in a moment of desire.

"Leave!" a booming male voice roared, but I couldn't recognize who it belonged to.

I backed into the wall, hugging myself.

In the intense silence, a terrified scream bellowed from deep in the room, then another.

Feet scuffling over the floorboards grew into a drumbeat, when the sharp shatter of glass smashing pierced the darkness. A girl cried out, her muffled sniffles deafening amid silence. Then others joined in with exasperated groans and shocked sighs. They realized what they'd been doing, how far they'd gone... there was so much more than a game of seduction going on here. But I knew exactly what it was... what allure the Sinful used over the girls to let themselves lower their inhibitions.

Except me.

Why hadn't I been impacted?

Blood rushed through me so fast my head spun as fear curdled in my chest.

Trevor rose in front of me, looking at me, but it wasn't his eyes I stared into. It was the monsters shifting in the dark. The fanged beasts who grinned with deadly intentions, who wrenched my suitor backwards, away from me. His cries of terror cut through me, and I turned away. Fear played on my mind that I'd failed the test, that those monsters hunting through the dark were coming for me.

12

"Don't kill me." *Please.* I whispered, leaving the last word lingering in my mind.

Laughter echoed from the shadows. The sound reverberated with not one growl...*but three*. Cries and whimpers from the other girls grew to a crescendo. But they weren't the ones who'd failed the test...they weren't the ones who couldn't make a desperate mortal guy be remotely attracted to her.

They weren't the ones who fought her own desires. I reached up and touched my lips, still feeling the brush of warmth. Memories rose in my head. Trevor's hands on my waist, the feel of his hips pressing against mine. But excited? Not even a little. Wasn't that supposed to happen?

I closed my eyes and looked down, hating how the floor seemed to be one massive hole I wanted to crawl into.

"What happened?" one of the girls whimpered. "I don't remember anything."

Another one started crying. Her blubbering was punctuated with snivels. I swallowed hard at the sound. We were all terrified.

Yes, but they completed the task, didn't they? Cassian's voice slipped through my mind.

Shudders raced along my spine. I glanced at the open door. Moonlight glittered from shattered glass shards, casting snatches of light against the ceiling.

"What are you going to do to us?" Willa called out in the dark.

"*What do you deserve?*" the stony voice answered next to my ear.

Cassian. I'd know his voice anywhere. I whipped my head toward the sound, finding only silhouettes of the other girls.

The fire had been smothered, leaving embers casting a faint orange glow. But it wasn't enough light to go on. I tried to get a bead on my captors, catching a blur of movement to my right. It wasn't anywhere near enough.

I sensed movement and tracked it in the dark.

The silver light of the moon seemed to grow brighter, like a spotlight in the middle of the dance floor. Arkyn stepped out of the shadows, and my breath caught in my chest. He looked like a god, all hard edges and sunken shadows. Savage. The word came to mind. I trailed my eyes along his body, unable to look away.

He cast a steely gaze around the room. "All but one of you passed the test. You have been chosen for the next trial. Go now, back to your rooms to sleep. In the morning, you'll find a reward and be given specific instructions. Tomorrow there will be a ceremony where you'll be given the gift of something pure...*something powerful.*"

All but one.

All I heard was the words. *All but one passed the test.*

Me. The thready boom in my chest grew louder. He was talking about me. I was the one who didn't pass the test. Desperation wormed its way under my skin. I shook my head and stepped backwards. "I'll try harder," I pleaded.

All I could think about was retribution as I searched for that steely rage that welled in my gut. But something else pushed to the surface, something that filled me with fear.

A flicker of need licked with warm, hungry tongues.

I wanted to stay.

I wanted to be here.

My own home drifted to the surface of my mind. Empty. Lonely. Jacob standing at the front door, *need* echoing in his eyes. His hunger for me was a fist around my throat. I was sucked dry around him, falling into an abyss of his desperation to have me...to have all of me, my body, my soul.

He'd consume me if he could.

That kiss rose to the surface of my mind, hard and determined, his hands clawing me, pulling me hard against him. With the memory came a predatory growl.

Is this your lover, Asena? Cassian's warning tore through my mind as steel clamped down on my wrist. *This...male that lingers in your mind. Do you want him? Do you think about him?* The words took on a harder edge, a more dangerous edge.

In that moment I knew what true fear felt like.

"Go now!" Arkyn roared to the others.

Panic filled the room and the sound of thunder followed. I jerked my gaze to my hand, expecting to see shackles...expecting to see steel. But it was a hand around my wrist as the blurs of midnight blue and red dresses flickered in the darkness.

The others raced from the room, snatching their skirts high and hurrying for salvation.

I tried to step away...tried to break the Vampire's hold.

"You're not going anywhere, Asena," Cassian murmured and in a rush of movement, my feet left the floor.

"No!" I whimpered. *I'm sorry.* I swallowed those words, fighting to remain calm. Tears filled my eyes, and through the blur, I caught the flicker of red hair as Willa raced along with the others, leaving me behind.

My pale blue dress billowed around me, swallowing my sight in a hazy blur as Cassian carried me through the ballroom and together, we plunged into pitch black.

"You didn't answer my question." The savage snarl filled my ears.

I tried to fight, tried to kick free. "Put me down...*I said, put me down.*"

In an instant, we were going down, descending past the upper floors. *No... this can't be happening.* I tried to get my bearings, tried to find the glittering, star-filled ceiling of the Night Room.

But he moved too fast, racing through one room and then went deeper still.

Cold licked my skin with hungry tongues, the sensation reaching higher as my skirt flew upwards with the flurry of movement. Hinges squealed for a second before my feet hit the floor.

"You won't answer?" One arm was yanked high. "Pity."

Bitter cold clamped down around my wrist. A weight sat heavy against my arm.

The clink of chains followed. I struggled, punching out with my free hand. "No, get off me...*I said, get the fuck off me!*" But it was useless to fight against Cassian.

I may as well have tried to stop a tide.

Links snapped tight, jerking my movement to a stop.

A cold gust of wind filled the room.

"Asena, Asena, Asena," Lorcan whispered, and the clucking of his tongue followed.

I tried to find a location for the sound, but there was nothing but blackness, nothing but cold.

A candle flared to life in the far corner of the room. In the other corner, another brightened, yellow rising slowly to cast a trembling, weak glow against the granite walls.

"You failed the test," Lorcan said, stepping into the light.

The blackened tips of another flame danced violently at my left as another blast of air swept through the room.

"You looked so pathetic," Arkyn murmured, striding across the room toward me. "Leaning close, trying to keep the attention of the mortal. Did he look at your breasts even once?"

The door closed with a *boom*, locks sliding into place even though no one touched them. I shook my head, terror driving from my chest and into my throat. I opened my mouth to speak, but there was only a hiss of air.

"She's trying to say something," Lorcan said as he stepped closer.

The last darkened corner brightened as a weak yellow glow splashed against the dark stone. All four corners shimmered and dimmed, casting faint hues against the three Vampires standing in front of me.

I tried to swallow, tried to voice the words that welled in the back of my throat. "Don't..."

"Don't?" Arkyn repeated. "Don't what?"

Cassian took a slow step toward me. I flinched at the movement, my heart pounding in my ears. "Don't kill me," I murmured.

"Is that what you think we're going to do?" Cassian whispered and reached out.

The frigid feel of his knuckles skimmed down my cheek. Something flickered in his eyes. Desperation. *Aching need.* Fear cut through my body like a surge of electricity.

They stepped closer, footsteps in synch...like they were one.

"Do you think you've come here to die?" Arkyn questioned.

They stopped in front of me, cold, still...*stony.*

"Show her, Cassian." Arkyn continued. "Show her why we brought her here."

I whimpered as the Vampire came closer, eyes glittering with savage, primal hunger. All my life I'd been afraid of the Wolves.

I hated the Vampires, hated them, until all I saw was their

blood. But not once had I ever been in fear of them...not true fear. But I felt it now. I felt it like a beast rifling around in my soul, scraping razor-sharp claws against the barrier between life and death.

Cassian's fingers unfurled, ice-cold tips carried across my lips. "You have the most perfect lips," he whispered. "Do you think mine are just as beautiful?"

My chest rose suddenly. My breath trapped. I wanted to fight the movement of my gaze, to find a stone on the wall and stare at that until my gaze blurred and my eyes burned. I wanted to do anything but find the beauty of his mouth.

His blood-red lips parting.

I lowered my gaze.

He took a step closer and I was reminded of just how he felt. Hard...unmovable, deadly. His finger slipped inside my mouth, so gentle...so slow. Heat flared in my core. White fangs peeked out over his lower lip, and I was pinned down by the sight. Millimeter by millimeter, the massive fangs were revealed as he smiled. "I can smell your desire. *We all can.*"

His finger slipped deeper into my mouth. My lips tightened around his knuckle. I hated that I was helpless...that they made my body react in ways I'd never felt before.

"Suck," Cassian urged. "Suck harder."

No, the word skimmed across the surface of my mind. But my mouth obeyed his command. My tongue skimmed the tip of his nail, and the soft flesh of his finger warmed in my mouth.

Danger sparked in his obsidian eyes. A deep growl of desire rumbled in the back of his throat. His fingers trailed downwards, leaving the warmth of my moisture along the curve of my chin and then lower.

"You're so beautiful," he whispered as he clamped his hand around my throat.

The frantic jump of my pulse pressed against his thumb as he stroked the long ridge of my vein.

"You're not like the others," he whispered.

My eyes widened. This was too real now, too focused, too everything. *Just kill me and get it over with.* I closed my eyes, anything to stop this torture.

"I can't seem to help myself around you."

His body pressed against mine and my nipples hardened in response. A brutal tearing sound filled the air, the frigid touch of cold air slipped lower, spilling over the tops of my breasts and a growl of desire filled the room behind Cassian.

They were beasts. Unbridled. Monsters who looked at me like I was their favorite meal.

"He was lucky." Cassian's cold breath danced across the tops of my breasts. "I would've gutted that mortal if he'd laid one finger on you. I would've torn the skin from his bones and left a pool of blood behind. I would've killed them all. Every. Single. One."

Fabric tore once more, arching my spine as the sudden movement jerked my hips forward. The icy tip of his tongue licked my nipple, tearing a whimper from my lips. I fought against Cassian's hold, shaking my head.

The rest of my dress was ripped with one savage yank of his hands. I shook there, dressed only in a corset and panties.

Cassian pulled away as the others moved. The shift of wind from their movements cast strands of my hair into the air.

"I want to see her," Lorcan snarled, hunger and danger filling the air.

I didn't dare move. Metal clasps pinged as they tore from my corset to hit the wall. I yanked on the shackles, trying to cover myself. But the chains snapped taut, leaving my arching fingers dancing in the air.

"You think we want to hurt you?" Cassian whispered, and lowered his body to the floor, coming to rest between my legs.

Eira's image came to me, naked, shackled...*bitten.* "You want to use my body? You're going to have to kill me first."

"I seem to think you're the one who's chained like an animal," Arkyn whispered, and lifted his hand to my chest.

But his touch was tender, dragging the back of a curled finger along the outside swell of my breast. "Or is it a monster? A beast, perhaps...or a *savage.*"

Cold lips pressed against my skin underneath my breasts as Arkyn's fingers moved upwards once more, heading for the sensitive flesh of my nipple.

I sucked in a breath as his finger danced across the peak. Soft lips trailed lower...and lower and lower. I was consumed by the sensations, fingers, lips...*hunger.*

"Kiss me," Lorcan growled from the other side. His hand followed, grasping my jaw, forcing my head to turn. He licked the corners of my mouth as Arkyn's fingers rolled the peak of my nipple.

A shudder coursed through my body. *Fight.* The need raged. *Fight them.*

The chains snapped taut as I yanked against the shackles. But their lips...*oh dear God...their lips...their tongues...their fingers.*

Pain raced through the puckered bead of my breast, cold slickness followed. I opened my mouth as Lorcan slipped his tongue inside.

The snap of my panties barely registered.

"Open for me, Asena. Open wide, let me do all the things I want to do to you," Cassian murmured against my navel. The skin trembled. My mind raced. I didn't understand what he wanted from me.

Lorcan broke the kiss and pulled away. But his grip stayed around my jaw, not too tight, holding me in place with a gentle touch. "Look into my eyes," he murmured.

Cassian's hand found the back of my knee. I was bare down there, bare for his eyes, bare for his touch. My strength was nothing. My will turned to water as I let him lift my foot from the floor.

All for you, Asena. Cassian's voice invaded my mind. I tried to shake my head. Tried to pull myself away from the brink of this chasm. My knee slipped over his shoulder. My heel skimmed his back as he leaned closer.

One lick of my slit, and I trembled. *"Please."*

He moved deeper, taking more of me...pushing his tongue deeper inside. My lips parted...a hiss of breath escaped as my eyelids fluttered closed.

"No, you don't," Lorcan growled, as Arkyn teased my nipple with his tongue.

The pointed tips of fangs dragged along the inside of my thigh. "Wider," Cassian commanded.

I was helpless to fight him. Lorcan drew my gaze down with a gentle tug at my throat. "Watch him. Watch what we will all take turns doing to you."

Cassian pressed his thumb into the groove of my thigh, then dipped lower, sliding his tongue inside the crevice between my thighs. Panic raced, but it went nowhere other than the insides of my thighs.

My heart thundered, My body trembled, something was building inside me. Some kind of foreboding urgency. Cassian pulled away, kissing the juncture of my thigh. The tips of his fangs seemed to mingle with the tremors between my thighs.

Danger.

Lust.

All swirled together as one. My body moved on its own, hips pushing forward to meet his lips. The tips of his fangs pressed harder into my skin as he slid a finger inside me.

I whimpered, mesmerized by his glistening lips. "I'm going to take all of you." Cassian's voice was deep and menacing.

His eyes glistened with insatiable hunger and he slipped his finger along to the tiny nub above my cleft. The building storm crackled inside me, lightning shattering my resolve.

"Asena," Cassian called.

I opened my eyes as my breath sawed and my legs trembled.

"Will you give in to us?" He lowered his lips and circled his thumb lightly against my sex. My back arched, thighs parting wider as electricity surged, sending me toppling off the edge of this chasm.

"Answer me," he growled, and opened his mouth, his fangs glistening as they hovered over the vein in my thigh, ready to strike. *"Will you give in to us?"*

The answer came at me with a scream…

An answer I didn't want.

An answer that tore apart everything I thought I was.

But the words stopped on my lips as Cassian drew his head backwards and, with a savage roar, sank his teeth into my body.

BOOK TWO

1

"Answer me," Cassian growled, his fangs glistening as they hovered over the vein in my thigh ready to strike. *"Will you give in to us?"*

Panic filled me, tearing through my veins. I pressed my spine into the hard, stony wall, cowering. I tried to get an idea on my location. Tried to scan my memories of the last few minutes to find out where I was. But everything was a blur.

I failed. That was all I knew.

Cassian had plunged the ballroom into darkness after the dance had ended and torn me from the room in the blink of an eye.

Were they going to kill me here?

The young geeky guy, Trevor, came back to my thoughts.

I'd try harder to seduce him, if given the chance. I trembled with the thought, while the chains dangling over my head clinked and shook. My hands were clenched into fists, chained high above my head. Steel shackles sat heavy against my arms. I trembled in the cold, bare to their gazes. My perfect chiffon dress now lay in tatters on the ground, ripped apart by Cassian's need. He hovered between my legs, his gaze ravenous. I breathed in hard and fast, torn between arousal and fear.

The Vampire waited for a second for my answer.

Then he drew his head backwards and, with a savage roar, sank his teeth into my body.

I jerked, driving my hips from the stony wall, pressing my body harder into the bite. Cassian's gaze was urgent, his fingers sliding in and out of me, hungry and insistent.

"YES!" I howled my torment into the void while my body responded to him, turning me on with such intensity, I trembled with need.

My body shuddered and jerked with the flare of delicious pain. He was merciless, brutal, his mouth clamped on the groove of my thigh. I jerked my gaze to the agony, before the sting melted away. His fingers glistened, moving in and out of me. With every smooth slide of his thumb against my clit, I shuddered.

My legs trembled and then gave way...until I didn't know where I was...until I didn't know *who* I was.

Still, the Sinful weren't done. The shackles came apart from my wrists, hands found me, carrying me to the mess of my torn dress. They lay me down as Cassian pulled away, leaving me with the other two Sinful. His eyes were wide and haunted. Blood seeped over his lips. *My blood.* The thought rose, then slipped away, weighed down like a body in a pond.

"Will you give into us?" Arkyn growled, and slipped between my thighs.

But something was happening to me. Something that raced through my veins like a bolt of power. Something *ancient and predatory...and powerful.*

"Arkyn," Casian growled, and lifted his hand to his mouth. His chest rose in great heaves. Color flushed his skin before it faded, and then, with a massive stride, the Vampire was striding back to me. "I want more of her."

"No!" the leader snapped, and lowered his gaze to my widened thighs.

But it was too late. Cassian was like a runaway carriage with all six horses galloping for speed. He lunged at his leader, grabbing him by his shoulders. "You don't understand. *I need her!*"

"*Cassian!*" Arkyn answered, rising to his feet, and turning on the other Vampire. "You *will* get more than your share, brother. *Look* at her."

They both turned to me. But that delicious predatory feeling flowed through my body. The juncture between my thighs was alive, senses firing, sending a hum through my bones.

A hum that called for them...that *wanted* them. I thrashed my head from side to side as both Arkyn and Cassian moved closer. Lorcan just stared at me, bewildered. Their gazes tracked every movement as I slipped my hand between my thighs and closed my legs. "What's happening to me?"

"The Calling," Arkyn whispered. His white fangs grew, sliding along deep red lips. "Open your legs for me. I want to look at you."

I shook my head, fighting the beast inside me. The one that slid against my insides, begging for more, who wanted them, who *called* them. But that hunger inside me was strong, surging to the surface, refusing to be denied. My hand shook, slipping as my knees parted.

Arkyn's body trembled as he lowered himself to his knees. His tongue skimmed his lips. Blood wasn't what he wanted in this moment as he reached out and gently dragged his thumb along my crease. "I'm going to fuck you now." A throaty growl tore from his lips. "Oh, my undead heart, hell have mercy, I want..." Danger flared in his eyes as he flicked his gaze to mine. "I want to take my time with you. I want this to last for eternity."

He didn't sound like himself. He reached out, his thumb

grazing the tight peak of my breast as Lorcan moved closer. His eyes glowed with an eerie glow. I closed my eyes as his thumb drew a circle around my nipple and then made the slow descent. I ached in the heaviness between my legs, ached with a kind of desperation I'd never felt before.

I needed him. I needed *all of them.* "Take the ache away," the plea slipped from my lips.

I opened my eyes to the three Vampires who looked at me with ravenous hunger. "Please take the ache away."

Arkyn lowered his head. Icy lips kissed my navel. "I would be honored to be your first."

I flinched at his words. "How did you know?"

"I can smell it all over you, along here." He lifted his hand, taking the swell of my breast as he kneaded, and lowered his head between my legs. "And here."

My spine arched from the floor as he licked the insides of my thighs. The heat was building once more, flicking out with greedy, languid tongues to drive my desire wild.

"Why me," I growled, trying to fight the need to splay open my legs and let him do what his lips promised to do. "Why the *hell* do you want *me?*"

They stilled. Hungry. Panting.

Eyes glittering with a darkness.

Until the sound of shattering glass outside filled the air.

"Fuck!" Arkyn roared and shoved to his feet. He jerked his head toward the doorway as a gunshot went off with a *BOOM!*

"Cassian!" Arkyn snapped. "Take care of that!"

Rage sparkled in the Vampire's eyes as he looked at me once more.

"Get out here, now!" a male roar came from outside. "Don't make us burn the house down, *Vampire!"*

Arkyn flinched at the words, then slowly licked his lips. The sight was seductive and sensual, as though he wanted to savor the feel of me, to draw it deeper inside him. "Lorcan."

The Vampire stepped forward without saying a word.

"Take Asena back to her room. Make sure she's safe and--" his gaze drifted to the torn dress underneath me. "Clothed. You will protect her with your life. Do I make myself clear?"

I flinched as the ache ebbed inside me. "But I failed."

"No." Arkyn gave the barest hint of a smile. "It wasn't you who didn't complete the task. That male wanted you. I can still smell his desire now. He was planning on taking you out of here."

"Vampire!" The roar filtered through the doorway once more. My heart lunged.

Will you show me around? Trevor's voice slipped through my mind. I jerked my gaze toward the doorway. *It was the same...*

"Yes," Arkyn growled and straightened his suit. "It seems our little mortal has plans for your future." Danger sparked in his eyes as he smiled. "And now we have plans for his."

One nod was all it took. Cassian and Arkyn tore from the room with a gust of wind that snuffed all four candles and plunged the room back into darkness.

"Don't fight me," Lorcan whispered against my ear.

His fingers slid over my breast, and then traveled down my body, lingering at the apex of my thighs. "I could take you right now," he whispered. "I'd fill you with my body, stretch you wide. I'd show you why we are both desired and feared."

Somehow, I knew he'd be risking the wrath of Arkyn and Cassian. Hate found me, filling my bones like marrow now that the hunger of desire was fading. "And risk your life in doing so?"

He stiffened. His fingers trembled, dancing at the entrance to my slit. "It'd be worth it," he whispered. "To have you writhing with pleasure underneath me. It'd be worth it a thousand times over."

I shuddered as that need rose with his words. I could see it unfolding inside my mind, see him parting my thighs. One slide of his zipper and he'd be inside me, plunging deep, sating that aching hunger inside me.

"Darkest hell." He spat, trembling. "No more...*no more.* Or I won't be able to help myself. I *want you...I want you more than I've ever wanted life.*"

His words shocked me. I stilled, letting the fantasy fade. The seconds seemed to stretch out in the darkness, before, ever so gently, he slid one hand under my back and lifted. My body ached with the weight as he settled me onto my feet and then grabbed the ruined dress underneath me.

I caught the movement in the darkness. Black on black shifted around me as he leaned close. "Your dress is ruined," he said, the words a hungry growl, as though he took great delight in knowing that.

He wanted to ruin it himself. He wanted to tear the dress from my body, to make it slick and wet. A moan slipped past my lips.

A dangerous, ravenous growl echoed in the air around me. "Don't try me, Asena, not when I'm riding this close to sheathing myself in your body right here and now."

A smile danced at the edges of my lips, cutting through the panic and fear like a light in the dark. I made them tremble. *I made them weak.*

The knowledge of that surged through me.

"Do not scream," Lorcan growled in my ear as there was a rustling of cloth. "You call attention to yourself naked like this, and I'll have to slaughter every male in this goddamn house who looks at you. Now lift your arms."

The possessive snarl reverberated in my ear.

"What?"

"Lift your damn arms, unless you want me to carry you through the damn house naked?"

I shoved my hands into the air so fast, I smacked myself in

the jaw. Pain flared. I opened my mouth, testing the tendons, and felt the dark ache.

"Humans," Lorcan muttered. "Let's try again, shall we?"

Soft fabric skimmed over my arms and raced along my body, dropping until the ends of his shirt skimmed midway down my thigh.

My feet were swept out from underneath me. His hard body and cool skin pressed against my side, stopping long enough to yank open the door.

The *crack* of a gunshot exploded through the darkness. Screams followed, unmerciful, haunting male screams. But they weren't just Trevor's. There were more of them, two or three more. Lorcan swept me toward the sound before he turned.

But yellow flames from a hand-held torch illuminated the darkness. There was a body lying in the middle of the floor. A woman, her dress fanned out around her. Blood darkened her chest from a gunshot. I recognized her instantly. *She was one of us.*

Arkyn glanced at the woman's body, then lifted his gaze to the mortal standing in the doorway, a rifle in his hand, the muzzle still pointed at her body.

"*No!*" Arkyn roared. "*No...no...,no!*"

Lorcan swept me away, carrying me along the hallway until he yanked open a door with candlelight already burning inside the room.

An old woman screamed and lifted her hand to shield her eyes, blinking. She wore muffs over her ears, soft pink things to muffle noise. Her eyes widened as she shoved to sit up in the bed, first looking at the Vampire and then me, standing naked in front of her bed.

"Dress her," Lorcan commanded.

"What?" the woman cried, dragging the muffs from her ears. "What did you say?"

"I said, *dress her*. See she is fed and cared for, then take her back to her room."

The old woman's eyes widened as she took me in from head to toe, lingering on Lorcan's bare chest.

"Mmhmmm," she muttered, and with a sigh, dragged her body from the warm bed. "I'll take care of her. Go on now." She bent, lit a candle for light, and shooed Lorcan away with a wave of her hand.

And the Vampire let her.

I watched his reaction. There was a flicker of a curl at the corner of his mouth, then he turned toward me. There was unfinished business with him...and with all of them.

That dull ache welled between my thighs and sprung to life as he stepped closer and lifted his hand. I tried to stop the flinch and the thunder in my head. His nostrils flared, fingers hovering inches from my face, but he dropped his hand and was gone in an instant, striding through the door... closing it behind him.

"Right," the old woman murmured. "This is something new, isn't it?"

I had no idea what she was talking about. Shivers ravaged my body, from both fear and the cold. The old woman glanced my way as I hugged my body and hurried, pulling on a robe and stepping into slippers. "Let me find you something warmer than that before you catch your death," she said, stiffening as she realised what she'd just said.

"Yes, well," she mumbled to herself, tied the sash around her body and made for a closet on the far side of the room. "It's one of the maids' uniforms, but it'll be warm enough." She yanked open the door and searched through the long dresses hanging there, then tugged one free.

It was white and sensible, With thick, warm fabric. I almost ran to her and yanked the damn thing on myself. I needed no encouragement this time to lift my arms. The old woman just glanced at the shirt, then mumbled something about leaving well enough alone and slipped the dress over my arms.

It fell around my body like a weight. Warmth wasn't there yet, but neither was the cold.

"Right, food, and a drink, and then back to bed for you. I need my sleep, so that means you need yours." She shooed me, just as she had Lorcan, toward the doorway.

I stopped dead, frozen by the memory of the body and the gunshots. "We can't go out there."

"To the main kitchen? No, love, we'll use the servants' hallways. This way." She seemed oblivious to the danger all around us, humming a soft tune as she yanked open the door and tottered along the hall.

I followed her as we left the spill of light behind from her bedroom. I focused on her back, my bare feet still icy against the stony floor. But I hugged the dress to my body, dragging in the seductive male scent of Lorcan.

"Damn Vampire is bad for my willpower. I was trying to cut myself out of the midnight snacking, now look what he's making me do." She turned, lingering in a doorway, and lit another candle on the counter for more light.

I had no idea where I was, another wing of the manor? I followed her into the small kitchen. There were pots of fresh herbs along the window sill and fresh fruit piled in bowls. "You live here?" I asked as she delved into the larder.

"Yes, going on eleven years now." She grabbed a plate of cooked chicken and some cheese and plonked it onto the counter. "Sit." She nodded to a small table and chair.

My knees still trembling, I didn't need to be told twice. I sat, watching as she grabbed a knife and sliced off thin shavings of chicken and cut sections of cheese before grabbing a wooden box on the counter and lifting the lid.

I glimpsed the half-eaten loaf of bread before she sawed the knife half an inch from the edge and placed the slice onto a plate with the rest of the food.

My stomach howled in hunger. Fear and desire had left me ravenous. *But not Cassian...he's had your blood.* I clamped my thighs together as heat raced to my face.

"You okay?" the old woman asked.

I nodded. "Yes, thank you, just hungry and tired."

She nodded to the plate, then turned, finding a glass and filling it with water before making her way over to me. "Eat up and I'll take you back to your room."

She slid the glass onto the table in front of me and turned to pick at the carcass on the plate. Two slices of cheese and the old woman sighed, giving in to a thin slice of bread, while I picked up the chicken and ate.

Food had never tasted so good. I was starved, biting into the breast and then the cheese before tearing off a corner of the bread, and ate until I was full. I sipped the water and leaned backwards against the chair.

"You're the one, aren't you?" the old woman asked.

Her words reverberated, echoing from the past.

"The one what?" I gulped the water, draining the glass.

"I don't know, but they've never cared enough about them to feed and clothe them. So I'm guessing you're different."

But different how?

She placed the chicken and the cheese back into the refrigerator, and then came for my plate and glass. Seconds later, the place was just as clean as when we first walked in.

"Right. To your room."

"They treat you well, don't they?" I murmured.

She stilled, head down, before she answered. "Yes, they do."

Then she stepped up to the doorway and hit the switch for the lights. I followed her, listening for the sound of her footsteps as we made our way back to what looked familiar.

She opened a small door to what looked like a broom closet

and reached inside. Keys jangled from a keyring as she pulled it free.

"Which one are you?" she muttered.

I neared my door, listening to voices from inside the room. Willa and Chaska would think her dead by now, or disappeared. I readied myself as the old woman neared the door and slipped the key into the lock.

I stepped close, hugging her and resting my hand on her arm. "Thank you, for everything."

She seemed surprised. Her eyes widened a little as she met my gaze and murmured, "I hope you make it through. I really do." Then she turned the key, and I stepped back.

The door swung inwards, but she didn't move inside. Instead, she stepped to the side, leaving me to enter my bedroom alone.

"Oh my God!" Willa shoved up from the seat and raced toward me.

I tried to smile, tried to think, as she bombarded me with a million questions.

"What happened to you? Where did you go? Were you with *them?* Did you see what happened? What about the Vampires?"

Exhaustion found me. I couldn't answer her...couldn't even think. The truth was, I didn't know what to say. "I don't know," I murmured and headed for the bathroom. "I got lost in the dark is all."

Chaska and Willa watched me like a hawk as I stepped into the bathroom and closed the door behind me. Silence found me, blissful silence. I leaned back against the door for a second and took a breath.

I can't tell them.

I can't tell them anything.

I pushed off from the door, made my way to the basin, and filled it with water. A small candle threw shadows across the room. All I wanted was to do was wash their scents from my body...and their touches from my mind. But I could barely stand...barely keep my eyes open. I needed sleep, and a lot of it, and maybe tomorrow I could find a way out of this mess.

I pulled off the dress I wore, leaving it to drop at my feet, before I grabbed a washcloth and soaked it into the cold water, then reached for my shirt.

It was halfway over my head when I heard the bathroom door open.

"I thought you might want some fresh clothes," Willa suggested and barged into the bathroom, eyeing me like she searched for something... an answer to her earlier questions perhaps.

I yanked the shirt down, covering my nudity as best I could, and jerked my gaze toward her.

"What the—" she hissed.

Her gaze was fixed on my inner thigh. But it wasn't my privates she stared at. I lowered my hand, covering the bite mark.

"They bit you?" She jerked her gaze high, rage flickering in her eyes as her cheeks blazed. *"The Vampires fucking bit you?"*

2

I was young when I lost my parents to the monsters, only eleven years old.

They were dead on the kitchen floor, fixed, vacant eyes staring at the ceiling, their throats torn open, their bodies white and drained of blood. Puncture wounds littered their bodies from bites… Vampire bites.

A scream had rushed out of my lungs, tears drenching my cheeks, and my heart seared me from the inside out. My knees hit the floor and I gingerly picked up my mother's hand, her touch already cold. I placed it against my cheek and closed my eyes. "Mommy, please come back."

I struggled to stay in that moment when the painful memory sliced through me, and tears already pricked the edges of my eyes. The ache inside me turned jagged. Images of my parents flashed across my mind. Father's hard gaze, but the kindest smile, his fingers always finding the right spot to tickle me. Mother hugged me too hard, too often, but now I longed for anything in the world to just hear that familiar voice that told me everything would be all right.

Monsters took them from me, ripped away everything I had,

and now... Now I placed myself at their mercy, desired them when I shouldn't.

Mumbled voices came from outside the bathroom, where Willa and Chaska talked about me, about the Vampire bite on my inner thigh.

With a quick wipe of my eyes, I pushed all the memories aside and dragged a nightgown over my head and down my body before stepping into the bedroom.

Both girls jerked their attention toward me, their voices silenced. I didn't want to talk about this, now or ever. Little from tonight made sense, let alone explaining what the Sinful had done to me. I saw the horror and jealousy in their gazes now, but I'd never asked for any of this. My intention was to come here for one mission, but everything was escalating, getting worse with each passing day.

How had I ended up in this situation?

"So," Willa snapped, then said nothing more.

I winced at the bitchiness. "I don't know exactly what happened."

"Try to remember," Chaska asked like she was genuinely concerned, but I knew they just wanted to hear the words, my admittance that the Sinful had claimed me, that somehow, they'd selected me, so the girls had even more reason to hate me. They wanted to think that I was in some way responsible for them missing out.

My heart was hammering. I sat on the side of the bed and slipped my cold feet under the blanket, before grabbing a pillow and hugging it to my stomach. I wished I could stop shaking so much.

Both girls just stood at the end of the bed, watching me, waiting for some kind of explanation.

"After the lights went out, my thoughts blurred. My date was taken away, then Cassian came and took me away from the chaos." I swallowed the boulder in my throat, fidgeting with the corner of the pillow.

"And?" Willa asked. "Then what happened? And where's your gown?"

"Trevor, my date, hurt me, he was aggressive and tore my dress." I loathed how easily I lied these days. "After the lights went out, I was so terrified, my mind fogged. The next thing I knew, I was being pushed into a servant's chamber by Lorcan to get dressed." I couldn't tell anyone the truth. Couldn't let them see how much I desired the Sinful or how much they yearned for me, how they'd cared for me when the human men returned to seek revenge.

Willa looked over to Chaska. "Do you believe her?"

The brunette shook her head. "I bet she went to the Sinful and threw herself at them."

I bristled and gripped the pillow hard. "Why would I do that?"

"Because you chose to come here of your own volition. Who does that?"

Willa was nodding, her eyes narrowed. They already hated and judged me. "Chaska has a point."

But I'd come too far, lived with darkness for too long, to let them get to me. Anger froze my movements and my voice climbed. "I already explained myself to the Sinful."

They stared at me incredulously. We were at the manor, not out of pleasure, but being forced into the situation for different reasons.

Willa's lips thinned. "And you just happen to be the first of us who the Sinful bit, right? Funny coincidence for someone who came here to kill them."

Chaska mocked me with her laughter.

"That wasn't the Vampire's bite." I searched my brain for a response, finding words that wouldn't make this situation somehow more insane. "It was just a damn spider that bit me."

"A spider! Right!" Willa rolled her eyes, emphasizing every word. Both of them turned away from me.

I felt sick to my stomach.

Tucking the pillow back on the bed, I slid further under the blankets and covered myself, curling into a ball on the edge, wanting to be anywhere but here. My mind was screaming to just run out of here, but it was too late to flee. The Vampires wouldn't let me leave, and I was completely terrified as to what would happen next.

The next morning, I woke up with a startled gasp, my skin drenched in sweat, and I clenched my thighs involuntarily. I may not remember my dream, but with the thrum of my heartbeat between my legs, I had no doubt it had included the Sinful.

Chaska rounded the small table and stared at me blankly, while Willa sat at the table, not even looking my way. They didn't question me, just remained quiet. Chaska wore a simple blue dress with a thin ribbon for a belt and long sleeves that fell loosely to her hands. Willa dressed very similarly, but in a pale yellow outfit.

"Those colors look good on you both." I pushed out of bed, feeling stiff all over, like I'd climbed a mountain. Why did everything hurt?

Neither said anything, and I awkwardly got up, loathing how my insides felt like ice at their cold treatment.

I wasted no time and padded across the icy floor to the bathroom to wash up. Their silence haunted me while, at the same time, I couldn't get last night's events out of my mind. The ballroom. Trevor's aggression. Cassian's bite… I'd pushed that thought out of my mind, not wanting to think about it too hard or what it meant.

Now it crashed into me like a toppling tree.

He'd bitten me.

Infected me.

Marked me.

And I knew what it meant. Once I tasted their blood, I'd become one of them.

A chill slithered down my spine like an icy touch. I didn't want to become one of them… a monster of the night. One of the fiends that killed mercilessly.

My hands trembled as I reached for a deep emerald green dress hanging on the corner railing where new dresses were left for me.

What if the Sinful intended to just keep me, like Eira, someone to feed upon? I shivered at the thought.

I undressed and drew the new gown over my head and down my body. With fumbling fingers, I laced up the ribbon straps that ran down the corset part of the dress. Long sleeves and a flowing skirt glimmered in the sunlight from the window. If I didn't feel like running and hiding from everyone, I might have admired the beautiful design.

Outside in the main room, the two girls lounged about on the chairs as the sun slowly sank over the horizon. We slept like Vampires most of the time. But on days like today sleep hovered out of reach. Instead I tossed and turned, unable to shake the hold over what I'd done.

I wandered over to a window and stared outside into the woods. A hawk glided past, freedom fluttering under his wings. If I flew, I'd travel the land and see everything it offered, never remaining too long in one place.

Turning back to my prison, I collected my book on the History of the Dark Ones and flopped onto the bed.

A knock came on our door later that afternoon when the sun dipped behind the mountains. Chaska opened it and found a guard standing tall in the doorway.

"The Lords have summoned your presence. We are to leave right away."

"Are they serving dinner early?" Chaska asked.

He shook his head.

We all exchanged quick, worried looks, then rushed to put on our shoes. After last night, I wasn't ready for another test.

I hurried to step into my shoes and followed him into the hallway, trying not to overthink what awaited us.

We were ushered into the study, where bookshelves covered the walls and Arkyn sat alone on the tallest throne. Cassian and Lorcan weren't in the room, and my stomach dropped at remembering the tension between Arkyn and Cassian over me.

As if programmed inside us, all eleven of us lined up in front of the Vampire.

He sat upright, legs wide, and even in his black pants with his shirt buttoned up to his throat, the collar high, he was devastatingly handsome. He unfastened his cuffs before folding up his sleeves over strong, muscular forearms.

Lorcan's words filled my mind. *I'd fill you with my body, stretch you wide. I'd show you why we are both desired and feared.*

Lorcan's devious threat from the previous night skipped into my thoughts, bringing with it a storm of desire, smothering me.

Arkyn's gaze slid over me, and all I wanted was for him to devour me. Did he know what effect he had on me?

When his lips twitched and an inferno blazed in his gaze, my nipples stiffened, responding to him. It just wasn't fair how easily he impacted me, how liquid fire quickly pooled between my thighs.

He was the enemy, yet I stood there sinking in his presence, needing his hands on me. The raw hunger inside me roared for me step toward him, but I didn't dare, not when I caught the side glances from the girls, the glares, the hatred prickling my skin.

"We are holding a rose ceremony as a small thank you for

your last test." His words carried a sharp edge, the kind that said there was so much more than this. What could possibly go wrong with a rose ceremony?

As if on cue, Lorcan strolled into the room, all in black, his shirt semi-transparent, hard muscles shifting with each step, and I closed my gaping mouth. Someone near me mumbled something softly about muscles and licking them.

"This small gift from me will bring you an unforgettable night's sleep."

I squirmed in my spot as Cassian entered the room carrying a silver tray with individual red petals and what looked like drops of something red inside each one. Blood.

Vampire blood? My arms trembled by my sides.

"Polaris," Arkyn called out first. "Come to me."

We all looked her way, and she hesitated at first, the color draining from her face. Her neighbor nudged her, and Polaris tucked her brown curls behind her ears, then stepped forward toward the Sinful.

"Kneel," he ordered, like she was nothing but a dog, and he'd follow it up with, *Good dog, here's your reward.*

Polaris dropped down.

The three Vampires watched her intently. Arkyn reached over to the silver tray in Cassian's hands, picked up a red rose petal with its red drop of blood, and looked down at Polaris.

She trembled, but didn't make a sound. I pitied her right then... pitied all of us.

"Open your mouth, little one. Let me reward you. It's a small token from us." Instead of further explaining, he tenderly set the petal into her mouth.

Token? What did that mean?

He offered Polaris a small nod, watching her until she ate the blood-topped petal.

"Aislinn," he announced.

Polaris quickly rose to her feet, returning to us in hasty

steps. Every one of us studied her, expecting we didn't know what, waiting for something to happen. But nothing came. She slid back into the line and shrugged to her friend.

One girl after another took their turn, until I heard, "Asena."

My insides tightened, and I forced my legs forward, trying to hold myself together, despite shivering uncontrollably.

When I glanced up, all three Vampires stared at me with the same ravaging look in their eyes as last night. And grins, of complete satisfaction. Goosebumps pebbled over my flesh, and all I saw was me beneath them, moaning, pleading for more. My nipples stiffened in their presence, but my mind knotted in confusion. I hated them. I desired them. What was *wrong* with me?

Cassian had bitten me, tasted my blood... One drop of his blood on my tongue, and I'd turn.

I breathed heavily, standing tall in front of Arkyn, hands curled into fists. I had to resist them.

Lorcan watched me from one side of Arkyn, Cassian on the other. All I could picture was me on the floor last night, spread open, naked, and their hungry eyes on me, starved fingers finding me, pressing into places they shouldn't.

My clit pulsed at the memory.

"On your knees." Arkyn's deep, throaty voice stroked me in ways no one's command ever had, and desire thrummed through me like a lightning strike.

I shouldn't do this, shouldn't let them walk all over me. For years, I'd prepared to come here, researched everything on Vampires, trained to wield a blade. So, I knew better and fought the fear choking me, yet my gaze searched those icy blue eyes for any kind of understanding, sympathy, but I couldn't find any.

Don't fight us, Lorcan's warning grazed over my thoughts.

"Kneel!" Arkyn's voice rumbled. He wore primal power and confidence, his presence both terrifying and turning me on.

My stomach dropped just as my knees caved and I fell before him, catching a smile from Cassian.

Someone behind me gasped. The girls saw Cassian's reaction. He'd offered no smile to any of them during their turn, none of the Sinful had. More reason for them to hate me.

Arkyn reached over with a red rose petal cradled in his fingers, his movement fast.

I pulled back, eyeing the offering. Wait! No blood sat on the petal. They weren't making me take blood, and my jaw dropped as shock jolted through my body.

He placed the flower petal on my tongue, and his finger lightly grazed my lower lip, sending a pulse of heat to the pit of my stomach.

Soft voices floated behind me, and I turned my gaze toward the other girls. Willa was whispering to Nilsine, both staring at me like they'd kill me if given the chance. Dread swallowed me, because I was in deep shit now… more than before, and all alone in the manor. Maybe I'd been wrong about thinking Willa was my friend. She was just like the rest of the girls.

I was trapped between the monsters who played their games, and the girls who'd destroy me to gain the title of Vampire Queen.

3

"The dream," someone hissed in front of me. "It was...*intense.* I saw...you know, *them. The Vampires. They were kissing me...*"

I flinched at the words and jerked my gaze toward the sound to find her.

Through the dim light, I saw one of the others lean close to another at her side. Giggles followed, annoying, silly little giggles that wormed their way under my skin. I ground my teeth as a flare of jealousy tore through me.

I clenched my fists, leaning forward, desperate to glean every sickening recount. It was the third time I'd heard about last night's dreams. The third time I had to hear about Cassian, Arkyn, and Lorcan unclothed, kissing, rubbing...*oh God.* A darkness welled inside me with the sound of their words.

They all had them.

Erotic.

Naked.

Demanding...

I licked my lips and shifted my stance as I stood in the hallway.

Maybe that's what I'd had…just a wild, *erotic* dream? Maybe this was all just that? A bad goddamn *dream?*

Wake up!

The words were a gunshot through my mind.

Just wake the hell up NOW!

But I didn't wake. This whole thing didn't just suddenly fade away. I stayed, as did that driving need to lunge toward that *bitch* who giggled and covered her mouth as she talked about them, as though she actually knew them.

I shifted my stance, felt the ache I carried in my hips, and casually lowered my hand, lingering for a second on my thigh, and pressed into the flesh.

A sharp throb followed in the bite mark. *That* hadn't been any dream.

No. That had been very…*very* real.

I licked my lips, remembering the feel of their hands, their lips…*their tongues.* I closed my eyes and felt the world sway. I shouldn't be thinking of them, not their bodies…not that ache inside me I carried all the time now, an ache that needed.

The heavy *thud* of the guard's footsteps echoed in the murky light. There was a grunt and a snarl close behind us. I flattened myself against the wall, watching as he passed and stopped at the door that lead us outside.

Locks snapped backwards, and the groan of the door handle tore through the air.

Sunlight followed, flooding into the hallway around me, piercing my eyes.

A reward. That's what the Vampires called this. I stepped outside, feeling like I'd been trampled by a stampede, and lifted my hand to shield my eyes. The sun's morning rays burned and a throb pulsed in my head.

Everyone moved slowly, moaning and grumbling as we followed the few mortal guards around to the gardens in the rear of the manor grounds. You'd think we'd be happy being outside in the morning sun after what'd felt like an eternity. But the truth was, we'd adapted to this nocturnal world, just like our captors.

Captors, the word rolled around inside my head. I swallowed and followed Chaska and Willa. My heels sank into the pebbled ground and I felt the world swirl around me. Everything was different for me now, in my body and in my head.

I carried the aching need for them like a sickness. My bones ached, my ligaments felt stretched. My breasts were heavy and full, but it was the weight between my thighs where I felt them the most.

It was a need...a *hunger,* one I felt every second of the day. Not even sleep helped me...not that I'd had much of that. And Willa...I winced at the thought of her.

She didn't believe me. I could see it in her eyes. She was careful around me, quiet, watching me from the corner of her eyes, especially now. She stepped toward the grassed area and then turned, glancing over her shoulder. The sun hit her eyes, but there was no flinch...and no hesitation as her gaze bore right through me.

She knew.

My heart sped. She knew what had happened, both with the Vampires after the masquerade ball, and last night at the ceremony, and she didn't like it. She was furious, and she'd turn on me, I knew it.

Muffled voices carried through the air. I lifted my gaze to the guard standing just out from the open door and then swept it through the others. A soft squeal of delight came from somewhere in the distance. Everyone surged forward, following the sound to a stunning field filled with vibrant colors of yellow and red and purple.

"Go no further than the far hedge!" the guard called.

But no one was listening, and I was captured by the excitement.

"Come on," Chaska called, grabbing for my arm to drag me with her.

The sight was stunning. Roses and daffodils, with tufts of baby's breath and other flowers I didn't know, were stuffed into tiny flower beds set into the towering hedges.

I rushed forward. We were to pick flowers for our rooms, any kind we wanted and as many as we could. This was our reward...but at what cost?

Chaska grabbed her dress and raced toward the towering roses. There were gardeners there with shears, ready to cut and de-thorn. She raced along the colors, reaching out to touch perfect, barely open buds. Her pale yellow dress flapped with the movement, flaring out behind her like liquid sunlight.

She looked beautiful.

I grabbed the skirt of my dress to follow, but was shoved from behind. I stumbled and threw out my hand, catching the movement as Nilsine and a few of the others pushed past.

There was no *sorry*, no comment of any kind as they swarmed around Chaska.

Bitches.

My breath caught as I recovered from the stumble and glared at them as Nilsine slowed and leaned close to Chaska, murmuring something in her ear. Chaska stiffened and jerked her gaze toward me, her cheeks burning red.

She'd believed me when I told her it was nothing, there was no bite. It was a sore that refused to heal, just something I'd had before I came here, and even though the two puncture marks were sore and red and swollen, she just smiled and changed the subject.

But the way she looked at me now said she'd clearly changed her mind.

Nilsine straightened, glancing over her shoulder to where I stood.

I broke her stare and strode away, toward a clump of

bramble bushes at the far side of the gardens. They all raced for the pretty things, for the tight little buds and deep red blooms. I went for the thorns and the deep purple delights they guarded ferociously.

They could have their pretty flowers.

They could have their gossip.

I bent and speared my hand through the belly of a spindly blackberry bush.

"So, is it really true?"

I stilled, and carefully dragged my hand back, empty of succulent delights, before I turned to her. "Is what true?"

Chaska's lips were thin, her jaw was clenched, muscles tensed. But it was her eyes that made me swallow hard.

"You were with them?" she hissed. "You *let* them. *Let them...bite...you?"*

Anger flared, hot, powerful...*consuming.* "I didn't *let* them *do anything,*" I barked.

The sound was loud, cracking through the air, drawing gazes toward us. I swallowed, took a breath, and lowered my voice. "I didn't want to tell you."

"Why not?" she asked, forcing the words through clenched teeth.

I could feel the weight of their stares. The *excitement* and thrill of tearing away what seemed to be my last friend in this place. "Because it's not something I wanted."

She flinched, but held strong. I expected her to cross the space between us and wrap her arms around me. I thought we'd grown close in the last few days. I thought I knew her...obviously I was wrong.

Desperation surged through me. I could feel their eyes on me, craning their necks, listening to every cruel word. The sound of a snigger cut through the air. This time they didn't even both to hide it.

A coldness cut across Chaska's face, and then, in the blink of an eye, it changed. "Oh, Asena," she murmured, and stepped closer, opening her arms for me.

Hope surged through my chest. Tears shimmered as I took a step toward her. "I promise you, Chaska. I didn't want this...I didn't want any of it."

Her arms wound around me, pulling me closer. "It's okay," she breathed in my ear. "I know you didn't mean for any of this to happen."

I stiffened in her arms. The way she said it made me feel like... "Wait," I whispered, and pulled away, searching her eyes. "You don't think I *meant* for any of this to happen, do you?"

Surprise flared in her eyes. Long brown hair lashed my shoulder as she turned her head toward the others. But they were already leaving, slipping between towering hedges, spilling out of view. "It's just that the others..."

"What about them?" I tried to keep the anger from my voice.

She turned back toward me and, in the sweetest voice, whispered, "They said you were the favorite. They said you go to them when I'm sleeping, that you do things with them...*sexual things.*"

My thighs clenched together as I scrambled for something to say. "I don't go to them, Chaska. You have to believe me. I'm as much a victim in this as you are."

"But you said you paid someone, didn't you? You paid someone to bring you to them."

A coldness washed over me. I barely heard my voice, barely felt my lips move, "Yes, but not for this."

"Then why?"

Her wide eyes begged for the truth, and I wanted to give it to her. I wanted to tell her everything that had brought me here. I stood on the precipice of the gaping hole of truth. *Tell her,* my own voice whispered. *Tell her everything.*

Memories rose up inside me. My parents, my home...even the old woman in the hills. I wanted her to know it all. I *ached* for her to know it all...to unburden myself from this neverending weight of loneliness.

Not even Jacob had helped me carry the weight of the past. He'd left me to stand and shoulder it alone. He left me to slip away in the darkness...knowing where I was going, and still...he never helped me.

A squeal of delight cut through the air. I whipped my gaze toward the sound, as did Chaska. Someone bolted from the gardens carrying the most beautiful apricot-colored rose.

"Oh," Chaska whispered. "look what she has, my favorite-colored rose."

She seemed to waver for a second, wanting to turn back to me, but then she took off, hurrying in the direction of where the other woman had come from. I followed her, desperation and the desire to find out what she had, rising inside me.

We hurried around the thick blackberry bushes, their tiny succulent secrets clutched tight in their leaves. I never wanted flowers. They wouldn't feed you, wouldn't warm you. They died...and they took their beauty with them.

Still, I followed, because Chaska wasn't like me. She wanted the pretty things, the perfect things...where I wanted the berries behind the thorns. Other girls raced off carrying perfect roses, groups of them. I caught Polaris as she strode after them. As her arms swung by her side, clutched in her grip was a perfect white rose.

But by the time we got to the gardener, he was already turning and walking away, his basket now empty. He strode past what looked like a stony shed with the wooden door opened. But it wasn't the shed he was going to. He slipped along the hedges and, in a heartbeat, was gone...leaving us alone.

"Oh." Sadness echoed in her voice. "We missed out."

Still, she kept walking, following the path of the gardener. My shoes sank into the lush green grass as I wandered past the open door of the small shed as she stopped at the end of the hedge, searching for her gardener with the flowers.

A splash of color caught my eye...a single rose splayed on the floor at the back of the shed. A triangle of light from the open door spilled inside, cutting through the darkness.

A chill raced along my spine. It was small...cold, dark. My breath caught as I stared at that rose, and then looked at Chaska, staring into nothing.

It was her favorite color.

Her favorite flower.

Her favorite everything.

I licked my lips, glanced around, and took a step toward the open door. *It'll just take me a second to reach it. I won't even have to step all the way in. She wants this...and I want to give it to her.*

Fear welled in the back of my throat, and then spilled like acid along my tongue. I tried to stop the shudder as I took a step toward the open door. The rose was on the floor, half buried in shadows.

I sensed movement somewhere outside. A patter of footsteps...or was it the thunder of my heart? One quick glance at Chaska as she still stared after the gardener, and I turned back and took a step further inside.

My heart was hammering, crawling through my chest as I neared the rose and bent down to pick it up.

Boom! I spun at the sound of the door shutting and a cry ripped from my lips. Darkness closed in around me. Darkness...and walls.

"Let's see how you like the darkness now," Nilsine spat through the closed door.

A little sunlight spilled in as the shadow of her body left. More shadows turned...they all left me behind...even Chaska.

"You think you're so special, don't you?" Willa's voice cleaved through the cracks in the door. "Let's see if you're special when you're dead."

"Willa...*Willa, I didn't mean for any of this to happen...WILLA!*"

Her sniggers were cruel, like a thousand cuts.

I lunged, grasping the handle and yanking. But there was no give...there was nothing. The door never moved, barricaded from the outside.

"Let me out!" I screamed. *"Let me out of here!"*

Laughter followed, and this time it didn't end...it spilled through the cracks in the door to smother me.

4

Darkness rose around me. I shoved against the door. Hatred followed. The stuff was so thick I had to swallow it, taking it down inside me...like poison.

Nilsine was behind this, and Chaska, to lead me here. I shook with rage, tears sprang to blur the darkness.

I throttled the metal handle, shoving it down, but the door refused to budge. Driving a shoulder into the wooden door, I pushed, but my shoes slid back over the stone floor. No windows in this shed for another way out, just blackness consuming everything in sight.

"*Bitches*," I cried. They'd barricaded the door. What was their plan? Leave me here until I withered and died?

Hands curled into fists, I banged them into the solid door, yelling, "Get me out of here!"

I couldn't stop, wouldn't stop.

My skin crawled, but my hits kept coming, echoing around me.

Straining for breath, I slouched forward against the door, my ear flush to the wood, and I listened for any sounds.

Silence.

No one was out there. They'd left me, left me all alone.

I kept banging and screaming for someone to hear me. Maybe the servants or the gardener would be near… they were human and would be running around the manor getting things ready for when the Sinful arose.

"Help!" I screamed, slapping my palms on the door, my throat raw, hands stinging and red. I glanced back at the darkness in the room behind me, felt it closing in around me.

I hit harder with every glimpse in my mind of my parents' empty faces, their lifeless bodies sprawled across the kitchen floor in the dim light.

I kept sucking in harsh breaths, my yelling turning to ragged cries, echoing around me. Broken and bloodied bodies on the floor.

Slamming my fists, I choked on tears, hitting harder and harder.

I was back in my parents' home, eleven years old, and locked in the closet.

"Angel, hush," my father whispered from outside the closet, his voice trembling. "Don't make a sound. Whatever you hear, don't make a sound."

"Daddy, I'm scared. Let me out." The darkness pressed in around me, and it smelled musty.

"Just cover your ears, please. We love you so much." His pleading voice shook, and it broke me. Tears rolled down my cheeks, my body wrenched with tremors. I struggled against the locked closet door. I had to get out, had to see what was going on.

A sharp scream came from somewhere outside the closet.

"Mommy?" I cried.

Footsteps thundered somewhere in the house, the creaky floorboards in the kitchen groaning like they always did when anyone walked heavily over them.

"T-They're here," my mother's words drowned in terror.

Glass shattered somewhere in the house, followed by an explosion of screams.

I flinched backward, hitting the closet wall with my back. The clothes hanging overhead were like hands grabbing for me, suffocating me. I slid to my ass, pulling my knees to my chest, and covered my ears. I couldn't stop shaking.

Don't make a sound.

Don't make a sound.

Don't make a sound.

A thin sliver of light sliced through the darkness from where the closet door refused to sit flush, and I had to see… had to know what was going on. So I pushed myself forward on hands and knees to peer outside through the tiny gap.

I stared at the hallway in direct view, gasping for air to fill my strangled lungs.

Something huge and dark darted through the hall, so fast I only saw a blur. I lurched backward, a cry spilling from my lips.

My father yelled, the sound sharp and jagged. Fear clung to my ribs, and I hugged myself tight, cries rising through me. I wanted to scream, to help my dad, but I couldn't move, and sat there frozen, gutless.

A loud huff came from outside.

Thump.

Thump.

Thump.

Shaking terribly, I pushed forward and risked another look to see what made that sound. All I saw was the top half of Father's body. He was on his back, eyes shut and throat torn. His body was being dragged down the hall, arms limp behind him on the floor, leaving a trail of blood.

I shoved backward, cupping my mouth with both hands, smothering my muffled cries.

My heart slammed into my throat, and I was back in the manor, pounding on the door.

Tears rolled from my eyes, and my knees weakened. I fell to the floor, hugging myself, remembering the horror of what was left of my parents, the savageness with which their lives were taken. The only reason I'd survived was my father's quick action to shove me inside the closet.

For years afterward, I slept with the fire in the heath glowing refusing to spend another moment in the dark.

The heavy ache in my chest faded as anger rushed through me at how shitty my life had become, how everything I tried failed, how alone I felt in this world... in this manor. Shivers wracked my body as I dreamed of how different my life could have been if monsters hadn't killed my parents.

I'd be happier, and dreaming of a brighter future. Maybe have found the right man...

Except now, I'd do anything to get revenge, to find some kind of closure, to make the Vampires pay.

Cassian came to mind... something about him called to me. It shouldn't have, but there was a softness behind his hard gaze, and it scared me that I let myself think such things about him.

Streaks of sunlight stretched from the gap beneath the door. How long before night fell? Before the Sinful discovered me missing, before they reached out to me through my mind? I paced back and forth near the entrance, not wanting the Vampires to find me out of my room. The thought of Arkyn's rage had me curling in on myself, arms wrapped around my middle, as images of how he'd punish me circled through my mind like vultures.

If last night's discipline was any indication of what was in store for me, I wasn't an idiot to think I knew what was coming my way. No matter how much I drowned in their desire, I couldn't let myself fall for them, because only two options awaited me.

Become a blood bride... a slave for them to feed on.

Or be turned, and become one of the monsters I loathed.

A skin-crawling sound came from behind me. *Scratch. Scratch.*

I froze, fear pricking the back of my neck. I slowly turned my head, peering into the impossible dark behind me.

My mind flashed with memories of my parents' dead bodies in the dark kitchen. What if there was a monster in here that would kill me, and when anyone finally found me, I'd be dead?

"H-Hello? Is someone in there?" I cleared my throat, then forced myself to take a step deeper into the room, squinting to look into the dark. I stuck a hand out, reaching for the wall, but my fingers brushed a thin wooden pole, and I patted it down, to find it was a shovel.

I stepped forward, but tripped over something and stumbled forward, kicking a metal bucket.

Something scrambled over my shoes, and I jumped, a scream rushing from my throat. I spun, and spotted the culprit, a huge rat darting across the room and into a shadowy corner.

My heart thumped so damn hard, and I let out a loud sigh of relief. "Shit, you scared the hell out of me." I grabbed the shovel, the wooden handle worn under my touch. "Don't worry, little one, I won't hurt you. You stay on your side of the room, and we'll get along just fine."

Marching across the dark room, I gripped the shovel and held it over my shoulder with two hands, then whacked it into the door, the sound ricocheting around me. Good, maybe someone would hear the noise.

After several more hits, the door showed no sign of yielding, and my insides died a little. So I swiped the sharp edge of the shovel across the handle, causing a deafening crack.

The metal handle snapped off and hit the floor with a clunk.

I rushed closer and pushed the door, but it remained jammed. Dropping to my knees, I prodded the gaping hole where the rest of the handle was to try to trip the lock or something, but the metal rod was already unlocked.

Sitting back on my heels, I sighed. "Bitches." What in the world had they jammed up against the door?

Determination pushed me to get up and keep trying. And I kept slamming the sharpened edge into the door, but I barely made an indent, barely chipped away at the wood.

My hands stung and when I stared at them, several red blisters had already started to form. I dropped the shovel, and the scream wedged in my lungs burst free. I wiped my wet cheeks and slammed my fists into the door. "Let me the fuck out!"

Sinking to the floor, I sat there, hugging my knees, exhaustion settling in.

"I'm going to end up stuck here, forgotten. No one cares. It's just me. It's always just been me, on my own." I rocked back and forth, staring into the dark.

I couldn't remember how much time had passed, how long I mumbled to myself, but the sun had slunk back from under the door, and the sliver of light I'd had was now vanished.

Panic slithered down my spine. I didn't want to be stuck in here in absolute darkness with just my thoughts and a rat.

Asena! Cassian's voice streamed over my thoughts.

I straightened and scrambled to my feet.

"Cassian?" I cried out, my heart pounding. "Is that you?"

He didn't respond at first, but within moments, a loud snarl came from outside the shed.

Shuddering, I recoiled from the door, dread smothering me.

Something scraped across stone, then the wooden door splintered, and I retreated further. A groan pierced the night. The door was ripped off the hinges and tossed aside as if it weighed nothing.

Cassian stepped into the doorway, his chest heaving, drawing great gulps of air into his body. Rage glinted in his eyes and, for a second, I thought I caught the red flames of Hell. His face was twisted with fury, lips cruel, fire burning in his eyes, hands fisted by his sides.

I whimpered and pulled into myself, wishing in this moment I was so small I was nothing. He looked like a monster, the beast everyone feared. His hard gaze flicked to me, seizing me like a predator captures its prey.

"Please," I murmured, sliding farther from him.

Cassian's shoulders rose, rage contorting his features as he wrenched his head backwards, and unleashed an ungodly roar into the night sky.

5

The savage, inhuman roar from Cassian shattered the darkness. I wanted to fight...wanted to be more than this pathetic, whimpering mess.

But I wasn't. I was weak and afraid.

Tears slipped from my eyes as he stepped through the doorway of the shed. I never moved, never lifted a hand to fight him. I was done...*broken*...still trapped inside that dark closet from my childhood, with the sound of my mother's screams in my ears.

"Asena," the beast above me called my name.

My chest heaved in great, consuming sobs. I closed my eyes, feeling the darkness shift around me as though this Vampire commanded the night itself.

Something brushed against my cheek, soft, slow...*tender.*

"*Asena,*" he growled.

His voice trembled with all the rage I wanted to muster.

"What did they do to you?"

Kindness brought me undone with the slow touch of an icy finger. His hand slid against my back, the other under my knees. The ache along my side left me as he lifted. I was so tired, so numb. I lifted my arms and gripped his shoulders as I buried my face in the juncture of his neck.

I hadn't the strength to fight, not him or my feelings. If he wanted to kill me, then he'd quite easily do it, after all, he was the monster, wasn't he? One blow of his fist.

One bite of his fang.

I shivered with the thought and a flare of heat swept through my body. Cassian turned his head, midnight eyes glittered as he stared into my eyes. "You want me," he growled. "I can smell your need, and your fear. Which one will win, Asena? Tell me, do you want to run away from me...or do you want to fuck me?"

His long strides ate the distance, taking me around the rear of the manor, where night swallowed the surroundings. He pulled me close. My breasts mashed against his hard body, my fingers curled around stony muscles, until one hand slipped from its grasp.

But my hand didn't fall through the air, it slipped along his arm. A surge of panic surged as he slowed long enough to open a door. I took that time to run my hand down his arm, and then over his chest.

His silent...empty chest.

Deep pools of obsidian glittered as he turned his head toward me. I was captured by his stare, held prisoner by his lips, and consumed by the silver shine of his skin. Waves of dark hair swept across my arm as he moved. I wanted to touch his hair, to sweep my fingers through the long strands. The vision filled my head...him kneeling between my splayed thighs, my fingers buried in the strands, guiding him as he lowered his head to that ache between my thighs.

The door closed behind us with a *bang*, tearing me from the vision. He smiled, that sinister, seductive smile. It'd be so easy to give into him...*so easy.* I fought to hang on to my last ounce of resolve. We were moving once more, stealing down corridors.

But this time, I never bothered to see where they led. This

time, all I saw was him. He carried me with the utmost care, not digging his fingers into my body, just sure and careful, until I was swept through a doorway, and the door closed behind me.

Night clung faintly to the room. There was a window, and the glow of the moon spilled across the comforter of a bed.

Springs howled under the weight as I was lowered.

"Is she…" Arkyn stepped out of the darkness.

His gaze swept over my body as he came closer. His hand traveled across the path he'd just made with his eyes, fingers skimming my cheeks, my breasts. My breath caught as he traveled lower, spanning out his hand to the width of my waist. Only then did he lift his gaze to my eyes.

A pressure built inside my head, not painful…but there, like the heavy weight of an arm across my mind.

"Let me in, Asena," Arkyn murmured, and closed his eyes.

The door opened, and then closed. A heartbeat later, Lorcan was beside the bed. White shone like a light in the dark as his lips peeled from his teeth, exposing fangs. Hate filled his eyes, hate so raw and thick I flinched at the sight.

"Tell me what happened…" Lorcan growled.

But the demand wasn't aimed at me as he cut a rage-filled gaze toward Arkyn.

"Let me in," Arkyn whispered. "I promise I mean you no harm. Open for me, Asena."

I shivered with the words. They were an echo of what they'd done to me…and my pulse raced. "Why? You've already been inside my head."

"You grow strong," he stared into my eyes and whispered.

But the pressure in my head was relentless. I fought, as panic reared once more, until Arkyn did something I didn't expect. He leaned forward and kissed me.

His lips grazed mine, before they took my lower lip. Soft, passionate…my lips trembled, heat flared just a little. I found my mouth opening for him…letting him in.

In the space of a breath, he was inside my mind, plunging deep into my memories. The force was an invasion. I sucked in a breath, ready to cry out, until the touch turned soft, *caring almost.*

"You have nothing to fear from me," Arkyn whispered against my lips.

I closed my eyes as his lips mirrored the touch inside my mind. Surging and ebbing, taking a little, before he pulled back.

Fragments flitted through my mind. Memories swept by so fast I couldn't catch them. Whispers. Giggles. Vicious stares aimed at me. Roses...perfect, beautiful roses.

Until *the* rose came to me. The one left lying on the floor in the shed.

A savage sound slipped into the room, like a beaten hound ready to make amends to his captor. It took me a second before I realized that sound had come from Arkyn.

Until he saw it...

Saw the moment the door to the shed slammed shut.

Memories turned into something else, something terrifying. My emotions surged to the surface with a rush. It was like trying to hold back the tide...or these Vampires.

He saw it all, the desolation, the loneliness. The darkness reaching up for me, and the sound of their savage glee slipping through the cracks of the shed door, and in the middle of it all was Willa's cruel smile...as she leaned close to Nilsine and whispered.

It was Willa's voice I remembered on the other side of that door.

Willa's sniggers.

Willa's cruel words.

You think you're so special, don't you? Let's see if you're special when you're dead.

He took it all, the pain as I slammed my fists on the door, the ache from the floor on my body. The cold...he swallowed the cold as though he was a hurricane, drawing all the pain from the core of me and into him.

And the past came with it, driving to the surface like a lie...

Like my lie.

His hiss filled my ears. He wrenched back, tearing from my mind like fangs from my body. I whimpered under the sting.

"They did that..." Something dangerous swirled around the room. "They did that to you?"

For a second I thought my life was over, that he knew everything. The revenge. The lies.

"They laughed while they locked you in there, knowing you...knowing you were terrified."

I swallowed hard and held his gaze. There was a flare of his jaw, a precursor for the wrath to come.

"They *dared* hurt you...they dared touch what's..." His top lip curled.

What's? I wanted to whisper. *What am I to you?*

The words seemed to flow through that unseen connection and I caught a flicker of the truth in his eyes before he tore his gaze away and stood back from the bed.

But what I saw wasn't enough. It wasn't anywhere near enough. The surge of desire was more than physical with him. Something else hovered under the surface, something I didn't understand.

"Bring me Xavier," Arlyn growled.

Lorcan took a step backwards, then turned. He moved too fast for me to track, yanking open the door, to leave behind a gust of wind.

Violence swirled around the room as I stared up at the two Sinful. Hate glinted in obsidian eyes. Their lips were bloodless and thin, just a slash on their grim faces.

"What...what will you do?" I whispered.

Arkyn lowered his gaze to me, recognition flaring like he'd

forgotten about me for a moment, so caught up in his own burning need for retribution he forgot I was here.

He moved fast, lunging toward the bed once more. His fingers, so gentle they were barely there, grazing down my cheek before he closed a hand over my breast. "I told you before, you had nothing to fear from me and I meant it. We'd never hurt you, Asena."

"Why?" The words came out of nowhere. I searched those endless pools. "Why do you want me? Why are you protecting me?"

There was the barest hint of a smile.

It was a chilling smile. *A knowing smile.*

But he pulled away, and barely a second later the *thud...thud...thud* of heavy boots slapped through the air. Darkness filled the doorway in the hulking outline of a man. He took one look at me, and then turned to Arkyn. "You wanted to see me, Sire?"

"Get them out of their rooms." Arkyn's voice was like thunder. "Get them *all* out of their fucking rooms."

I caught the flinch from the guard. "Sire?"

Arkyn swiveled in an instant and roared. *"Get every fucking one of them out of their rooms right now. I want them in the ballroom...I want them to see what they have done!"*

The mammoth guard took a step backwards, then, in an instant, he nodded and made for the door. The blood in my veins ran ice cold as Arkyn turned toward me, took a step forward, and held out his hand. "If I may?"

The sudden change in him was chilling. I knew in that moment he was riding the killing edge. His face was a mask of perfection, composed and controlled...yet underneath...

Underneath was rage.

My hand trembled as I reached up and took his hand.

"Are you cold?" he whispered, and stared into my eyes.

I wasn't anything in that moment, not cold, not angry. I was empty, like a vessel waiting to be filled.

"No," I answered. "Thank you."

With a nod of his head, he turned toward the doorway, holding my hand in the crook of his arm. I followed, my steps a haunting echo of my pulse, and stepped out of the doorway.

"It's not far," he murmured.

Faint echoes of cries and questions slipped through the darkness. My stomach hardened with the sound.

"You have nothing to fear now." Arkyn stroked the back of my hand with his fingers.

The feeling was strangely comforting as the faint sounds of distress became louder. We entered the ballroom from the upper level. I glanced at the closed doors, expecting to see boarded up areas from the attack after the ball.

But there was no evidence anything had happened at all. The doors were closed and locked. Sheer black curtains covered the nighttime view. But inside the room was utter darkness.

Arkyn lifted his hand and, in an instant, the fireplace came to life with a *whoosh* of flames. Amber flames brightened the more they grew, and soon enough they were licking the sides of the stone hearth. But we still stood in the darkness...out of view.

The other women filed into the ballroom under the growls of the guards. Doe-eyed and frightened, they clung to each other, holding hands and casting panicked glances all around.

"Stay here, Asena," Arkyn warned, and let my hand go.

I didn't dare disobey him...not in that moment. All I could do was stare in terror as Arkyn and Cassian strode toward the stairs leading down to the dance floor. From the corner of my eye, I saw Lorcan meet them before their descent, and as the faint fire glow reached the Sinful, those who'd left me for death whimpered.

"It's come to my attention that we are missing someone," Arkyn barked.

A chill cut through the air with the words, making me tremble. They others didn't dare whisper a word, not to the Sinful or each other. I glanced at Chaska, feeling the stab of betrayal like a knife in my chest.

I'd trusted her, but she'd fooled me into lowering my guard. She cowered, her big eyes stretched wide as she glanced from Arkyn to the others. But the one who hurt most was Willa. She never blushed with guilt, never answered.

Arkyn's gaze skimmed across her, and she stared right back at him like she was a statue. It was her laughter that echoed inside my head, her painful words that cut like a knife.

It felt like months since that night we'd been taken here. I'd thought we were friends, at the bare minimum, I'd thought we were allies.

"Does anyone want to comment?" Arkyn looked straight at Willa when he spoke.

Still she said nothing.

"Do you take us for imbeciles?" The threat was clear. "Mere idiots of the night?"

Chaska shook her head…

"WELL, DO YOU?" The roar trembled the flames in the fire and shuddered the windows like a gale-force wind.

"No. God, no…"

"No."

Cries echoed through the room as the women stumbled backwards in terror, clinging to each other.

"Please," Chaska cried, and fell to her knees. "Please…I."

"Shut up!" Willa jerked her gaze toward Chaska and snapped. "Just shut up."

I took a small step forward and caught Arkyn turning his head to stare at the floor with my movement. One small shake of his head stopped me. I stepped backwards, obeying his command.

"Do you like to play games?" Arkyn's question was not a question at all.

I shook my head as desperation roared to the surface. My heart thundered as he stalked the women like a beast on the hunt.

"Well? A cruel game, perhaps? One involving a shed."

Some of the women shook their heads, confused. But there were others who were frozen with fear.

"She deserved it," the whisper cut through the room.

Willa turned her head, and defiance raged in her eyes. "She took what was ours...all of ours. I hope she's dead...and I hope it was painful."

I slapped a hand to my chest at the words. "No," the word slipped from my lips.

"She didn't die." Arkyn stopped in front of her. "Asena is very much alive...which is more than I can say for you."

And with a sickening, savage growl, he lunged, grasping the woman where she stood and sinking his fangs into her neck, until, with one terrifying wrench of his head...he tore her throat out.

6

A single scream ripped through the ballroom, an eerie, dreadful scream that would haunt me for eternity. I stared in disbelief as Willa's limp body slipped out of Arkyn's grasp and hit the floor at his feet with a dull thud.

Throat ripped out.

Blood rushing onto the floorboards.

Eyes wide and void of life.

He'd killed her.

Dead.

Gone with that single moment of rage.

Grimacing, I froze on the spot, barely able to draw a breath into my lungs, unable to stop shaking. Other girls screamed, drawing away from the body, and their cries sliced through me like blades. Tearing me apart, taking me to a place I never intended.

Hatred and guilt.

This was my fault. I should have made more of an effort to get out of the shed before the Sinful woke up, should have begged Arkyn not to kill her, should have made him understand we were all terrified here, willing to do anything for survival.

That was what being at this manor had become... it had always been this way, but I'd let myself believe otherwise.

Now, reality lay on the floor, bleeding everywhere, and I choked on my tears. I'd let myself get carried away with my desires and seduction, except us being here came down to one brutal thing. A lesson in survival, nothing else.

"Return to your rooms," Arkyn snapped, lips and chin covered in blood. Red stained his gray shirt. Darkness crowded behind his eyes, his fury silencing the cries. His tight face carried no sympathy, no warmth, just rage. He turned swiftly on his heels and marched out of the room.

My nerves were a jumble, and I wiped my eyes dry.

Lorcan approached Willa's body and lifted her into his arms as if he'd done this dozens of times before, then followed Arkyn into another room. The girls all raced out of the hall, vanishing out of my line of sight, their whimpers fading with their footsteps.

Except me. I stood there, still shaking, staring down over the railing at the puddle of blood left in the now barren room.

What had I done?

Footsteps closed in behind me, and I jerked around to find Cassian striding toward me. His midnight blue shirt sat wrinkled and untucked over his strong torso, his feet bare, shaggy hair falling to his shoulders. He'd rushed out of his death-sleep to collect me from the shed, not paying attention to his appearance. The startle of waking up with fear still clung onto his gaze. Was he really that terrified of me getting hurt?

"You need to return to your room." Impatience peppered his words. His hand reached out for mine, offering me a lifeline, and all I could do was stare at his large palm, curled fingers, and the power behind them. A Vampire who'd murder without mercy. Arkyn had proved that tonight.

I gazed at Cassian. "Why kill her?" The words slipped past my trembling lips, but I had to know.

"She hurt you," he replied, like the answer was clear, like I was too dumb to see the answer right before my eyes.

I stared at him. "You'd kill me if I hurt another girl?"

Something shifted behind his pale green eyes, and confusion flashed over his stilted expression. "We need to go," was all he said.

I toyed with the idea of pushing the point, making him answer, though part of me knew the response he refused to voice.

Why were they treating me differently? Why me?

Frowning, I accepted his hand and let him guide me into the hall and toward my bedroom.

"They won't touch you anymore," he explained. "None of them would dare."

But his words did little to comfort me or soothe the knot bunching up in my chest. I'd caused Willa's death, and I didn't deserve the Vampire's sympathy.

"What will happen to Willa now? Will she..." Eira crossed my mind, chained to the wall, fed upon.

He raised a brow. "Will she become one of us? Is that what you want to know?"

I nodded.

"Well, that depends."

"On what?"

"This is not a conversation we're going to have." A brittle smile pulled at his lips that looked more dangerous than calming.

"Because it might one day become my destiny? And you don't want to scare me?"

His green eyes widened for a heartbeat, and the corded muscles in his neck flexed. "Our protection over you does not give you the right to defy our decisions or to question them."

Even though his response wasn't a surprise, it still rattled me, and the silence between us grew as cold as a frigid winter.

Releasing his grip of my hand, I pulled back.

"Go now. Get some rest until tomorrow." He didn't wait for my response, but was already striding back the way we'd come, leaving me in the dimly lit hallway. He marched with the poise of a predator tonight, tall shoulders and deadly silent, and his warning chewed on my confidence.

I feared them.

Desired them.

They'd always be the enemy and I'd always remain the prey, dominated by them. I gritted my teeth at the constant games, the pulling and pushing of my emotions.

Stepping to the side, I reached for the door handle, my stomach tightening, and shoved into the bedroom.

A candle flicked on the bedside table, tossing shadows over the walls like a grand puppet show of ghouls and monsters. Except scarier things lived in this manor with us.

Chaska sat on the bed, still in her dress, knees pulled tight to her chest, her muffled cries flooding the night. An ache pierced my chest because, if I'd thought the girls hated me before, now they'd hide it, but they'd aim those invisible daggers at my back, waiting for the right chance to drive them into me and make me pay.

She lifted her tear-filled gaze to me and scoffed. "Are you happy now?"

My stomach dropped. Fast feet carried me closer and I slid onto the side of the bed. "Chaska, I never wanted any of this to happen to Willa. Why did you all have to lock me in that shed?"

Her lips clamped to paper-thin lines, but only more tears spilled from her eyes. "We fucked up. You and being the favorite did this to Willa." Her sobs grew heavy, and I reached over to touch her arm, to let her know she wasn't alone.

But she shoved my hand away. "Don't." Her voice came out vicious. Up on her feet, she crossed the room and sank into a chair, bringing her knees to her chest, and just stared outside through the window into the night.

There was nothing I could do to change what happened, or stop feeling like the worst person in the world. I wanted to scream back at Chaska that *they* did this to Willa, not me... but it wouldn't change a thing.

Willa... what would the Sinful do to her? Desperation swirled inside me as I kept picturing Arkyn ripping her throat out, the splatter of blood, the wet sounds, her last whimpering cry.

Crawling into bed, I curled in on myself as loathing spread through me, hating what the Sinful had done to me, that they made me desire them, that I couldn't control myself around them. It was what they wanted from me... from all of us.

Icy fingers wrenched my heart. I'd come here for one mission, yet I'd lost my way.

My mind reeled, always coming back to Willa. I couldn't sit back and let this pass...

<hr>

With everyone busy, I picked the lock once more and crept down the hall on silent feet. It was becoming a habit now, picking locks of doors, leaving when I wanted. I'd seen the others do the same.

Black stone walls flanked my path, darkness crowding in around me the deeper I moved through the manor. From one empty room to the next, I wound my way back to where I'd found Eira. A single burning torch hung in a metal bracket on the wall, barely slicing through the dark.

Pushing open the door, the hinges gave a small groan, and I peered inside the room. Part of me expected to find Eira. Except she wasn't there. Only the chains were, hanging from a metal ring on the wall. Nothing else, not even a window.

Sighing, I turned to retreat, when heavy footfalls came from the direction I'd come from earlier.

Dread slammed into me, and my heart pounded. I scrambled down the hall, into the clutches of shadows, and reached for the next door.

A quick glance over my shoulder revealed a figure coming in my direction. Shaking violently, I darted into the dark room before closing myself inside. Fear crawled over my flesh, my breaths coming too fast. Was it a guard? Had he heard me?

A spray of light spilled across the wooden floor from a door ajar across the room, and I moved in that direction.

From the doorway, I stared inside. Two black chaise lounges filled the space, the bronze chandelier blinking overhead from candlelight, and a whimpering sound came from the far corner. Someone crouched there, her back to me. Tangled brown hair hung halfway down her back in loose, knotted curls.

My heart slammed harder, more ferociously.

"Willa?" I inched forward, something terrifying in the air, like I was being watched. The hairs on my arms stood on end.

The crying sounds ceased, and she twisted toward me in slow motion, staring at me, her nose wrinkled and eyes narrowed.

"You came to laugh at me?" She sounded like her normal self.

It took me a moment to find my voice. I scanned her, my gaze lingering on her throat, and she saw me looking. "I'd never laugh at you."

As she lifted herself to her feet, the clang of chains sounded. Metal shackles circled her wrists. She stepped into the light and lifted her chin, showing me the bite marks on her neck. Two tears down the sides had left her skin barely healed and were blushing pink from where Arkyn had torn her flesh with his bite. Sickness churned in my gut at seeing her in this state. Were the Sinful using her for feeding?

I cringed on the inside, shocked she was still alive. Chained up meant she couldn't have been turned... not yet.

"I was terrified for you and had to see if you were still alive," I murmured, unable to get my feet to move forward as shivers crawled up the back of my legs.

Her gaze lowered for a moment. "I did this to myself."

I rocked on my heels, not convinced I'd heard right, but when she met my gaze, I saw the truth in her eyes. She owned her mistakes, but she'd fooled me once before.

Willa fidgeted with her shackles. "I just wanted to be selected, you know. Back home in Windtorn, I had no friends, and no one ever gave me a chance. I had no boys interested in me, either, and Father threatened to trade me to an old man in a neighboring town for a herd of his sheep." Her lips thinned as her chin trembled. "I was glad to be sent here for payment. Better than marrying some old man who'd already had two wives."

The agony crossing her face touched me. I wanted to protect her, soothe her, take away the pain, but she'd been instrumental in locking me in that shed.

Her cries tugged at my heartstrings and, without a thought, I closed the distance between us and dragged her into my arms.

I expected her to fight me, shove me aside, maybe bite me, but instead, she softened against me and cried louder.

I wasn't sure who the real Willa was, in all honesty, as she now resembled more of the girl from when we'd first arrived at Nightingale Manor, a terrified girl who'd been putting on a brave front because it was the only way to deal with such terror. Except, was that really her or was this just another game?

"I'm sorry," she blubbered and broke free from my embrace as she wiped her eyes. Whatever jealousy and anger she held for me seemed to evaporate from her sorrowful face. "For trying to kill you, for even thinking that way. Something's broken inside me. I deserve this and so much worse." She clenched her hands into fists, fingernails digging into her palms, her eyes scrunched tightly shut.

I understood that sentiment too well. "You're not broken, just barely keeping your head above water, like the rest of us."

Her teary eyes slid open, and a ragged whisper slipped through her lips. "I need to make it right. To show you I mean it. I'll tell you everything I know. Everything I find out, I'll reveal." She was nodding her head fast, like she half-talked to herself. "The Sinful know everything about you. They want you, and they will have you. You need to find a way to escape from this place."

I loosened my fingers and dropped her hands. "Why me?"

She blinked several times, her expression sharp and controlled, expressing so much concern that I wanted to believe Willa had changed and this wasn't her pretending. "I don't know why."

"Then help me find them, to end this for all of us. Where do they sleep?" I felt the blade in my boot, the weapon I'd started wearing more often these days.

Darkness flickered behind her eyes, but she didn't hesitate in responding. "They're down in the crypt. Go out in the hallway and turn left, keep following it, then take the first three lefts and the fourth right, until you reach a final door. That's them."

I swallowed uncomfortably. Was she telling me the truth or leading me to another trap?

But the reason I'd come to the manor was to finally secure revenge for my parents' deaths. Yet my bravery fled in an instant, leaving nothing but fear in its wake.

"Let me free you," I offered but she was shaking her head.

"Be quick," Willa reminded me. "Do it now while the sun stays high and death keeps them at bay. While the guards take their morning break."

Her voice said it all. Get caught and I'd die.

"Go now," she insisted. "Stop wasting time."

I stared at her, tried to decipher her words, read the expression on her face, searching for any hints of deceit.

"You have every reason not to trust me," she began. "But I've lost and my hatred is for the monsters who put us in this danger in the first place."

And I wanted to believe her words… but I'd been too trusting, and it was my turn now to take what I could to help further my own agenda. There was no harm in checking, and at the first sign of a guard, I'd bolt in the opposite direction. So I retreated into the hallway. I checked for any sign of whoever was there earlier, only to find the place empty. To my left lay a passage swallowed by darkness.

Goosebumps slid down my arms, and I reached for the fiery torch on the wall, dislodging it from its metal bracket.

Without hesitation, I sank into the darkness and made hasty steps along the descending steps. The deeper I traveled, the stuffier the air grew, smelling of fresh soil, while the walls were no longer black, but made of raw stone. With each step, my stomach clenched, but I followed Willa's instructions, passing other underground tunnels. The place was a maze, but I was completely alone.

And all I could think about was me trapped in the closet.

I winced, imagining the roof and walls crashing in on me, engulfing me, burying me alive. That robbed me of all other thoughts.

With heavy breaths, I hurried down the corridor, following a curved path that led me to death's door all the way at the end.

This was it, and I was going to be sick.

A huge black door stood before me. I clutched the icy cold handle and pushed it down. To my surprise, the door swung open. A flurry of stale air greeted me.

The fire from my torch fluttered, its light stealing the darkness of the room. I paused in the doorway, glancing inside, at three king-sized beds, black bedposts carved with elaborate cravings. Black bedsheets draped over the mattresses, yet part of me expected them to sleep in coffins as the rumors had said. The Vampires lay there, dead to the world.

I scanned the room. Bare walls without any brackets for the torch, and aside from the beds, only a wooden writing table sat against the wall nearest the door. There I found papers and gloves and candles. I stepped closer and lowered the flame to the wick. Once it caught alight, I took the torch outside and slid it into a wall bracket. Back inside the room, I shut the door and retrieved the blade from my boot.

One woman.

Three Vampires.

I turned to the beds, Cassian in the closest one, and I stepped closer, my heart banging against my ribcage like thunder.

Dropping my gaze to Cassian's face, I lowered myself and placed a gentle kiss on his lips. I shoved aside all feelings and gripped my blade tight.

"Tomorrow," I whispered. "Tomorrow we'll all be free."

7

*D*o it...*do it now.*

My palms slick with sweat, the handle of the knife slipped. I clenched tighter, forcing the tip of the blade to stop trembling, and pressed it to Cassian's chest.

Shadows of the blade danced from the faint glow of the candle.

It's me or him...

I tried not to look at him. Tried not to remember the way he carried me from the shed...the way he whispered in my ear. *It's okay. I have you now. You're safe with me.*

You're safe with me.

That's what he'd told me...that's what they all told me. *Safe.* The word resounded from the depths of my soul. I swallowed hard and stared at his lips...soft, perfect. Pressed together. I let my gaze roam to his closed eyes, long, dark lashes against pale skin.

He was a mask of serenity.

The blade trembled once more in my grasp.

You want me, I could still hear his voice. *I can smell your need, and your fear. Which one will win, Asena? Tell me, do you want to run away from me...or do you want to fuck me?*

Fuck me. That was what he'd said...I lowered my gaze, roaming over the hard swell of his chest to his muscled stomach. All that power, that raw, unbridled power. I remembered what he'd felt like between my thighs, remembered his lips and his tongue...remembered the way he'd moved slowly, drawing every tiny quake from my core.

Heat moved through me with the memory. His touch had branded me, his lips had chained me, and his fangs had marked me. I was forever changed because of him.

Forever different, even standing here, with a knife pressed to his heart, I felt it.

A shift of desire.

Do you want to run away from me...or do you want to fuck me?

I lowered my hand and closed my eyes as the room swayed around me. My pulse sped...my knees trembled. Tears sprang to my eyes as I stood above my captors. I conjured the memories of my parents.

With a shuddered breath, I was back there, tiny fingers speared through the cracks in the closet, my nails ripped down to the soft bed as I scratched and clawed, desperate to find a way out.

Their blood...*oh God, their blood.* I could still smell it, thick and cloying, like a rag stuffed down my throat. They screamed when they were murdered. They screamed and screamed...I opened my eyes and stared at these monsters--*and screamed.*

These...*beautiful, deadly monsters.* I knew in my heart it was them. Still, there was an echo of uncertainty. I shook my head, trying to dislodge the claws of mistrust.

All these years...these years I'd trained, all these years I'd hated.

All the years I'd planned their deaths.

And here I was....

The candle cast shadows on the wall. I lifted the knife once more and swallowed hard. *Kill them...do it now. It's the only way you can escape them...the only way.* I glanced at Arkyn, so vulnerable now...unlike the night before.

He'd terrified me. A phantom touch grazed down my cheek. I kept the knife in front of me and reached up with my other hand to follow the touch...just like he'd done, and his words filled my head. *They did that to you? They laughed while they locked you in there, knowing you...knowing you were terrified. They dared hurt you...they dared touch what's...*

What?

What was I to them?

I left Cassian and stepped closer to Arkyn. "Tell me." My voice rang out in the dark room. "Tell me what I am to you."

A scurry came from the corner of the room. The sound scratching, *scurrying.* Panic drove through my veins, born from a fear that ran deeper than my soul. Images scattered inside my head...*rats...rats everywhere. Over my face. Crawling through my hair. Get it off me...GET IT OFF!*

Reflex drove me, and a cold rush of power ripped through me. I was all instinct, unmerciful, venomous, and very much alien as I lashed out. The knife left my hand before I knew, impaling the black blur to another desk in the corner of the room. In a heartbeat I was back here...in this room...in the manor. I sucked in hard, sawing breaths as the memories that were not my own faded.

My heart thundered, filling my head with a deafening roar. My breath came out in a rush as I stumbled toward the tiny creature that still kicked and fought, flicking dark drops of blood across the desk as it moved.

"No," I whispered. "Oh, no."

I yanked the blade from deep inside the rodent's chest. It hit the desk with a *thud* and stayed there, unmoving.

"I'm sorry," I whispered and reached out with trembling fingers.

Its black, beady eyes shone in the darkness. I jerked my gaze toward the weak candle flame on the writing desk near the doorway and strode toward the light. The flames flickered as I reached out, as though the yellow teardrop of fire cowered from my touch.

A lump grew in the back of my throat as I lifted the light and turned to the twitching little dark body. Blood spilled in a trail, to slowly drip from the edges of the slanted wooden desk.

I stepped closer and reached out, touching its matted, thick fur, and pulled away. Its little chest moved in panicked pants until, with a slow sinking, the rat stilled. Tears slipped down my cheeks with the sight. "I didn't mean…"

My voice was husky and deep. I didn't understand what had happened. My reflexes were never that good…never that accurate. I'd trained for months, throwing knives and axes. I'd even found a quiver of old dusty arrows and an old bow.

Day after day, month after month, I'd trained. I closed my eyes, remembering the cold December winds and torrential rain. I'd aimed those weapons at tree stumps and markers and even came close to hitting them a few times.

But I'd never been this close. I looked down at my hand, at the blade, then lifted my gaze to the three sleeping Vampires. I'd never been anywhere near this close. I turned back as the blood dripped and stepped closer.

The desk was filled with papers and a small row of ink wells.

Asena.

The sight of my name caught my breath. I neared, grasped the rodent as gently as I could, and lowered it to the floor before I rose. My name peeked out from under another letter. I pushed it aside, tainting the edges with the rodent's blood.

I winced at the sight, but I couldn't care about that now....
All I saw was my name.

Asena is the one you seek.

My heart lunged at the sight, the heavy *boom* echoing through my body. *Asena is the one you seek.* I shoved the top letter further, unveiling the scrawled writing.

Dear Arkyn...

I couldn't concentrate, couldn't focus on the words.

I had a very interesting visitor today.
A young woman, Asena.
She came seeking information about the Sinful, and even though she refused to tell me the true reason why she sought you out, it was enough for me to become intrigued.
All the markers are there, Arkyn. Everything you've been searching for, she carries within.
She has come to seek you out, but I urge you to take her into you, so you may know the truth in her heart.

I swear this is truthful.
I swear on my allegiance.

Domina.

Domina?

I swallowed the panic as it rose swiftly, like a storm. Still, terror was all around me, sharp and bitter like the choking scent after lightning struck. I snatched the letter from the desk and re-read the words. *Domina.* I knew that name. I closed my eyes, conjuring fragments of the past.

*The old woman...*the old woman in the hills, that's who she'd said she was. A noise came from the other side of the door. A soft scrape was followed by another...and then another.

The candle flickered in my hand as the door handle slowly turned. Inch by inch, the brass handle turned...my heart pounded, the sound deafening. I shook my head, backing up and lifting my hand as the door creaked open and a shadow moved inside.

"Asena?"

I flinched at the femine whisper and lifted the candle. Chaska stepped into the dim light and glanced toward the candle. Air left my lungs in a whoosh. I crumbled against the desk, sucking in great gulps of air as she stepped onto the room and eased the door closed behind her.

"What are you doing?" she whispered loudly her own candle adding to the glow in the room.

I winced at the sound and grabbed the letter from the desk, folding it along the creased edges and slipping it into the pocket of my dress. "Are you following me?"

She narrowed those big doe-eyes and stepped closer. "You didn't answer the question."

"You first," I growled, as a flare of betrayal reared its ugly head.

She glanced around the darkened room. But the candlelight was weak, barely reaching in front of me, from over here at the desk she wouldn't even see their feet.

But she'll see the knife, won't she?

"What's that?" She came closer, her gaze drifting to the floor at my feet. "Is that a rat?"

I turned, grabbed my knife, and nodded. "Yeah."

"Yuck." She winced and came closer to prod it with her foot.

I took the opportunity to bend, hitch up the bottom of my dress, and slip the knife back into the pocket of my boot before I straightened.

"What is this place?" she asked.

"What do you want, Chaska?" I growled.

She swallowed hard. Her throat muscles worked overtime as she scanned the dim room. "I followed you...found you when you came back down the hallway. I saw you were looking for something so I hung back and yeah..."

"Followed me for what?" The candle flickered, the flame dancing so violently it almost spluttered out.

"To say I'm sorry. I'm so sorry, Asena. I... I acted like a bitch and I hate myself for what happened. I didn't know it was going to go that far. I thought, I thought they were just going to scare you, that was all. I begged Willa and Nilsine to let you out of the shed, but they wouldn't listen to me."

Redness crawled into her cheeks as she fidgeted.

"Chaska, look at me." I lifted the candle.

She did, and there were tears in her eyes. Honest tears, the kind you couldn't fake.

"I believe you," I murmured and took one look behind me before I jerked my gaze toward the door. But I'd be careful, always remember my own agenda here. "How about we get out of here?"

She gave a nod, lifted her hand to swipe the tears slipping from her eyes. "Yeah, I'm kinda tired. Following you around all day is exhausting."

I smiled as she opened the door and stepped back out. I gripped the candle with one hand, the folded letter crunching in my pocket, as I grabbed hold of the door and stepped through, turning at the last minute.

I didn't need the glow of the candle. I could see them inside my mind. My thoughts tumbled together in a panicked knot. The old woman betrayed me, writing the Sinful a letter to give them my name. I didn't understand them, nor did I understand this power these Vampires held over me.

I wanted answers...needed to understand what I carried that intrigued them so...and I needed them alive to get those answers.

I closed the door behind me and turned. The torch I'd left changed the hallway from utter darkness to faint light. I grabbed the torch and climbed, following Chaska as we made our way through the sleeping Vampires' lair to the far wing where our bedrooms lay, but I took a moment to return the torch to its original bracket

My body felt the effects of the last few days. I'd pushed hard to not only stay awake, but to hunt the Vampires in their own home. I knew where they slept now, and I knew they kept secrets from me.

Chaska opened the unlocked door to our bedroom and slipped inside, smothering a yawn with the back of her hand. "You need to stop picking the locks and leaving. Between you and Polaris, I'm exhausted."

I stilled and stepped inside, closing the door behind me. "What do you mean, Polaris?"

Chaska flopped onto the bed, letting her body bounce. "She's just like you, always searching, finding hidden doors. Best lock that in case the Sinful come."

My hand froze at the laces to my boot. I would lock the door, in moment. I was too busy captured by what she said. I lifted my head. "What hidden doors?"

Her eyelids were heavy as she shoved her elbows against the

mattress and pushed upwards. "The one behind that big painting of the Vampire."

My thoughts raced. The manor was big, big enough for secret rooms and hidden passages. The more I thought about it, the more my resolve started to gather.

I wouldn't kill them...not yet.

Soft snores came from Chaska as she lay sprawled out on the bed. I yanked off my boots and lay them on the floor and then quietly made my way to the bottom of the bed. There, I gently untied her laces and eased her boots from her feet.

She never muttered, never woke once.

I had to bide my time and play my part. I'd be the good captive...I lifted my gaze. I'd make sure I didn't step out of line. I wouldn't draw their attention, not the Sinful or the other women. I crawled higher in the bed, falling to the mattress beside Chaska.

A yawn consumed me, stretching my jaw muscles until they strained.

When I was awake during the day, I'd search the manor, inside and out.

And I'd find out what they were hiding.

And why they wanted me.

Daylight slipped away in slumber. I woke to the sounds of chatter and then plunged back into the abyss. Dreams haunted me. The shrieking sounds of rats followed me, filling my heart...making me panic.

I was back there in the shed, but it wasn't a shed. It was someplace else and my heart was pounding in my chest. Death was coming, Death shrouded in darkness. But I couldn't see...*I couldn't see.*

I woke with thunder in my ears and a scream trapped in my throat.

Pounding...*pounding...*

"Hold on." Chaska dragged herself out of bed and crossed the floor.

Still the banging became louder.

Chaska opened the door and Polaris all but shot inside the room. She was panting and heaving. She lifted a hand, her words nothing more than gasps of air. "Willa...*Willa.*"

Chaska froze as the blonde beauty lifted her head and gripped my gaze. *"Willa, she's back from the dead!"*

8

"**B**ack from the dead?" Chaska gasped, shutting the door to our room in case anyone was listening. She turned to us, pressing her back to the door, her eyes round like the moon. "They turned Willa already? What happens to her now?"

I just saw her, and she didn't look turned, but what if being chained to the wall was part of the transformation process? Did that mean Eira was now one of them, too? I sucked in a sharp breath that whistled through my front teeth, and Chaska cut me a strange look.

"Are you certain?" I asked. "If she hasn't taken Vampire blood, she'll--"

"This isn't something I'd lie about. You need to see what I did." Polaris scrubbed a hand through her brown curls, minus her usual black eye makeup. But she still had the three dots down the bridge of her nose. She wore a simple black dress today, following the curve of her body, unlike Chaska and me, still in our nighties. I suspected Polaris had been spending the day spying through the manor.

"So, what did you see?" Chaska asked.

195

"Something I'll never get out of my head." Her cheeks still paled.

"Was she eating someone?" Chaska cried.

"Eww. Vampires don't eat people," I corrected. "They drink their blood."

Chaska was shaking her head. "I bet they do. Did you see how quick Arkyn attacked Willa? How he ripped out part of her throat? That shit is terrifying, so what if Willa was caught eating a human servant?"

I rolled my eyes.

"She wasn't eating anyone," Polaris piped up, her voice stern. "You need to have a look for yourself or you won't believe me. So, are we going?"

"Where is she?" Chaska stepped into her shoes. "Asena," Chaska called out, "you coming?"

Alarm bells rose through me, rather than curiosity. The last time Chaska asked me to go somewhere with her, Nilsine locked me up in the garden shed. Then Arkyn ended up attacking Willa and now she was a Vampire. A vicious circle that ended with nothing good as a result.

I padded across the room to look outside where dusk approached over the landscape. I hated how the smallest thing panicked me. Hated that I didn't feel safe from the girls during the day and the monsters at night. Hated how easily I'd become just like them, sleeping most of the day, only to roam the castle at night, waiting for them to find me. But I'd let my guard slip, let the Sinful sweep me up in their desires, and now Willa's dead... And it could be me, too, if I didn't focus on my mission.

Revenge.

Make the Sinful pay.

"I believe you," I answered over my shoulder. "They probably did turn her."

"And you don't want to see?" Chaska demanded. "We're

stuck here, which means learning what we can about these creatures and how to survive."

She carried so much passion in her voice, unlike previous times where she'd held something back.

Polaris shrugged. "If she doesn't want to come, that's fine, just the two of us."

Chaska stood between us, her eyes pleading with me, clearly she preferred safety in numbers. "What have you got to lose? Come on, I really want to see this."

So many answers swept over my mind, but instead, I gave a small nod, convinced neither of them were setting me up. And if they were, I refused to feel an ounce of guilt if the Sinful turned on them. All lies, I knew, but it was the only way I'd convince myself to trust them again.

Chaska stepped closer, her palm extended, and I accepted it. She smiled, while Polaris opened the door and checked the hall.

"I know why you hesitated," Chaska whispered, her eyes sincere. "I'll never trick you like that again, I swear to the gods."

"You better not." I yanked off my nightie and grabbed a dress. Part of me wanted to ask if that comment had anything to do with fear of what the Sinful had done to Willa. But everyone made mistakes, so I wanted to believe her.

Out in the hallway, Polaris took the lead, signaling for us to follow with small hand gestures.

The stones under our steps barely made a sound under our long strides. Dark walls crowded around us, and I hoped Willa was kept somewhere close so we'd return before night fully encased the land. With my pulse thumping fast, I rushed with both girls, wasting no time.

"How often do you go out on your own?" I asked, curious as it seemed no one played by the rules.

Polaris glanced over her shoulder. "Does it matter? We all do it."

"I'm not judging. Just curious."

"Enough times."

Chaska looked at me with a raised brow, and we returned to traveling along the hall, then down a set of stairs. The air smelled stuffy, like it had when I made my way to the Sinful's room. Only the occasional torch on the wall chased away the shadows.

"You sure there are no guards around here?" Chaska muttered.

"Shhh." Polaris glared our way, whispering, "If there weren't, there will be now." For the rest of the descent, no one said a word.

We took a sudden turn left down a passage, and right into the first door. "How in the world did you find this place?" I asked, figuring I ought to spend more time familiarizing myself with this manor.

But my attention swung to the three locked prison cells along one wall. A single flickering torch lit the place, while my attention fell on the figure lying on the ground inside the first cell.

All three of us inched toward the metal bars. Light gleamed off her brown hair and thin, frail body curled in the corner.

Chaska gasped out loud, shaking her head. "That's disgusting. Why is she eating rats?"

Half a dozen dead rat carcasses peppered the ground around her. Bite marks scored their tiny bodies, blood staining the stone ground. More crimson mess coated Willa's hands, tucked against her chest. She slept like she used to when we'd shared a room. Except, she was dead now, and once the sun fell, she'd rise. Heaviness settled in my muscles at seeing her in this state.

"Maybe she's getting used to her new Vampire hunger?" Polaris suggested.

"Well, she's definitely a Vampire." Memories of my last conversation with Willa crashed over me. How she hadn't lied, and said she regretted her actions, then promised to tell me information about the Sinful. Was that why they turned her? That awful ache settled in my gut, and I prayed it wasn't because of me.

"Let's go back," Polaris ordered, already pulling the door to the room open. Chaska retreated and hurried out of there, while I took one last look at Willa. I couldn't help but wonder if this was destiny for all of us.

I turned away and the three of us made a hasty retreat back to our room. We encountered no guards or servants, like everyone spent most of the day concealed, as well as their Lords.

Chaska shut the door to our room, then lit the candle on the table, and the three of us gravitated to the bed, where we sat cross-legged, facing one another.

"So," Polaris said. "Back home, my father once told my sister that once a Vampire was turned, the transformation would either kill the person or transform them, but that the majority of the time they didn't live. Which was why we don't see so many Sinful around."

I scrunched up my nose. "But there are quite a few Sinful guards in the manor."

"That's the thing," she whispered. "It all depends on whose blood they drank. The more ancient the blood, the more likely they'd survive."

"How old do you think the Sinful are?" I asked, remembering my conversation with the old woman, and with the thought came the memory of the letter I'd found in the Sinful's bedroom, her betrayal. Was anything she'd told me true?

"My grandpa said close to five-hundred years," Chaska added.

"Wow!" What would it be like living so long? I'd be bored out of my brain.

My stomach groaned and they both looked at me. "I'm starving," I said.

"Me, too," Polaris and Chaska said in unison.

"Anyway, I should probably head to my room." Polaris hopped off the bed and crossed the room. "See you girls soon." She slipped out and shut the door behind her.

"I like her," Chaska admitted. "She's just trying to survive, like the rest of us. And she came to us first about Willa."

"Probably because we shared a room with her, but I know what you mean. She seems nice. A bit of a take-control kind of person."

"You know, it's got to do with living in Sparrowfire. That town is dominated by dragons. Those things kidnap people right out of their yards, and no one sees them again. So everyone is brought up a warrior there, to fight off dragons."

"Shit, and I thought living with Wolves hunting us in our town was bad."

"I'm going to get changed." Chaska climbed off the bed and headed to the toilet.

I flopped onto my back on the bed, hands tucked behind my head, and let myself think what a life with dragons would be like. Horrifying. Everything wanted to kill humans in this world.

Hours later, a knock finally came on the door.

I rushed to open it, and a guard stood there, tall, broad shouldered, and wearing a sneer. "Your meals are being prepared. Until then, everyone is invited to the study."

My jaw flexed and I took a step back to find my shoes, but my insides coiled tight. Was this another summoning by the Vampires?

Chaska and I followed the guard through the dark hall, curving around the corridors, passing closed doors and finally reaching the study, where bookshelves lined the walls. The other girls were already inside, sitting around chatting, or poking around at the books. No sign of the Sinful.

I looked back at the guard with a raised brow.

"Get inside and wait until we call you for dinner." His wry frown left me shivering, and I moved into the room rapidly.

What was going on? Where were the Vampires?

"Come with me." Chaska snatched my arm and drew me deeper into the room toward the far corner behind the three black thrones. "I have to show you something I found."

At the back of the room, I kept glancing back to see the guard just standing there, watching us. The air felt thick tonight, something was happening.

Chaska nudged me in the ribs, and I winced. "You have very bony elbows."

"Look at this." She turned her back to the rest of the room and grasped a thick, leather bound book in her arms.

I reached over and opened it to a random page, the spine creaking with resistance. Both pages were filled with two rows of girls' full names and their ages. All of them were twenty-two-years old, the same age as me. "What is this?"

Chaska shrugged. "Are these all the girls they've kidnapped?"

I flicked the pages, and many names were crossed out, hundreds and hundreds of names. I hurriedly flipped through the book, and glanced up to see a guard looking directly at us. My stomach dropped, so I rushed through the pages, until I reached a page where the names stopped.

Running a finger down the last names, I passed Nilsine, Chaska, Willa, and so many others. I paused when I reached my name, underlined twice. Ice filled my veins. "What does this mean?"

Chaska quickly shut the book and shoved it back onto the lower shelf, then pushed it deeper so it sat out of sight. She jumped to her feet and casually threw a gaze over my shoulder.

"Is he still watching us?" I asked.

"Yep. Damn bastard. But there's more books like that." She casually strolled toward the slanted desk on the opposite wall that had more leather bound books.

The guard turned and left the room, and we lunged for the books, flipping through the pages to find more names, just lists of girls' names, lots crossed out.

"What are they searching for?" I fumbled with the next book, looking back at the entrance before opening another text.

"Could they be lists of girls they've turned, or are going to turn?"

"But why?" I asked. "Why keep records? After five-hundred years, did they forget who they turned?"

"The question is how many damn girls they tortured with these tests? And if they turned so many, where are they now?"

Dread sank through me at her words. She was right. With trembling hands, I pulled open the small drawer of the writing desk. A smaller book sat there, wrapped in worn brown leather with an exposed, bound spine.

I flipped open the book to find even more names, when a strange sensation coursed through me, something that just didn't feel right.

The lights dimmed, and the earlier chatter silenced. I rubbed my eyes and lifted my gaze, my surroundings no longer in the study at the manor but a completely different place.

Wind blew through my hair, as I stood outside, overlooking a grand, expansive open land and the sea in the far distance.

Dark stone walls were on either side of me, crenellations jutted up in front of me, and I stumbled backward. This was a castle.

My head pounded, and it hurt to try to make sense of anything, as panic slithered up my spine.

A war cry bellowed from my right, and I whirled around. I cried out in shock and fear, my body shaking convulsively.

An enormous man dressed in battle gear charged toward me, wearing a worn leather coat pulled tight with metal buckles, black baggy pants, and a sword raised over his head with both hands. I caught the emblem above his heart--a silver shield with a battle axe sitting over two crossed swords.

I'd seen darkness before, the kind that turned my life into a living hell, but this... this made no sense. I screamed and flung myself in the opposite direction, my heart about to explode, feet punching the stone balcony. I darted into the castle through an arched opening, and everything changed in a flash.

I stumbled forward, a cry on my lips.

Chaska grasped my arms. "Asena? What's wrong?"

Paralyzed with fear, I scanned my surroundings, at all the girls staring at me. I was back in the study, my breaths racing, and all I saw in my mind was the warrior with a sword lunging for me.

A whimper fell past my lips, and I stumbled over to the back wall nearby, where I leaned against it to catch my breath. What had just happened?

Looking back at Chaska who stared at me, terrified and puzzled, I noticed the brown leather book I'd been holding earlier lying on the floor.

"Put that away." I pointed to it, too terrified to touch it, and Chaska looked down at the book before she leaned over and tucked it back into the drawer.

"Are you all right?"

"Yeah. Just had a head-spin." Maybe I was hallucinating.

"What you need is some food, since you started freaking out and screaming."

"I think that's all it was. I need food."

"Shit. Does anyone have any snacks on them?" she called out.

Just then, two guards dressed in black stepped into the room, looking ominous and deadly. Their expressions were stiff and focused.

I bristled, the hairs on my arms standing on end as they scanned all the girls. They were searching for someone.

They marched inside and grabbed Nilsine by the arms.

She yelled and batted them away, her face terrified. They wrestled against her kicks and screams, but she stood no chance against them. They dragged her out, and an invisible hand squeezed my heart.

"What's going on?" another girl asked.

Chaska and I moved closer, as did everyone else. Terror settled in my gut.

Several servants emerged from the hallway and waved for us to follow them. "Dinner is ready."

But no one moved… no one dared, not when Nisline's cries ricocheted from down the hall where the guards dragged her.

***

I lay in bed, tossing and turning as the day crept away. Sleep evaded me after last night. No one told us where they'd taken Nisline last night. She never returned to join us for supper. What did the guards do to her, and why hadn't the Sinful joined us? I shifted in bed, Chaska's soft snores keeping me company.

So many thoughts crammed in my head, buzzing endlessly, and I kept coming back to the books in the study with the rows and rows of names. What did they mean?

I pushed my legs out from under the blanket and lowered them to the cold wooden floor. The only way I'd uncover the truth was to go back and study them more carefully, try to make sense of it all.

My head spun, which might be from the lack of sleep. And I just prayed I didn't have another insane hallucination, whatever that had been about. I pushed those thoughts aside and slipped into the bathroom to quickly change clothes. Then I crept out of the room, gently shutting the door, and ran all the way to the study, eager to spend a few hours in there before anyone noticed me gone.

I pushed down on the handle and the door swung open easily. Quickly, I scrambled inside, except it took my brain a few moments to make sense of what I stared at... At the nothingness.

The room had been gutted, all the books removed. It was almost completely empty.

A whimper fell past my lips and my knees wobbled.

Everything was gone.

9

The room was empty...

Except for a large, dark leather sofa on the far side of the room. But everything else was...*gone.*

My heart thundered as I peered into the darkness. "No...no way." I stumbled around, stepping on the same spot where bookshelves had been towering in the back corner, the books all gone now. I rushed to the slanted writing desk and pulled open the drawer. Empty. Books that gave me names...*books that gave me answers.* "Goddamn it."

They'd been right here...*right here.* I scuffed my boots along the floor in the same spot where I'd stood and flicked through the pages, searching for names.

Searching for my name.

And now...now there was only darkness, and the hope I had felt slowly slipped away.

I clenched my fist as anger lashed like a whip deep inside. I could *never* win with them, could I? They always seemed one step ahead...tearing the answers from my grasp.

"Looking for something?"

The words were barely a murmur but I heard them like a

lion's roar. I jumped, and then spun, to see Lorcan leaning casually against the wall. He had his arms crossed, watching me like an owl watches the scurrying little mouse. My heart pounded at the sight. I quickly scanned the shadows, searching—

"They're not here," he murmured. "Busy doing whatever Arkyn and Cassian do best."

I flinched at the words. I ground my teeth. I knew exactly what they were doing, finding a new place to hide their secrets. I eyed the Sinful in the dark as black on black shifted, but somehow, I could track him. Still, one Vampire instead of three. It didn't make me feel a whole lot better.

"Were you looking for something, Asena?"

His husky words danced across my skin, all carnal and dangerous. I stiffened, waiting for him to come closer...waiting for him to touch me. But he didn't. Not a brush of my shoulder, not a flick of my hair. I trembled as the tension inside me grew.

"Like to break out of your room, do you? My little lockpicker," he murmured, coming closer. "You like to invade and steal what's not yours, to break poor Arkyn's rules."

"I wasn't going to—"

My hair flipped from my shoulder, dancing in the air with a *whoosh,* stopping my words cold.

"Wasn't going to...*what?*"

Fear crawled along my spine, stealing my breath. I became aware of him...*very aware.* The inches between us...the fact that he was *terrifyingly* dangerous and all alone.

"The others aren't here now," he whispered against my ear. "Not to save you."

Goosebumps broke out along the back of my neck. I clamped my jaw tight, swallowing the whimper.

"It's just you and me."

Swallow...*swallowswallowswallow.*

"You know what I do when someone breaks the rules?"

The shake of my head was a tremble.

His finger found the place under my ear, the touch soft and tender, trailing all the way to my shoulder. He pressed against me, hard muscles and icy breath. I closed my eyes as his lips touched my bare skin and he whispered, "I punish them."

A whimper tore from the back of my throat, like a gasp of breath, as he reached around and cupped my breast, driving me back against his body.

"I *like* to punish, Asena...*and I do it very...very...well.*"

That hunger between my thighs flared to life. It was a beast of its own, *ravenous and unsated,* always waiting for a trigger.

The Sinful was that trigger.

"You're all alone." He kneaded my breast and breathed the words. "Are you scared?"

I wasn't scared.

I was goddamn terrified.

But the terror mingled with the ravenous fire inside me, and it was like his words fanned the flames. My breath came in sharp, short bursts, pushing against his hand around my breast. The hunger moved deeper, stalking me like prey as I closed my eyes and answered, "No."

"You should be," he growled, and spun me around to face him.

My hair lashed my face, blurring him from view. But his hands were gone, leaving me to stumble backwards in the dark. He was threatening, long, languid strides eating the distance no matter how fast I recoiled.

A candle came alive in the far corner of the room. I wrenched my gaze toward the sight as a cry slipped free. Another flared with a yellow flame, and then another...and another, until they brightened the room.

"I like to see what I'm eating," Lorcan growled, and stalked forward.

I tripped, stumbled, and threw out my hand into the empty

room to right myself. Still he came forward, long strides swallowing up the distance...until I hit the far wall.

My fingers skimmed the smooth leather arm of the sofa. Panic roared through my veins like a thousand horses galloping inside my chest. The sound echoed, filling my head with the roar.

I had nowhere to go...nowhere I could run to.

And finally, a whimper tore free, desperate and urgent, stinging as it left me.

"All alone," Lorcan repeated. "And I am so very hungry, Asena..." He licked his lips as his gaze traveled over my breasts and lingered between my thighs.

My heart slammed against the confines of my ribs.

I knew what he wanted.

And it wasn't my blood.

I lifted my hand as he stepped closer. *Not again...not this again.* But there was no shake of my head, no whisper of *No* from my lips as my hand met his chest.

Piercing green eyes sparkled in the candlelight. His fangs grew, sliding over his deep red lips. The sight of that did something to me. My pulse jumped, desire flared, and a slow, seductive curl of his lips followed.

He grabbed me by the shoulders, and then spun my once more. I was helpless to fight him, whipped around like a rag doll until my hands smacked the arm of the sofa.

He was behind me, pressing his hips against the curve of my ass. Something hard prodded against me, slipping into the hollow of my thighs as my body met the end of the sofa...and had nowhere else to go.

"They've had their turn with you," he growled in my ear, and the savage sound sent shudders along my spine. "And I've waited so long...*so very long.*"

My mind raced with the feel of him, but my body responded

to his words. My hands splayed on the arm of the sofa, almost as though I was readying myself. *But for what?*

For his fangs...

For his body...

His hands ran along the small of my back, thumbs stroking my spine, until the expanse of his grip captured my waist while he pressed against me, and then eased away, rocking me like the incoming tide.

Surge and retreat...surge and retreat, making that need inside me grow with it. I felt my head lower, my spine arch. I hated the way they made me give in... how they stroked that ache inside me like I was nothing more than a game to them...like I was a *plaything.* And as much as I hated it, I wanted him desperately.

"Darkest hell, you're beautiful."

I clenched my eyes tighter, my focus drawn to that hardness pressed against my thighs with his thrust. Warmth spread between my thighs. He stilled, hands lingering on my hips. I waited...waited for him to tell me what he wanted.

A touch on my breast made me flinch.

"Easy now," he murmured.

His fingers worked the laces of my dress, cold air slipped inwards, spilling between the valley of my breasts. "Do you want me to stop?" he whispered against my ear. "You can leave this room, if that's what you want. The door is open and I won't stop you. You can run back to the others, and tell them all about how terrifying I am... *or, you can stay, and you can let me do what I so desperately want to do."*

I tore my gaze from his fingers as they slipped the neckline of my dress wider. The open door was right there...but salvation seemed so far away, hidden under the icy touch of his fingers, and not in the protection of a locked door.

Echoes of a memory slipped into my mind, one where I knew him...I knew his body...*I knew his love.* His name rose inside me, so achingly familiar. "Lorcan."

"Yes?" he murmured and kissed the hollow of my neck. "Say it again, *call me. Call my name.*"

I closed my eyes, someone else moving within my body, someone with memories that were not my own. *"Lorcan."*

His sigh was a thousand years of suffering. I caught the tremble in his fingers as he worked the last of the binding free and slid his hand across my bare breast.

"I want you." His words were desperate and dangerous. The tips of his fangs met the nape of my neck, making me flinch. "I want you so much I can't bare not touching you."

But the sharp points grew longer and pressed harder. The pain was instant, not enough to break the skin...but enough to speed my heart.

"That's the way," he growled. "Be afraid of me, just a little...just so you know there is *nothing* I will not do to claim you."

And with a barbaric wrench, he tore the dress from my shoulders, and the fabric spilled to the floor, falling at my feet with a *thump* of satin and lace.

My panties were all I had left...panties and boots.

My knife.

The image filled my mind, silver glinting, the tip honed to a point. There was a shift in the air around me and his touch came again, sliding down my spine, making me tremble.

"Oh yes," he murmured, stopping his touch at the top of my panties.

His lips kissed the place where fabric met skin. His breath was a cold blast, making me tremble...*or was that the feel of his mouth?* He gripped the top of my panties and, with a jerk of his head, the sound of shredding fabric filled the room.

"Now, Asena," he whispered as he slid his hand straight up between my thighs, "brace yourself."

My legs were shoved even further apart. I fell forward and threw out my arms to brace myself on the sofa seat. But his touch was gentle, lingering just above the inside of my knees and going no further. He kissed the curve of my ass, sliding his hand around my hip to shove my body away from the comfort of the leather.

My hips drove backwards, pressing my ass against his mouth. He dragged those fangs down my skin, over the swell of my ass, lingering long enough to press his lips in the crease. "Like a peach," he growled. "I'd forgotten how much I enjoy them."

I shuddered, curling my fingers to dig into the leather as he pressed his face deeper into the crease. The pressure of his hands grew stronger, forcing me wider. The grip of my boots slipped, sliding my stance apart.

His icy tongue met fevered skin as he licked at the entrance of my core. A growl followed from his lips, something demanding, *something inhuman.* I dropped my head, unable to save myself as his hand drifted higher.

"Perfect," he murmured against my softest flesh.

His finger slid along my crease, finding the part of me that made me whimper. That hollow ache between my legs was roaring now, forcing my legs even wider, letting him go where he wanted to be.

My body was not my own, heat flared, making me press back on him as he moved between my legs.

"Mmm," he growled, spreading his other hand over the curve of my buttock. His thumb slipped as he drove his face deeper, his hungry tongue seeking that tender nub, and all I could do was hold on.

"Please," my whimper was weak and mewling.

I slid a hand behind me, fingers skimming his cheek and then the long strands of his hair. I curled my fingers, muscles trembling as I lifted my leg and hooked my knee over the corner of the sofa.

I didn't care what I looked like, open and bare for him to

see...for him to taste. One frantic press of his head and he took control, sliding his thumb along the crease of my bottom as he drew his other hand away.

His mouth took over, lips, and tongue, and fangs...*oh God, the fangs,* pointed tips skimming across my pulsing flesh. I pressed against the back of his head, needing more than just his mouth. I ached inside...*I throbbed.* But I had no time...and I didn't have the words.

I shoved my ass against his fingers, and my slit against his tongue. He sucked, drawing tender flesh into his mouth. The sound of his swallow made something in me give way. I trembled, and an urgent gasp of "again" filled the air in the sound of my voice.

He complied, pressing his thumb against my opening, only it wasn't the one he licked and breached with a pointed tongue. I didn't have the will to stop him. Hard pants came again as his tongue probed deeper, moving in and out of me, and this time...so did his thumb, stretching my muscles, invading a place that was sacred.

I wanted something else moving in and out of me. Something harder, something bigger...something to stroke that wicked longing between my thighs.

His thumb pressed harder as he buried his face between my thighs, finding that part of me that pulsed with a beat of its own. I was blown apart by the invasion as he breached my defense over...and over again.

I was burning on the inside, fevered and sick. Still, I held his head against me, angling my hips for him to be where I needed him to be, and like a sudden bolt of lightning, the tempest tore through me.

I shook...shuddering, drawn to the sensation of his thumb moving in and out of me.

My hand dropped from my hold on his head, my knees suddenly weak. He slipped free of me, catching my hips, holding me steady as he licked the last traces of my desire...*and swallowed.*

"Like I said." His voice was pure animal. "Utter perfection."

I closed my eyes with his words. I throbbed with that ache, like a low-grade fever I couldn't shake. I wanted more...more than this, more than fingers and tongue. "I need..."

He rose from behind me, sliding his hand under the back of my leg to lower my foot to the floor. "What do you need, Asena?" His body moved against me, that hard length straining against his trousers.

Even though I was sated, I felt my body respond, warming to him...*aching for him.* Shame and disgust flooded me, but still I reached behind me, my fingers grasping for the juncture of his thighs, until he caught my hand. "Not yet. I want..."

I closed my eyes as he let the tips of my fingers skim across that hard length punching against the front of his trousers. He gave a moan and lowered his head to kiss my spine.

"I want your first time with me to be perfect."

A gust of wind buffeted my face. My hand dropped to my side, and then fell to the leather of the sofa. It took me a second to register...Lorcan was no longer there.

I sucked in hard breaths, waiting for that need to slip away.

But it never did. Eventually, I bent and grabbed my dress, slipping it over me. I fixed it the best I could and, with one last glance at the empty room...I left.

10

One touch, and Lorcan's intoxication had consumed me. I'd underestimated him... underestimated all of the Sinful, believing I had the strength to resist them, to watch them until I found the right moment to strike. That time had come and gone, but with good reason, yet the irresistible allure I feel toward them was unraveling me. They were murderers, the enemy, the villains. And yet, I'd willingly given myself to Lorcan, begged him for more.

Shaking those thoughts away, I had to refocus and remain calm, always calm. I repeated it in my mind as I paced my room. Chaska was changing in the bathroom, and I refused to tell a soul what I'd done last night.

I want you so much I can't bare not touching you.

His words threw me off, and a slice of arousal dipped between my thighs as I remembered his tongue and fingers on me, his icy tongue meeting my fevered skin as he licked at the entrance of my core.

Liquid heat spread through my stomach and my nipples tightened. I threw open my eyes and shook my head.

"God, no," I mumbled. "No, no, no." I wouldn't let him affect me so much.

I paced around the room, tucking such thoughts away, or I'd never survive another day without giving in and losing myself to the Sinful. I was starting to understand now why they were called that. Most believed it came from their savagery and unquestionably ruthless killings, but I wondered whether it had more to do with their hypnotic seduction.

Letting myself fall wasn't going to help my mission. The Sinful had no idea what was coming their way, but first... first, I'd uncover their secrets about me, then I'd finish this.

A small shuffling noise came from across the room, and I glanced over to find a small folded page sticking from under the door.

I marched over and snatched the door open, then scanned the hall left and right. No one. So I picked up the note and shut the door. Walking over to the window, I unfolded the piece of paper that had been torn out of a book.

Asena.

22 years old.

Parents: Unknown

Lineage: Powerful.

I reread the half-torn page and refocused, but nothing changed.

What the hell does this mean? Unknown parents? Lineage, powerful?

Confusion blurred my thoughts, no matter how many times I read the handwritten words. I reeled. Someone wanted me to know this, but why?

Chaska emerged from the bathroom, and I stuffed the page into the pocket of my dress. I intended to discover what it meant before I told anyone else. I didn't need wild rumors spreading or somehow getting back to the Sinful. If I kept my mind closed to them, they wouldn't be able to pry into my thoughts without permission.

Bang. Bang.

I flinched away from the door.

"Geez, why are you so jumpy?" Chaska stared at me strangely and moved to open the door. A servant, an older man with cold eyes, stepped back and waved for us to follow him.

I pushed off the wall and joined Chaska, both of us following the servant down the familiar hall. Sleeping during the day, and awake during the night. Even this castle was starting to feel like it was…normal. I almost laughed at the word, because nothing in this placed was normal.

When we were led into the small open courtyard in the middle of the manor, I beamed with joy. I'd take being outside over indoors for a change, even if we were tired.

Two long wooden tables stretched out in the middle of the yard. They were filled with bowls of porridge, nuts and fruit, loaves of bread with butter, and jugs of juice.

I joined Chaska and sat next to Polaris on the fur throws on the benches. Everyone was already diving into their food, and I helped myself to a bowl of porridge topped with cinnamon and sugared apples. Around us, the manor sat like a sentinel, watching over us, but in the doorways, I spotted guards keeping an eye on us. Servants ran back and forth with more food and drinks.

"Did you hear about Nilsine," Aislinn mumbled, sitting across the table from us. She glanced over her shoulder to ensure no servants were near. "She's been heard screaming."

I stiffened in my seat, lowering the spoon from my mouth. "Where?"

"Out in the woods," Devika said, the breeze tossing her blond curls.

"What's she doing there?" I asked.

The five of us at our table leaned close as Aislinn whispered,

"My room's near the servant's quarters, and I heard them talking about her. They said Nilsine was heard screaming out in the woods, not far from the manor. One of them swears they saw her out there."

"Wait. She's out in the woods alone?" The words burst from my mouth, and I cringed at being so loud. "Why?" I murmured.

Devika's lips twisted. "Because the Sinful are demonic sons of bitches who only want to make us suffer. Is there any other reason needed?"

Her anger came from her own humiliation at the hands of the Vampires, but this was different. "There are Wolves in the woods. She can't stay out there," I added, my insistence fueled by fear.

"Where did they see her?" I asked.

"Somewhere behind the manor, apparently. So, what are you going to do?" Aislinn joked, half laughing. "Go out and get her?"

Silence.

"Asena, you can't." Chaska murmured.

"I didn't say I would. Just that she's in danger out there."

"But what did she do to anger the Sinful?" Devika asked, her big dark eyes widened.

"Could be anything," Polaris piped in before scooping a mouthful of porridge into her mouth.

"How can you eat at a time like this?" Chaska chided, gaining herself only a shrug from Polaris.

"She's done something bad." Devika leaned forward further. "Why else would they throw her out to the Wolves. Did she uncover a secret?"

Her words sat like stones in my gut. No one deserved such punishment, and just like the others, I had to find out what was going on with Nilsine. Sure, she wasn't my favorite person in the world, but she didn't deserve to die.

"Was it punishment for hurting the princess?" Aislinn swung her attention to me, her forehead furrowed.

A rush of blood hit my chest, and my cheeks burned. They called me 'the princess'?

"Back off," Chaska snapped, stealing my words. "If Nilsine is being punished, it means she did something she shouldn't have. So don't go blaming Asena."

"Wow, big words from someone who, if I remember correctly, lured her into the shed."

Devika and Aislinn stood from their seats, sneering at us, then took their bowls over to another table.

"Bitches," Polaris muttered.

"Thanks," I murmured. "That conversation escalated fast."

"They're jealous of you," Chaska whispered, leaning closer. "They all see how the Sinful look at you and want what you have."

My brain seemed to have numbed, as finding responses today had become a chore. "A-And what's that?"

"Your sex appeal," Polaris butted in, taking another mouthful of porridge. "You clearly are the type of girl they're into."

Memories of Lorcan and me flashed into my mind, of how Cassian made me feel, of Arkyn's words about me being safe here. Except, was it sex appeal? Considering I'd never really been with a man, I struggled to believe that reasoning.

"That's crazy," I said and picked up my spoon to finish my food.

After the meal and the tables were cleared up, the servants brought in wooden boxes with games. Chess and checkers and a bunch of others I didn't recognize.

Nilsine kept swirling in my thoughts.

Nilsine was seen out in the woods, not far from the manor. She was tied up out there.

I glanced over at the two entrances to the courtyard, both patrolled by guards. I took a seat next to Chaska and joined in the games to pass as the day slipped into night.

By the time the first faint stars sparkled, I leaned back and stretched my arms in the air, and noticed one of the entrances to the courtyard was unattended.

My stomach tightened. I had to go find Nilsine for myself, go find out if it had anything to do with me, try to make sense of all the things happening at this manor. I would be a fool to ignore that it did feel like things might revolve around me, that the Sinful played favoritism. It killed me that Willa was now turned, so I couldn't live with knowing Nilsine was ripped apart by Wolves because of me.

"I'll be back" I nudged Chaska in the arm. "Just going to the toilet."

Without waiting for a response, I cut across the yard. A quick glance over my shoulder and no one looked my way, so I slipped into the dim hallway and ran toward the servant's kitchen on the ground floor. I'd been here long enough, watched where everyone came and went in the manor, and kitchens always had a back door for produce delivery.

Keeping to the shadows, I followed the stone passage.

Footsteps rang out from up ahead, and panic hit me in the chest. I glanced around, left and right, then ducked behind the curved wall, in full sight if anyone looked back.

The steps quickened and two female servants, their hair braided down to their waists, hurried down the hall I'd just come.

Waiting until their steps completely faded, I spun, darted around the curve of the corridor, and reached a wooden door. With shaky hands, I pushed it slightly ajar and peered inside.

A man in black clothes and a white apron stood across the room, his back to me as he chopped up vegetables. In the opposite corner was another door. My heart banged so hard I shook, and I crept inside. A quick sweep of my eyes confirmed no one else was there. Hunched low, I darted across the room and grabbed the handle, praying I was right.

A loud sigh reached me, and I dove back behind an oversized

table in the middle of the room, holding myself still. What was I doing?

When no other sounds came, I peered out from the table, to see the cook was still chopping.

I rushed to the back door and pushed it open just enough for me to slide out into the darkness. I wedged a rock in the gap to avoid it closing completely, just in case it was locked from the outside.

Leaves rustled across the forest floor, trees swayed in the breeze, and just being out here left me feeling like I'd broken the worst rule ever. Fear clawed through my chest that I'd get caught, but I couldn't think that way or I'd never take another step to find Nilsine. I burst into a run, staying close to the manor, and headed to the back of the building. Darkness stared back at me from within the tree line, coving me in shivers.

Around me, enormous pines towered over the land, reaching for the clouds. Nothing but trees and woodland in every direction, and I kept imagining the Wolves.

No one goes into the woods. That's where the Wolves hunt.

Father's words haunted me. I breathed rapidly and moved with haste, careened around the enormous manor toward the rear and scanned the forest.

No sign of Nilsine. Had I been wrong to come out here? To risk capture and punishment?

I kept moving, trampling over twigs and dried leaves, the stone manor at my back. The building was enormous, but I ran the length of it, searching the woods. *Where are you?*

A crow cawed in the distance, and I stared in its direction, diagonally from the manor, and then I saw something. I squinted, and saw a figure standing up against a tree. My heart leapt, and I darted over to her, running like a madwoman, praying no one looked out this way from the manor.

Up close, her head jerked toward me, her eyes wild and panicked, her hands tied around the black tree trunk with thick ropes. She wasn't naked or bleeding anywhere. The guards hadn't beaten her, which was a small reprieve.

Her muffled cries bludgeoned my heart. She wriggled against the restraints binding her.

I dashed to her side and wrestled the gag out of her mouth

She burst into tears. "They're trying to kill me, Asena. Get me out before the Wolves come."

"I will." I shifted behind her, fumbling with the rope keeping her tied.

My fingers strained as I pulled at the binding, the knot refusing to budge. I desperately tugged at her ties, but it was useless.

"Hurry up, please." Her panic leached through me.

"I'm trying." Reaching to my ankle, I tapped my leg and, of course, the one day I needed my blade, I'd worn my slip-on shoes, not my boots. Hell!

I pulled with all my strength at the rope, then reached down and grabbed a rock, starting to smash it into the knot. But that barely made a difference and I'd be out here till dawn to make any indent.

Her cries grew louder, and she'd attract every animal in the woods.

"Why did they put you here?" I asked out of curiosity, and needing to silence her wails.

"Something about me not being the chosen one. What's taking so long?"

"These knots are impossible to untie. I need to go get a knife. I won't be long."

"No, don't leave me," her pleas broke me, her voice quivering.

"I'll be back in no time. I give you my word."

She stared at me with sorrow in her eyes, fear clung to her because she knew what was coming for her if she remained out here.

I turned to leave.

"Asena," she murmured. "Thank you. And you have to leave this place. Help me, and we'll run together. They know who I am now and they're coming."

Ice filled my veins. I paused and glanced over my shoulder at Nilsine, my brow furrowing. "Who are you, exactly?"

"Just get that damn knife and I'll tell you everything. Hurry."

My heart raced and I nodded, then I ran back toward the kitchen for my life. My lungs fought for air, but I kept going. Around the far corner of the manor, I slammed into someone.

I stumbled backward and fell over my tangled feet.

"Watch it!" a girl snarled.

I waited a second for my head to stop spinning and looked up at Chaska and Polaris, who offered me her hand. "What are you doing here?" I accepted her hand, and she wrenched me to my feet.

"Well, do you really think I believed you were just going to the toilet?" Chaska said.

"Did you find her?" Polaris glanced over my shoulder.

"Yes, but I need a blade to cut the rope." I pushed past them, but Polaris snatched my arm, her fingers strong, and pulled me back. "I have a blade. Let's help her."

Gasping in relief, I pushed into a run with both my friends, cut through the dimming woods, and headed straight for Nilsine.

But when we reached the tree... the tree I swore she'd been at, she was gone.

"What the hell?"

The sound of a lone Wolf baying cut through the forest. Chaska gave a whimper and spun, searching the dark.

"She was just here," I growled and looked around the dim woods. "I swear to you. I saw her and came straight back."

Polaris was a quick flash in the night as she strode past me and bent at the base of the mammoth tree. "Well, it looks like someone beat us to it." She lifted a fist full of cut ropes.

They flapped in the air like snakes, all they had to do was hiss and spit. I stared at the severed ends as she rose and dropped them back again before lifting her gaze to me. "Now what do we do?"

A guttural sound of panting filled my ears, followed by a low growl. Silver blinked like the glint of coins in the darkness of the trees.

"Oh shit," Polaris muttered and turned to face the beast as it slunk forward.

It was big...as big as a horse.

"Just stay back," Polaris warned, and lifted a hand. "Don't make me hurt you."

The snap of a twig behind me made me spin. I caught movement from behind a mammoth bush. One glance toward the manor and my heart clenched with fear.

But the snarl came once more, only this time those glinting silver eyes were fixed on Chaska.

"Asena," she cried.

"Easy." Polaris took a slow step, placing herself between the Wolf and the other woman.

She was fearless, piercing blue eyes shining with power. "We're not here to hurt you," she spoke to the Wolf. "We came to find our friend."

The monstrous beast stepped forward, hulking shoulders rolling as it moved. It sniffed the air, fixed its deadly stare on the warrior, and ended the growl.

"That's better," Polaris murmured. "See, you're not so bad."

The Wolf curled its lips, baring honed white teeth.

"Why did you have to say something like that?" Chaska whimpered.

"Because," Polaris kept her hand in the air and took another step, nice and slow. "I've seen beasts that will burn you alive as soon as look at you, seen winged monsters so big their steps shake the earth when they walk. I've seen these nightmares become men in front of me...and I *never* want to see that ever again."

She took another step and slowly lowered her hand. The Wolf relaxed, sliding its top lip into place and lowering its head.

"There you go," she murmured. "See, we're not here to take anything from you. We just wanted our friend."

I glanced over my head to the manor, feeling the weight of the darkness like a cloak around my shoulders.

Polaris never said a word, just stared into the beast's eyes as it flared its nostrils, drawing her scent in deep, then turned and slunk back the way it came.

The other Wolves followed, slinking back through the trees as the shadows stretched around us and closed in like a fist.

"She's not here," I murmured. "And we have to leave."

Polaris sucked in a hard breath and turned toward me, casting one last gaze at the bonds left behind. "Whoever came for her wasn't a damn Wolf."

"How do you know?" Chaska followed the woman's gaze.

"Because the rope was cut with a knife, not torn with fangs."

The words made me flinch, and my mind raced with possibilities. "Who could do that?"

"Not the Sinful." Polaris nodded toward the manor and we hurried, backtracking the way we came and racing for the side kitchen entrance.

Dark clouds were gathering as a wind whipped up, casting strands of my hair into the air. Power raced along my arms, standing the hairs on end.

"Do you feel that?" Polaris murmured and lifted her gaze to the sky. "Something is coming."

I felt it, too.

It was more than the bruised clouds or the bitter scene of ozone. It was the panicked sound of my heartbeat. Movement drew my focus to the edge of the forest. The monstrous Wolf stepped out of hiding to stare at us.

"Lord, that's creepy," Chaska muttered, and rubbed her arms.

But the animal never moved, just stared at us as we turned. Polaris grasped the handle, opened the door, and we stepped back into the manor once more.

I glanced around the small kitchen, to find it dimly lit and empty. We rushed out of there fast and into the hall.

"I don't like this." Polaris said, staring right through me. "It doesn't feel *right*."

"When has any of this felt right?" The words slipped from my lips.

But as soon as I said them, an echo rose from the depths of

my soul...one I'd felt before. I reached down and touched the torn page in my pocket. I had two pages of their deceit now, the letter from the old woman and the one pushed under my door.

Two pages that spoke of their lies. My lineage...*unknown.* I carried power, too, though I had no clue what that meant. Lies all around me. Lies in the words the old woman told who had betrayed me.

I was betting Nilsine knew more than she was telling, but now she was gone from the neatly severed bindings and it made a seething anger rise in me.

"We have to tell the others." Chaska's words pulled me from the hatred.

"Tell them what? That someone *other* than the fucking Wolves is out there ready to snatch us away? God, could this be any more sickening? We're miles from a house, or even a town...and we don't know who we can trust."

"We can trust each other," Chaska murmured.

But her words were a lie. The only person I could really trust was myself. I knew that better than anyone. A deep rumble came from outside. I shook my head. "Whatever we do, we'd better figure it out fast. The storm is coming and the Sinful could rise any second, and I don't want to be out here running through the hallways when they do."

No, Lorcan breached my barriers and whispered through my mind. *Because we all know how that ended, don't we?*

Heat lashed my cheeks as Polaris took a step and then stopped, turning her head and looking at me over her shoulder. "You coming?"

All three of us raced back to the far wing and to our rooms. A storm was coming, sending a snarl across the sky over the manor. The sound slipped through the cracks as we rounded the last hallway and Polaris stopped outside our door, her chest heaving in hard pants.

She turned, meeting my gaze, and then Chaska's. "Okay, so we just wait, right?"

Fear echoed in her eyes. She clenched her fists, then unclenched them and rubbed her hands over and over. Instinct drove me. I stepper close and pulled her against me in a hug. "It's going to be okay. Whatever happens, it's going to be okay."

I felt her nod before I let her go and she stepped backwards, then I turned for the door. Chaska was already through our bedroom door before I knew it.

We were all alone...listening to the rumble of the storm.

"First Willa, and now Nilsine." Chaska's eyes were so wide they looked like saucers in the dimming room. "Is all this part of their test?"

I shook my head and reached for her. "No, it's not."

"I don't want to die here," she burst out, crying and shuddering. "I want to go home."

"I know." I ran my hand down her hair, making soft comforting sounds.

"They've not even chosen any of us. I don't get it."

My hand stilled for a heartbeat as my cheeks burned. I closed my eyes, hating what the Sinful had forced me to become, and when I touched Chaska's hair once more...my fingers trembled.

I felt the Sinful shake off the weight of slumber inside my mind, felt them come alive with a savage need, and that ache deep inside me rose with them. I dropped my hands and took a step backwards from Chaska.

It didn't feel right touching her, even as simple as offering comfort. I remembered how easily I'd struck that rat with my blade, with the quickest reflex, without thinking about it.

Lineage: Powerful.

Was there something inside me? Something dangerous? Footsteps resounded in the hallway outside our room.

I whirled as the lock turned and the door opened, and in

came the old woman who had taken care of me after they rescued me for the shed.

"You've all been summoned." she announced, and nodded toward the bathroom. "Best make yourselves pretty. They're not in a good mood."

They're not in a good mood?

I'd never wanted to put my fist through a wall so goddamn bad. I just gave the old woman a small nod and turned to Chaska. Tears shimmered in her eyes and glistened on her cheeks. "We *will* get through this," I growled. "Whatever it takes…"

She turned and hurried to the bathroom, then closed the door. Sounds of splashing water followed. I turned to the open door. I wanted to rage, and kick, and scream.

I lifted my head at the rumble of power above.

I wanted to rage.

She emerged minutes later, her hair combed, a new dress perfect against her voluptuous curves. "There," she murmured. "How do I look?"

"Perfect," I answered, giving her a smile.

Then it was my turn. The dress laid out for me was the same one I'd worn to the masquerade ball. It seemed they wanted me to whore myself again.

No more. No…goddamn more.

I turned away from the dress and strode into the bedroom.

"What are you doing?" Chaska asked, watching me with wide eyes.

"Not wearing that damn dress, that's for one," I snarled, and turned, finding the row of simple dresses hanging up. Dresses we were to wear during the day when we weren't dressed in nighties and asleep, leaving the chiffon and lace, *and fucking velvet,* for when the Sinful commanded.

But no more, not for me.

I ran my hands along the plain cotton and grabbed the

drabbest garment I could find before marching to the bathroom once more. I yanked off my worn dress, hurried to wash, and then slipped the gray, three-sizes-too-big dress back on. "There." I smiled at myself. "Now I'm ready."

The pages were the last thing I grabbed, slipping them into the pocket of my new dress, and I strode out of the bathroom, watching Chaska's mouth drop open. But this time, she didn't say a word, just followed as I went to the door and stepped into the hall.

We fell into line, just like the good captives we were. Every step pounded a nail into my coffin...*thud...thud...thud...*I lifted my gaze to the others. They looked almost...*excited?*

There was something really wrong with this, something festering and *rotten.*

And it wasn't just the circumstances. *It was us.*

We were becoming what they wanted us to become.

I strode along the hallway and headed to the ballroom, bypassing the study and its emptiness. Energy coursed through me with the memory. Every stride stroked that hunger inside me, every surging memory of his fingers...his lips...*his fangs.* I closed my eyes, then opened them, trying my best to push that into the darkness, and strode into the ballroom with the others.

The girls' heads were lifted, their gazes were fixed. There was a catch of breaths as the Sinful stood on the steps above us, looking regal and every bit the cold-hearted monsters they were.

Arkyn shifted his gaze, his cold, stony eyes glinting when he took in my dress, and the tips of his fangs lengthened as he spoke. "Thank you for coming. You all look...*ravishing.*"

There was a giggle from one of the girls.

I stiffened with the sound and ground my teeth.

Arkyn took a breath, lifted his chin into the air, and announced, "We have another trial. A simple one, but we are getting to the point—"

"No." I clenched my fists and growled out the word loud enough for everyone to hear it...*especially the Sinful.*

He jerked his gaze to me, brow furrowed for a second, before a twitch appeared at the corner of his eye. "As I was saying," stony words followed as he held my gaze. "This test will give us a clear indication of who we wish."

I took a step forward. "I said, *no.* No more tests, no more trials, no more *seduction.* I want answers, *and I want them now.*"

There was a gasp. Hands fluttered to cover mouths, as if they could somehow stop what was coming.

But they couldn't stop me, no more than they could stop the storm.

There was a flinch as Arkyn moved closer, taking a step down to meet me. He lowered his head, and sniffed the air around me before the Vampire's top lip curled, and a savage snarl slipped from his mouth.

He whipped his gaze to Lorcan, who held the alpha's stare.

"I can smell him all over you," Arkyn growled, turning back to me. A savage glint sparkled in his eyes, one that made my heart speed with terror. "Between your legs and all over your skin."

The gasps from the others made me flinch. Heat raced to fill my cheeks.

Rain pounded the roof of the castle, the deluge so great it was deafening. Thunder and lightning followed. The blinding flashes illuminated Arkyn's cold stare. But he never flinched, not from the *boom* as a bolt of lightning struck the ground outside, or from the screams of his captives behind me.

My hand trembled as I reached into my pocket and withdrew the papers. "I want answers," I growled.

Still the torrent continued, thumping against the windows so hard that one shattered. Someone screamed, but the sound was swallowed by the howling wind.

Movement came into the corner of my eye. The old woman

who'd cared for me hurried forward, terror on her face. Arkyn's head snapped toward her movement, stilling as she neared cautiously, then lifted her hand, covered her mouth, and whispered something in his ear.

The Vampire stiffened, and that tic appeared at the corner of his eye once more. "You'll have to excuse us. It seems we have an urgent matter to attend to... *As for you,*" he lowered his glare to mine, "I *will* find you later."

In a blink of an eye, Arkyn turned, letting out a menacing snarl at Lorcan as he neared, and left. Then Lorcan and Cassian left and, seconds later, the old woman scurried behind them. The guards left, as well.

Heat burned my cheeks at the Vampire's words. I wanted the ground to open and swallow me whole. Tears came, sliding hot down my cheeks.

Until the soft touch of a hand came at my shoulder.

Chaska stood at my side, her expression showing nothing more than concern.

Still the rain pelted the windows...and tears slid down my cheeks.

12

Sheer black curtains hung torn from the rod in the blown-out window. An upright sculpture toppled and smashed to the floor with a *boom!* I flinched at the sound and stepped backwards.

Half the candles on the chandelier snuffed out, while the burning torches in the walls sconces flickered wildly but weren't going out anytime soon.

The other girls scurried like frightened mice into the middle of the room, clutching each other for dear life. Paintings flapped and smashed back against the walls, thin wires the only things keeping them in place.

"What do we do?" someone called behind me.

I turned, to find them all staring at me.

"They've gone, haven't they?" another cried. "They've left us here to die."

"No one's going to die," Chaska snapped. But her voice wavered, like she didn't believe her own words.

"It's going to be okay." I stepped closer and shoved the two folded pages back into my pocket.

I wanted answers, but more than that...I wanted to stay alive. *I wanted all of us to stay alive.* Wind howled through the shattered window, casting glass like knives through the air. "We need to stay safe."

"We need to run back to our rooms!" one shouted.

"No!" My heart thundered as I looked at the middle of the room and remembered the towering windows behind our beds. "We're safer here." I lifted my hand. "But we need something to cover that." I pointed to the broken window.

"The table?" Chaska turned to me. "The same one we used outside. I saw it standing upright. It's big enough to cover it."

"Good," I nodded. "Yes, that will fit perfectly. She needs a hand to carry it."

"I'll go," a blonde murmured.

"And me," someone else called.

Before I knew it, there were five of them hurrying from the ballroom, holding hands.

"We need to clear away the glass." Polaris looked at the flapping curtains. "And check the others."

"Maybe we need to open a few windows?" Chaska looked from Polaris to me. "So there's not so much pressure in here?"

"Good point." Polaris scowled with determination and looked around. "I'll see what windows I can find, but let's open them as far from us as possible."

I turned to Chaska. "Wait here, okay?"

She nodded and wrung her hands. I hated leaving her behind, but somehow we had to ride out this terror. My hair lashed my face, stinging my eyes. I lowered my head and shoved forward, treading carefully on the shattered shards as they flew across the floor with the gusts.

Rain slanted down through the broken window. I slipped, but caught my fall on the slick floor, thankful I hadn't fallen on any glass. I stumbled to the closest intact window and pressed my fingers to the pane, staring out into the wrath-filled sky.

Lightning flared behind charcoal clouds, and I was caught by the illumination. A memory slipped into my mind, and a sickening sense of deja vu surfaced. I'd stood like this, facing a great storm...waiting for...*what?* Something terrible to come...the more the memory filled me, the colder I became.

I spun, staring at the empty place where the Sinful had stood earlier, and knew in my heart they were at the center of all of this. I closed my eyes, lips moving in a soundless prayer that we'd survive the night.

A howl echoed somewhere outside. Wolves. Was that where the Sinful had rushed to? Eliminate the enemy on their doorsteps? Why were the Wolves here in such numbers tonight?

A young maid in a black dress and white apron scurried past the ballroom entrance, catching my attention, and I rushed after her. "Wait," I called out.

She looked over her shoulder, fear-stricken. "There's no time to wait. The rains are flooding the manor. The south wing is under water."

"Shit." Before I could ask her where we could find brooms to make the ballroom safe, she swept back around and darted out of sight down the hall. Well, that explained why the servants weren't around.

With the floor still wet near the open window and covered in shards of glass, I rushed over to another window. "Chaska help me."

I grabbed another curtain as she joined me. Together, we wrenched it free, dragging the rod down with it. Rushing closer, I ripped the material off the wooden pole and turned to Chaska. "We use this to sweep up the glass and water a bit so no one slips."

We each took an end of the material and laid it on the floor, then swept it over the mess, pulling as much of the glass as possible up against the wall.

Water pelted against us when the girls returned, carrying in the wet table, all of them drenched, and they hurried towards us. I jumped in and helped them place it upright, flush against the window. It already thumped back and forth from the wind.

"It's not going to hold," Chaska stated the obvious.

I scanned the room. "Fine, let's grab one of those bookshelves." And hastily, we all gravitated across the room and removed all the small vases and books. We wrenched it out of its spot, and it barely moved. "Shit, how heavy is this thing?" But we worked it out in shuffles and slid it over, the base screeching across the floorboards, and then we shoved the bookshelf against the table.

Stepping back, we all watched our masterpiece.

No movement or rain rushing inside. Job done.

Everyone else just rushed around sweeping more of the glass off the floor... we all needed something to do other than stand around and worry.

I stared out through the uncovered window, where rain hit the glass, where trees slashed through the night. The wind howled, and my skin crawled.

Nothing felt right about the night.

"Where do you think the Sinful went?" one of the girls asked a friend.

She shrugged. "I don't understand half the things they do. If it wasn't raining this insanely, I might consider running home."

"Crystie, no. They'll come for you, and then..." She paused like she struggled to say the words. "You heard what they did to Willa and Nisline. They're monsters and will show no mercy." Then she plunged into a list of things that made them horrible.

I turned away and padded toward the staircase that led up to the next floor... the same place where I'd had my date with Trevor. He'd turned out to be crazy.

But these tests by the Sinful were nothing more than trying to break down our defenses.

I flopped down on the third step, hugging myself, unable to stop shaking. Not just from the cold, but from the fear swallowing the air tonight.

My thoughts swept to the folded-up pages in my pocket. The unanswered questions, the mounting confusion in this manor, the Vampires, all the secrets and lies.

Parents: Unknown

Lineage: Powerful.

Those written words revolved in my head, making little sense. I knew exactly who my parents were because they were killed by the Vampires, so why 'unknown'? And the power. I hurled my blade at that poor rat so easily and accurately. I'd practiced for years to face the Vampires, but I'd never been that precise, even on my best shots. So, what more was there to me than I ever thought?

All the markers are there, Arkyn. Everything you've been searching for, she carries within.

The old woman's words danced in my thoughts. What did I carry inside me?

And on top of everything, I'd offered myself so easily to Lorcan. I sighed heavily, loathing myself.

Heat burned through me even now as I replayed the memories in my mind, dulling my guilt, but I changed my thoughts to my mission I had to focus on what mattered, on changing the direction of where my future was headed if I did nothing but allowed the Sinful to mold me into their plaything.

Voices drew my attention to the girls huddled in the middle of the ballroom, sitting cross-legged and close to keep warm. They were frightened. We all were.

Polaris and Chaska strolled over in my direction and took a seat on either side of me. We pressed up close.

"We've been talking about the Sinful," Polaris said. "I think they're out there fighting the Wolves. That the Vampires put

Nilsine out there as a sacrifice to them. That's why her ropes were cut. They weren't going to eat her, but claim her as their own."

Her words had some merit. I'd heard of Wolves taking humans as mates, but the poor girls rarely survived such a primal and barbaric life.

"And I think there's something else," Chaska added. "I think the Wolves brought the storm. There are legends of Wolves so powerful, their connection to the moon can influence the weather. It's a full moon tonight, so if you're going to attack the enemy, you bring all the force you have, right?"

"Yeah, and we're stuck in the middle of their war," I murmured, unsure how to feel about the Sinful battling for their lives. I wanted to ignore the ache in my chest and reminded myself they kept us here as prisoners.

Thunder cracked outside, the walls of the ballroom shaking. Chaska clasped my hand and squeezed. "For all our sakes, I hope you're wrong about your idea, Polaris."

"Me, too," she muttered.

An explosive boom came from the double doors right in front of us. The three of us flinched in unison.

We froze, and the other girls' chatter died.

"Was that thunder?" Chaska asked.

Boom. Boom. Boom.

She jumped, and I startled just as hard, jolting to my feet with fright. Who'd be knocking on the door during this storm?

"Go open it, Asena," Aislinn called out. "You're the first to stand."

I scanned the room, waiting for a servant or guard to appear, but none came.

"I'll join you." Polaris climbed to her feet, and I could have hugged her.

"Me, too." Chaska put on a brave voice, but I saw the fear on her ashen face. "Could it be the Sinful?" she asked. "Or one of the servants who locked themselves outside?"

"As if," Polaris replied, sarcasm rolling through her voice.

Adrenaline fueled my steps forward, coupled with curiosity as to who'd be knocking on that door now.

The girls in the ballroom rose to their feet, inching closer, dread spreading over their expressions.

Polaris gave me a tight smile and a nod. I stepped forward and unlatched several of the locks, then I reached for the handle.

"Who is it?" Chaska called out, and her voice had me flinching once again.

I had to calm down or my poor heart would just give out. It banged inside my chest like a drum.

"I can't see who's at the door from here," Devika blurted, and I looked over my shoulder to see her face pressed to a window, staring outside.

Taking in a sharp, ragged breath, I pulled open the door, only partially at first.

Standing under the door ledge's cover were three men, tall, broad, and shrouded in shadows. I didn't recognize them, and they weren't dressed like the guards. The middle one, with a short dark beard, stepped into the doorway, his hand splayed on the door, nudging it wider.

"Asena?" he questioned, deep blue eyes finding mine, and I trembled under his gaze.

How did he know me?

He was formidable, tall, and had to be in his thirties. Short black hair stuck to his head as rain trickled down his square face. He never blinked, but studied me from head to toe. There was a harshness about him, like he wasn't a man who backed away from a fight.

He wore a fitted coat, pulled tight across his broad chest,

glinting onyx buttons racing down the front, and a high-collared shirt underneath. The only other people I'd seen dress this formally were the Sinful. Except these men weren't pale. Their cheeks were red from the cold outside, chests rising and falling with life inside their veins.

"Who's asking?" Chaska snapped, hands on her hips.

The stranger with deadly eyes stepped inside, rain dripping off his body, the other two following close behind, and the three of us recoiled. The air grew suddenly heavier, and my skin shivered with the way his gaze lingered on me. Alarm bells rang in my head to run... to escape this very moment. This was the warning I'd been feeling all day, the danger that tore into these woods, riding on the storm's back.

With a sharp wave of his hand, he stated, "I am Lord Emin Reis, and we have traveled a long way to find you, Asena." The words rolled off his tongue with a husky timbre in his voice, distinctly foreign. An accent I didn't recognize, but then again, not many travelers came to my hometown.

He stretched his arm out to me, wanting me to accept his hand, and hesitation froze me on the spot. My attention fell to his wrist, and the shine from his cufflink, a silver shield with a battle axe sitting over two crossed swords.

My mind raced with thoughts. I'd seen that crest before... recently, in fact, and the image flashed in my mind. The hallucination back in the study pushed forward. The warrior with the axe chasing me... he'd had that exact emblem on his coat just above his heart.

I slipped backward, my mind failing, struggling to formulate a plan. My gaze went to the open door, to the girls around me, to the two men behind Lord Emin... guards. They were his guards.

"Why are you here?" I demanded, holding back the terror swirling through me. I had to know the connection, how it related to me... why I'd seen that emblem earlier?

"Asena, please. You need to come with me." He reached out for me once more, but I stepped backwards, shaking my head, panic strangling me. What if my hallucination was a vision of what would come?

"She's not going anywhere with you," Polaris hissed through her teeth.

Chaska stiffened beside me.

"You're not welcome here. Leave," I demanded.

"Asena, you don't recognize me, but I am your real father."

Several girls gasped out loud, and my jaw dropped open. "Is that the best you can come up with?" Yet his words were claws, digging into me, imprinting on my mind, which spun to make sense of it.

My father? No, he couldn't be. My father died.

"I need to get you out of here and away from these monsters, now."

The hairs on the back of my neck lifted. Something wasn't right here… something wasn't… right.

Lord Emin lunged for me, lightning fast, and snatched my wrist. I fought back, hurled a fist into his face, but his guards moved just as fast. Their hands were so large and powerful when they grabbed me, so strong, I was just a twig in their grips.

Polaris and Chaska barreled into the men with fists and kicks, but it was useless.

They dragged me toward the door, my feet skidding, and I screamed with terror as they pulled me out of the manor and into the night being thrashed by the storm.

I strained against their violent actions, as they tugged me roughly down a pebbled path drenched in rain, my feet stumbling to keep up. "Let me go."

Screams sounded behind me.

They didn't listen, their grips squeezing, hurting me, and hauled me toward a carriage the color of midnight, drawn by four black stallions.

Fear paralyzed me, blackness feathering at the corners of my eyes, and all I saw was my demise.

Finality.

My demise.

Death.

BOOK THREE

1

ord Emin...

My father?

I stood in the middle of the foyer and stared at the stranger. A stranger who called himself kin.

"Come with me." His dark eyes glinted as he stepped across the foyer and reached for my hand. "I can give you all the answers you seek. I can tell you everything. I *am* your real father, Asena. Let me prove it to you."

Rain pelted the shattered window, the storm relentless. I tried to find a flicker of *anything* for this man...but all I felt was confusion.

Black hair darker than my own glistened with rain. But it was his face that captured my attention. He was all jutting cheeks and hard-angled dark eyes, which were fixed on me. He looked too young to be my father, too harsh...too *everything*.

My gaze dropped to his sleeve. Silver cufflinks glinted as a crack of lightning brightened the room. But I was captured by the crest stamped into the middle of the stud. A silver shield and a battle axe sitting over two crossed swords.

For a moment, the present world wavered... the man in

front of me shimmered, riding the ripples like a stone cast into the pond. Only as he stepped closer, I knew in my heart I was that stone.

I was sinking...down...down...*down...*

Shadows crowded the doorway. I raised my head at the movement as men invaded the foyer, flanking each side of us. In a heartbeat, Emin lunged and grasped me by the hand, sharp nails piercing my skin. The sting was enough to wake me, tearing me from the frozen state of fear.

My heart thundered, senses on fire, screaming...*let me go!* And the words bubbled up to the surface as terror kicked in. "Let me go!"

I yanked and twisted, trying to tear free from his grasp. *"I said, let me GO!"*

His face was a mask of savage horror, dark eyes impossibly wide, teeth bared to the blinding flash of white light as a bolt tore through the sky. Thunder followed, booming overhead as Chaska and Polaris screamed.

They were a blur in the fading light, all chiffon and lace whipping through the air, slaps and shrieks unleashed.

The sight of them drove me. My shoes skidded on the hard stone. I yanked my hand backwards and struck. But there was no open-handed slaps, and no raking of nails. I curled my fingers, knuckles finding his cheek. His head snapped to the side, as a look of surprise froze on his face.

"Get her outside!" he roared.

Hands grabbed me, lifting my feet from the floor as they carried me toward the doorway. I bucked and kicked, wrenching one foot free, only to lash out and strike a guard in the chest.

He stumbled...losing his hold. I saw it, pain...*recognition.* I was stronger than I was before. Energy surged through me. I wasn't a victim, I *could* fight.

Fight. The word filled me, once again carried on the rippled pond.

I was sinking lower, but not falling anymore…

No, this time I dove.

Head first, arms flung wide. I screamed, twisting my body as my feet were carried through the door. My hands found the doorframe, nails clawing the wood, tearing so hard they buckled. *"Get off me! Get the fuck off me."*

Four massive beasts waited for me out on the drive…glistening midnight coats, eyes so wide the whites were blinding. The horses snorted, flaring massive nostrils, and pawed the earth, jostling the carriage forwards and backwards.

My heart lunged at the sight as I was shoved.

"No!" Polaris charged forward, slamming into Emin, tearing free my hold on the doorframe. I fell, arms cast behind me before I hit the stairs, hard.

Air rushed from my body. Dark spots flared in my eyes. I tried to suck in a breath, but my chest refused to move, wedged in place… pain tore like fire through my lungs. But Polaris was like a banshee in the night, screaming and wailing. Her eyes mirrored the four black stallions waiting for me.

She whipped her head toward me as she landed on the stairs in front of me, lips curled, baring her teeth as she growled, *"Run!"*

My feet were heavy, my reflexes slow. I shoved against the marble stairs and stumbled to stand. White light flared across the sky, turning my world ashen gray. I stared at the towering horses, their slick obsidian coats gleaming like an oil slick as I coughed and gagged…and with a *pop,* air rushed in.

Bitter air filled with oxygen rushed in. I gasped in big gulps, easing the fire inside my chest, as a pale blur rushed toward me.

"Asena." Willa grabbed my hand. She cast a terrified glance toward the intruders and shoved me forward. "You have to run…*please…Asena…RUN!"*

One of the stallions rose on its hind legs, its front hooves driving through the air. I stumbled backwards at the sight, barreling into one of the guards. Two more raced toward us. I caught sight of Polaris on the ground. She shoved her hands into the dirt and pushed upwards to stand. "You want to take her? *Then you're going to have to go through me!*"

Her face was filled with savagery.

She's a fighter.

She'd die if needed.

More came. Chaska stumbled down the stairs behind Polaris, her fists trembling out in front. She was timid and terrified, but prepared to stand and fight. To save me. Devika and Aislinn followed, heads raised high, lips curled into sneers.

"Get in the carriage, Asena." Lord Emin swiped his hand across his mouth.

There was a line of blood on his cheek, a remnant from Polaris, no doubt. Still, he looked like he'd fight forever. He lifted his head and gave a nod to the guards behind me as thunder rumbled once more.

"No one needs to get hurt here. We only want you...we *only* came for you." Emin sucked in a breath and took a step forward.

The horses pulled the carriage, surging and ebbing, an endless tide in an endless storm.

"She's not going anywhere." Willa shook her head and bared her fangs. "Not without a fight."

The guards behind me moved fast, sweeping my feet out from under me. Their jarring steps rattled my bones as Emin yanked open the carriage door. "Hurry!" he roared. "Get her in!"

Adrenaline was in the driver's seat as I fought once more. My hands were heavy, fingers swollen, nails ripped down to the bed. Still I kicked and punched, desperation tearing through my throat in a guttural scream.

Blood followed, sickly sweet, slipping down the back of my

throat. I couldn't fight them, not forever...and they made ground.

Those massive horses loomed over me, so close I felt the hot gust of their breaths.

"No!" Willa lunged at one of the guards, slamming into his body and driving him to the ground.

I fell with them, hitting the hard pebbles beside mammoth hooves as big as my head. Willa and the guard were a blur of movement as they fought. She was savage and unbridled, opening her mouth wide before she struck.

My fingers curled around the biggest rock I could find. I did all I could, turning to pelt the stone into the stallion's hindquarters as hard as I could.

Others followed, lunging forward to fall to the ground. Pebbles were hurled through the air in a shower of stones. The horses kicked and screamed, pulling against the reins.

"Whoa!" the driver roared as lightning coursed through the sky.

"Stop!" Emin howled, lifting his hand, but he was smacked in the cheek by a flying shard. "I said *STOP!*"

An iridescent bolt of energy curled downwards, throwing off veins of white through the midnight sky. I stumbled backwards, the rock falling from my grasp, as the lightning shot downwards into Emin's hand, and then outwards.

The current was a weapon, tearing through the air before it smacked into Willa. Her hands few outwards as she was tossed through the air. Her mouth opened, although no scream came until she landed with a sickening crack, face-up on the ground.

Through the blinding glare, I saw the blackened hole where her chest used to be. Her skin, so pale in the glow, it was nothing more than eyes. She looked at me...and lifted her hand, her fingers curled toward me.

I'm sorry, her eyes screamed. *I'm so sorry.*

And as the white-hot light ebbed, she turned to ash in front of me...*and was gone.*

Horses howled, moving in a blur of blackness past me. Emin gripped the handle on the side of the carriage and, legs pumping, slammed his shoes into the ground, running alongside the carriage, then jumped.

In an instant, he flew through the air and the open door, landing inside with a thud. His face was a savage mask, staring back at me. The ground trembled with the pounding of hooves as a terrifying roar came from the manor...and in an instant, the Sinful were there.

Arkyn tore past me and hurtled toward the carriage.

Lorcan was a blur, stopping long enough to touch my hand. "Did he hurt you?"

Tears filled my eyes. I shook my head and glanced over my shoulder to the blackened mark on the ground. "Willa..." was all I could say.

"Get inside. Lock the doors...we'll protect you." The Vampire growled as he wrenched his gaze toward the clatter of hooves.

Cassian tore from the manor, meeting Lorcan on the pebbled drive.

They were gone in an instant, leaving me behind with the smell of ash lingering in the air.

2

Blinding white light ripped over the unsuspecting sky. The woods came alive in a flash, revealing the Sinful moving with unimaginable speed, chasing after the intruders, the storm exposing a mere glimpse of their strength. In that shared moment, I felt something other than my fear in the brightness... a flicker of desperation, but not for me, for the Sinful. With it came a sliver of an image pulsing through my thoughts. Something I didn't recognize: A savage storm tearing me away with violent intensity, carrying me into the air, and I screamed from the excruciating pain of being skinned alive.

Just as quickly as the vision came, it vanished, and the darkness swallowed the Sinful once again, stealing the breath from my lungs. I was standing in front of the manor, the storm roaring all around me.

I stumbled, my chest throbbing with agony, my mind confused by the vision. It made no sense, but it stayed with me, like everything else. Heavy on my mind and shoulders.

My pulse punched through me, pounding in my ears, and I licked the rain from my lips, shivering in the downpour. A thunderous boom crashed around us, always calling its warning moments too late.

Tears blurred my vision, while something inside me twisted as I looked down to where Willa had raced to rescue me, and all I saw in my mind was the lightning striking her down. I glanced around in a frenzy, part of me wishing she'd come back, that it was one massive mistake, putting the agony wrenching through me to an end. Tears fell as I stumbled closer to the edge of the worn path. Falling to my knees, I grabbed handfuls of grass, dirt, Willa's ashes.

Willa!

I choked on my tears.

She was dead.

Gone.

Taken.

Because she tried to help me.

Dread grew wildly inside me, reminding me nothing in life was a certainty, and my jaw tightened. The wind howled around me, ripping at my hair and dress, the cold digging into my flesh.

I sucked in a shaky breath, and suddenly in my head, I was back in my hometown, kneeling in front of the barren grave for my parents. So many similar graves surrounded me for all the lost people, a place for those left behind to grieve. Those beautiful memories of my parents, making me laugh, teaching me to fish, tucking me in bed, were now shards of glass cutting my insides. Every memory played like a ferocious storm in my head, and anxiety swam through my veins.

I couldn't stop shaking.

Too many emotions and memories battled inside me.

"Asena." Chaska's voice came before her hand found my shoulder. "We need to go inside."

My head whipped up to her as rain flowed down her face, her lips pale and trembling from the cold. She stood in her blue dress, an arm outstretched to me, and I accepted her hand, then climbed to my feet.

Once inside, where the other girls waited and stared at me, Chaska shut the door.

No one said a word, or maybe they expected me to explain what had happened, except I didn't understand anything.

"What did you do?" someone finally said, and I lifted my gaze to Nascha, her dress clinging to her body and curves. She heaved each breath like she'd run around the manor ten times. Except, she was scared, just like everyone else in the room.

"Shut the hell up," Polaris snapped. "Didn't you see she was being attacked?"

"But... Willa?" Nascha murmured, and wrapped her arms around herself.

"Willa was turned," I stated loud enough for everyone to hear. "She protected me. And those men killed her." My voice quivered with those words, with the admittance out loud.

"Your real father, you mean?" Aislinn snarled, facing me like somehow I'd brought on this storm and the attack.

"He's not my father," I spat though, in truth, I had no idea. There was so much I didn't understand... what if my parents had lied to me? What if they'd found me abandoned as a child and never told a soul?

Lies. Was that all my life came down to... Lies seeping from the torn throats of the people I'd thought were my parents?

I wanted to scream because none of this was fair.

Instead, I lowered my gaze and walked to the lavish staircase with the elaborate black handrails and took a seat. Despite feeling everyone's eyes on me, it made sense that we stayed together until the Sinful returned, until we understood what was going on. Polaris and Chaska sat next to me.

I opened up my curled fist, staring down at the cufflink in my palm. The shield with the crossed swords and battle axe looked up at me. The same one I'd seen in my vision the other day.

"What is that symbol?" Chaska asked.

"I think I've seen it before," Polaris admitted, and I jerked my head up to her.

"Where?"

She reached over and picked up the cufflink, studying the emblem. "When I was young, merchants came to my hometown to sell wares and expensive spices. I remember one of the guards wore this symbol on the sleeve of his coat."

"Where was he from?" I asked, accepting the cufflink she pushed back into my hand.

"All I knew was that they came from across the Black Sea."

"There are so many lands over the sea," Chaska added. "And witches come from those areas. Did you see that man call the lightning strike to hit Willa? No ordinary man could do that. He used magic."

I pursed my lips, trying to wrack my brain for anything I'd heard on magic users, but I'd only read bits and pieces in books, information so insignificant, it offered no help.

"Regardless, it's clear the Sinful hate them, and whoever that man was, he was scared of the Vampires, and now they're gone," Polaris added.

Two maids walked into the room and stoked the fire, and it wasn't long before their heat reached us.

The rest of the night dragged and still there was no sign of the Sinful. Girls started heading back to their rooms, until it was just the three of us left in the ballroom.

"Let's head back." Chaska climbed to her feet, running her hands down her creased and still partially wet dress. "I'm tired and want to change my clothes."

"You go," I suggested and glanced over to the closed front doors.

"You'll see them tomorrow." Polaris rose to her feet and combed a hand through her damp hair while lifting a brow.

"It's not them I'm waiting for, but…" I swallowed hard. "I want answers…and they are the only ones who can give them to me."

"And you think they'll tell you?" Polaris mocked. "They don't even tell us what's going on here."

I shrugged and rubbed a hand over the back of my neck. "I have to try."

"Come, let's go. She's not leaving." Polaris took Chaska's elbow.

"You sure, I'll wait with you if you want?" Chaska asked, her words fueled with sympathy, and not the same tough girl I'd met when we first arrived at Nightingale Manor. But neither was I… this place changed us, forced us to become something else to survive.

"I'll be fine. You both head back. I'll be there soon, I promise."

Chaska finally nodded, and Polaris looked over at me one last time. "Just so you know, I'm not judging you. I'd do the same in your position, I just don't know if it's the right decision, that's all."

Without another word, the two girls strolled hand in hand out of the ballroom, leaving me alone with the roaring fireplace.

Right decision.

Was I being foolish, believing the Sinful would treat me any differently and disclose such information?

I pushed myself to my feet and strolled closer to stand in front of the fire, sticking my hands out, warming the cold from my fingers, drying out my dress.

The floorboards creaked behind me suddenly, and I turned, expecting Chaska to have changed her mind. But it wasn't her.

Arkyn stepped into the room, meeting my gaze, thick curls stuck to his forehead, his clothes dripping water onto the floor.

"Why are you here?" he asked, his voice rough, and the blood on his fingers didn't escape me.

"I was waiting for your return," I admitted, suddenly feeling dumb for doing so, realizing that we were so close to morning they wouldn't waste their time now. Yet, the questions in my mind teetered forward about what had happened, and did they kill those strange men?

Two shadows shifted from either side of him and emerged into the ballroom. Lorcan wore a bruising scratch down the side of his cheek and neck, his black hair still slick and somehow perfect, despite the rips and tears in his coat and pants.

Cassian limped forward, blood dripping from a bloody gash across his ribs. He winced with each step he took.

I stared incredulously as he shuffled forward. These were Vampires...beasts incapable of feeling anything, let alone pain. So, if he was suffering now, how badly was he hurt? They'd protected me from the attackers, and gotten injured because of it.

My legs moved forward of their own accord, but I stopped myself. All three of them watched me, as if shocked by my reaction. Blood raced through my veins too fast. "What happened?" I asked. "Cassian, I can clean your wounds."

But he didn't respond.

Arkyn scoffed and grabbed my attention. "No."

"Let me help, *please*." I hated that word, hated they made me beg. More than that, I hated feeling like my whole world hinged on their decisions. I shouldn't need to beg to help someone... it ought to be an automatic acceptance.

Cassian stumbled, and I steeled myself, ready for him to fall over.

Lorcan cleared his throat. "Just let her help. He's a mess."

Arkyn's lips pinched, and only silence stood between us.

I held my chin high, having no reason to fear him when I only offered help.

Finally, he nodded with a frown, then turned away before vanishing into the darkness of the hallway. Lorcan followed him, while Cassian remained standing in front of me.

"Why?" he asked, sincerely shocked that I'd ask for such a thing.

"Because you got hurt trying to protect me. Because you can barely stand on your own feet."

I stepped closer and took his arm, placing it over my shoulders to help him, not waiting for him to give his approval. And he didn't protest. We moved into the hall with him leaning gently against me.

Even with his injuries, he took the lead, but we didn't travel far before he pushed open a door and we entered a chamber. A large bed sat in the middle of the room, a table and two chairs, a wardrobe, and a door that I guessed led to a bathroom. Several lit candles sat on the table, lighting the place. Just another room like the one I shared with Chaska, except this one looked untouched.

"Quickly, let's get you lying down." He hobbled closer, already shuffling out of his coat, which I helped drag down his arms.

I hurried to stand in front of him, my fingers shaking as I reached for the buttons of his black shirt. There was blood through the gaping tears of the fabric. I froze, my eyes widening at the savage gashes in his side.

Quick fingers flipped open the buttons, and I moved farther down, my heart racing, my insides burning up at being so close to him, so close that I could slip my hand under his shirt. The slightest touch on his skin left me breathless. I stared up at him, lost in those pale green eyes, and for those few moments when I imagined him leaning closer, tasting my lips, and euphoria climbed through me.

"Thank you." His fingers reached for my face and pushed loose strands of hair behind my ear. I shivered under his touch.

So vulnerable. I swallowed the lump in the back of my throat and lifted my gaze to meet his. This wasn't the Cassian I knew, but I liked him this way. Something about the way he stared at me, at the way pain twisted his expression, left me feeling raw. Maybe I was being stupid for feeling that way, but I wanted to keep him protected and safe.

I winced for him as he reached to pull his shirt off, the fabric sticking to the wound, and he ripped it open in one go. Blood spilled freely from the injury, rolling down his hip bone and over his pants. I hurried and drew one sleeve off him at a time. He lay down, and I bunched up the shirt before placing it against the wound. His eyes were shut, jawline tight.

All I could do for those few seconds was stare at him spread out on the bed, at the perfect lines of his cheekbones, the ruggedness of his jawline, his long lashes. And those kissable lips. He was so perfectly handsome. I usually took fast glances at the Vampires, but to be this close and have Cassian needing me, kindled something within me. My gaze traveled to the strong planes of his chest, the thin line of hair trailing down the middle of his stomach and vanishing into his pants. The thought of tracing that perfect line with my finger pressed through me, fire searing in the pit of my gut, and I blushed at the image of my lips leaving a trail.

God no.

Absolutely not.

But I couldn't push the thought away.

His eyes opened, and I flinched. I quickly took his hand then placed it over the shirt pressed against his wound.

"Hold this, I'll be right back." I darted into the bathroom, my cheeks on fire, barely catching my breath. Could I be any more obvious, any more desperate ?

God help me, but the idea of climbing on top of him,

straddling him, crossed my mind so ferociously, the heat between my thighs pooled into liquid lava. His strong hands sliding up my thighs, pushing my skirt up, fingers devouring me, rubbing me, guiding his cock into me were all I could see in my mind's eye.

I was breathing so hard, my back pressed to the wall, my hand gliding down my body.

Shaking my head, I stopped. What was I doing? I couldn't do this, and especially not here.

I set about finding towels, a small bottle of pure alcohol for disinfecting wounds, which we had in our bathroom, as well, and a bucket. I filled it with water and rushed with everything back into the room.

Cassian twitched every so often, as though he rode a wave of pain. With the bucket next to the bed, I would have preferred warm water, but I figured it wouldn't matter that much to him.

"I'm just going to clean up this wound first, alright?"

, He nodded, and I soaked part of the towel before I wiped the blood away from the edges of his injury.

"Was this a bite mark?" I asked as I lifted the bunched-up shirt and wiped at the mess, finding teeth marks in his flesh, and I cringed at how much that must have hurt.

"Fucking Wolves," he groaned.

"You might need this stitched up."

"No. Just clean it and I'll heal soon enough." Pain engorged his voice, so I just set to washing the blood and dirt away from the wound as best I could.

"So, that Lord who came to the Manor. Did you know him?" I grabbed the small bottle of alcohol and pulled out the cork. The strong alcoholic stench stung my nostrils.

A growl rolled through his chest in response, but I couldn't tell if that was with regards to my question or the smell from the bottle.

"This is going to sting a bit."

The corded muscles in his neck tensed. Not wasting a moment, I pulled back the fabric and splashed the clear alcohol over the bite mark.

Cassian hissed, his eyes clamped shut. I snatched a clean towel, folded it in half the long way, and pressed it to the wound, tucking the edges in around his waist like an oversized bandage. I kept my hand over the wound for pressure, hoping to stop the bleeding.

"I thought Vampires healed fast," I teased to lighten the mood a tiny bit.

"We still hurt, and even fast healing isn't instantaneous." He pushed the words out through clenched teeth.

His eyes kept slipping open and closed, and I drew a chair near, sitting there while holding a hand on the towel.

"I miss this." There was a longing in his voice I hadn't heard before.

"Miss what?"

"Just having someone care for me not because they had to, not feeling obliged." Exhaustion washed over him as he yawned.

"Where did you live before... when you were human?" All Vampires started human.

He responded while his eyes remained shut, like it pained him too much to keep them open. "In a small town just over the mountains. It's long gone now. A memory I hardly remember anymore."

All these years after losing my parents, some days it felt like they'd died just days ago, other days, it seemed like a lifetime away. Still, the ache burrowing in my heart never left me. Was it that way with Cassian, too, after so long?

Looking over at him, his lips were slightly parted with soft snores. His body had to be healing itself, so I lifted the towel, to see most of the bleeding had stopped. I sat back in my chair and waited. I let my eyes close.

Cassian murmured in his sleep, and I slid open my eyes to

see his nerves twitching under his skin. He grumbled and moaned, and it made me wonder if Vampires had dreams when they fell dead to the world to sleep.

"Aelin!" he bellowed. *"No! Come back."*

I bristled in my seat, listening to the torturous agony in his voice, while an inferno of fire burned a track over my heart.

Who the hell was Aelin?

3

Sweat beaded across his forehead as he fought unseen battles. I swallowed that ache in the back of my throat and reached for a cloth, dampening one corner to sweep across his brow.

He looked so vulnerable like this, so *normal.* I'd be forgiven for thinking I was tending just any man. My gaze drifted down to his perfect lips, lips I'd kissed, lips that'd found places on my body that no one had ever seen. For some strange reason, I thought of Jacob.

Was he still waiting for me, still pining for something he'd lost? But the truth was, you cannot lose something you never had. I wasn't his to love, wasn't his to care for. I wasn't his to take...not my body, and not my heart.

"Aelin," Cassian whimpered. His fingers curled into fists. Desperation strained his face, lifting his head until the tendons along his neck pulled tight.

Who was she?

Who was she to him?

The questions welled in the pit of my stomach as I pressed the cloth to his face. *Talk to him, you idiot...*

"Aelin...*please don't leave me.*"

Say something.

"It's okay," I whispered and smoothed his hair. The long strands slipped through my fingers, so soft and luxurious. I bent closer and breathed deep. Deep, heady spices filled my nose. God, he smelled good...*so very good.* I closed my eyes once more, my heart thundering as I inhaled.

What would it be like to be the kind of woman who loved a man like Cassian? I stilled, the thoughts slow...but insistent. To belong to one meant you belonged to all of them...

Heat flared deep inside me. I closed my eyes and sat back down on the mattress beside him. The memory of what I'd done returned with a vengeance. Shame filled me, burning my cheeks, setting my soul on fire. My hands trembling, I gripped the bedsheets to still the quake.

If the room swallowed me whole, then I'd be okay with that.

I'd be okay with disappearing, just drifting away. Because the truth was, I wanted them. So help me God, I wanted them like I'd never wanted anything before in my life. I opened my eyes to find his perfect face, With the high cheekbones and strong jaw. He was more mystery than he was man, and I wanted to understand him...as well as myself.

I dipped the cloth back into the water and smoothed his hair back once more. Those scratches aren't just any scratches. I was betting they were from a Wolf. What else could affect him like this?

Vampires and Wolves.

Men who pulled lightning from the sky.

I shifted my focus to my pocket and the silver cufflink. I wanted answers--I focused on the man in front of me...*no, not just a man... a Vampire.*

"Who is Lord Emin?" I whispered.

Cassian's brow furrowed, a flare of desperation cut across his face. "No," he whispered. "No, you cannot have her."

I stiffened at the tremor in his words and leaned forward, catching the lines in his face and the ends of pointed fangs growing long enough to peek between his blood red lips.

"I'll die to protect her."

I flinched, my heart pounding. He loved her...*he truly loved her.* My mind raced with questions. *Who was she? And where was she now?* The creak of a hinge had me whipping around, grabbing the stool beside the bed for a weapon, and raising it over my head.

But the blur of movement was so fast, it took me by surprise. The stool was yanked from my hands. I was lifted from my feet and driven across the room. Arkyn's dark eyes flashed with danger as he pressed me to the wall.

I struggled to breathe under his grip as Lorcan followed the leader into the room and closed the door.

"A stool, Asena?" Arkyn growled. His hand splayed around my neck, but he never tightened his grip, just held me against the wall as Lorcan neared the bed and looked down on the wounded Vampire.

"You've cared for him, haven't you?" Arkyn drew my focus. "Wiped his brow...did you kiss him, Asena? When no one was looking, did you lean down and brush your lips across his?"

He lifted his hand and gently swiped his thumb across my lips, stilling in the middle and curling inwards. My lips parted under the pressure, mouth widening. He looked at me like I was his last meal and he hadn't eaten in a very...*very...long time.*

Lorcan pulled the towel from Cassian's body and inspected the wound. "He's healing, but slowly. Goddamn Wolves."

But Arkyn wasn't listening, focused solely on his thumb sliding into my mouth. The pressure of his thumb dug into the dull points of my canines. There was a flare of disappointment, as though he expected...*more?*

Did he think Cassian in his weakened state had changed me into a monster like them? *Or maybe he hoped.* I stared at the flicker in his eyes. Yes. It was hope that welled there. Hope with its dark inclinations.

I pulled away from him, letting his thumb slide free. Saliva glistened on his skin...I sucked in a breath and met those unfathomable eyes. "I want answers, and I want you to give them to me."

His eyes widened for a heartbeat...which wasn't long considering mine was galloping like a thousand horses. "Is that so? Tell me, Asena. Which questions are burning you up on the inside? Is it the need to know who that man was...or is it that hunger inside you, the one that makes you wet between the thighs?"

I shook my head. "I don't—" And froze as his hand slipped between my thighs, driving the fabric of my dress against my core.

"I could be here in a flutter of that fragile heart of yours," he growled. "You wouldn't even fight me, would you?"

Panting breaths filled my ears. Satisfaction roared in his gaze, but there was no smile. He was every bit an animal.

"I'd tear your panties in two with my fangs and bury my face in that slick heat. I'd lick you, drawing every quiver from your body, and then I'd take you, stretch this wide," his finger moved against me, slow and forceful.

There were no more panting breaths.

No more of anything.

I closed my eyes to the feel of him and fought with everything I had. But his touch rocked me...back and forth...back and forth...pressing a little harder with every slow thrust. My hips slowly tilted forward as that ache bloomed. I wanted...*I wanted...*

"Tell me," he murmured. "Tell me what you want?"

His other hand went to my chest, fingers fanned outwards, the groove of his thumb circling the base of my neck, and my pulse sped with the movement.

I was so fragile...so utterly fragile.

I opened my eyes and saw the need that rode him. His pointed fangs grew long, and he drew in a deep breath. "Is this what you want? Do you want to feel me inside you, stretching you, claiming you? Do you want me filling you until you cry out my name?"

My knees moved on their own as I grew wet with his words. I wanted this...I hated this. I was lost to the torment and the pain. I glanced at the bed, to find Cassian's eyes open, his fangs elongated with need. "Yes." I answered, and wrenched my gaze to Arkyn.

He was the alpha...the commander...the one they obeyed. "I want you inside me. I want you between my thighs and at my breast. I want to feel your fangs on my skin and your thickness rammed to the hilt. I want you to be my first..." *I want all of you to be my only.*

I swallowed all those words, leaving them to linger in my mind. But I knew it was as hopeless as the curl of Arkyn's lips. His hand slid from between my legs and hiked my skirt up in one fluid motion.

His hand against the base of my neck moved higher. His fingers curled, pressing against the pulsing vein. One yank, and my hips jolted from the wall, and the room was filled with the sound of tearing fabric.

His splayed fingers slid lower, cupping my breast hard as he knelt in front of me. Cold air rushed in, licking my fevered skin as he lowered his face to the juncture of my thighs and, with a brutal savagery, he tore my panties free.

His touch was so tender, sliding along the outside of my leg, before he curled his grip inwards and grasped my thigh. A hard, barbaric shove and my legs splayed wider. I was open, exposed, desperate for his gaze, his tongue...his length. I clenched my ass and drove my hips forward.

Fire consumed me. I wasn't the sweet, innocent woman

they'd brought here. Cassian had me...Lorcan defiled me. Still I wanted more, more between my legs and in my heart. I screamed these tormenting words. "You want me? Then claim me. *Choose me, Arkyn...choose...me!*"

With an animalistic growl, he set his mouth where I wanted it the most. I was the one being pleasured. I was the one being owned...but the power was all mine. They didn't want any of the others. They only wanted *me.*

"Yes." I threw my head backwards. My hand moved to his over my breast. "More...I want more."

Hungy, barbaric...*beasts.* He speared his tongue inside me, pushing deeper than ever before. Growls echoed to fill the room as Arkyn rose from between my legs, gripping my knees with one hand.

Cassian and Lorcan watched as Arkyn left my breast to fumble with the button on his trousers. This was more than desire, more than need. This was him staking his claim.

Something hard and thick slid along my crease as he lifted his hand to grip the neckline of my dress. I tried to catch my breath, but I was unraveling on the inside, grinding myself on his length.

"You want to know who he is." Arkyn's lips shone with my desire.

He yanked my thighs wide, readied himself, and then plunged deep with one unmerciful thrust.

I cried out with the force of the assault as he drove in deeper, stretching me wide. I couldn't go any further, blown apart by his hunger as he surged inside me and slowly withdrew.

"Do you?" he repeated, his dark eyes so wicked and lethal, like a honed blade ready for a kill. *"Answer me! Do you want to know who he is?"*

He drove his body inside me, brazen hands yanking the hemline of my dress as he surged like the ocean.

"Yes," I gasped, and squeezed my eyes closed. *"Tell me!"*

He drove inside me, tore the dress from the neckline at my breast and, with a feral growl, roared, *"He's the man who wants to take you from us! Is that what you want to hear? Is it? He's your death, Asena...he's...your...DEATH!"* And he bit.

Fangs pierced the skin of my breast as he rode my body higher and higher, tearing me apart from the middle--reaching that point of no return.

I knew now what that ache was inside me. It was more than unbridled lust.

It was love.

Love for all of them. Love for their brutality and their kindness. Love for their non-beating hearts and their icy touch, love for their longing and their lust. I cried out as a wave crashed over me, sparks flared behind my eyelids. I grabbed hold of his arms and felt the power in his body. He lifted his head, the tips of his fangs red with my blood.

"He wants to take you from us." He slowed the thrusting between my legs and lowered his head to nuzzle my neck. "I won't let that happen."

I couldn't speak, But I could feel. My body throbbed, aching and needy, my limbs loose as Arkyn slipped from me. He was still hard...still aching. I lowered my gaze to his body. The thick head of his cock glistening with a small smear of blood.

"I'm glad I was your first," Arkyn murmured as he bent.

His hands went to the backs of my thighs before he lifted my feet from the ground.

"We need to sleep now," he murmured, so soft and kind.

"But you...I mean," I stared into his eyes. "You didn't...finish."

His lips curled into a smile. "There'll be plenty of time for me later."

Heavy breaths controlled me as Arkyn carried me to the bed and laid me next to Cassian. "Will you continue to care for him? *For my brother.*" I glanced at Cassian, his eyes closed, but his fangs still long over his lips. "Will you keep him safe?" Arkyn murmured.

"Yes." The tide surged inside me. "Yes, I'll take care of him. Yes, I'll keep him safe."

Arkyn slid his hands out from underneath me and fixed his trousers, and still the smile on his lips lingered.

"You know," I murmured staring up at him, "you're quite beautiful when you smile."

He bent in an instant, pouncing like a predator. "And you, Asena, are beautiful all the time, especially when I'm between your legs. I haven't even started with you yet. I'll take my fill of your delicious taste, and I'll do it over and over and over again. There's no escaping the inevitable. I'm glad you finally realize that now. It'll make things a lot easier."

I flinched at the word. "Easier on who?"

The sparkle in his eyes was not the answer I wanted. But it was all he gave me as he straightened from the bed and glanced at Cassian as he cracked open his eyes. "Sleep well, brother. See you in the dark."

With a gust that cast strands of my hair into my face, they were gone...the door opening and closing without a sound.

"Was it good?" The croak of Cassian's voice drew my focus.

I pushed up on my elbow and met his sleepy gaze. "I'd be lying if I said no. My body...it aches."

His eyes closed as his lips curled into a smile. "He took it easy on you. You just wait until it's all three of us."

My breath caught. Panic raced, but it was followed by excitement.

"Oh yeah," he muttered as sleep came for him. "You're going to love every minute of it, as will I."

I searched for something to say, but he was already gone, claimed by blissful slumber.

There was a soft knock at the door. I flinched at the sound

and, swinging my feet from the bed to the floor, hurried to the door.

"Mistress," the soft voice came from the other side. "The master sent me with fresh clothes and food."

My stomach snarled with a warning. I clutched my torn dress and opened the door. This tearing of dresses was getting old. I needed something that was more...*accessible.*

Heat raced to my cheeks with the thought as I met the young maid's gaze. "Thank you." I took one step backwards. "If you can put them over there."

She carried in a tray with a steaming bowl of soup and sliced fresh bread, with thin slices of meat and cheese, as well as dried apricots and nuts.

But she froze when she saw Cassian. Her eyes widened before she whipped her gaze towards me. I moved swiftly, taking the tray from her hands and eyeing the knife next to the food and the steaming soup. I'd cut her...I'd burn, and hit, and main.

I knew that now.

It didn't matter who it was. If they came for him, then they came for all of us. "Thank you, that will be all," I commanded and held her gaze.

There was a flush to her cheeks, before a small nod.

Then she left, closing the door behind her. Cassian slept while I set the tray on the floor beside the bed. I dug my sharp knife from my boot and changed dresses, working the straps as fast as I could, and dropped the ruined dress to the floor, using it as a pillow as I sat.

I ate slowly, watching the candle flames cast shadows on the walls, and when Cassian called for the unknown woman, it was me who answered.

Me who wiped his brow.

Me who cared for him.

"It's okay," I whispered and saw the tension in his body ease. "I'm here now. I'm not going anywhere."

And slowly, the candle melted away until it was nothing more than a stub.

"Asena." The harsh whisper of my name floated to my ears.

Scratches came from the other side of the door. I palmed my blade and shoved up from the hard floor. The muscles of my back were screaming, but I gripped the hilt and went closer. "Who is it?"

"It's me, Devika."

Devika?

I twisted the handle and yanked the door open. "How did you find me?"

She smiled and shook her head. "Been searching the manor through the day. But I just wanted to make sure you were safe."

I opened the door just wide enough for me to slip through and closed it behind me.

"What are you doing in there?" She tried to peer around me, until I moved to block her view.

"Nothing. What time is it?" I searched her gaze.

"Almost night. That's why I wanted to make sure they didn't turn you like they did Willa. Anyway, I see you're still...*you.*"

She gave a soft smile and turned away. "By the way...we're sorry we treated you badly."

I gave her a smile, nodded, and watched her leave. Something didn't sit right with her tone and, after a while, I stepped back into the room and took my position by the bed.

Night was coming...and that meant Arkyn would be back.

I smiled. I liked the idea of that...*very*...much.

4

Night swallowed the woodland around the manor, bringing with it shadows and dangers. Dangers with pointy canines, with malicious intent, and no sympathy.

I, along with half a dozen other girls, pressed our faces to the windows in the ballroom, staring outside as Arkyn strolled down the pebbled path, his black cape fluttering behind him in the wind. A guard opened the door to the carriage, just like the ones we'd been picked up in on our initial arrival to the mansion. He climbed inside swiftly.

Going to get reinforcements and supplies was all he'd said. None of us dared ask more questions, but we knew it was for mending the manor from the fire and flooding damage.

Two Sinful guards climbed up onto the front seat of the carriage, taking the horses' reins, and quickly they sped off, riding down the path like they flew through the air. The trees whipped and thrashed from the sudden explosive gusts raging through the woods tonight.

I watched Arkyn vanish from view, and my heart beat faster at remembering him from the night before, my neck and face flushing with heat. I shouldn't let myself fall for these

Vampires, shouldn't melt in their presence, and I hated myself for being so weak around them. I ought to remember my mission, work information out of them, even when my body betrayed me in their company. Determined, I promised myself to do just that.

The girls around me made soft sounds, and I turned to find Lorcan striding into the room. Black pants tight across strong thighs, a leather jacket buckled to his throat, and he looked like death swooping in to collect his next soul, except every girl in this room wanted to be *his* chosen one. I couldn't stop staring at those golden eyes, like fire burned behind them, or his midnight hair cascading over his shoulders in soft waves. He had a delicate and fierce look about him that captivated me. His presence called to me, and everything in my body stopped functioning. The things these Vampires did to my mind... to my body was explosive.

Warmth ran rampant down my neck and chest, fire filling my body as I remembered our time together. The things I'd let him do to me, how much I'd craved him, how much I still did.

My insides had burned with lust and hunger for him from his touches, his tongue. I couldn't believe I'd let this stranger, this Vampire, this enemy touch me that way, and I couldn't get enough.

His gaze shifted to me, and a grin pinched the corners of his mouth like he knew... he fucking knew I wanted him. But I also knew he craved me just as much.

Wonderful job of not falling for their charm, I chided myself.

I tore my gaze from him and lowered it to my feet, remembering the books in the study, the rows of girls' names. How many had they been through and eventually turned?

Feeling eyes on me, I turned to see Polaris watching me. "You're so fucking obvious," she whispered.

I huffed in response. "You don't know what you're talking about."

She snatched my arm. "What do you think happens when a monster becomes bored of its toy? It eats it."

Agony ripped through my chest, because she was right, and my emotions were so damn transparent. I kept thinking of last night, but now, when my eyes were wide open, I started doubting my feelings.

Blinking, I looked around at several girls standing near Lorcan, staring up at him with such admiration as he ordered them to collect brooms and buckets to start cleaning the ballroom. Hell, they'd clean up the place naked if he asked.

"How do you do it?" I turned to Polaris.

"Do what? Resist the spawn reincarnated who wears sheep's clothing?" She stared at me long and hard, her resistance to the Vampires' allure unconditionally strong.

"I know it sounds insane, and I fight it every day, but when I look at them, I… I melt. There's a danger about them that terrifies and excites me at the same time," I whispered, unable to believe I'd admitted that out loud. "It's the best way to explain it. How do you resist that?"

She reached out for my arm and drew me farther from the cluster of girls and Lorcan. "I feel it, too," she admitted. "But I fight it with every ounce of my body. The trick is not to let them into my thoughts, to stop fantasizing, to see them as repulsive if they touch me, to stay as far from them as possible."

Well, I'd done the complete opposite, and I chewed on my lower lip because I felt so far gone. The Sinful were in my thoughts, in my dreams constantly. How did I stop that?

"Back in Sparrowfire, where I grew up, we battle ferocious Dragons constantly, but those beasts aren't only in the air. They walk on two feet and take human form, and they are the most fucking dangerously addictive men you'll ever meet. But their tempers are ferocious and they take anything they want. I've seen first-hand what falling for a monster could do to someone, how their life is ripped to shreds, and they lose everything, including their will to live. So just be careful."

"I will," I said, not wanting her to know how much they'd really affected me already. And her words worried me that I would somehow let myself fall too far too quickly.

"Good luck, my friend, as the Sinful already have their eye on you and you've already given yourself to them. But it's not too late."

I blushed, remembering Arkyn admitting that out loud in front of everyone. They all knew.

"I don't plan on dying here, and I focus on that. What about you, Asena,…what do you want?"

Her question hung in the air. I thought I knew what I wanted… no, I did know. Avenge my parents. I glanced over my shoulder at Lorcan, who watched me intently, and something inside me shifted. Polaris was right. They were monsters and I was their prey.

"Ladies," Lorcan called out. "Before Arkyn returns and while Cassian heals, we will all work together and clean up the storm's mess." There was no asking, but more of a command.

Several of the girls returned with brooms and mops and water-filled buckets.

"Nascha and Aislinn, you're responsible for the ballroom."

"On our own?" Nascha blurted out before slapping a hand to her mouth for arguing back. Her gaze lowered, but Lorcan didn't pay heed and paired us to assigned locations.

"Polaris and Asena, grab a broom. You're sweeping the hallways near the courtyard."

In an explosion of activity, everyone burst forward in a flurry. Polaris nudged me in the ribs and we hurried forward to collect brooms, then we headed out into the hall. Guards were everywhere, more than before, watching us as they tidied up, as well.

"At least we're only doing the small stuff," Polaris added.

"Poor servants need to clean out the flooded and burned down parts of the manor."

I nodded, still consumed by her earlier thoughts about being more in control of my emotions. Yet the memory of the Vampires and me smothered my thoughts and emotions. I'd barely kissed Arkyn last night, and he'd wasted no time in clamping his lips around my clit. The wet sounds he'd made with his mouth were intoxicating, and my panties already felt so wet.

God, what was wrong with me? I had to keep my head straight.

Under the glow of lanterns, I swept the mess of leaves and twigs and dirt blown into the hall from the open courtyard, but there was so much to do, we'd never get this done in one night. I'd work nonstop if it meant my mind stopped returning to Lorcan.

A laugh came from the courtyard where Devika and Sarai, a short-haired blond girl with the palest blue eyes, carried overblown chairs back to the tables, giggling like this was a night of fun.

I recalled Chaska's ramblings one night about where each girl came from. Sarai lived in the great northern mountains, where it snowed every day.

"I don't see why we should clean up this mess. This isn't our home, but our prison," Polaris groaned. She leaned a shoulder into the wall, pushing her broom around in the same spot.

Suddenly, the chatter died, and my head snapped around as Lorcan strode into the courtyard from the opposite entrance, his eyes everywhere. My chest tightened. Polaris pushed off the wall, sweeping at once. My cheeks grew warmer at his presence, my body completely betraying me.

"Are we done here?" he asked casually, coming off aloof and cool, which was a facade.

Devika and Sarai hurried with straightening a bench and

rushed to his side, like good little puppy dogs, and it made me wonder if that was how I looked to everyone else when I fell under their spell.

"We're almost done," Sarai said. "Where would you like us next?" she asked in a sultry voice, implying so much more than asking about cleaning up, and a blaze seared under my heart at hearing the honey in her words.

"Head to the dinner room, there's broken glass everywhere in there."

"Of course," Devika answered instantaneously, sticking out her chest and curling a lock of hair around her finger.

I wanted to gag.

But when Lorcan looked my way, I forced a smile, then he turned and walked back out the way he'd come. Apparently not thinking about him constantly was out of the question, so I returned to the menial task of cleaning, doing something to keep myself busy.

"Look at you both, playing house with those monsters," Polaris scolded.

I glanced up to find her cutting across the courtyard, arms swinging by her sides, her posture stiff.

Sarai grunted at her dismissively. "You're just jealous."

"Of what?" Polaris narrowed her eyes. "Being treated as a slave, being threatened, cleaning up our prison?" she scoffed, turning her nose up at the girl. "You need to rearrange your priorities."

The tension in the air billowed, and it pressed heavily on my chest.

Sarai's nose wrinkled, her shoulders went rigid. "You have no idea what being a prisoner even means. Try living under the command of the fae, then come cry me a river," she snapped. "This here for me is a chance to escape from under their dominance."

Polaris burst out a forced laugh. "You're swapping one

monster for another. At least back home, you have your family, those close to you."

Silence threaded through the air, and I saw the torment flash across Sarai's face. Shit, Polaris hit on a sore point, and I hurried over to her side before she dug herself deeper.

"Leave it," I whispered, but she shook off my hold.

"The fae stole my parents, my sisters, my friends. They take everyone into their world and sell them off, so don't act all high and mighty like you understand my problems." Sarai's chin quivered, and Devika drew her friend by the hand.

"Nice work, Polaris. You're such a bitch sometimes," Devika snarled. "Go fuck yourself with that broom."

Polaris charged forward, but I seized her arm harder and hauled her back. "Don't, it's not worth it," I hissed. "Leave them alone."

Silence.

Polaris glared at them, her breathing loud and raspy, her cheeks red. In an instant, she spun around. "I fucking hate this place." She ripped free from my hold and marched back into the hall, tossing the broom side.

We all had shit in our pasts because we lived amid beasts who took and took what they wanted with no repercussions.

The rest of the night passed in a blur of sweeping and cleaning rooms affected by the storm. My stomach growled for food and by the time our meals were served, I moved back to the dining hall.

Once we stepped into the room, the table was overflowing with food and my mouth salivated at the smell of fresh bread and butter. Everyone rushed to the table, then someone moved in alongside me.

I looked over at Cassian, and my heart froze. Where had he come from?

He stood with slouched shoulders, yawning, the whiteness of his pale skin drawing out the greenness of his eyes. His unruly brown hair stuck outward and I wanted to run my fingers through his hair, tame the wild strands back down.

I dropped my gaze to his side, and the new crimson shirt he wore showed no sign of bleeding from his bite mark. Had he completely healed?

His eyes roamed over me.

"You feeling all right?" I asked.

He nodded and shrugged at the same time. "Feeling strange." His voice was raspy, and he licked his dried lips. He rubbed the back of his neck. "I need fresh air."

"Want some company?"

With a nod, he retreated out of the room into the dark corridor, and I noted he still walked with a slight limp, meaning he wasn't fully healed. That bite must have really impacted him, maybe even poisoned him.

The food wouldn't disappear, but it wasn't often Cassian was this accepting of having me near, so I hurried on quick steps after him.

"What's going on?" I asked, seeing the worry on his face.

"I'm sensing something that's not right."

I pushed closer to his side and let him loop an arm around my shoulders as we moved faster down the winding hall and finally reached the ballroom.

"What are you sensing?"

But he never answered as we stepped inside the huge room, and his attention swung toward the front doors.

I turned and froze at the sight.

The most beautiful woman I'd ever seen stood at the end of the room with the door behind her wide open. A howling wind swept inside the building, blowing hair red as the sunrise after a storm over her shoulders. Porcelain skin seemed to gleam under the chandelier. She was tall, her black corset pushing curvy breasts high, black, skin-tight pants hugged long legs, and she wore heels thin enough to pierce someone's heart. Her pale eyes scanned us, crimson lips pulled into a deadly grin.

I hated her before she said a word, hated her beauty, hated that Cassian had sensed her and rushed to find her so fast.

"Corvina, what are you doing here?" Cassian boomed, fury curling around his words.

She smiled, sharp fangs slipping out, pressing on the fleshy pillow of her red lips. "Nice to see you, too, Cassian."

5

Corvina?

I flinched at the name and felt Cassian's arm slip from my shoulders. The woman jerked her gaze toward me, and for an instant, I knew what it felt like to be a mouse in the path of a viper.

She was a predator. A cold, ravenous predator.

I stiffened as Cassian took one slow step in front of me, consuming her attention.

"You don't sound enthused to see me, Cassian?" she murmured.

I shifted a little to the right, just enough to see her better. She was partially obscured from view by shadows, until she turned and lifted her hand. Long black satin gloves caught the flicker of the fire. She slowly pulled each finger of the glove, peeling the fabric from her skin and glancing around the foyer.

A horse whinnied outside on the graveled drive. The sound was followed by a grunt as an old, gray-haired man hurled a suitcase through the open door and stumbled in after it. His face was red from exertion, grunting and groaning as he dropped the suitcase further onto the stony floor before he sucked in heaving breaths, and stared at her.

"What?" she snapped, barely giving him a second glance.

Then with a huff, she yanked the rest of the glove from her hand and pulled up a small clutch. "Fine," she grumbled, and plucked a silver coin from her purse, casting it in his direction.

She never turned her head as the coin smacked the old man's belly and then clattered to the floor. Never acknowledged his presence as he bent and clawed for the money he'd earned with the sweat of his brow. She just stood there, staring into the foyer, as he grasped the money and rose.

"You should be paying me," she snarled, her fangs growing long over her lower lip.

She was beautiful, but she was cold...colder than the Sinful and probably twice as deadly.

"The rest of your bags are outside." The old man left with a scurry, almost launching through the open door, leaving the thud of his steps behind. The sound of horses followed. Whinnying and neighing slipped through the air before the crack of leather on flesh.

The thunder of hooves followed and slowly faded. I lowered my gaze to the case at her feet and felt that icy twinge of fear take root.

Was this the woman Cassian had been calling out for in his fevered state? Or, was it someone like her? A past lover? Maybe a wife? The thought of that made my stomach clench.

Say it wasn't so. Not someone beautiful...like her.

There was no denying it. She was someone you called out for, someone you pined over. Someone you never let go. I could see them loving someone like her, see all three of the Sinful passing the centuries with a Vampire like her.

"Planning on staying?" Cassian murmured, and glanced at the bag.

But she never answered, just took a step and wandered

around the foyer, glancing at the missing curtains and the boarded-up windows, remnants from the violent storm. "This place isn't as grand as I remember."

She'd been here before?

I clenched my jaw at the words as faint chatter spilled in through the hallways. Corvina stiffened with the sound and swiveled her gaze toward the bark of laughter in the distance.

No...God no.

The others were coming, jostling and howling, invading the hallways of the manor like some unwelcome poltergeist. It was the sound of mortals...the sound of life, and this undead immortal was drawn like a moth to a flame.

Corvina's eyes lit up as they spilled through the far doorway and into the foyer. They didn't even notice her, not at first. Devika walked in with her chin jutting into the air, haughty and refined. Chaska lingered at the rear of the others, caught up in the whirlwind of excitement. Polaris walked behind her, staring daggers at Sarai's back, still pissed off and angry, seething from the argument earlier.

Their hair was disheveled from their labor to repair and clean the manor. Their dresses were smeared with dirt and soot. Boots were muddy, leaving clumps of sodden earth behind as they kept walking. Those at the rear, consumed with chattering, did not notice the ones in front had stopped.

They slammed into each other, sparking a fresh wave of anger that lashed the air, until Corvina took a step toward the stairs leading down toward them and murmured. "Oh...how exciting."

In an instant, the chit-chat stopped and a chill filled the air, sparking a fresh wave of hunger, only this time, *we* were the meal.

"Corvina," Cassian warned as the female descended the stairs and strode towards them.

"I had to come and see for myself," she whispered, her eyes alight with excitement.

"See what?" Lorcan stepped out from behind the women and cut through the room, tearing a pent-up breath from my chest.

"Why this, of course," she grinned at the others. "Your little...*buffet.*"

I swallowed hard as Cassian left my side, moving slowly and surely, forcing each step to count, like he wasn't weak, or injured. But the gray, sickly tinge of his skin was a dead give-away.

"Where is my *warrior?*" Corvina whispered, stopping in front of Devika. "Where is Arkyn?"

Devika's eyes widened, fear trapped in the whites of her eyes as she looked to Lorcan.

"On his way back," Lorcan answered.

"But not here, correct?" She lifted a hand, long, tapered fingers catching a blonde curl of Devika's hair.

"You must be exhausted after such a long journey." Lorcan took a step forward. "Maybe you'd like to freshen up a little? I can have one of the maids—"

Until a savage snarl from Corvina stilled him in his tracks. "Don't try to manipulate the conversation, Lorcan. It might not be my blood that turned you, but you *are* of my line. Show a little goddamn respect."

Not her blood? The words resounded. So Lorcan...and maybe Cassian weren't hers. But of her line...that's what she'd said. Which meant...*Arkyn. He was of her line...he had to be.*

"I meant no disrespect." Lorcan bowed at the waist.

But the sharp bite of anger was soon smothered under her interest in the others. I wanted to move toward them, with my knife making a mark against my leg, itching to be used as a weapon.

But the moment the need swelled inside me, Cassian gave a slow shake of his head and lifted his gaze toward me.

No, his eyes pleaded. *Don't move...don't even flinch. Stay right where you are...and pray.* A shudder coursed through me, cold, deadly. Cassian was scared...*really scared.*

"So, is anyone going to answer my question?" Corvina slowly walked to another, only this time she drew a long, pointed nail down her jawline, dragging a whimper from her prey.

Corvina's eyes sparked with the pathetic sound, and her lips curled. "Maybe it doesn't matter...I'm sure I could entertain myself in the meantime."

There was a shift in the line, a tiny step forward dragging Corvina's attention like a lightning strike across a midnight sky. Polaris shifted, lifting her head and scratching her cheek, then muttered, "Look, we get you're dangerous and all that crap, but can we just get this all over with?"

It wasn't Corvina she spoke to. She stared into Lorcan's gaze with the kind of burning desire that'd only get her killed.

"Well...well...well. What do we have here?" Corvina murmured, and took a step toward her. "You are a beauty, aren't you?"

Polaris just stared at her as the Vampire strode toward her.

"Sire," one of the maids scrambled into the room from the hallway, all in a fluster. "The grain...it's all ruined."

Lorcan hissed, and the deadly sound echoed around the room, drawing every gaze...including Corvina's.

"Tell me, Lorcan. What exactly happened here?" Corvina murmured. "And don't insult my intelligence by telling me it was the Wolves. I've seen the burns on the front lawn...and smelled the stench of the newly dead."

The maid froze as Corvina turned toward her. "I want to see what's become of my warrior's home. Take me."

My breath caught. I clenched my jaw, waiting for Cassian or Lorcan to say a word. It was Cassian who took a step forward, lifted his hand, and growled, "It's okay, Lira. Save what you can.

Arkyn will be back soon with more supplies. Corvina, we would love to entertain you as our guest until Arkyn returns. But as you can see... we are in the middle of something with our...contenders."

"Hmm...*contenders*," the word rolled along her tongue like it was liquid fantasy.

Maybe it was. The idea of that chilled me to the bone.

"Tell me...*you*," she stared at Polaris. "What wicked little deeds have you performed for your master?"

Polaris flinched at the words and jerked a searing gaze to Cassian. *"They* are *not* my masters."

"Really? Such insolence. If you were mine...*well,*" Corvina growled, her gaze peeling the dress from Polaris's body.

"We...*danced,*" Devika murmured.

Corvina glanced toward the tiny sound. "Danced, hmm? I like the sound of that. Show me."

Lorcan took a step closer, his lips curled. Possessiveness raged across his gaze. But there was no more movement toward her. If he did...*she'd tear him apart.*

I..." Devika jerked her gaze to Cassian, and then to Lorcan. "I don't know."

"Don't look at them," Corvina held her stare. "I think you'd look lovely dancing."

She took a step away and opened her arms. "Show me. Come on...all of you, *dance for me.*"

Panicked gazes cast my way and then to each other. It was Devika who started to dance in her muddy boots and dirty dress. The bottom of her mud-encrusted skirt scraped against the stony floor as she swayed.

Then more joined in, Saria the next, lifting her hands and swaying.

"We have no music." Displeasure filled Corvina's tone. She jerked her gaze toward Cassian, who just winced, trying to keep from collapsing.

He looked gray...and sick. I caught the tremble in his legs and knew he was seconds away from toppling.

What would happen then? He was weak, and Vampires were sadistic predators who killed anything less than powerful and perfect. She'd tear him apart in a heartbeat. Darkness swelled inside me. There was no way that was going to happen...

Not while I was here.

I took a slow step closer as she swiveled toward the dancing women. Panic was etched across their faces, lips trembled, hands shook.

We weren't getting out of this...

The thought hit me like a blow.

We'd not survive...her.

"Corvina, what the hell are you doing?" Arkyn pushed through the doorway and strode into the room...looking every bit the warrior she'd said he was.

He jerked a gaze to the dancing, frantic women. "Thank you, ladies. You may stop now."

6

---

  rkyn's lips twisted, eyes narrowing on Corvina like he might lunge for her throat. The anger sizzling off him thickened the air, and goosebumps pricked along my bare skin.

I wanted to look away, but couldn't get myself to move. Not when everyone in the ballroom was frozen on the spot, caught in the tension.

For those few moments, there was nothing but an unspoken dance of power between the two. Arkyn's unimpressed sneer. Corvina's flippant eye rolling, like Arkyn was but a child to her, yet the pinch at the corners of her mouth said everything. She loathed his reaction, but pretended it didn't affect her. That small pretense made her seem almost human… almost.

Arkyn schooled his frown and took off his long coat. A servant ran up behind him to collect it, then hurried away.

"This must be an auspicious night, to receive your company." He spoke with bitterness in his voice and strode across the room, his boots hitting the floorboards with force.

Corvina simply stood there and stuck her arm out. Arkin placed his under hers and walked her across the ballroom

288

toward the hearth. There was an elegance in the way they both almost floated across the room, hypnotizing to watch.

This whole time, I'd always associated the Sinful with males, but of course there'd be female Vampires, and this one was beautiful and powerful. I couldn't help but wonder why the Sinful in this manor wasted their time with human girls when they had a goddess like her, who'd live through eternity with them. But I knew the answer... we were the toys they played with, a way to feed easily. And I loathed thinking that was all I was to them, which made me feel even worse for wanting them to like me. But I did, in a twisted, unhealthy kind of way.

"Come, warm by the fire and let's talk," Arkyn announced, having eyes only for her, like no one else in the room existed.

That ache slowing growing in my gut intensified.

Corvina's gaze tossed over his shoulder and landed on all of us girls, caught in her web.

Arkyn followed her line of sight and stared at us like he'd forgotten we all stood there.

"Everyone back to your rooms. Now," he snapped, not even looking my way.

Guards rushed inside, herding us away like we were nothing more than cattle. I caught Lorcan and Cassian watching Arkyn, their eyes wide. Yep, no one was happy with her arrival.

With most of the girls leaving the room, Chaska took my arm and drew me out into the hall. "What do you think she wants?"

"What does anyone with power want?" Polaris butted in, stealing my words. "More power. Or she's an ex-lover and has come for a bit of fun." She smirked, while I cringed on the inside. And I shouldn't react that way. I shouldn't, when I kept reminding myself of my mission. That was the focus.

Get revenge.

Make the Sinful pay.

Not give them my heart.

I'd trained for so long to kill Vampires, not sleep with them.

But I hadn't expected the sheer boiling intensity inside me when Corvina arrived, insisting on the men's attention, the moment punching through my chest.

What was she going to tell them?

"Or she's here to feed on us?" Chaska whispered as a guard marched ahead of us. We trailed alone behind the line.

I kept looking back down the hall as someone pushed the doors closed, but they didn't shut and remained ajar. A sliver of light pierced the dark of the corridor.

"I'm going to stay and listen," I said in a low voice.

Chaska squeezed my wrist. "Are you insane? We don't even know who she is and you saw how intense it got in there."

"Don't you want to know who the new player in the manor is? If we should be running for our lives or not?"

Polaris shrugged, showing little interest in our conversation as she examined her fingernails. "She has a point."

"Whose side are you on?" Chaska murmured. "Her getting caught and dying, or being smart and surviving?"

"I'm on the side that makes the most sense, and when danger arrives, you find out what you're dealing with. That's rule number one back home."

The more Polaris talked about her hometown filled with Dragons, the more I wasn't sure which was worse, Vampires or Dragons?

I didn't think about it any further and steeled myself. With a sharp intake of breath, I checked the hall ahead and behind us. No guards, so I darted back down the pitch-black corridor, ignoring Chaska's gasp.

I pressed my back to the wall near the door, swallowed by shadows, until I was certain no more guards came back searching for me.

I half expected Chaska to join me, but she never did. I stayed there, silent as a mouse and strained my ears.

Distant voices came from within the room, but I couldn't make them out, so I crept toward the door. I stood there, feeling vulnerable and exposed. I wouldn't stay long.

Leaning closer, I peered through the crack between the doors, with a thin view of only Arkyn. He stood with his arms folded across his chest, jawline clenched, and the fire's light danced across his frustrated expression.

"It's too dangerous," he said with a flat voice, like he'd trained his voice to conceal emotions.

"I wasn't asking you if this was too dangerous." Corvina stepped up to him, her hand lifting to his shoulder and she circled him, her fingers trailing over his back, his arm, and paused over his chest. Her hand splayed, she looked up to him with a smile, studying him, admiring him, and my chest filled with fire.

"I know exactly what you were asking," Arkyn snapped, and turned away from her, walking out of my line of sight.

She lowered her hand to her side, her gaze following him. "Then you know I didn't come here to plead for your help. You're my fiercest soldier, no one compares to you, so I'm calling for you to join me, to fight for me." Her response was like silk, soft and smooth, but her words carried venom. "And you will follow me, as will those who are under your command." She turned to someone near the fire, then moved toward them, vanishing from my sight.

"Cassian, dear. I will need you completely healed, because we aren't going to lose this war. You understand that, right?"

War?

Who were they fighting?

"Don't condescend to him," Arkyn snarled. "I heard you, and I will consider your offer."

"You seem to have misheard me." She strolled across the room, her heels clicking on the floorboards, and tossed her red hair over a shoulder. "The old Arkyn would already be in his battle gear, roaring to feel fresh blood dripping down his skin, but you… you're pathetic. I say we're going to war and you want to stay here to play with your dolls. Didn't your mother ever tell you not to play with your food?"

Arkyn stepped up to Corvina, strong and untouchable. He wasn't afraid of her, towering over her. She didn't even flinch.

"And what sort of greeting have you offered me? I should rip your ice-cold heart out of your chest for disrespecting me. I'm your maker, and you should grovel in my presence, yet you talk back to me?" she reproached.

They glared at each other, and I held my breath.

She held power over him, so what stopped her from taking any of us, killing us?

Arkyn said nothing back in response, but he also didn't bend a knee to her.

"There you go." She leaned in closer, pressing her breasts against his chest, staring up into his fuming gaze. "Opposing me won't end well for any of you, especially after I pulled a lot of strings with the other elders to secure this piece of land for you." She licked her lips, and ran her tongue over her fangs. "You were once my favorite, do you remember those times?" Her hand trailed down his tight stomach, over his belt, and paused on his cock.

I shuddered as an inferno flared through me, my heart racing so hard, it pounded in my ears.

Arkyn didn't move or react, he simply held her stare with his own icy glare. In a flash, she whirled away from him, pivoting on the balls of her feet, and walked away. "Okay, if you're not interested in showing me respect, then I'll take matters into my own hands in this manor."

I swallowed hard.

Arkyn stepped after her. "Tomorrow night we'll hold a celebration in your honor," he announced, his jaw clenching. "One unlike anything you've seen in years, and no cost spared.

Give me until tomorrow night to show you the kind of welcome you deserve, my queen."

I wanted to gag at hearing him grovel, and I shook with anger.

The faintest of grins graced her blood red lips. "I shouldn't have had to ask, but I'll accept. Make it worth all my while because, after that, you're all coming with me to remind those fucking Dragons who's in charge and show them why they'll never dominate this world."

Dragons.

War.

I breathed faster, and everything in my mind fell silent. Too silent, because I couldn't make sense of my thoughts. What would happen to us? Would we be set free or locked up until the Sinful returned? *If* they returned, because who battled a Dragon and survived?

"Take me to my chamber, will you, Arkyn." Her sickly sweet voice had me close to gagging, but instead, I spun and threw myself back against the wall where the shadows deepened.

Seconds later, the door opened and a flood of light sprawled over the hall.

I held my breath.

Couldn't move.

The distinct click of heels on stone grew close, and I pressed my spine against the wall.

Waiting.

Watching.

Sweat dripped down my neck, but I didn't dare move.

With her hand draped over Arkyn's, they strolled down the hall in the opposite direction to where I hid. Cassian emerged next and trailed behind them, shoulders curved forward, defeated.

Chewing on the inside of my cheek, I froze, my breaths wedged in my lungs, when a shadow fell over me.

I snapped my head up, a gasp falling from my lips. "Lorcan," I whispered, my heart pounding, and pulled myself deeper into the shadows. "I didn't mean--"

"Let's go," he growled and I flinched back, except he leaned in close and grazed his lips over mine, the kiss unexpected, thrilling, and... and I wanted more.

I pushed myself closer, kissing him back with a burning fever, with a desperation to feel something other than the fear shackling me to the spot, to somehow feel wanted and not just be one of their dolls.

His hands closed over my hips and he pinned me to the stone wall, kissing me longer, his aggressive tongue pushing past my lips. My hands reached up and tangled through his long hair as he drew my lower lip into his mouth. I melted under him, and I was already dripping. I kissed him harder, remembering the way his mouth had felt between my thighs. Sparks of pleasure soared through my body as his fingers cupped my breasts and pinched the nipples hard. Pain twisted with pleasure and I needed so much more.

He pulled back, and I stumbled. I'd thrown myself at him, and my cheeks burned with embarrassment.

"I should go," I said.

"You have nothing to fear from me," he whispered in the dark.

My pulse was racing as a shiver of arousal and fear swept over my skin. "Who should I fear then? Corvina?"

Dread tightened his expression and his hands squeezed mine. "Come, I'll get you back to your room. Tomorrow will be a big day for all of us."

So many questions pressed on my mind, and asking them wouldn't gain me the answers I sought. Not tonight, at least.

With his hand in mine, he drew me out of the shadows and we walked quickly down the curved passages, through arches, and alongside the courtyard, until we finally reached my door.

"Sleep well," was all he said before pushing hair out of my face, staring into the depths of my gaze like he might say something, but the words never came. Only the howling wind outside spoke of beasts in the woods, of monsters in the manor.

Without another word, he walked away, blending into the shadows.

I hurried into the bedroom and shut the door behind me, my heart thundering, my lips tingling from his kiss.

"Soooo, what did you hear?" Chaska's soft whisper curled through the air, and I turned to find her sitting upright in bed, her eyes wide beneath the moon's rays coming in through the window.

"I learned why that Vampire came to visit."

She patted the bed, her mouth in an O shape, and I rushed over, joining her. "Tell me everything. Who is she? What does she want?"

I grabbed a pillow and hugged it to my chest, then the words fell from my lips and I told her everything about who Corvina was, what she wanted... but not the part about kissing Lorcan. Or how my body still sang with arousal. That part was staying guarded in my heart.

Chaska gasped, her fingers clasping my hand. "They're holding a party? Like the last one where we had to seduce those men?"

I hadn't given it much thought, but when she put it like that, my stomach dropped like a stone sinking in the sea.

7

A party? The idea of that kept me awake. I tossed and turned, grateful for a soft bed, but still, there was no comfort, not when Corvina was here. The energy in the manor was different now. Gone were the times we were in fear of the Sinful, now we had an even bigger predator to worry about.

Chaska snored softly beside me, but I rested my head on my arm and looked up at the ceiling. Corvina wasn't the woman Cassian had cried out for in his dreams, of that I was sure. But his breathless cries still haunted me, dredging up a flicker of jealousy.

I turned, dragging my knees higher in the bed, staring into the growing morning light. I needed to sleep, and more than that...I needed to stop wanting *them.*

Darkness slipped into the brightening room. I closed my eyes as the emptiness called me and drifted down...into the emptiness, where the panic waited.

The squeals of rats drifted to the surface. My heart thundered with the sound and I lifted my hand to shield my face.

He's the man who wants to take you from us! Arkyn's roar resounded from the darkness.

Something scratched my neck. I threw out my arm, trying to drive the rats away in the dark, and hit something beside me. I shoved hard, scrambling away. I was in some kind of hole...*a shaft.* The words came to me. Down here the light never reached.

But death did...death came in its savagery. In the murky gloom I saw it. A silver shield and a battle axe sitting over two crossed swords.

A cry ripped from my lips with the sight. I lifted my gaze and stared into an open mouth. Glazed eyes stared into nothing. But it wasn't the man who came for me. Not his savage sneer, or his hate-filled gaze. Blood was smeared around the open gash of this throat. Fangs marks punctured so deep I could see the white splash of bone.

A moan bubbled up to the surface, low and nauseating. I slapped my hand over my throat and tasted acid in the back of my throat.

He's your death, Asena...*he's...your...DEATH!*

Arkyn's words followed.

My death.

My death.

"My death. My death."

"Asena, wake up. You're calling out in your sleep."

I cracked open my eyes to see Chaska leaning close. Sunlight speared through the window. I blinked into the glare and rolled over. "Sorry," I whispered, my voice raw and fragile.

Something tickled the edge of my nose. I swiped at the sensation with my fingers and caught a tear. From the depths of desperation, I ached for who I was in my dreams. I ached for her loneliness and her fear. I closed my eyes, wanting to go back to her. To comfort her...if only with a ghostly touch.

But there was no well filled with rats waiting for me as I

sank into the depths once more. Just nothing...bitter nothing. I tossed and turned, rising to the surface and then falling again and when I woke, sometime later, I was aching and exhausted.

I yawned, trying to rub the grit from my eyes, and felt the sting.

"You look like hell. I was kinda hoping you'd stay wherever you ended up last night. The bed was comfy when I stretched out and hogged all the covers on my own."

Chaska eyed me standing at the bottom of the bed. Her gaze slipped to my chest. I glanced down, finding the puncture marks on my breast. One jerk of my dress and the marks were covered. I slipped from the bed and made for the bathroom. I needed to wash, and then some coffee...*yeah, coffee...*

"So, this party. What do you think it's going to be like?" Chaska followed me as I strode into the bathroom. I turned and gripped the door, but she stood in the way and then glanced away. Chaska might've wanted me out of the damn bed, but she was sure getting clingy when I was here. I sighed and then made for the toilet, hunkered down behind the privacy screen to do my business, then stood.

"I don't know," I answered.

But she never really wanted my opinion, swaying while she twirled a strand of her hair around her fingers. "I used to love parties," she mused.

I could only shake my head and make my way to the basin. I filled it to the brim, then sank the cloth into the water and peeled my dress down, an inch at a time. But there was no need to glance Chaska's way. She was off with the fairies talking about the parties she used to have.

I only ever had funerals. I thought about my parents now, hating myself for believing the lies.

Asena.

22 years old.

Parents: Unknown

Lineage: Powerful.

The torn page of information reared its ugly head. I dipped the cloth into the water and ran the soap across it. I soaped and rinsed, taking my time to run the cloth along the back of my neck, and before long, I wasn't thinking of my parents anymore.

I was thinking of Cassian.

And Lorcan…

And then Arkyn.

Liquid sunlight spilled between my thighs. I clamped them together, trying to still the memories. But they surfaced, and I hated they were so easily called. His lips…his tongue…his…I closed my eyes as my hands fell to grip the edge of the sink.

"What? What's wrong, you sick?"

I jerked my gaze up to Chaska, standing in the doorway. She looked at me like I'd just interrupted the most important conversation of her life.

"You're all flushed," she muttered.

"I'm fine." God, I needed to stop this.

Get control of yourself. The words surfaced as I grabbed the washcloth and lifted my gaze to the mirror. The fang marks on my breast had closed over and were healing. I pressed the cloth against them and winced.

"I wonder if they'll give us pretty dresses again?" She shoved away from the door.

Finally.

I hurried, slipping the dress down low and washing the rest of my body before I emptied the basin and refilled it. I met my reflection as I grabbed the soft towel and wrapped it around my body. My hips jutted out a little harder than they ever had before, and there were bags under my eyes.

I was changing, turning into someone I didn't know, someone who wore the marks of Vampires on her body as well as on her soul. A knock came at the door, making me flinch and grip the towel tightly. Chaska almost sprinted to the door, yanking it open before she ushered whoever it was into the room.

"Oh my God, *yes!*" she howled. "Thank you. I'll see Asena gets hers."

I rolled my eyes and filled the basin once more. It seemed the dresses had arrived. I grabbed the shampoo and the jug, washing my hair as Chaska cooed and gushed in the next room.

I lathered my hair and rinsed the lengths with the jug as she bounced into the bathroom carrying a midnight blue velvet dress. "This one is mine. God, it's beautiful."

I smiled and as she pranced from view once more, and then her tone changed. "Oh, yours is boring."

She could barely contain her excitement as she flung the dress into the doorway. It was the palest of blue, plain, no chiffon or lace this time. Just a simple dress, like the ones we wore through the day, and part of me sighed with relief.

"Maybe they aren't into you anymore?" she called.

"Maybe." I wrung the water from my hair and grabbed a fresh towel, wrapping it around my head.

Chatter echoed through the walls. I stepped out of the bathroom and eyed the dimming sun. Night was coming, and I was betting that the dance would be underway as soon as the last sliver of light slipped from the sky.

I dressed, listening to the others as they chatted and laughed. I'd just slipped the dress over my head when the door opened.

"There's carriages in the drive," Devika gushed.

I slipped the dress down and yanked the towel from my hair before reaching for the comb.

"How many?" Chaska stepped closer.

"I dunno, *a lot.*"

"Did you see who they were?"

I turned away from the gossip, feeling more like an outsider than ever before. I strode back into the bathroom, grabbed a ribbon, and tied up my hair as I stared at myself in the mirror.

Fear stared back at me, fear in the glint of my eyes...fear in the stone in my belly.

This wasn't a party I wanted to be part of...*and neither should they.*

The door opened once more. Hurried voices echoed before Chaska popped her head through the doorway. "I'm going with the others."

"Sure." I forced the word through clenched teeth and smiled.

One minute they wanted me around them, and the next I was discarded like a used tissue. I sighed, and lowered my gaze, finding solace in peace. I took one look at myself, and gave a slow nod. The faint sound of horses slipped in through the open door. I gave a sigh, touched my hair, and headed for the chatter that spilled along the hallway.

I closed the bedroom door behind me, and lifted my gaze to the others. They were beautiful...stunning even, a kaleidoscope of pinks, blues, greens, and red. Bold red...*blinding red.* Devika turned toward me, her smile wide, eyes sparkling as she grabbed the soft velvet skirt and twirled.

Only Polaris stood silently to the side, arms crossed, glaring at the others as they fussed. I headed toward her, not bothering with the others.

"Gonna get themselves killed," she muttered as I turned and leaned against the wall next to her. "Or worse...*bitten.*"

I winced and thought of Willa. We all knew how that ended.

"Ladies," the guard growled. "If you will, please follow me."

They were in a hurry, giggling and falling in line, any excuse for a party...as long as we weren't the favors. Polaris shoved off the wall with a huff, and I followed, hanging toward the back of the group with my boring blue dress.

Music drifted along the hallway, growing louder the closer we came to the ballroom. Servants rushed from the lower floor, laden with massive golden trays. The smell of cooked meat drifted through the air, making my stomach growl with hunger.

More trays were carried through the opening. Maid after maid with their gazes downcast, scurried in after one another. Squeals of laughter spilled out, swallowing the normally quiet manor.

Corvina was there, front and center, dressed in a sheer dress that dipped down between her creamy breasts. She turned her head as we entered and raised a glass.

"Here they all are...*aren't they adorable?*" she gushed and swiveled around to watch us. I slowed my steps and searched the room. Arkyn sat at the opposite end of a mammoth table, legs crossed, and a glass of the darkest red wine in his hand.

I don't think that's wine.

I stiffened with the thought and caught my breath. Cassian strolled behind him, and lifted his gaze. Our eyes locked, and a current of desire flared through me, and all of a sudden, I was conscious about the boring dress...and the unflattering way it fell over my bony hips. But he never seemed to notice anyone else.

And neither did the other women around me.

"Come in... come in, don't just stand there," Corvina gushed.

I scanned the room, searching for Lorcan, and found him over by the bar, alone, seemingly uninterested in the party that was in full swing.

Movement caught my gaze from the other side of the ballroom. The guards were showing other guests through the foyer, men who looked every bit the predator Corvina was.

They strode ahead, leaving the guards behind.

"Corvina," one guy called, and opened his arms.

Perfect hair, perfect smile. His voice boomed through the room, swallowing the music and laughter. I winced at the sound and took a step backwards.

"I brought you a present. Well, three of them, to be exact." He chuckled and turned, motioning someone forward.

"Oh my God," Chaska muttered, staring as three of the

biggest men I'd ever seen in my life strode into the ballroom, wearing nothing more than black sheaths across their groins.

"How delicious," Corvina murmured, and rose.

The three men went straight toward her. One bent low, meeting her lips, and captured her waist.

Hands roamed over her body. Her growl of excitement filled the air.

More guests arrived, scantily clad women, who made Devika and the others stiffen. I lifted my gaze to Lorcan as he turned and grabbed a tumbler filled with amber liquid. Our gaze connected, and a quiet desperation passed between us. *Stay back,* it whispered. *Stay back...and stay quiet.*

I took another step backwards.

"Come. *You, blondie. Come over here,*" Corvina called.

Devika flinched, her eyes widening to saucers. She never glanced at Arkyn, just took a step forward. Arkyn clenched his jaw, the muscle bulging, but he never made a move to stop Devika as she took a tentative step forward, enraptured by this predator who laughed and smiled. He didn't like Corvina here, didn't like her taking over his home, didn't like her ordering his captives around.

I thought about that for a moment. He was a captive himself in this moment, and he didn't like it, not one little bit. The music grew louder, the wine flowed more freely, and soon three almost-naked men became six, and then eight, and the women followed.

Corvina called Chaska, and the others moved forward at Corvina's command, and I was once again struck by that same flare of desire from Lorcan to stay silent...and hidden in the shadows.

The music slowly consumed the room, fighting the raucous laughter. The louder they became, the more wine that flowed, it made little difference because, in the middle of it all, still nursing the same glass of wine he'd had at the beginning of the evening, sat Arkyn.

He was a statue, legs still crossed in the same position. His fingers were pinched around the stem of the wine glass, slowly turning...turning...*turning,* hypnotized by the movement.

But I knew the pretense was a lie. I felt this current of untapped rage flowing through him. It was enough to make me catch my breath...and stay very...very still.

In a surreal shift of movement, he slowly lifted his gaze and met mine. There was no one left around me now. Corvina had called them all to her side, all the pretty dresses, all the laughter and the wine. I knew then...knew why the boring dress. I was sure he'd hand-picked it for me.

It was so I'd look exactly this, *plain...boring.*

Uninviting.

And that was how I looked. A flare of excitement surged through me. He wasn't punishing me, wasn't hurting me. *He was protecting me.* He knew exactly the type of flame he was dealing with that sought to attract these moths. He knew exactly the triggers he needed to push to keep me out of harm's way.

And it was working.

"I just *adore* this color on you," Corvina growled, and fingered the neckline of Devika's dress, then let her hand slowly drift down, over the rise of her breast.

Devika's breath caught, her cheeks reddened with a flush. I glanced at Arkyn, who still stared at me from the far end of the table, motionless as stone, like he could see this all playing out in his head. His stare nailed me to the spot.

"But I'd like it better off you," Corvina murmured.

And suddenly the tone of the music changed. Gone were the lighter, flowing sounds of the harp, it was turning deeper...darker...*hungrier.*

Skin on skin glistened under the amber glow of the fire. One of the scantily clothed men reached over and kissed

Devika. The movement like a trigger, as Corvina leaned forward and grasped Devika's jaw, gently coaxing her to turn her head so the Vampire could take her mouth with her own.

There seemed to be a possessiveness, a push and pull. One wanted to kiss her, and the other fought for control.

The music played, becoming deeper, and more dangerous. In a heartbeat, there was more kissing, more touching, more skirts lifted to explore the hidden secrets underneath. The laugher was replaced by moaning, gasps of desire, and the rush of excitement.

Lorcan turned from standing at the bar and glanced at the others, but he made no move to stop any of that...until a hard bark of laughter tore through the room, low and growling, filled with sex, as women kissed women.

Still the almost naked man kissed Devika, bowing her backwards so she lay across the table. In that moment, *she* was the meal, her lips, her heartbeat as he splayed his hand over her breast. I was frozen by the sight of his powerful back as he drove his powerful hips against hers.

Corvina stilled, consumed by the sight of such a beautiful act. Until, with a sudden lunge from across the table, she landed on his back, flung back her head, and bit him in the side of the neck.

Blood spurted from the wound, splashing Devika's face and her dress with the bright crimson mess. Corvina was a savage, gorging and sucking, until there was no fight left in the man twice her size.

Screams erupted, howls of terror. Devika's piercing wail was like a nail driving through my head. She kicked and shoved as the dying man slumped against her. I slapped my hand over my mouth, stifling my own scream.

"Enough!" Arkyn roared.

"Corvina! Jesus Christ, *what have you done?"* The posh man

who'd brought the naked men to the party shoved up from his chair and stumbled backwards.

But the Vampire just smiled and wiped her mouth with the back of her hand.

Arkyn was out of his seat in an instant as the room was filled with the hiss of deadly vipers. But this was no snake pit. This was a Vampire's lair. The other women cried and whimpered...everyone but Polaris, who stepped backwards, her face white as a sheet.

"Lorcan," Arkyn raised a hand and snapped, "get rid of that!"

Lorcan left his drink at the bar and strode toward the twitching body that was slowly sliding off Devika.

"Goddamn you, Corvina!" the man roared as he stared down at his gift to her.

"Let's go," Cassian growled, striding toward him.

I could see this all getting out of hand, even more than the blood and the bodies.

Still Corvina stood amongst it all with a blood-smeared grin. "I enjoyed my gift, thank you."

There was a shake of Cassian's head as he ushered the guest from the ballroom, and then the house. Arkyn followed, leaving us alone with a murderer.

I'd heard the stories about the Vampires. I'd listened to the warnings. They were about creatures like her...monsters who killed on a whim. Beasts who had no heart...and no soul. I lifted my gaze as Lorcan heaved the body over his shoulder and carried it around the table with long strides.

The ballroom was deadly quiet. There was no whimper from the others, no sound from the harp, until Corvina whipped her gaze toward the woman sitting in the corner, cradling the instrument. "Play!"

The music started once more, but with some missed notes as the terrified woman made the beginning stutter, until her fingers found the rhythm, slipping across the strings like they were plucking air...and the ballroom was filled with the seductive sounds once more.

"Sit." Corvina snapped. "Drink, smile...*laugh.*"

Still, she never moved, just stared at them, until they slowly sank to their seats once more, even Devika, as she trembled and wept silent tears.

I pressed my spine to the wall, watching them as the room slowly returned to how it had been before the incident. More wine was poured, and forced laugher followed.

"Oh, *her?*" A voice slipped through the madness. "You mean Asena? *No, no one's allowed to touch her. She's 'off limits'.*" I jerked my gaze toward the sound.

Chaska sat at the far side of the table, her hands shaking as she brought a glass of wine to her lips.

I shook my head as the words slipped through the room, loud enough for all to hear.

And slowly, Corvina turned her head...and that viper's gaze settled on me.

I knew then that the players had been played. Not once had she come near me, not once had she looked my way. She'd called the others forward one by one, leaving me alone. But as the smile curled those red lips, I knew it'd all been a play, just like the attack on the man was nothing more than a ruse to lure the Sinful away from me.

I lifted my head and stared at the empty foyer. My protectors were gone...

8

Corvina glared at me, her predatory eyes burrowing into my soul, seeing me for who I was… someone who'd taken the interest of three Sinful.

I'd grown thicker skin since moving to this manor, but her menacing stare was something completely different and terrifying.

It left me shaking. Because in her gaze, I saw death. So much of it.

My chest caved as if someone punched me.

Her jawline flexed, and to me, she looked like a killer.

She *was* a killer. One didn't get to their status without leaving a trail of corpses in her wake.

And she'd kill *me* if given the chance.

I saw the threat written all over her beautiful porcelain face, a face of deceit and lies.

All this debauchery and celebration in her honor revealed her for what she was… power hungry, and as soon as she took the Sinful away, there was nothing to stop her from attacking the girls… from attacking me.

The music around us picked up in beat, and other guests

rushed onto the dancefloor with the girls. Those huge, gorgeous men lingered around Corvina, hands draped over her body, but she didn't seem to notice.

Chaska spun in front of the Vampire in her elegant dress with an enormous skirt that looked incredible and also reminded me of a cloud. She was happy to be the entertainment.

So much fake merriment surrounded us, fake smiles, fake laughter. It made me sick.

I slipped backward, letting the shadows near the hallway swallow me further, but Corvina's gaze found me beyond the dancers, and my skin crawled.

Arkyn returned to the room and his gaze swung my way, too. Then he hastily swept in front of Corvina, taking her hand in his with elaborate movements before leading her onto the dancefloor, but Corvina's face distorted, and she shoved a hand into Arkyn's chest, sending him reeling backward.

My heart jolted with fear, and I flinched at her swift moment. One moment, she was across the room, the next, she was in front of me, the faint breeze from her speed a whisper through my hair.

She now stood in front of me like a starving lioness, a malevolent grin splitting her lips, revealing sharp, pointy fangs.

A shiver rushed through me, and a small cry pressed on my throat. But I stood my ground and faced her, lifting my chin.

Never run from a predator, Father would say. *It shows your weakness, and monsters love to hunt.*

So, I stood there, shaking on the inside, but I schooled my features to appear like a calm girl who didn't give a fuck. No one needed to know I was a twisted mess of fright on the inside.

Her gaze raked over my body, the corner of her mouth curling. "Such a plain, boring dress for such a celebration." She spoke loud enough that those standing nearby turned in our direction.

Heat slithered over my cheeks.

She stared over her shoulder at the dancefloor, at everyone's beautiful gowns. Elaborate stitching, large ribbons, silk trims, plunging necklines, and suddenly, I didn't want to be here, not looking like this.

I lowered my gaze to the boring blue dress hanging off me, my cheeks on fire. No frills or lace or silk, but just a simple dress that most of us had been wearing during the day, so why would the Sinful request I wear this tonight? I reminded myself the Sinful had a purpose for everything they did. But I was a toy to them, so it shouldn't matter what I thought. But it did and it churned in my gut. I was mortified that she was drawing so much attention to how I looked. I stood, soaking in her laughter and the judging eyes.

"You don't seem like their type," she continued, her face twisted with hatred and disgust. "Maybe a nice fit for a maid, but not pretty enough to claim as a queen." Mirth danced behind her words, and she was sneering, enjoying the belittling. It was becoming a pattern with her, yet she still got to me.

Anger slithered inside me, colliding with hurt and embarrassment. I looked down and quickly swiped at my eyes, hating that she affected me so much, hating that she made me squirm in my own skin, but my blood was boiling.

Don't let her get to you.

The words swirled in my mind, over and over, the more I clenched my fists.

"In my plain dress, I shouldn't be a threat to you." The words slipped from my lips too fast and I regretted them at once. I should have shut up, said nothing, smiled, and played the scared dumb girl. But I'd had enough of being pushed and prodded.

She seethed, narrowing her eyes at me. Leaning down toward me, she snatched my wrists, iron fingers squeezing the life out of them. "It's mine," she hissed. "All of this, all these men, all of you, mine. And I tread on vermin who dare talk back to me."

I blinked hard and my hackles rose.

Arkyn was at her side in a heartbeat, his hand on her arm. "Corvina, don't waste your time, come and enjoy the night. This is all for you, my queen."

She ripped her gaze from me, her glare morphing into a dainty smile, and she had the audacity to bat her eyes at Arkyn. I doubted this woman knew happiness, but in manipulation, she was a master.

I wanted to kiss Arkyn so hard right then for taking her away from me.

"Yes, yes, you're right," she cooed and whipped around, turning her back to me like I no longer existed.

Which was perfect for me. I wanted to be nowhere near that dangerous lunatic.

I watched them vanish into the crowd and Lorcan emerged from the shadows, his hair and clothes blending in with the dark. He stood so close to me, my skin pricked with anticipation that he might place a hand to my back, touch me, something, but he maintained his distance, like even he had rules to follow tonight.

"You may want nothing to do with the monster," he started. "But the monster wants everything to do with you, it seems." He stared out at the celebration, as did I, standing side by side in the shadows.

"Why do you think that is?" I couldn't hide my disappointment in my voice that someone like Corvina was paying me attention. "Why would she be threatened, in her position?"

He didn't answer, but just kept watching the dancers. "I used to hate dancing before I become a Sinful. I had two left feet and no matter how much I practiced, I stepped on everyone's feet. I still do." He laughed softly. "Just because a monster wears a mask doesn't mean they can hide who they really are."

"I guess. So, why did Arkyn turn you? If you don't mind me

asking?" I had no clue what was etiquette on asking such questions of the Sinful.

"I lived during a time of a great war and was conscripted to fight, along with all the other men in our town. Needless to say, I didn't survive my first week on the front of the enemy lines, which, I didn't know at the time, were also Vampire feeding grounds. Arkyn found me dying and took pity on me." He spoke with no emotions about how he'd died, but his story speared a blade into my heart.

His story sat with me a long while, imagining the terror of war, the fear of being brought back a Sinful. I turned to Lorcan with words already spilling from my mouth, but he was gone. Only darkness kept me company.

Instead, Chaska strolled toward me in her gorgeous gown, her breaths racing, her cheeks blushing wildly. "I swear I'm going to kill someone." She gritted her teeth, staring back at the crowd with hatred. "One of those Vampires stuck his hand up my skirt and pushed his hand inside my underwear like I was just there for his pleasure." She was trembling with fury, with shock. "I managed to get away from him, but if he finds me again, I'm scared what he'll do. I don't want to be like them," she whimpered.

"Let's sneak out of here," I suggested, taking her trembling hand in mine.

She whipped around toward me. "We can do that?"

"If no one sees us, why not? Maybe let's find Polaris."

As if on cue, Polaris slid out of the crowd and marched toward us.

"I don't want to stay here," I murmured, especially to have Corvina coming to find me again.

We slipped backward through the shadows as I scanned the ballroom, not seeing anyone looking our way. Once in the hallway, we ran for our lives, the shuffle of the girls' gowns sounding, the light clicking of their heels, our racing breaths.

We didn't stop until we reached the courtyard and paused to catch our breaths, checking that no one had followed.

An inky mist swirled in the night sky, and everything out here was silent, too silent.

"Holy donkeys," Chaska blurted before collapsing on a wooden bench with a great huff. "What sort of party was that?"

"Whatever she wants it to be," Polaris added. "Did you not see the fire in her eyes? She has no fear, none of them do, because they're already dead."

But I remembered the fear in Arkyn's eyes and it had everything to do with what Corvina would do to me if given the chance. He wanted me for himself, worried what she'd do if she got a hold of me.

"What do you think will happen to us if she makes the Sinful leave?" Chaska asked.

Neither Polaris nor myself responded, because we all knew the truth, but voicing it made it too real. I doubted Corvina would allow us to just walk away, to return to our towns.

The breeze brought with it a cold shiver, and I rubbed my arms.

Across the courtyard, a shadow raced down the hall and shot past the second entrance to the courtyard, so fast it had to be a Sinful. My heart slammed into my ribcage, and I shuddered. Had someone followed us? The guards never ran around like that.

"Did you see that?" I whispered, inching closer to the girls.

They froze, then looked at each other and at the entrances on either side of us.

"What did you see?" Polaris asked in a faint whisper.

"A shadow rushing past."

An eeriness fell over us. "Something's wrong," Polaris muttered, glancing around us as if expecting something to jump out at us.

The hairs on my nape bristled. She was right, I felt it, too. Something was there with us, watching, playing a game.

"We should return to the party." Chaska jolted to her feet, the blood draining from her face.

We gravitated toward the hall in a tight group, when the raspy sound of something dragged across the stone. It came from the direction of the ballroom.

Chaska squeaked, and my heart was close to exploding. We spun and ran, shivers racing up the back of my legs.

"Faster," Polaris cried, taking a fast left, and we scrambled after her, when a huge shadow rose before us, blotting out the torches on the wall, stealing the light.

I shook my head, my chest constricting. *This couldn't be happening, no fucking way.*

This was a nightmare coming to life. I recoiled, snatching Chaska and Polaris by the arms, hauling them back.

Chaska was murmuring unrecognizable cries, frozen on the spot, while Polaris's hands curled into fists as she readied to fight. And I pulled them to leave, to run, because whatever we dealt with was going to win. The manor was filled with Vampires... this was their night and we never should have left the ballroom.

"Run!" I called, and the three of us scrambled out of there and rushed back the way we'd come, running in circles while death chased us.

Laughter rose around us, echoing off the walls.

"It's her," I snarled. "It's the Vampire bitch."

"God, she's going to kill us," Chaska murmured, her inhales hitching. "I don't want to die here, not in this damn manor. I want to see the world, do something with my life."

The corridor ahead of us curled away into infinite darkness, but the faint chords of the harp reached us, singing through the manor. The ballroom was near.

My feet slipped and my stomach lurched, but it was Polaris who caught my arm to steady me. "Careful."

That was when the impossibly dark shadow reappeared and I flinched as it grew in size before us. From within the dark, a face emerged, mouth gaping open, fangs long and exposed.

I couldn't breathe.

Corvina stared right at us, and I was frozen.

Chaska grabbed the back of my dress and yanked backwards to get me to move.

I spun and we scrambled down another passage, not caring where it led, as long as it was as far from her as possible.

She was toying with us, enjoyed seeing us scared to death.

"Corvina, please don't do this." Fear quaked through my voice.

Chaska took a sharp left, and we followed her, straight into the courtyard again. My breath came in short, sharp spurts, the three of us stood in a tight circle with our backs to each other. I was shaking ridiculously hard with fear.

"Please, God, let me live," Chaska prayed, her expression pure panic.

Glancing left and right, a scream shoved to the edge of my throat, my lungs pumping hard but there wasn't enough air going inside them.

The clack of heels hitting stone came from my right and we all jerked our heads in that direction.

Corvina reared up from the shadows in the hallway, staring at us with hunger in her now-black eyes.

Frozen, we huddled close, watching her, waiting for her to attack.

"Little mice running.

"Running for their lives.

"Lives that are mine.

"Mine to take, and take I shall."

She charged at us so fast, we didn't see her moving until it was too late.

Chaska screamed, but Corvina snatched her first by an arm and whipped her away across the yard. Her screams shattered my ears as she hit the ground with a loud *oomph*.

Shoulder to shoulder, Polaris and I faced the monster and retreated.

I reached down and snatched the blade from my boot, gripping the leather hilt with a sweaty palm.

Fast hands shoved Polaris aside and one grabbed my throat, the other seizing my fist with the weapon.

She stared down at me, her smile more of a grimace, her expression vile. "You will taste the sweetest. After tonight, my hero will no longer have need for any of you."

Panic numbed my brain, and I clawed at her iron fingers around my throat with my free hand. She stole my breath, suffocated me.

"He'll never love you, none of them will. They don't have beating hearts, girl."

Stars danced in my vision just as Polaris threw herself at Corvina's side, driving a vicious kick to her ribs.

It didn't dislodge Corvina, but the shock had the monster's grip loosening. Instinct owned me, and I wrenched my arm free.

With a vicious thrust, I drove my blade into her gut. It slid into her like into soft butter, making a horrible squishy sound.

Her eyes bulged out, and I recoiled just as Chaska rose from our side, a chair over her head, and she slammed it across the Vampire's head. The timber seat broke into pieces, but Corvina barely seemed to feel it. She just glared at me, and I suddenly regretted everything.

She grabbed the hilt of the blade and wrenched it out, her face writhing with pain, yet she still cut me a furious glance. Blood rushed out of the wound, dark crimson dropping down her dress.

"I will skin you alive with my bare hands," she spat.

She lunged.

I screamed as death flashed in my mind.

Everything happened too fast then.

A flash of movement blasted past me and crashed into Corvina, driving her backwards.

She fell to the ground on her back, and Polaris scrambled off her.

I couldn't make out what I was seeing, at first, as my head spun, my insides churning with panic.

The monster lay on the ground between us, with a wooden leg from the broken chair piercing her chest… into her heart.

Blood trickled from the corners of her mouth and eyes, and for those few moments, I could have sworn a wisp of a shadow lifted from her body and dissolved on the breeze.

"Oh, fuck!" Chaska cried out. "You killed her. You killed the master Vampire!"

"Shut the hell up," Polaris retorted.

I was pacing. "Oh, fuck. Oh, fuck." We were in so much shit for this.

Corvina lay on the ground, her expression frozen, her body unmoving, dead eyes wide open.

Terror closed in around me, squeezing, stealing the life out of my lungs. What had we done? We'd killed one of their kind. They'll butcher us, all of us!

"Isn't she meant to disintegrate or something?" I asked, and started nervously chewing on a hangnail.

The scuffle of feet came from the entrance to the courtyard, and we all flinched, jolting our heads up.

Arkyn, along with several other Vampires, stood in the doorway, their faces shocked, and their gazes locked on Corvina.

9

"What the fuck just happened?" Arkyn growled, his wide eyes staring at the unmoving body on the ground.

"She was going to kill us." Polaris stood and swiped the hair from her eyes.

Everyone stared in horror. Every mortal...and Vampire who'd gathered near the courtyard. Had they all sensed our fight and come running out here? How long had they been watching?

"Well," one of the male Vampires murmured. and lifted the napkin he'd brought with him to pat the corners of his mouth. "I must say, Arkyn, your parties are *never* dull."

I swallowed hard and glanced at the others, then at Polaris. Corvina attacked us. Had they seen that part? But would that mean anything in the Vampire world?

I didn't think so.

A few Vampires started to retreat back down the hall, and Arkyn's face changed. He raced right behind them.

Panic strangled me.

With a quick exchange with Chaska and Polaris, I quickly

retrieved my blade from Corvina's dead grip, wiped the blood on her dress, and tucked it back into my boot. Then we darted right after them all, down the hall and into the ballroom, where many of the guests and girls remained sitting around the decadently decorated table, startled and frozen in their seats.

Arkyn lowered his gaze as one of the Vampires headed toward the front door.

But Arkyn was faster, stepping into his path and blocking his escape, shaking his head. "Now, Orion, you know I can't let you leave."

There was a huff and a smile from the Vampire, then one glance over his shoulder at the others sitting still and quiet at the table told him all he needed to know. This party had turned deadly...and the night was still young.

"Arkyn." Orion met the Sinful's gaze, and his voice grew colder. "You know I won't tell a living soul."

Arkyn took a step toward the other Vampire, closing the gap. "See, that's the problem, Orion. You *do* tell. You're what's called...*a gossip.* That's why I brought you here, but that's not going to save you. I'm sorry."

There was a shake of Orion's head before he cast his gaze toward the door.

Don't do it, the words filled my mind. I took a step forward, out of the shadows, as Orion lunged for salvation. But Arkyn was faster and stronger, moving with brutal precision.

He grabbed Orion by the neck and lifted, until the Vampire's feet left the floor and tap-danced in the air.

One sickening *crunch,* and his head came clean off his neck...leaving his body to fall into a heap on the floor.

I cringed and hugged myself.

A sickening moan slipped through the air. I turned toward the sound as Devika shuddered and shook, slowly rising to her feet from her chair at the table and then, with a slow exhale, crumpled to the floor.

Others of the girls rushed toward her, grabbing her from where she lay in a heap. Her arms flopped by her sides, her eyes remained closed.

"She's just fainted," Polaris muttered, and glanced at Arkyn as he cast the head of the dead Vampire aside and strode towards them.

"Lorcan, see the ladies to their rooms and make sure they're secured while I deal with this mess."

"Arkyn," one of the female Vampires said, but made no move to stand, "tell me what you're thinking. You can't possibly think to kill us all."

He flinched and lifted his head, and I knew in an instant that was precisely what he was thinking...and what he'd do...to protect us.

No, to protect me.

And just like he was thinking the same thing, Arkyn lifted his head and glanced my way. "What do you suggest?" he asked as he stared at me. But the words weren't for me.

He was giving them a way out of this nightmare.

"We know of you, Arkyn. We know how you've fought for us. We know the... *sufferings,*" the female Vampire murmured, and this time, she moved to rise, *but slowly.* "And we know what you'll do if word of this gets out. So take my hand, let me pledge on this unforgiving life of mine, then look into my head and know I speak the truth."

My breath stilled. The entire room waited for his answer.

"Arkyn," she pleaded, "please make the right choice here."

He glanced around the table as Lorcan bent and grasped Devika by the arm. "Let's go," he murmured. "All of you, to your rooms."

A sigh of relief swept through the room as, one by one, the other girls stood and hurried for the doorway. Even the woman who had played the harp rose to her feet.

"Not you," Lorcan snapped, and wrenched his gaze her way.

The poor woman just clasped her hands together, her eyes wide with fear, then sank to her small stool once more.

Polaris glanced down at the blood on her hands before she moved with the others. She'd saved me. I looked around at the shell shocked gazes. *No, she'd saved all of us.*

I reached out as she stepped past and grabbed her hand. "Thank you, thank you for everything."

Tears shimmered in her gaze. She turned to me and leaned close. It was like she needed comfort, but hadn't the words to ask. I wrapped my arms around her and held her trembling body close.

"I can't do this anymore," she whispered, her voice brittle and sad.

I had no words of comfort to give her. We were playing by their rules, bowing to their whims. It was brutal and bloody, in a world mortals weren't meant to survive in.

"Let's go," Lorcan urged.

"We need them to help with the cleanup." Cassian's voice cut through the room. "Everything she brought with her needs to be burned as soon as possible. The faster we eradicate her trace here, the safer we all are."

Something passed between Cassian and Lorcan. I *felt* it more than saw it, a surge of desperation, of fear, even.

"I'll stay," I answered.

"Me, too," Chaska said, and stepped forward, staring at the pool of blood on the floor.

"Good," Cassian murmured, meeting my gaze, then lifted his gaze to Lorcan.

The others were ushered out and back down the hallway, the clatter of their heels ricocheting off the walls as they ran all the way back to their rooms.

"What can we do?" Chaska asked, glancing at Cassian and then looking at the floor.

She was being nice and weird. Something felt *off*. But then again...I glanced around the room at the blood splatter from the dead Vampire and the remaining guests, too terrified to move.

"Hannah," Cassian called one of the maids forward. "Take Asena and Chaska to Corvina's room." He met my gaze. "The three of you can dispose of all her belongings. Take them down to the incinerator...time is of the essence. We'll take care of everything here."

I nodded, feeling a surge of desperation, feeling like he wanted to get us out of the ballroom as they cleaned up. What were they going to do? Kill every Vampire guest?

I admired Cassian for wanting us out of the way, for us to not see what was coming. Maybe I was getting too close to them, starting to feel protected by them. It also seemed I was wanting the same things as they wanted. Sex, love...they were a hunger that burned inside me until I was nothing more than an inferno. But I couldn't think of that now.

The maid gave a nod. "Yes, Sire. Ma'am, if you please, follow me," she answered, and turned toward the hallway.

I took one last glance at Arkyn and left, with Chaska by my side. I didn't know what would happen to the others. Whatever decision he made would have consequences, both for him and for those who remained.

Other maids rushed forward, carrying empty trays into the ballroom to clear away the tables that hours ago were laden with food and wine. The servants didn't look terrified, just focussed, as though their very lives were measured by how fast and how efficient they were.

We hurried past them, following Hannah along the hallways to the guest wing of the manor. I'd walked along here once before, opening the doors and peering at the opulent suites with the four-poster beds, laden with lace and velvet--rooms fit for a queen.

That was where we hurried now.

"Just up ahead," Hannah urged and stopped at a towering red

cedar door, carved with ornate flourishes and swirls. She hovered at the door for a moment, then twisted the handle and gently pushed the door wide. "I shall leave you to it."

One bow of her head and she was gone, hurrying back the way we'd come, throwing over her shoulder, "Collect all her stuff in a pile and I'll bring a cart to help us carry it to the basement."

"Holy shit," Chaska murmured, and stepped inside, casting a gaze around the room. "This is gorgeous."

I didn't care about how pretty the paintings were or how luxurious the velvet cover on the bed felt. All I cared about were the bags Corvina had left behind and to get this over with. I hurried to the large suitcase and the smaller carry bag that sat neatly beside the bed, while Chaska ran and launched herself at the towering bed.

She hit the middle of the mattress with a bounce and threw open her arms, running the backs of her hands along the covers "This is *gorgeous*, Asena. Come up here, lie with me."

I knelt at the smaller case and yanked on the handle, ignoring her as best I could. Glass clattered inside with the movement as the clasp flipped open and unearthed Corvina's secrets. There was a flare of dishonesty as I upended the contents and spilled vials of blood and tiny gold canisters onto the floor in front of me.

"Oh, that looks interesting, let me see." Chaska jumped from the bed and landed with a *thud* next to me.

She sank to the floor and reached out, automatically going for the gold.

"Careful." I grabbed her hand, her fingers almost touching the vials. "You don't know what's inside them."

She stiffened, and glared at me. "Are you just saying that 'cause you want all the pretty stuff for yourself?"

I flinched at the words and let go of her hand. "No, I was trying to save your damn life."

Nothing was going to stop her, not even the fear of death. She just plucked the golden vials from the floor and cradled them in the palm of her hand. "They're so pretty, what else does she have?"

I just shook my head, leaving her to pick through the rest of the contents, and moved to the large suitcase. The metal buckles clanked as I unhooked each one and threw open the top. Clothes were packed neatly, lace and frills and satin. But that was only half of the bag, the rest was filled with books. Two small black velvet bags were wedged in the corner. I poked them, listening to coins clatter inside.

"Oh, my God." Chaska reached over and plucked a bag from the middle of the suitcase. One bag became two as she went back again, until all three bags of coins sat in front of her. "How much do you think this is?" she whispered.

More than we could spend in a lifetime, I wanted to answer. But I didn't care about the money...all I saw was what they unearthed.

There was a stack of letters.

All neatly folded.

The writing on the front was elegant and sprawling, and in a language I couldn't read. I grasped the small stack and placed them in my lap. I opened each letter carefully, setting aside those I couldn't decipher, and stilled at one I could.

It was addressed to her. *Countess Corvina Elenor Bathory.* I stiffened, reading her full name. *Bathory.* I knew that name, had heard it whispered about a deranged countess who liked to bathe in the blood of innocents. Was this really her? And we'd killed her!

"I'm keeping it." Chaska grasped one bag and tried to stuff it down the neckline of her dress.

I lifted my gaze to her, but she never cared who this woman had been...or the danger she'd brought to our door. She cared about gold and velvet, about pretty things and greed.

That was what sparkled in her eyes...*greed.*

I turned back to the letter and peeled open the envelope with shaking fingers.

A single page slipped free, the writing small and neat, and in words I could read.

Corvina,

The fight isn't coming, it's already here, and if we are to survive against these winged beasts, we will need an army. Arkyn must be at the head of that army. He <u>must</u> heed our call to arms, and you, my dear, must make him.

Go to him, to his manor, find out why he has those mortal women, and bring him back with you...or don't return at all.

I lifted my gaze. *They wanted him to fight...but why was he so important in that fight?*

Polaris's voice filled my mind. Her stories of the Dragons rising in great numbers to build an army. I lowered my gaze to the rest of the letter.

If you cannot encourage him to return with you, then find the woman. You find her...and you will control Arkyn.

My heart gave a tremble, and then sped without warning. *Find the woman.* Those words were a scream inside my head. There was no signature on the bottom of the letter. No hint at all as to who had sent it.

I scanned through the rest of the letters and stopped at a grainy black and white image. I recognized Arkyn instantly...and Lorcan with his long, flowing hair, and Cassian standing just a little apart from the others.

There was a woman standing between them. A beautiful woman staring directly at the camera. My heart was thundering, filling my head with a roar as I lifted my hand and stared at her face.

Find the woman. The urgency was all I felt. I stood on the edge of a precipice, and all the answers of my life were right in front of me. All I had to do was look into her eyes, and I'd know...

I'd know it was—

The words died in my head as I focused on the grainy picture, at her wide smile, her dark, glinting eyes, and her hand on her hip, one leg cocked casually in front of her. But it was her chin jutting in the air that made the guest bedroom where I sat slowly start to spin.

I'd seen that look before.

"They won't know," Chaska muttered, trying to wrestle the third bag filled with gold coins beside the swell of her breast.

She lifted her head, her dark eyes catching mine, then lifted her chin, staring at me with the same expression. "Don't look at me like that," she snarled. "It's not my fault you care more about a stupid photograph than you do about money."

I couldn't speak.

Couldn't breathe.

The room swirled faster as I lowered my gaze to the image once more, and I stared at the woman who was the spitting image of Chaska.

It was her...it'd *been* her all along who the Vampires wanted, who the letter must have referred to. I closed my eyes as my world collapsed.

Pain came, spearing across my chest with an unseen blade, the tip so hot it scorched the flesh as it plunged deep.

*Find the woman...*the letter said.

And it looked like I'd done exactly that.

I'd found the woman the Sinful had wanted all along.

And it wasn't me....

10

I glanced at Chaska, who adjusted the small bags of gold coins she'd tucked down her dress before grabbing one of Corvina's bags. She seemed so engrossed, so caught up with her treasure, while I felt hollow, somehow forgotten, betrayed, used, and so many other emotions that thickened my throat. Tears prickled in my eyes that it wasn't me the Sinful had wanted all along. Was I just a means to an end... an entertainment?

"Asena, you going to help?" Chaska asked as she lugged a leather trunk of clothes across the floorboards toward the door.

Swallowing past the boulder in my throat, I quickly wiped the tears from my eyes, furious that I'd let myself feel this hurt from not being selected, for not being as special as I originally thought. Was Chaska being treated the same way as me, having secret moments with the Sinful, and I hadn't noticed?

I hesitated at first, my fingers clamping tight around the photo and letter in my hand. Back in the ballroom, Corvina had called Chaska to her a few times, watched her. The Vampire had known all along Chaska was important and that she might be the one who could influence Arkyn's decision.

So, who exactly, was this woman in the photo? Her mom, aunty, grandma?

Looking down at the image, I stared at the lookalike. "Chaska," I began, "have any of your past family members or relatives been taken by Vampires? Worked for them?"

Her head jolted up, her features twisted with confusion. "What are you talking about?"

"Just curious."

She shrugged, her lips pinched tight. "Doubt it. Why? Did you find something?" Her gaze fell to the photo and letter in my hand.

"I was just wondering, that's all." I turned away and folded my findings before tucking them down the front of my dress.

"A few years back, a woman in my town crossed paths with a Vampire in the meadow and was taken by him," she added. "A shepherd saw her bitten before they vanished. But that happens occasionally in my town."

All I could picture was me with Lorcan, with Arkyn, Cassian's endearing words. And I wanted to murder them for making me think I meant something to them. It seemed Vampires just took and took from everyone.

Their constant reassurances that they wouldn't harm me had fooled me.

The flirting.

The stolen stares and tender touches.

Was it all a game?

I wanted to scream.

Or was I reading too much into it? Everything hurt... my head... my heart. The room was spinning around me.

Chaska huffed as she dumped the bag near the door and pressed her hands into her lower back to stretch. "It's heavier than it looks, and she's got like half a dozen more. Why was she carrying so much stuff around for a simple visit? Almost looks like she was moving out."

Bring him back with you...or don't return at all.

So, if she was so terrified of her master that she planned to run away, then I never wanted to meet that Vampire!

*Find the woman...*I thought back to what the letter said.

I growled under my breath.

Chaska's eyes narrowed. "What's wrong?"

"I'm exhausted and so much has happened tonight. Let's get this finished." Shoulders curled forward, I turned away from her and grabbed another bag, closing it and hauling it to the door.

It wasn't long before the maid returned with a metal baggage cart on creaky wheels. We piled the bags onto it and helped her push the thing down the hall.

"You sure you're okay?" Chaska whispered, looking over at me. "You're acting strange."

I nodded, and offered her a forced smile. "I'll feel better once we're in our room, away from everything."

She accepted my excuse, and I was left alone, drowning with my thoughts, with confusion and uncertainty. For a while there, I'd felt I was starting to understand my purpose in this manor with the Sinful, they'd made me lower my guard, and now I hated myself for falling so easily for them. It made me sick to my stomach to feel tricked.

The manor was empty around us, no voices nearby, just a deathly silence.

Finally, the maid came to a stop at the top of a set of dark stairs.

"You each take a bag and we need to carry them to the basement." The woman with chestnut hair grabbed the big trunk and heaved it off the cart. I rushed to her side to help, but she batted me away with a hand.

Chaska groaned but was already lugging another bag down the stairs. The continuous thumping sound reverberating against the stone walls. I took another bag with both hands and carried it down the curving steps. The deeper we descended, the mustier the air grew.

At the bottom of the steps, we dragged the bags down a dark hall and into a room where heat engulfed me the moment I stepped inside. I choked on the pungent, heavy air that clung to my throat. Covering my mouth and nose with a hand, I looked up.

"Oh hell… this is hell," Chaska murmured alongside me.

Black char coated the ceiling and stone walls as if this basement had been set on fire before. Across the back wall sat an incinerator, with a large metal door hanging open and flames leaping and flicking inside. If Hell did exist, that right there was how I imagined it an endless burning pit of torture.

"Hurry, bring the bags over," the maid called out.

Chaska didn't move at first, but I stumbled forward, dragging the trunk behind me. My face burned from the intensity of the flames, and I was sure I'd have no eyebrow hair left if I moved any closer. With the maid's help, we lifted the trunk and shoved it into the doorway.

I stepped back, with the flames popping and crackling at the new fuel, and the maid grabbed a long metal stick before shoving the bag in deeper.

Sweat slid down the sides of my face. Maybe I should have felt pity for Corvina and how horribly we disposed of her belongings, but she'd tried to kill me.

"Don't just stand there," the maid snapped. "Go get the rest of the bags."

So I rushed out of the room, thankful to escape the overbearing heat, and Chaska joined me.

"Do you think that's where they stuffed Corvina's body?"

I didn't want to think about it or have the image in my mind. "Who knows what the Vampire ritual is with final death."

Dragging the last bag into the room, I wiped the sweat from

my brow, catching my breath as Chaska took her turn to help the maid push bags into the fire.

Wooden crates and boxes lined the walls. Were they all items to be burned? Maybe garbage, because it reeked in here. The flicker of light from the fire caused something to glint in the opposite corner and I squinted for a better look.

My legs moved on their own as my mind tried to make sense of what I was looking at. Up close, I crouched down and spied a book with elaborate golden text on the spine. Behind it sat several tall piles of books. They were from the study... all the missing books. Water stained, most were ruined and buckled.

My stomach clenched. What information could they possibly contain that they needed to be burned? With greedy hands, I snatched the first one and cracked it open, to pages of print. These weren't the books I searched for. Shuffling deeper into the dark, I scanned the piles for leatherbound books with no words on the cover.

Finding one, at the bottom of the pile, of course, I pulled bundles off the pile until I reached the bottom one and grabbed it. My heart raced as I opened the leatherbound book. Rows and rows of handwritten names and ages lay in my hands. I flipped toward the back, searching for my name and Chaska's, except every page was filled with other names. This wasn't the recent edition I'd found in the study. But why were they burning this book when it didn't look water damaged? How many more were down here?

I scanned the other piles, reaching for another leatherbound volume, and collected it into my hands.

Someone cleared their throat behind me.

I flinched around. The maid stood there with a red face, her hair frazzled and sweat bubbling on her upper lip. She sneered at me and snatched the book out of my grasp.

"You are meant to help me, not go through the garbage." She tossed the book into the incinerator.

"No!" I lunged after it, but was too late as she shut the door with a loud thud. "Return to your rooms," she ordered.

I gritted my teeth.

Chaska touched my arm. "Let's go."

We wasted no time turning and running out of there.

"What was in that book?" she asked breathlessly as we raced up the stairs.

"I thought it might have given information on Corvina and the Sinful," I lied way too easily.

"I'm glad she's dead," Chaska murmured, "or it might have been us in the furnace tonight."

"You're probably right." I kept thinking back to why the Sinful would burn those books. What secrets were hidden inside? There was something they didn't want us to know. Something that told me I was foolish to think I could ever trust them.

"You know, Polaris is scary at times, but I'm glad she's on our side."

"Maybe the three of us need to stay together more often." To watch if Chaska went and spent time with the Sinful on her own.

We rushed back to our room, my skin crawling at being out in the halls tonight. Unease hung in the air. Back in our room, Chaska and I barely exchanged words as we washed, changed into our nighties, and jumped into bed.

My head still swirled with the night's events, the revelations, the deaths. I had no idea what Arkyn would do to us in the morning, but I closed my eyes and tried to sleep, tried to forget that it wasn't actually me who was special to the Sinful, tried to ignore the breaking of my heart.

The last trickles of sunlight vanished from our room. The candles flickered and swayed.

I sat cross-legged on the bed, staring up at the shadows dancing on the ceiling, while Chaska counted her gold coins at the table. The jingling filled the silence in the room we'd been in here since waking up in the afternoon. Apparently Arkyn wanted us locked away from whatever was going on out there.

A knock came at the door, and I caught my breath.

I jolted off the bed, while Chaska swooped her treasure into a bag, the clank distinctive, but it didn't stop her making so much noise. She'd claimed those gold coins from Corvina and no one was prying them out of her grasp.

The lock clicked and door opened, to reveal a large guard all in black standing in the doorway. "You have been summoned for dining." He stepped back. Chaska and I wasted no time and hurried after him.

Tonight, we were led to the study, where a long table had been set up for us. Food and gold jugs of drinks waited for us, while glass vases spilling with gorgeous red roses brought color to the room. Many more dishes were being brought out, roasts and vegetables, and breads and butters. But my attention fell on the bookshelves that had been returned to this room, filled with books. Did the collection still include all the handwritten books with girls' names? Or were they all down in the basement being burned?

There was no sign of Arkyn.

Cassian and Lorcan stood at opposite ends of the room, watching us streaming inside. Expressions tight, they gave nothing away.

My heart kicked harshly, making me lower my gaze, my chest burning at seeing them, my mind spinning at remembering the letter in Corvina's bag.

Taking a seat across the table from Chaska, I quickly filled my plate with food, as did the other girls. Chaska was chatting away with Polaris, not even noticing the Sinful.

I kept glancing between the Vampires and her. But tonight, they seemed distant, barely looking our way. I hated feeling this vulnerable, but I had to find out more about who that woman in the photo was and why she looked so similar to Chaska.

Once everyone had finished eating, the maids cleared the table and replaced the food and plates with card games. It seemed we were back to being closed up in one room, and I was on my feet, unable to sit around like nothing bothered me.

I shivered and just wanted to scream at the Sinful to tell us what was going on. But I wasn't fool to think they'd answer, so I kept quiet. I always kept quiet.

Moving over to the bookshelves, I ran a hand over their spines, eyeing the writing desk in the corner where I'd found some of the books with names. Had they been taken away, too?

I felt the heaviness of stares on my back, and I randomly pulled out a book and opened it, but my attention swept back to the bottom shelves, where the other books had been hidden previously.

"Your interest in the sex life of plants astonishes me," Cassian murmured from behind me.

I shuddered that I hadn't heard him approach and glanced over my shoulder. "I'm fairly certain it's a necessity for anyone owning a home or manor."

He snorted. "Does it help to read it upside down?"

I shot a glance at the book and almost died at seeing he was right. I slapped it shut before shoving it back onto the shelf.

My cheeks heated up as I looked up at him. "I've read that book before." I held his gaze, trying to find that callous monster behind the mask.

If Chaska was the woman they'd sought all along, then what was I?

The bait? The stupid fucking plaything? I was a slit between my legs, a warm body to play with...and a heart to break.

He leaned toward me. "Are you all right?" There was something intimate behind his pale green eyes, a tenderness, and every inch of me warmed up.

Yet his words caught me off guard, and I wasn't sure how to process them. This was the Cassian who'd been crawling into my thoughts and desires, but then, who was that woman in the photo? Why was she crucial to Arkyn?

"What is Arkyn going to do to us?"

"You mean with regards to Corvina's demise?"

I nodded.

"That's not for us to discuss."

I swallowed hard and a chill ran through me. I stood still.

"You seem different tonight," he suggested. "You've been keeping your mind guarded and closed lately."

"A girl's got to have her secrets." The first words to come to mind tumbled out, and I felt stupid saying them, but Cassian's lips curled upward, already accepting my response.

Loud voices came from near the table, and I glanced past Cassian to see Devika and Aislinn attacking each other, both of them hitting and pulling hair. What was going on now?

Lorcan, who'd stood talking to Chaska, whipped around and stared at the brawling girls, just watching, doing nothing to stop them.

"So, you couldn't see that coming with your mind reading?" I blurted. "You can't read minds now?"

Cassian looked across at me, the bridge of his nose wrinkled like I ought to know the answer. He scrubbed a hand over his mouth. "No, only yours."

His response startled me, and I stood there while he marched over to the fighting girls. This whole time, I'd assumed the Sinful could read all our minds, but I'd been wrong. They could they only read mine...

11

*F*ind the woman...

Find the woman. Find the woman. Find the woman.

I couldn't get the words out of my head, and each time I saw those words, the agony moved deeper. Cold spread with icy fingers through my chest, stinging and freezing as it went. I didn't know how my heart was still beating, how the blood still drove through my veins, how it wasn't hardened and icy.

I looked at Cassian, *really looked at him,* and I saw him for what he truly was.

A monster.

A beast.

I'd rather Corvina, at least you saw her fangs coming. But not the Sinful...no, they were manipulative and wicked. They pulled you in, made you...made you...*made you* want *them.*

"Asena, what's troubling you?" Cassian took a step closer and lifted his hand.

My body moved on its own, heart thundering, even as it shattered into a million pieces. I stepped backwards until my spine hit the bookshelf, and cowered from his touch.

He froze, his brow furrowing, dark eyes glinting. "Asena?" he whispered.

I hated my name on his lips. I wished to hell he'd never said my name. I wanted it wiped from his memory...and the memory of him wiped from me.

I wanted the perfection of his lips to burn like fire.

His seductive whispers in my head to die and decay.

I wanted the hardness of his body under mine to be cruel and brutal. *Taking me without an ounce of care.* So help me God, I wanted to hurt him just as much. I clenched my fist by my side as the image of that drifted to the surface. I'd hit him. I'd hit and bite and scratch.

No. I wouldn't.

I'd use him like he used me.

I'd tear the clothes from his body. I'd make him stand there naked before me. I'd ride his cock. I'd take and take and take, and then maybe that hollow inside me that yearned for all of them would be full.

But instead of being filled with their love.

It'd be full with my hate.

I'd take a piece of them, like they'd taken a piece of me. I'd become a beast...nothing more than a monster. Sinful. Ashamed. I waited for tears to fill my eyes, but there was nothing. I was empty, void of even a single...*goddamn...tear.*

"Did you think I wouldn't find out?" The words were barely a whisper.

His eyes widened, and Chaska's voice shrilled from further in the hallway. Screams echoed, screams of rage and anguish. Cassian bared his teeth and growled. He lifted a hand and stabbed a finger through the air at me. "I don't know what the hell you're talking about, but I'm going to find out. Stay right there. Do. Not. Move."

The screams from the others grew louder, *insistent.* But I was done with obeying his commands. *I was done with it all.*

I turned, giving him my back, and that savage sound deepened. But he was gone in an instant, leaving me alone. *Leave.* The need swallowed me. *Leave this place and never return.*

I sucked in a breath and looked around.

No, the word was a roar in my mind. *Not until I have some goddamn answers.*

I stumbled from the study, and back along the hall. They'd burned the books to hide them from me. But maybe they hadn't burned them all?

Maybe there was something else? My pulse raced. I spun, scanning the darkened hallways, and still I couldn't escape the sound of Chaska's voice. Her words repeating over and over…

Maybe they aren't into you anymore?

Maybe they aren't into you anymore?

Maybe they aren't into you anymore?

I clenched my fist tighter, driving my nails into the flesh of my palm. The sting saved me from unraveling. I wanted something…something more than the lies that spilled from their lips.

The old woman's letter. Maybe there were more…I spun, my heart leaping as I hurled myself down the hallway to where they slept. I was desperate enough to take anything, any piece of information. My steps boomed inside the hallway and filled my head.

I was in a precarious position, and this time it had nothing to do with fangs or control.

This time, it had everything to do with my heart.

"*Asena!*" Cassian roared.

He was coming for me. I could feel him tearing through the study, like a hound on the scent of blood. The stampede in my chest was a thousand horses, trampling and kicking, bruising me from the inside. I spun, scanning the hallways, losing my way for a second.

*Asena…*Cassian's voice cut through my mind. *Stop this…stop.*

"Get the fuck out of my head," I snapped, and stumbled, throwing my hand against the wall.

I pushed off the wall and ran, losing my sense of direction. I didn't care where I was running now, didn't care about the need to understand. I just wanted out of there, and away from them.

I ran from the Vampires, only now it was for a different reason.

Asena. Arkyn's stony voice slipped through my mind. *Stop running. Stop this panic. Tell us what's upset you.*

They couldn't feel it, not this pain, or this anguish. I slammed my palm between my breasts, and pressed down, trying to still the ache. They couldn't feel my heart, even as it broke.

Find the woman.

Chaska. Chaska with her snide comments, Chaska who'd betrayed me more than once, luring me to that shed--and now...taking then from me.

I ran until my legs shook and my lungs burned, and found myself in a part of the manor I'd never been in before. A part that made me stop and stare.

It was all glass...every bit of it, from the walls to the ceiling, where stars sparkled overhead. It was an atrium. A giant glass dome designed to let in the light. The air was sweet, and sultry, and warm.

I sucked in great gulps of air and tried to slow the roar inside my head.

Asena. Tell us where you are. Arkyn's voice tried to pierce through my mind.

I closed my eyes and focused on shutting him out. I'd not let him take another thing from me, not my innocence, and not my mind.

I'd come here for revenge. I came to avenge the death of my parents, and somewhere along the line, I'd lost sight of that. I really was as gullible as Jacob had said I was.

So stupid.

So fucking stupid.

I balled my hand pressed in the center of my chest into a fist and yanked it through the air, unleashing a punch.

The blow hit my cheek, and an ache followed, beating like a pulse. But still it wasn't enough, not hard enough…not painful enough.

My fist trembled as I wrenched it back once more and released again. I closed my eyes as my knuckles hit, the impact thrusting my head to the side. Pain flared, spreading along the bone and into my eye.

Relief followed. I was pain. I was agony. I was lost in the sensation. I pressed my hand to the throb and pushed them out of my head, and out of my heart.

I'd come for justice.

I'd come for revenge.

Do not move from there, Cassian growled. *Asena, do you hear me? I'm coming to find you. I'm coming.*

I lowered my hand and reached into my boot. I'd come for justice for the parents that'd been taken from me. Parents I'd known, not lies they told me. I held onto that now and dragged the knife from my boot. I remembered the woman who'd taken care of me when I scraped my knees, and sang to me when I couldn't fall asleep.

I remembered the jovial man who'd gone to work out in the forest and worked all day, cutting down tree after tree. I remembered Jacob and the way he was at our house more than he was at his own.

I remembered the life I'd had. The simple, innocent life standing in the light. I'd been so strong then, so sure of myself. I gripped the handle of the knife and stepped backwards, waiting for the beasts to find me.

Freedom waited in the depths of my blade. I sank into that

feeling. There was no pain down there, no sting of betrayal, no hunger for their touch, no nothing.

Just movements, practiced movements.

A blur of motion tore through the doorway, then slowed.

"Asena," Cassian's eyes glinted as he called my name.

But he couldn't see me, not all of me. I stood partially hidden in the shadows, my hand with the knife unseen at my side.

Movement came into the corner of my eye from one of the other doorways leading into the atrium.

"Where is she?" Arkyn growled, and scanned the darkness...and stilled on me. There was a flare of desperation in his eyes, of something quite fragile. Lorcan swept into the room behind him, his hair disheveled, wide eyes searching the shadows until he found me.

And that battleground in my chest gave a roar.

They were here, all of them...ready for me.

I clenched my fist around the hilt and, sliding my hand behind me, stepped forward.

They never glanced at my hand, never even wondered what I was hiding. All three of them surged forward with desire and desperation in their eyes.

"You scared the hell out of us," Arkyn snarled, striding forward like the alpha he was.

"Talk to us," Cassian urged. "What were you trying to say to me? *Did we think you wouldn't find out* what?"

Arkyn flinched at the words, and lifted his hand toward me, slowing his steps. "What's got you rattled, Asena? Talk to us."

Find the woman...

The words rattled around in my head. But it was the grainy black and white photograph that made me shake.

"Hell, you're shivering," Arkyn growled. His fingers moved fast, unbuttoning his jacket before he shrugged it free in an instant and stepped closer.

"Don't." The word slipped from my lips before I could stop it. "Don't touch me. Don't come close to me. I want...*I want...*"

He stilled, eyes widening. There was a second where his brow furrowed, and that pressure in my head increased. It was him, trying to open my doors wide, trying to figure out what was going on.

"Get the fuck out of my head, Arkyn," I snapped, and slammed the steel doors down inside my mind, shutting him out.

I stared at them, all standing there with heartache in their eyes.

"I hate you," I spat the words and took a step closer. "I wish I'd never laid eyes on you."

Those dark eyes glinted from each one of them. But there was a dullness now. A hardness that hadn't been there a second ago. Arkyn swallowed, throat muscles working. Lorcan gave a tiny shake of his head, like he couldn't quite believe what I was saying.

"Of all the women you brought here, why did you pick me?" The fresh ache bloomed in my chest. "If you wanted Chaska all along, then why use me? Why toy with me? Why break my goddamn heart? Why not just take her?"

There was a hiss of pain. Cassian shook his head, as though he refused to hear the truth. With the pain came that dark need inside me, the one that wanted to hurt them like I hurt.

"You fucked me...forced yourself on me. You did things...you did things to me I'd *never* let another living soul do to my body. You made me..." The horror and the pain in their eyes sealed the deal. I held the knife by my side and reached up with my other hand to grasp the neckline of my dress.

I wanted to end it, end this misery, end this torture. No more lies, no more...*Sinful.*

With a brutal yank, I tore the neckline of that painfully plain dress. The thin fabric gave way, tearing down the middle, exposing my breasts.

The cold night air reached out with a lover's touch. My nipples tightened with an icy brush. "You wanted me like this, didn't you? Wanted me craving you…wanted me desperate for you, wanted me…l—"

Arkyn's fangs punched from his mouth at the sight. The jacket slipped from his hand to hit the floor as Lorcan and Cassian both surged forward.

"Asena," Arkyn whispered, his lips moving over the long, tapered points. "I don't know what you—"

"*I know everything!*" The shrill sound of my voice made me flinch.

My hand was trembling, nails poised over my chest. I dug in and clawed the flesh all the way over the tender skin of my nipple.

Arkyn was mesmerized by the movement as the sting followed. Blood welled in the gouges and the heady scent of my own blood filled the air.

"I know she is the one you want. I know she is the one Corvina was meant to find."

"No!" Cassian exclaimed, and stepped forward, coming closer than Arkyn.

Reflex took over. I wrenched the knife upwards in my other hand, but instead of pointing the blade at them, I spun the handle, and pressed the sharp point to my own chest. "You wanted me hurt…you wanted me bleeding. Then you've succeeded."

With cold, savage control, I thrust my hand into the air, gripped the hilt, and plunged the knife toward my chest.

12

"*N*o!" Arkyn's roar filled my ears.

I was hit from the front and my hand wrenched to the side, before the clatter of the knife followed.

Silver sparkled in the moonlight as the blade spun on the stony floor and came to rest. My one hope for salvation now gone. I hated him for that.

"*No!* Do you hear me?" Arkyn gripped my chin and tore my gaze to his. His wide eyes were filled with terror. "Never that...*never that!*"

"*Find the woman!*" I screamed at him, unleashing my pent-up rage. "That's what they told Corvina. She came to you to fight for her, didn't she? She came to make you lead her great goddamn army against the Dragons. But she had a fail-safe in case you said no. Did you know that?"

His grip relaxed around my wrist. Still he held my jaw, and I saw why Corvina wanted him. The savagery that dwelled in those eyes chilled me to the bone. But I was too far gone to care about all the death that lingered in those bottomless pits.

My heart wanted to lash out.

"In case you didn't *heel like a good little Vampire,* she was to find...*the woman.*" A harsh bark of laughter tore from my lips and rebounded in the room. "The woman you supposedly loved. But you found her. She was right under my nose all along. I saw the image, Arkyn...I saw you standing with a woman who looked exactly like Chaska."

He shook his head and dropped my wrist.

"You hurt me," I bit out. "You hurt me so much, I don't know who I am anymore."

A wounded sound escaped from his lips.

"I feel like part of me is dying, standing in front of you. I want to hurt you. I want to hurt you like you hurt me. *This* is what you've done."

I lashed out, hitting his cheek with a *slap.* He never flinched, never moved. His stony gaze stared back at me. *Uncaring. Cruel.* Poison spilled from that dark pit inside, infecting and festering, making me lower my hand. "Take off your clothes."

"What?" Arkyn whispered.

I knew what it was now. That hatred. That *hurt.*

Jealousy.

"Take your clothes off, or so help me God, I *will* leave this place and you'll never see me again."

Surprise flared in Arkyn's eyes. But it wasn't just him I wanted. They'd *all* hurt me. They'd all made me want them...they'd all made me love them.

I stilled with the word and the knowledge sank like a stone.

Love...I loved them.

Arkyn slowly lifted his hand to the first button on his shirt. "You're wrong about—"

"Shut up." I shook my head. "Just shut up. I don't want to hear the lies. I'm tired of them...the lies and deceit. I want to be done with you. I want this and then I'm done. If you don't do this, I'll hate myself forever. *But I'll hate you more.*"

"Take me." Cassian's voice was thick and husky. "If you want someone to hate, then hate me."

That icy heart of mine cracked open. "I do hate you. I hate you so much, I can't think straight. I hate you so much, I can't sleep. I hate you so much, there's a constant ache inside me, and I can't eat without thinking about you...about all of you. You're in my veins, in my dreams. So this is me ending this. This is me saying goodbye. I want you to get undressed and I'm going to ride you. I'm going to have my fill of all of you, and when I'm done, you won't see me anymore."

Arkyn shook his head. "I forbid you to leave."

"YOU FORBID NOTHING!"

My scream was a crack of thunder. But the storm was still trapped inside. There was a tremble in my words, a painful longing. I tried to hold to the last thread of dignity I had left.

And this was how I'd exorcise them from this relentless hunger inside me.

Heat bloomed between my thighs as Cassian slowly unbuttoned his shirt and peeled the fabric from his skin. He shone under the moonlight, perfect and strong, powerful shoulders tapering to his waist. His stomach rippled, the muscles cording and releasing as he lowered his hand to the waistband of his trousers...and that hair. That long, glorious midnight hair fell forward.

My pulse sped as Cassian stepped closer. Only this time, there was no cocky swagger. This time, there was only sadness and despair. "I *never* wanted to hurt you. I never wanted you to feel anything more than desired and loved. But if you're looking for someone to hate, then let it be me."

He was the first Vampire who'd kissed me. The first who'd turned my world upside down. The first who took my breath away, so it seemed only fair.

"You're consenting to sex?" I needed to make sure he understood what was happening here.

"I'll always consent to you." Cassian peeled open the front of his trousers and let them fall.

He was naked underneath, and fully erect. His cock thick and long, standing straight out from between his thighs. My breath caught at the sight. I took in the fearsome sight of him naked in front of me and then lifted my gaze to meet his eyes.

He wanted me. He ached for me...he was hurting as much as I was. "Lie down," I commanded.

But the words were not my own. I wasn't this cruel, sadistic person. I wasn't the kind of person who took things because I wanted then, not caring about their feelings. But here I was, stepping forward. I hiked up the skirt of my dress and yanked down my panties, letting them fall at my feet before I stepped free.

He dropped to his knees in front of me as I neared, and lifted his hands. His fingers ran along the outside of my thighs before I stepped away. "No. Don't touch me. You don't get to do that. It's me...it's only me."

One nod of his head and he was quiet.

"Lie on your back," I demanded.

Lean muscles stretched as he leaned backwards. I gripped my dress and parted my thighs, straddling his body before I sank lower and reached for his ready length. He closed his eyes as my fingers curled around the base of his cock, and a slow hiss echoed through the air around me.

I wanted them to watch. I wanted them to hate. I wanted them to feel the sting of betrayal that I'd felt. I scooted closer, spread my thighs wide. The thick head of his cock pressed against my core, and I was done with waiting, and wanting. I held him steady, and with one growl, I sat down on his erection...hard.

His grunt echoed with mine, and it was followed by a threatening roar from Arkyn. The master Vampire strode closer, his gaze riveted to mine. I held onto his stare and rolled my hips, grinding against Cassian.

I was a monster just like them in that moment. I was a

pitiless, remorseless, reckless animal. I ground myself onto Cassian, riding his body with every savage thrust until that ache inside met the fire. Arkyn sank to his knees beside me and gripped my jaw, forcing me to hold his stare.

With a guttural growl, he yanked my skirt to the side and lowered his gaze to where our bodies collided. A surge of power tore through me as he watched. I wanted him to see the slick my body left behind. I wanted him to *need and seethe.* I wanted him to see me riding Cassian's cock every time he looked at him.

The same way I saw those words in my head.

Find the woman...

"Harder," the command slipped from his lips.

Still, he never looked away from the juncture of my slit and the length of Cassian's erection as I took my fill. *"I said, harder."*

His hand clenched around my jaw, just enough to shock me. I pumped my hips and Cassian's length gorged me, stretching me wider, driving deeper, working the spot inside my body that made me gasp and groan. I leaned forward, using the friction to climb that crest inside me.

Moonlight spilled through the glass ceiling of the atrium and over Cassian as he looked at me. His dark eyes glinted, but there was only love in them for me, only desire, only the same craving I had inside me.

"Do you see?" Arkyn demanded, pulling my focus to his gaze. "Do you see now?"

I stilled, heart pounding, breath escaping. The air rushed in and the tears flowed. They didn't hate me, no matter what I did to them...no matter if I used them. "She wasn't me." The words spilled free as slick tears raced down my cheeks.

Disgusted, I climbed from Cassian's body, leaving the sheen from my hatred on his body behind.

"She has always been you." Arkyn growled, and shoved his hand into his pocket, drawing the faded black and white image free. I stiffened at the sight.

Arkyn closed his eyes and inhaled hard before skimming his tongue across the sharp points of his fangs. Then with ferocious clarity, he lunged forward, faster than I could track, and in the gentlest way, drove me backwards. My ass hit the ground, and he was between my legs before I realized, holding that black and white image in front of my face. "Look at it."

I shook my head. He was nothing but a blur through the sheen of tears. "No."

"*Look. At. It.*" He hurt me then, his fingers squeezing the flesh of my cheeks until it ground against my teeth. But it was the surge of his hips, and the hard ridge that surge revealed, that made me stiffen.

My eyes went to the grainy image, and yet still, all I could see was Arkyn standing next to Chaska with a lovesick smile on his lips.

"She wasn't me!" I tasted blood with the words, as though they ripped me raw.

"No, *she wasn't.* But look in my eyes, Asena, and see the woman I looked at all those years ago. Let me give you a goddamn hint, it's the same woman I look at today."

His lips slid back from his teeth, those wicked fangs ready to rip and kill. Only his eyes shone, not with hatred, but with a determination that blinded me.

I saw myself in the reflection. I saw my wide eyes, my parted lips. I saw shimmering tears and pale skin.

"You are the *only* woman I *ever* looked at. *Look!*" he roared. "Tell me who you see?"

I shook my head.

"*TELL ME!*"

"I see me." I cried, and closed my eyes. "I see me. But that isn't me."

"Yes, it is. Who do you think is taking the photograph?" he growled, and lowered his head to the curve of my neck.

The heat was gone from his words, leaving desperation

behind. "Who do you think I look at?" When he lifted his head, a blood red tear slipped from the corner of his eye. "Look at the picture again, Asena. I beg of you. Look at the picture again and know the truth."

The world seemed to tilt. I was sliding, falling off the axis, as I blinked my tears away and turned my gaze once again to the image. It wasn't the lens he looked at. His focus was shifted from center...to the person behind the camera.

The woman he loved. *Yes,* that was what reflected in his eyes...that was what reflected in all of their eyes. Not betrayal, not cruelty...but love.

Love for me.

"Yes," he whispered. "Now you see it."

He let go of my jaw to slide his hands along my cheek and spear them through my hair. "Don't you know there's nothing we wouldn't do for you? Nothing we won't endure...*nothing we won't give you?*"

I shifted my gaze to Cassian, who'd pushed up from the floor and now rested on his elbows, his cock still hard and ready.

"You want our bodies? They're yours, any way you want them. You want to use us...we'd love nothing more to see the pleasure on your face and feel your body quake above us."

"Who am I to you?" the words slipped free. "Tell me, who am I?"

Arkyn lifted his head and met my gaze. "The woman we love, the one we'd lay down our lives to protect. You want the truth? Yes, Corvina wanted me to fight for her, and yes, we tried to protect you, but she would've eventually found you, and then..."

He stopped, but he didn't need to finish. I knew what would've happened...it was the same thing that did happen.

"Chaska." I murmured. "How...why?"

"Arkyn." Lorcan stepped forward. "We don't have time for this. We need to get rid of all the evidence. They'll come for her.

It might take days...might even take weeks, but we need to be ready when they do."

They? Arkyn's gaze clouded with purpose as he slowly gave a nod. "I will answer your questions, I promise. Just not tonight."

"Then tomorrow?" Hope surged inside me.

He leaned close. "Tomorrow. I promise. Can I trust you to keep yourself safe?"

Heat raced to my cheeks. I felt like such a damn fool.

"But Chaska can never know about this, okay? She doesn't...doesn't remember. Not yet, anyway. So, you stay close to her, but I want you to stay on your guard."

He met my gaze, drove his hips forward in a slow thrust between my thighs, and then pulled away with a look of longing. He shoved upwards, then bent to pick up something from the floor, and reached out his hand for me.

"As much as I'd love to drive this steel into the ground for ever lying against your skin, I need you to keep it. But you must promise me to never...*ever*...try to harm yourself again. I almost lost you...I cannot lose you again. That's a fate worse than death."

"I promise." He grasped my hand and lifted me from the ground. Cassian followed, yanking on his trousers once more. Arkyn stepped close, pressed the blade into my hand, then leaned down and licked the deep gouges on my breast.

I shivered as his tongue ran from my collarbone over my nipple. My hand fluttered, landing on his shoulder as he drew my peak into his mouth. I clenched my other hand around the hilt of the blade and never wanted this feeling to stop.

I was in love with them.

Hopelessly...*dangerously* in love.

"Now, you need to get back to your room before I tear that dress from your body and make you remember all the delicious ways we've had you."

My breath caught with the images in my mind as Arkyn

tucked my breast into the ripped neckline of my dress. But it still gaped.

"Here." Cassian stepped closer, holding out his white shirt, and slipped my arms into the sleeves. He took the opportunity to leaned down and murmur in my ear. "Next time, I want a replay of what we just did. I want to look up at you in the moonlight and see that look of determination on your face as you climax...*over and over again.*"

With that, he buttoned the front of his shirt, then grabbed the tails and, in a neat tie, cinched it around my waist. "You could wear a potato sack and still be the most ravishing woman in the room."

He gave me a soft, seductive smile. I couldn't help but chuckle.

Because they were telling the truth.

Lorcan stepped closer, then reached up and caressed my cheek, before kissing me. His lips moved on mine as he pulled away. "I promise you, when this is over, it's just us...it's always going to be us."

I nodded, hating the way my chest hurt as he stepped away...as *they all stepped away.*

"Hurry now," Arkyn urged. "Straight to your room and put that knife back in your boot."

I nodded, bent, and slid the blade back into place before stepping past them and through the door. Questions filled my head. *Who were 'they' and what did they want with me?*

Days, Lorcan said. In days they might be here...

Tomorrow. Tomorrow I'd get the answers I needed. Tomorrow I'd figure out what I could do. I was done being helpless. If Arkyn and the others needed to fight, then I wanted to fight, too.

I walked until the hallways became familiar, and then picked up my pace, hurrying to my room. But as I turned into our hallway, I saw a flash of brown hair at the far end of the hallway by the door that led to the kitchen. The same way we'd used to go outside.

I raced forward, my boots loud on the stony floor, and followed her into the empty kitchen, entering just as she slipped past the door that led outside.

Polaris raced through the darkness of the woods in the distance, her brown curls streaming out behind her as she clutched her cloak close.

A twig snapped somewhere, but I was too busy stepping forward, the words, *Polaris no! Don't leave,* trapped in the back of my throat.

But that was where they stayed. I sucked in those words as I watched her race for the trees. She would be gone by the morning, heading back home to her sister, maybe.

I felt the loss as keenly as I would my own flesh and blood. She was the only one I felt a connection with.

Footsteps padded softly.

A breath in my ear.

A hand closed over my mouth before I had a chance to scream, and black was shoved over my eyes.

"This is the one I saw through the glass with the Vampires." The words were a savage growl.

I kicked and bucked and screamed against the icy hand muffling the sound. Pain lashed my head, sharp and cruel...like a kick. Darkness swallowed me, racing from the depths of my mind.

Arkyn! I screamed inside my head. *Arkyn...*

Then, I knew no more....

BOOK FOUR

1

---

ootsteps echoed behind me. The rush of a heavy breath followed, dragging my gaze from Polaris as she raced across the front gardens of the castle, leaving us behind.

A scuffing sound came from somewhere near me.

"Chaska, is that you?" I turned to find her.

Darkness took me by surprise. Black cloth slid against my cheek and wound around my neck.

"What are you doi—" I fought for air, clawing the binding around my throat.

"This is the one I saw through the glass with the Vampires." The words were a savage growl. A man's voice...a *stranger's* voice.

I bucked and punched out as an icy hand slammed against my mouth, muffling the sound. *Arkyn!* I screamed inside my mind. *Arkyn...*

Pain lashed my head, sharp and cruel, and my knees buckled. I tried to catch my breath and moaned.

"I wouldn't try that again," another male growled in my ear. "Not unless you enjoy pain."

My heart thundered as I stumbled backwards and my feet were wrenched from under me. *ARKYN!* I caught a flicker of Arkyn's mind, but he was snatched away by the cleaving roar of agony, leaving me alone.

Run...run now, desperation soared.

I shoved against the hands around my arm and wrenched my hand back to strike. *"Get off me! GET OFF ME!"*

But my blows were useless. My fists struck a muscled chest before someone grabbed my wrists. Hands were everywhere, one slid around my neck and yanked me forward until I hit a hard body.

"I can smell them all over you," my attacker snarled. "Mortal *whore.*"

The words were a bucket of icy water.

My blows stopped, panic narrowed down to a single thought. This was no normal attack...they wanted me...to get back at the Sinful. I dragged in a breath and the bag over my head with it. They were going to hurt me...because of the Vampires I loved. That thought drove me harder. I fought like a wildcat, kicking and screaming as they carried me away.

Cassian!

A searing unseen dagger plunged through my head, buckling my knees. I dropped to the ground, before I was wrenched to my feet, cruel fingers gripped me...crueler words followed.

"I told you not to do that," the male growled.

Tears welled and sobs caught in the back of my throat. I tried to remember what happened. The atrium...pain sliced through my heart. Chaska's face filled my mind for a second, and my heart thundered in response. They didn't want her. *They didn't love her.*

But this wasn't about her...

*Corvina...*the Vampire's name rose in my mind, and terror followed.

We'd killed her...we killed her and got rid of the body. Her memory burned through me like wildfire. She was the reason...she was why they were here. It had to be.

The black and white photo filled my mind, and the letter that accompanied it. *If you cannot encourage him to return with you, then find the woman. You find her...and you will control Arkyn.*

Corvina was sent to find Arkyn. My slow, panicked thoughts finally pieced everything together… she wanted him to lead an army against the Dragons.

And if he refused...then she'd use me to do it.

Me.

Not Chaska.

The past rose with cold clarity. Fingers clenched around my arms and gripped my ankles. I was carried over the pebbles until the sound gave way to silence. This had been her plan all along, force him to fight for her, or else…

It just so happened to be that *'else'* was me. I'd been a toy for her, someone she could manipulate.

The image. Had she known all along I'd find it? Was her plan to slip it to me in some dark hallway and pretend to care while my heart broke in two at the sight of Chaska standing there smiling next to them, and not me?

Cruel. So fucking cruel. My heart still ached from that hopelessness.

But I knew the truth now.

I'd felt it in their kiss.

I'd seen it in their eyes, in the pain of their desperation.

They loved me.

The wanted me.

They chose me.

The snap of a twig was all I needed to get my bearings. We were in the gardens that backed onto the forest. We were close...so close. A surge of desperation clawed its way along my throat. They could still get to me...they could still save me. I was jolted and bounced. My teeth gnashed, yanking me from the thought, until the soft nicker of a horse sounded.

They were taking me away...away from *them*.

"No!" I kicked my foot and was rewarded with a grunt. I tried again, yanking my foot backwards. *"Cassian!"* I roared. *"CASSIAN!"*

A blow slammed into my jaw, snapping my head to the side. White sparks flared behind my eyes as that low, merciless growl demanded, "Do that again and I'll hurt you so much, you'll beg for death."

Cloth slammed against my lips as I sucked in hard breaths. In a daze, I was lifted and thrown through the air. My dress flapped wildly. The white shirt Cassian had given me slapped against my neck. I hit the floor of a carriage with a hard *thud*, knocking the air from my lungs. I tried to gasp and suck in a breath, but none came. Tiny gasps bowed my belly, until, in a savage wheeze, cold air rushed in.

The carriage shot forward, the horse moving quietly. I sucked in heavy breaths.

There was only one.

One horse. One driver...*one man to hold me down.* I focused on my breaths, and tried to think. The carriage rocked and swayed as we moved. I could hardly tell which way was up, still, I shoved my boots against the floor of the carriage and lunged, driving myself through the open doorway, and toppled out.

Air rushed up to greet me, until I hit the ground with a brutal *thud*. I rolled, thrust my hands out in front of me, and shoved against the ground.

A roar came behind me, panicked and pissed off. The sound was all I needed. I shoved my boots into the packed earth and tore the black hood from my head, until, in an instant, I was yanked from the ground.

Hooves thundered, trampling the ground. I screamed and

kicked, but my abductor never made a sound, just gripped me around the waist. "Let me go!" I screamed. *"Let me go!"*

My feet jolted, head snapping back and forth as the horse picked up speed.

"Sire." The rough familiar snarl came from my attacker.

"Here, lose her again and you lose your head," my captor threatened.

Silence claimed me. I was handed over like a rag doll and sat inside the carriage once more. There were more of them...more men to hunt me.

More men to make Arkyn fight in their war.

"Why are you doing this?" I forced the words through my fear.

The horse whinnied and stepped forward. The air grew thick and hostile as I sucked in hard breaths and waited for an answer. But all that came was the snorting sounds of the horse, and the galloping thunder as the beast shot forward.

The carriage pulled ahead with a jerk. I turned around, only to be shoved forward. Pain flared through my wrists as I shoved them out and hit the floor before a boot pressed against the middle of my back. "One more attempt like that, and I'll drag you behind with a noose around your throat, like the filthy slut you are."

Terror speared through me.

Real terror.

The kind where your life danced on the edge of a blade.

I stayed silent this time, as the carriage jolted and bounced. Tears came, sticking the hood to my eyes and my cheeks. He hated me...truly hated me, and not for who I was...but for what I'd done.

Love.

That's why he hated me...he hated me for love. I clenched my eyes closed and splayed out my hands, rocking with the movement of the carriage. The feel of his boot at my back was crushing. He never let up, not when the sounds of snapping branches from the forest floor gave way to the quiet worn path of a dirt road.

But the pressure was in my chest, wrapped around my heart like barbed wire. The motion of the carriage lulled me, pulling me away from the sounds of the night all around us to the hurt inside.

Would Arkyn look for me?

No. He expected me to be in my room and fast asleep. Chaska was the only one who knew I wasn't there. Would she come looking? A surge of desperation cut through me. My emotions were a turbulent storm inside me as the black and white image surfaced once more.

I had more questions than answers. Why was Chaska in the photo? And why had Arkyn warned me against her? I tried to think as the carriage jerked and swayed. My stomach tightened the more I thought about it. For some strange reason, I had a feeling that was important.

That that seemingly insignificant image was at the heart of everything in my life. The carriage turned. I spread out my fingers, trying my best to remember how long we'd been travelling.

Too long.

The answer was choking. "Where are you taking me?"

There was no answer, not that I'd expected any. I turned my focus to everything I remembered; from the page I'd torn from the Sinful ledger to the Vampire I'd helped kill. But the problem was, I didn't know truth from lie.

All I knew was what my heart said...and also my fear.

I opened my mind and reached out to Cassian with a tiny flicker of hope. *Please hear me...I love you.*

I waited for a response as the horses galloped and the night grew colder.

But none came. My teeth chattered, and the feel of the boot at my back seemed to melt away.

"Cold," I whimpered. "I need a blanket…"

There was no mercy. No warmth.

Nothing but a shift on the seat, and that numb pressure at the middle of my back. The gnashing of my teeth made my jaw ache. I clenched my mouth still and tried to shift, to curl my body.

Slow, savage movements dragged my knees toward my chest. I opened my eyes and tried to see through the weave. His boot wasn't in the middle of my back…how long? How long had that aching feeling been nothing more than a phantom?

I pulled my knees closer and gripped them tight.

The knife.

My breath caught. The chatter stopped for a second.

"Hey, you dead?" A jab of his boot at my side made me moan. "Fine. Here."

Something heavy was thrown over me. A blanket…one that stank like horse. But it was better than nothing. I reached up with trembling fingers and tugged it all the way from under my chin and kicked out with my boot to shove the covering lower.

The rough fabric scratched against my skin, but still, I clutched it like it was my last hope. Time slipped away under the thunderous hooves of the horses.

I shuddered and shook, my knuckles burning with the chill as I was carried to somewhere I didn't know. My breaths were a countdown. I timed each movement to the rush of air and slowly dragged my knees higher as I slid my hand down the outside of my leg to the secret hollow on the inside of my boot.

The horses snorted, and the wind howled. I inched my shaking fingers down, my muscles jerking and quaking. I used the tremors to hide the movements until my fingers skimmed the top of the knife hilt.

The carriage turned once more, and then once again.

I was lost, confused. The tips of my shaking fingers skimmed the cold steel of the blade. I pinched the edges of the hilt and dragged the weapon free as the horses picked up speed once more...and slowly...*slowly* I pulled the knife to my chest.

"You still alive?" A kick to my foot made me jump as a cy tore free.

"Just stay that way...that's all I need you is alive."

I clutched the blade to my chest as the roar of hooves filled my ears.

Stay alive. That's all I thought of...all that consumed me. Stay alive long enough for my Vampires to come.

I lost track of time while the horses snorted and galloped through the darkness. I was a long way from hope, or any flicker of warmth. But when the call came from the driver to slow, a surge of heat tore through me. I could do this. I could fight and survive. I could find a way back to Arkyn.

I could find a way back to hope.

I gripped the hilt of the knife as the horses turned hard. My back slammed against the boarding. I dared lift my head.

"*Whoa!*" the driver roared, slowing the carriage.

My heart thundered, filling my head with a deafening boom as the horses pulled up hard. The carriage shuddered as it settled on its springs.

This was it....

I gripped hilt...

"Hey. Time to move," my captor snarled.

I waited, shivering and terrified, and lowered my hand when the blanket was yanked free. My muscles trembled, my mind slow to respond. But when he kicked me, I shoved upwards and lashed out.

The knife carved air before it sank deep. A grunt was followed with a bellow so loud it ripped like thunder through the air. "*Fucking bitch!*"

I didn't wait, and yanked the hood free before lunging for the open carriage door once more.

"Fucking whore bitch!"

My trembling hands slipped on the doorframe as I hit the step and then the ground. But he was right behind me, snarling like a Wolf, ready to tear me limb from limb. Hinges on the carriage howled before the wheels bounced. I heard a grunt before I plunged forward and sank in the cold, filthy quagmire.

He hit me like a horse at full gallop. I was slammed to the ground, the mud swallowing my hand and my knife along with it.

"Where the fuck is it?" he howled, and yanked my hair.

My head snapped upwards, the darkness a blur under the sheen of tears.

"Where's the fucking knife?"

All I saw was his massive fist, driving through the air.

"That's enough." The cold, cutting command stopped the blow.

I blinked and tried to lift my gaze to that voice. It was from the man who'd captured me, the man who'd carried me on horseback back to these vile thieves.

The man who controlled everything.

Mud-coated strands of hair stuck to my face as I lifted my head. Steely eyes stared down at me. The slash of long pale hair was neon in the dark. I tried to focus on him, tried to understand what kind of monster I was dealing with.

But I couldn't.

My gaze was drawn to the towering monolithic mansion behind him. The huge midnight structure consumed the space. Tall towers reached from the corners of the roof, like swords standing upright, ready for war. In the middle of the roof at one end was a gigantic midnight cross, which I figured marked a place of worship, maybe a chapel or temple of some kind.

But this wasn't a place of hope, nor of comfort. This was a place of pain and death.

"I should kill you right here," my captor said above me.

I tore my gaze from the monstrous building behind him and met inhuman eyes. Black irises consumed the whites of his eyes. He looked down on me like I was nothing.

Like I wasn't even here.

But I *was* here, kneeling at his feet in the filth.

I knew in that moment where this would all end, for me...and my Vampires. There was no getting out of this, not anymore.

"Get her up. I want her into the cells before anyone sees."

My warden wrenched his gaze upwards, and stared behind us. Hands grabbed my arms and yanked. My hands tore from the mud, the suction tearing the blade free. My last line of defense now gone.

"Little bitch lost her little blade." The vile pig yanked me toward him. I slammed into his big, brutish body and lifted my gaze to yellow teeth as he sneered. "I'll give you a good poke. How 'bout that. Eh? I'll give you a real good poke."

"That's enough," the pale-haired Vampire snapped. "In the cells...now."

As I was yanked forward, I swore I caught the faint howl of a Wolf behind me in the distance. In the blinding sweep of a midnight cloak, the Vampire above me turned and strode toward the Gothic mansion.

2

"*Wait!*" I roared, and lifted my gaze to my captor as he strode toward the shadowed mansion.

But he never stopped, he never even slowed...he was gone in a heartbeat, leaving me alone with the foul excuse for a man.

"What's he paying you?" I wrenched my gaze to his and his grip tightened around my arm, thick, calloused fingers driving the flesh against the bone hard enough to bruise me.

But I'd never cry and I'd never plead...that was what he wanted.

He smiled a sickening, terrifying smile and shoved me forward. "Move."

There was no negotiating with some men...men like him. It didn't matter the money. He was probably doing this for a warm meal in his belly and a roof over his head. Some men just liked to hurt those who were weaker.

That was what I was now.

Someone weak, someone captured, someone who had no weapon to arm myself with. All I had was my wits, and three Vampires who'd come for me.

They would come...of that my heart was certain.

I looked at him now, this gigantic, festering slug of a man with his cruel, glinting eyes and even crueler hands. "They'll kill you when they come for me, you do know that, don't you? You'll die screaming and I'll enjoy that *very* much."

That flicker dulled in his eyes. His thick, protruding lips curled, pulling away from broken yellow teeth and festering red gums. But there was no witty come-back, no threatening words to give him the strength he needed.

He just shoved me toward the stairs. I stumbled and threw out my arm to save my fall, but the mud gripped tight to my boot, wrenching it free. The suction held tight, holding onto the leather as I hit the ground. I turned, reaching for my boot, and was yanked upwards.

"My boot," I cried as he grabbed the collar of my shirt and shoved me forward once more.

With one boot missing, I stumbled up the slate stairs. Rage mingled with my fear. I was helpless, careening toward this ancient, medieval-looking mansion with its shimmering windows high up in spear-like towers.

I was a slave to circumstance out here in the middle of nowhere. I turned my head and caught a glimpse of the looming obsidian mountains behind us before a fist at my shoulder drove me forward.

"Don't bother, there's nothing but war in those mountains. A little thing like you wouldn't last a day. Then again, you might not last a day here, either."

Breath shot out of me with another blow to my spine. I dropped to my knees on the hard, stony steps, then reached up with trembling hands to the stair above.

"That's it...crawl like the gutter tramp you are."

Tears welled in my eyes. I tried to catch my breath. But fire raged inside me. Burning and searching, I drove my bare foot down against the frigid step as I pushed upright.

A snigger came from behind me. I focused on the step ahead.

My world became that step, narrowed down to the movement of my body. Climb. Climb. Climb…

Higher I went, not daring to lift my gaze to the horror awaiting me. Still, I felt this place like a weight bearing down on me--crushing me from the inside. Heavy steps echoed behind me. His harsh breaths were something that would haunt me forever.

Forever.

It seemed like such a fragile word. I gripped my knee and bore down, using my strength to meet the next stair. I wouldn't give in, not to this place nor to these people.

I'd fight for as long as I could…for as long as I had to until either my will, or my body, broke. The massive wooden front door swung open as I neared the last section of stairs.

But there was no one who stepped out of the darkness…just a rush of dark mist that slipped from inside and was carried on the wind. The piece of shit behind me froze, his breath caught with a wheeze.

Still I climbed, using sheer desperation to get to the top, knowing exactly what he'd do to me if I failed.

My head still burned from his grasp on my hair, and my back from his fists. If there was an excuse to hurt me, he'd find it. So I climbed the stairs to the open doorway and stopped at the top.

My sawing breaths mingled with the howling wind. I sucked in the bitter gust and glanced around at the rolling black mountains all around us. Nothing looked familiar…not even the moon from this height. Even she pulled away from me.

"Inside," my abuser gasped and jerked his head toward the open door.

I followed his command, slipping in through the door to stop in the pitch black.

There were no sounds, no laughter, no chatter. No frantic steps of the maids as they took care of a herd of young women for the Sinful. A tremor tore through my middle as I stood in the doorway to a void. I'd give anything to go back there, to the place that now felt like home.

I wanted to be amongst the others...but most of all, I wanted to be with *them*.

Arkyn. Cassian. Lorcan. The moment they filled my mind, agony carved through my head. I clenched my eyes shut and shoved out a hand to brace myself against the door, feeling their loss drown me.

"Told you not to do that." There was sadistic pleasure in his tone, as the foul male took great delight in my pain. "Soothsayer is not one you want to mess with."

I pulled away from the memory of my Vampires, and the pain slipped away into the abyss inside my mind.

"Walk." He shoved my shoulder.

I stumbled forward not more than a few steps before a torch came to life with the rush of fire further in the darkness. I made my way toward that small burst of heat with slow, tentative steps.

Cold trembled inside me spearing icy fingers deep inside. I lifted my hand as I neared the orange flames of the torch, but the second I came near the warmth, the flames sputtered and went out.

That spiteful chuckle spilled through the air once more. "You'll find no warmth here for you, you nasty slit."

I swallowed the foul names, dragging them into the pit of my stomach. A lump formed at the back of my throat. I swallowed and swallowed as an amber glow flared in the distance and another torch burst into flame.

I dropped my hand and kept walking.

Whore.

Slut.

Slit.

Words and fists were their weapons. But I'd survived worse.

I focused on that torch and kept walking, and this time when I neared, I didn't lift my hand.

"She learns fast."

The torch died away, leaving one more to flare in the emptiness. Like a lamb to the slaughter, I kept following the glow until it stopped outside an open door...and through the doorway came the birth of fire.

Stairs shimmered with flames. A spiral staircase hugged the stony wall, sinking lower until it melted into nothing. This was one of the towers I'd seen, one of the spears stabbing the sky. My feet stopped at the opening of the doorway and refused to move.

"Walk." A fist slammed into my back, shoving me forward.

But I grabbed the doorframe and held on. "No. I'm not going down there."

The cold, bitter stench of pain wafted through the doorway. Terror waited for me down there, terror and death. I knew if I stepped foot down there, I'd never come back.

"I said *move.*"

"No."

My nails sank into the hardwood of the doorframe. My captor clenched his massive paw around my hands. My knuckles crunched, until one popped under the strain.

Agony flooded through my hand, tearing a shriek from my lips.

He pressed his face against the side of my head and growled, "I won't tell you again."

I couldn't move out of fear. "I can't..." Tears slid down my cheeks. "I can't do it."

His grip around my hand eased. In a breath of panic, I envisioned him shoving me into the blackness, leaving me to scream and claw the air until I found my death at the bottom of the well.

At the bottom of the well?

The words drifted from out of nowhere as I was grabbed and shoved through the door. The faint memory of the dream I'd had before rose inside me. Screams burned my throat and rebounded off the walls.

But they were an echo of the screams inside my head.

Howls of terror.

Arkyn! A woman's voice echoed inside me as I hit a steel railing.

"Have you got it?" he snarled.

I could only nod as tears slipped down my face. My feet moved on their own, descending into the darkness. The thud of my boot was followed by the silence of my bare foot. I felt nothing as I gripped the railing and stepped downward.

Heavy steps followed, making me flinch with every thud. I worked my way down until my boot splashed water. The dank, putrid stench of well water filled my nose. I swallowed the air and tried to keep from retching.

"Over there," he snapped.

I lifted my gaze in the murky gloom. Through the darkness, metal bars glinted in the faint moonlight spilling from the windows high above. "What is this place?"

"It's your new home." He shoved me forward.

My bare foot splashed the water until my toes grazed against hard stone. The sting was instant, slicing deep between my toes, but there was no time for tears, no time to swallow the pain. There was only the open cell waiting for me.

"Get inside. If you don't, I'll hurt you."

A numbness swept through me as I stared at the tiny cage. I was pushed inside and the door swung shut before I knew it.

"Wait!" I turned to him, ready to do whatever I needed. "Please don't leave me down here, I'm begging you."

"Now you're ready to beg?" He grinned and stepped toward the bars.

I trembled at the sight of him. I'd faced ravenous Vampires

with nothing more than the sharp edge of a knife and still hadn't been as terrified as I was right now.

But that spark of rage deep in the depths of my mind refused to die. I gripped the icy bars of my cell as he waited for my answer.

"That's what I figured," he finished, then turned and walked away.

The heavy thud of his boots cracked like thunder as he climbed. I gripped the bars and closed my eyes. My world swayed under the rising panic.

With the fading boom of his footsteps came the scurrying of something in the cells around me. Fear bloomed like a deadly rose. I opened my eyes and stared at the tiny room. There was a steel bucket and a rusted metal bedframe shoved into the corner.

Water sloshed at my feet as I stumbled for the skeletal remains of the bed. A dark blur raced along the outside of my cell, followed by a shrill squeak. The rusted metal howled and twanged as I climbed onto the frame and balanced my weight.

Rats scurried through the water on the filthy cellar floor. I curled my bare foot underneath me and wished for my knife.

"They look hungry tonight."

I flinched with the sound of his voice and scanned the darkness. There was nothing, no movement...no shadows, just emptiness. "Who's there?"

Tiny claws scratched, sloshing through water and rasped on the stony floor.

"The rats." The voice came once more, floating out from the corner of the big room. "They look hungry."

Dark mist caught a breath of air. The smoke drifted in tendrils until they gathered substance and, in an instant, became a man in the center of the room.

A cry tore from my lips. I gripped the rusted frame of the bed and shoved backwards. He stepped closer, moving without sound toward the cells. 'I fear the sound of them, as do you, I see."

He stepped into the faint silver glow of the moonlight and stopped. Dark, inhuman eyes tracked my every movement. This was no man...this was a *Vampire*.

"What do you want from me?" I searched for a flicker of warmth in his gaze but found none.

"Answers, that's what I want." He stopped at the locked door of the cell and I had a feeling he could pass right through it if he wanted.

He was nothing more than mist. Nothing more than a cold, heartless, dead *thing*. He'd kill me in an instant and never even blink. I was nothing to him, a means to an end...an answer...

"Where is she?" he murmured. "Where is Corvina?"

I flinched at the question. My hand trembled against the rusted frame, the decrepit thing squealing and howling with the movement. "I don't know."

"*Lie.*"

I shook my head, tears threatening to come. "I'm telling the truth." The image of her dead body lying on the ground floated to the surface of my mind.

I conjured darkness, swallowing the image. If he could turn into a mist, then he could read minds. The thought chilled me to the bone.

"I know you're lying. But unlike you, I have time." He turned his head to the rodents that raced along the floor and whispered, "Have a good night, mortal."

In an instant, he was gone, leaving the whisper of darkness trailing in the air like ribbons. The rats froze, beady black eyes shone as they sniffed the air. But the air had changed, gone was that predatory feeling. They turned their gazes toward me.

One massive rodent stepped forward, leaving the others behind. I stared at the creature as it boldly opened its mouth and unleashed a piercing squeal.

Hunger roared in the shrill sound.

Sickening, ravening hunger.

I slammed my hands to my ears and screamed. Still the terrifying sound found a way inside my head. Images of darkness and blood filled me. It was the same memory I'd had before.

I lay on the rusted bed, cold, terrified, and in pain. The scratching of tiny claws echoed all around me. I knew they'd come for me now, biting and scratching, going for my eyes. *Arkyn...*

The whisper of his name cut through the memory that wasn't my own, tearing me from that desperation and slamming me back into my own body once more.

I lowered my hands. There was silence, no scurrying, no shrieking. Something had frightened them...something—

Through the windows high above the sound came with the wind, haunting and ghostly. It was the howl of a Wolf...

The call of a predator.

One I felt in my bones.

3

I struggled to get out of bed, having no clue how many days had passed. Three, maybe four, they'd all become one big blur. a jumble in my mind. And the more time that passed, the more the knot in my chest tightened.

A clawing sound came from somewhere in the cell, and I turned my head to see a tiny blur dart across the stone floor. Rats. This placed was infested with them.

I had cuts on my hands and tiny bite marks from where I'd fallen asleep and they'd come. I'd known they would...eventually.

My Vampires hadn't come to my rescue, as I'd hoped... Not yet anyway, and it had everything to do with our mind-link, or the lack of it. Pain cut through my head every time I tried to reach them, until I cried with the agony.

A spell, that was the only thing I could think of. The only thing I knew that could poison the mind connection I'd shared with my Vampires. I tried everything I could think of, even trying to reach Chaska in the hopes that she might somehow feel me and convey my desperation to the Sinful.

The only thing that came back was pain, time and time

again. I was alone with these violent creatures, alone and cold and hurting. I gripped my ankle and felt that deep throb grow stronger. The cut on my foot was getting worse. At first, it was the sting of a new wound, then the ache moved deeper, morphing into something far more threatening.

The squeal of hinges came, and I jolted my head up, to see a shadow coming down the stairs. Despite the aches and lethargy claiming me, I pushed my legs out of the worn bed that groaned with my movement and padded across the damp stone floor to the bars. I winced each time I stepped onto the cut on my foot. After losing my boot, I'd stepped on something, and now it stung like hell.

The burning torch on the wall lit up the maid with blond curls approaching. She carried a bowl in both hands, meeting my gaze with a tiny smile. "Evening."

I liked Mary, as she called herself. She looked me in the eyes, talked to me, while the others treated me as less than a rodent.

"I have soup for you today, and I snuck in a piece of bread to put some flesh onto your bones."

"Thank you." I retreated as she set the soup on the floor and unlocked the cell door.

A guard would be standing outside the big room. So even if I could slip past the maid, I wasn't going anywhere. There was only one small window here that hardly let any light in, and it sat high up on the wall in the next prison cell.

Mary entered my cell and handed me the bowl, with a slice of bread and a wooden spoon. I didn't waste time and took a large mouthful of potato soup, savory, and lacking salt and some warmth, but it tasted better than what they'd given me over the past couple of days. I needed to keep up my strength.

The maid studied me with pity in her soft eyes, but said nothing, just stood near the open door.

I tilted my head up, staring into her deep brown eyes. She

was a human, a slave just like me. "They're going to kill me, aren't they?" I whispered.

She winced at the words and cast a nervous glance over her shoulder before she turned to me once more. "They'll kill you on the spot if you try to escape. I've seen the things they do to those who don't follow the rules. It curdles my blood." Fear dulled the shine of her eyes, the kind of fear that was always there...day in, day out. The kind you lived with until you couldn't live anymore.

I pushed more food into my mouth, chewing and swallowing like it was my last meal on Earth. It very well could be. The bread was a large lump in the back of my throat. I swallowed hard and winced as the food went down.

Heavy breaths consumed me. The food hit my stomach, sending shudders of pain through my insides. The last time was a small bite at the party.

The party.

My hands shook as I reached for the last morsel of bread and placed it in my mouth. I chewed more slowly this time, swallowing the pain as well as the food. I was lost here...lost, knowing what had happened to Corvina. My life here hung by a thread, this might even be the last meal I had before they came.

I bit down on the bread and chewed.

"There must be a way to escape," I whispered again, staring at her and wiping my mouth with the back of my hand. "A weakness in the building? A time no one is around? A way out? Please, I don't want to die here."

Her lips pursed, the crease lines deepening at the corners of her mouth, but she was shaking her head, her eyes widening, breath catching. I knew she wanted to talk to me, but she was scared. My insides crumpled with despair.

She studied me hard before answering, "I have never seen anyone escape these Vampires. But if you ever see the chance to escape, you run. Don't look back. Just run like the devil himself is chasing. You understand, girl? Until then, don't fight them. Do as they instruct or they'll hurt you."

I nodded.

Fear gripped her voice, and she wasn't just talking about me, but herself. Something she'd been holding onto for so long. Many took escape for granted in a world ruled by monsters.

"They took my sister," she murmured, almost to herself. "They murdered her in cold blood. I cried for days, until they offered me an option. Serve them, or they had no need for me. I guessed they took pity on me, but they are monsters. And none of us mean a thing to them."

A dark pit of sorrow opened up inside me, and I reach over to touch her hand, to let her know I was there for her, even if just an ear for her to speak freely.

But she shook her head, grumbling like she was angry with herself for opening up old wounds.

She collected the empty bowl and spoon from my hands, turned her back to me, then left. Without a word, she locked the cell and vanished down the hall. Only the squeal of the hinges announced her departure.

I pressed against the cold metal bars as a cough racked through me. My chest ached, my breath making raspy sounds with each exhale. I tried to remain calm, tried to tell myself I'd get out. The prison was cold and run down, it was dark and infested with vermin. It was meant to scare me, but I wasn't giving up.

I hobbled back to the bed and collapsed onto it, drawing my knees to my chest and hugging them. I'd been through so much.

Closing my eyes tight, I tried to summon sleep, but like most nights, I lay in bed awake, and my only distraction was thoughts of my time with the three Vampires. And me praying to survive another day.

I dreamed of them, of dark corners, and soft lips. I dreamed of Cassian and Lorcan and Arkyn. Lightning shattered the night sky in my dream, casting the heavenly glow out into the room. They were between my legs, and at my breast. My fingers were tangled in Cassian's hair as he kissed my neck and murmured, "You belong to us, Asena...forever and always."

I cried in my dream, thick, slick tears slid down my cheek. Their words echoing inside me mingled with the boom of my own heart.

"Get up!" The words punched through me.

I snapped open my eyes to a balding guard who looked like he'd eaten a lion for breakfast, his grubby hand on my arm, dragging me out of bed.

My heart was in my throat, and I scrambled to find my feet. "W-what's g-going on?"

"You've been summoned." Icy cold eyes grazed over my body and my exposed neck. Hunger darkened his gaze.

He wanted me. Wanted my blood...I was his for the taking. So why didn't he take? My father always said there was always someone faster and more dangerous than you out there...maybe it was the same for him?

Maybe that faster and more dangerous Vampire was the one who summoned me now?

No one was safe here, no one. We were all replaceable things. The guards and maids knew that, but they played the game to stay alive for as long as possible.

He hauled me by an arm out of the cell and out of the big room, my injured foot screaming with pain. He didn't pause when we reached the stairs, but pulled me along, despite the dark and that I couldn't see the steps.

I was icy all over, my brain numb, and I acted on pure adrenaline, while panic drummed in my mind.

We moved fast until we reached two doors, splayed open. He shoved me ahead, and I stumbled forward, tripping on a lush red rug.

I fell, my knees slamming the floor, my pulse on fire.

Head tilted back, eyes wide, I stared at the enormous room made of dark wood. A bright half-moon shone through one of the arched windows lining the walls. In front of me were four golden thrones, facing a grand table with carved legs that resembled animal legs and paws.

Golden poles tipped with burning torches surrounded us, tossing shadows, stretching them into hideous beasts. We were inside the section of the castle known as the keep, tall towering walls with a lofty ceiling and expensive windows high up, letting in air, sunlight…and rain. Rain that ran down the inside of the walls. Rain that left everything in here rot. I tried to imagine how majestic this place might've been…if it hadn't have fallen into the hands of the Vampires.

The same three monsters before me on their thrones.

My gaze caught on a man with silver-white hair that seemed to gleam in the light, as did his eyes.

Fear made it difficult to breathe.

On the wall behind the Vampires hung several painted portraits of different heroic warriors in battle gear, on horseback, holding a sword. Then I found a familiar face. Arkyn stared back at me from the largest picture. He stood tall and proud in silver armor splashed in blood, while behind him lay a field with fallen soldiers. Hard jawline, perfect full lips, piercing blue eyes, he hadn't changed one bit. Still gorgeous, but there was a fierceness in his face, a dangerous man who'd take no pity, who'd slaughter without care. That wasn't the Arkyn I remembered.

"He's one of the best and most ruthless warriors," the white-haired Vampire stated. "Singlehandedly massacred a quarter of the Turkish invaders on our land. He's unmatched in the battlefield, unstoppable."

The way he spoke of Arkyn left me both intrigued and scared that Arkyn would kill so many. Except, this Vampire had said Turkish invaders, and my thoughts flew to the stranger who'd invaded Nightingale. The man who'd insisted he was my father, and he'd said he was from across the Black Sea. Turkey lay beyond the sea... I racked my brain, trying to see the connection. Could he have been someone from my family line who fought the Vampire here? That would explain why Arkyn was furious at his arrival, why he chased after him in the woods. But how could he be my father? There was so much I still didn't understand!

The white-haired Vampire flicked a hand at someone behind me.

In a flash, hands were picking me up, and I glanced back at the two guards who drew me closer to him. They lifted me off my feet and lay me on my back on the table in front of the all-powerful Vampires.

My heart was shuddering, and I couldn't stop shaking. "Please don't hurt me."

He rose from his throne with the poise of a Wolf about to strike, staring down at me, pushing some white strands out of his face. Up close, I could see he was older, wrinkles deepening at the corners of his eyes. When he made a hissing sound through his teeth, his pale lips thinned, and I winced, seeing my own death at their hands. They'd kill me here, I knew this, and no one would even be aware of what had happened to me.

"She's too thin," a young man with a long face and thin moustache cooed like he cared. I turned my head, to see him reclining on his throne, legs crossed, dressed in a frilly black shirt with puffy sleeves, black hair slicked off his face. If I wasn't lying there about to be butchered, I might have laughed at how he looked like a pirate, but I didn't care for anything but my own survival. His green eyes raked over me like daggers, and my skin crawled with the way he studied me, like he wanted to do more than feed on me.

"She's not here as our guest," the white-haired monster

snipped, venom in his voice. In a sudden movement, he snatched my wrist and lifted my arm to his nose, sniffing me.

I swallowed my scream and froze. I didn't dare move. He'd kill me in an instant.

Don't fight them. Do as they instruct or they'll hurt you.

Mary's words whirled in my mind.

He hissed and dropped my hand. "He drank from her, I can smell him in her blood."

"So she's not pure. Well, I'm not surprised," the third Vampire murmured, already on his feet and circling the table, running his fingers over my legs, over my dress, up the side of my ribs and over a breast, then to my neck, where he paused. "She's so scared, trembling. Oh, how I love them scared," he muttered, staring at me with a desperation as his tongue flicked out, tracing his long fangs. With short golden hair, he had the palest gray eyes, and I could see in his gaze he was old, ancient He'd been a Vampire for so long, nothing fazed him anymore. So he enjoyed the chase, the game, something all Vampires had in common.

The head Vampire's hand fell to my thigh, fingernails pressing into my flesh. "Tell me, Asena, what befell Corvina? She visited Nightingale, correct?"

I blinked hard, my heart pounding, and already I felt the first trickle of sweat at the nape of my neck. I stared up at the monster, at the wickedness in his expression, and swallowed past the pain traveling up my leg.

"Yes, she came to visit Arkyn," I answered in a soft voice.

"And?" He dug deeper, and I winced.

If I could just get past my nerves, I might be able to lie without looking guilty. I just had to breathe and slow my heart, as they'd detect me panicking. I grasped onto the edges of the table, squeezing harder.

"She left," I said. "She and Arkyn argued and screamed. Then she left."

His eyes narrowed down at me, his fingernails never letting up. Tears pricked my eyes.

"I can tell you're lying." He was shouting now, and the pain was terrible. It fucking hurt so much. My vision faded in and out.

I shouldn't defy them, but surrendering would end in my death. I couldn't tell them, *couldn't.*

Gray-eyes gripped my chin, pinching it as he pushed my head back to stare him in the eyes. I reacted quickly, shuddered, tried to resist, convinced he'd bite my neck.

"You would never lie to us, would you?"

A small cry slipped past my lips unbidden when he huffed in a low sound that came with a grunt of fury. His words sent a flurry of hatred through me, more determined than ever to make them believe me.

I shook my head. "No, never," I whispered. My heart beat erratically.

The other Vampire pulled his nails out of my thigh and glared down at me.

"I didn't see the argument between them," I began. "But the other girls and I saw her storm out. She was furious. She and Arkyn had fought. They both had bloody scratches on their faces and arms."

The lies tumbled from my lips freely, I'd say anything to survive, anything to make them believe me.

Silence fell over us. Too silent.

"Take her back to her cell," the white-haired Vampire barked, and my gut twisted at his sudden outburst.

The guard seized my arm and hauled me off the table so roughly I slid to the ground. But the bastard didn't stop, he dragged me as I stumbled to find my feet.

I glanced over my shoulder at the three Vampires who looked like death to me, and they had their sights on me. They watched me with anger blazing in their eyes. *God, please let them believe my lie.*

My world hinged on that moment. The fantasy came flooding through me, conjured by pure hope. Maybe they'd believe me. Maybe they'd send me back. Maybe they'd throw open the cell's door and let me find my own way?

I'd take that chance...I'd take any chance.

I followed my captor in silence, making my way back to the door that led to the cellar and the cells below. One heavy thud was followed by the muffled tread of my bare feet. "Can I at least have some blankets for warmth?"

"Move." The guard drove me forward with a punch to my back.

I staggered ahead, stumbling down the last stairs, and splashed in the puddles at the bottom. Bile rose in the back of my throat with the sound. "I need fresh water and food. Please, I...." *beg of you.*

Still he made no sound. Just stepped up to the cell door and waited for me to enter. I made my way to my bed, the wound on my foot flaring with sharp pain. I slumped down and dragged the dress up over my thigh, finding the bruise already forming from his fingernails, the indentation in my flesh. He hadn't broken the skin.

My shoulders rose and fell with ragged breaths.

Dread cloaked around me and my tears fell. Exhaustion danced over my body and I curled in on myself on the bed, clasping my eyes shutting, praying with everything I had that this was a horrible dream and I'd wake up back at Nightingale, that Arkyn, Cassian, and Lorcan found me.

A single howl sliced through the silence, a menacing sound that reminded me that even if I managed to escape, I might never make it alive through the woods.

4

I cracked open my eyes at the squeal of hinges. My movements were slow, thoughts even slower. A sting came at my leg, sharp and cruel. I opened my eyes more and shoved up on the rusted bed.

Beady eyes glinted in the darkness as the rodent looked at me. I screamed and lashed out, driving my foot into the air, dislodging the little beast. Pain flared, burning. I yanked the bottom of my dress aside to find blood.

The bite was deep, claw marks around my leg stung. I grabbed my leg and rocked forward, tears welling in my eyes. I had scratches on my hands and welts on my face from my abductors. But the worst was the cut on my foot.

The filthy, rat-infested puddles had probably infected the open lesion. Would the Vampires care? *No.*

An impossible tiredness pulsed through me, dragging me deeper and deeper back into sleep. I didn't want to move or do anything but lie here.

Scratch. Scratch. Scratch.

The rats were clawing at something again. I pulled my foot higher as the squeal of a hinge came once more.

The thud of footsteps cracked through the darkness. "Who's there?"

Thud.

Thud.

Thud.

A whimper slipped free from my lips. My heart slammed against my ribs. I pulled myself upright as my abductor came into view.

"Looky here," he chuckled. "You're still alive. I would've bet you wouldn't have made it through the night. But here you are...still looking at me with disgust."

I jerked my gaze away and sucked in hard breaths, but out of the corner of my eye he came, boots hitting the damp floor to stand on the other side of my cell. "Looks like the rats have had a taste. They'll be back with a vengeance now, you won't stop them, not until they've had their fill."

I winced at the words and turned my head. "What do you want?"

He just stood there, smiling and silent, until smoke drifted through the air. I tightened my grip on the bedframe and watched as the pale wisps melded together and turned into a Vampire. It was the same male as before, the one with murder in his eyes.

Eyes that found me now.

"Let me try this again," the Vampire said, stepping closer.

Rage lashed the air like a whip. I stiffened with the sting and the bed underneath me trembled. My foot throbbed harder, the heat reaching into my ankle. But in that moment, I didn't care about sickness or infection. I only cared about him.

Anger simmered under the surface, barely controlled. One wrong word and it would all be over for me. He stepped up to the bars and stared down at me. "Tell me what happened to Corvina?"

Images flooded me, violent and terrifying. I tried to shove

the images away, but I was weak...too weak. I closed my eyes as the slow thud of my heart pounded in my ears. "I..."

"Lie to me this day and I will end you. Look into my eyes and see I speak the truth."

I trembled and obeyed, opening my eyes and staring into the unholy blackness of his stare. "Tell me what happened to her," he commanded.

"I..." the words were stuck in the back of my throat, wedged tight by the clench of fear. "I... don't know."

"TELL ME WHAT HAPPENED TO CORVINA!"

I flinched with the fury of his roar. Rats scurried away in the darkness. I looked at my vile abductor. He was silent and unmoving. Not even his chest rose with a breath.

*Please...please...please...*I clenched my hands to still the tremble. I'd beg, if it came to that. I'd fall to my knees and beg for my life. Tears welled in my eyes. I felt my hold on this world slipping, falling into a pit of despair.

The pale-haired Vampire stiffened, my abductor slowly and quietly stepped to the side. Through the emptiness, something slithered into the room, and that same sickening hiss followed. I knew who it was.

The dangerous one...the one filled with venom.

The younger of the Vampires appeared beside him. Long, languid strides made no sound. "She was mine you know."

"Ours," the white-haired Vamp hissed through his teeth.

But the younger fanged beast paid him no mind. "I loved her."

I closed my eyes as the last pieces of the puzzle slipped into place. They'd loved Corvina...and we took her from them.

So, it was only fair, right? Tears welled in my eyes. Fair that they take what the Sinful loved. The only flicker of happiness that I'd ever had in my life was snuffed in an instant. I tried to hold onto my sanity, but my grip was slipping, and so was my life.

One wrong word…one wrong move, and it'd be over.

"So, I'm going to ask you once…I want to know what *they* did to her. I want every excruciating detail."

He stopped…waiting. It felt like I left my own body, like a sack of flesh and bones just fell away from me and I stood outside the vessel, waiting for the end.

"The party…" the words just seemed to spill from my lips.

"What about the party?"

The cell swayed. I tightened my grip around the bedframe and tried to hold on. "She was there, everyone was there. Drinking. Laughing. Arkyn." The scene unfolded in my head.

Arkyn tearing into the middle of the party. But we weren't laughing anymore. Blood all around us and Polaris standing there with wide, terrified eyes and blood all over her dress.

The whole room had fallen silent. There was no laughter, no almost naked men to dance and flirt and pour wine into greedy, open mouths.

"Arkyn." The young Vampire urged. "What did Arkyn do?"

I jerked my head upwards and met his gaze. In my head. Arkyn's savage gaze was fixed on the body on the floor. His roar filled me. *What the fuck just happened?*

"Arkyn--" I whispered.

A howl tore through the air, this time louder…*closer.* The baying sound magnified and multiplied until the haunting sound was all I could hear.

Wolves…

Wolves were here.

A tremor raced through my body as the Vampires snarled and lifted their heads. Moonlight washed over their faces as they closed their eyes.

Goosebumps raced over my arms. Terror made the hair on the nape of my neck rise. Something was happening…the piercing howls seemed to end in an instant, leaving hollow silence behind.

The past rose in that silence. I held on while fragments of a memory that wasn't mine slipped into place. Only this time there was no well...and no rats. This time, the howling cries of Wolves surrounded us. It was here...and past, but not my past.

"This has happened before, hasn't it?" I murmured, and opened my eyes.

Pale hair shone as the older Vampire met my gaze. "Yes. Blood, death...disaster. It seems to follow you, doesn't it, Asena?"

I winced at his answer. Nothing made sense...not here...not now, and not in my past, either, and as I tried to put the pieces together, a *boom...boom...boom...*echoed from up above.

I flinched, my heart hammering. Panic danced across my mind like a shooting star across the night sky. Some kind of knowing stirred in me, an aching...a *reaching,* and as the two Vampires in front of me curled their lips and bared their teeth, I knew whatever had come here wasn't what they expected.

Or what they wanted.

The pale-haired Vampire straightened and adjusted his jacket, staring at me. "She makes one sound and you have my permission to quieten her anyway you see fit."

In a breath, they were gone, tearing up the stairs in a frenzy before the howl of hinges echoed through the air once more and the door up above me closed with a bang.

"Any way I see fit." The pig in front of me smiled and took a slow step forward.

I slid my feet from the rusted cot, unable to tear my gaze from him. But all I was listening was for any hint of a sound from the front door. "Who is it?" I dared. "Who has come...who don't they want me to know about?"

The vile scum just grinned wider and took a step closer to the cell door. He reached into his pocket and pulled out a set of keys. Keys that no doubt fitted the lock to this hell I was in.

My heart thundered...desperate to tear from the confines of

this body and soar high above. I knew without saying the words...I knew without question.

Arkyn had come for me...

My Vampire was here...

5

ARKYN

Darkness descended over me. I clenched my jaw tight, the wind whipping my face. I'd endure a thousand lashes...a hundred thousand lashes...maybe then that infernal rage inside me would ease.

I wanted to fucking kill someone. I'd tear the whole damn forest apart to find Asena. She was taken right out of my home. Ripped from under my protection, and I was beyond livid.

On top of my mammoth black horse, I rode furiously through the woods, his breaths heavy, sending gusts of white fog into the air with each snort. Large hooves hit the ground, and we flew along the worn path.

Asena.

I could barely sense her now. Even when she'd closed down her mind, I'd picked up on her presence, faint but always there. Except now, no matter where I traveled to search for her, the sense never strengthened, and that terrified me. I couldn't lose her, not after everything we'd gone through to find her.

Before me rose the black temple like a mountain. It towered over the woods like a giant, the home of the elite, ancient master Vampires who ruled over this continent, who made the rules and tried to keep peace with the other four species living in this territory, Wolves, Dragons, Fae, Humans. But they failed miserably, because we were all warring.

I was fucking sick of it all, tired of the endless battles. Burn everything down to the ground for all I cared.

Except for Asena. I'd suffered too long without her, and now… I drove my horse harder up to the building. Now, I'd find out if the master Vampires had taken what belonged to me. I'd tread lightly, well aware that if I tore the place apart, it would be an all-out open war I couldn't win.

Several howls pierced the night. The Wolves were out in droves tonight, encroaching on our land. Something was happening… tension hung thick in the air, death lingering over all our heads.

I hurriedly dismounted, the horse heaving for breath. "You've done well, my friend." I stroked his neck and turned toward the door, where four guards emerged from their shadowy posts.

Tall fucking brutes, who were more muscle than brain.

"Lord Arkyn," the one with a hooked nose stepped into my path, wrapped in a black coat that fell to his ankles. "Were my masters expecting you?"

"Step out of my way if you want to see the night through," I hissed through my teeth.

Without hesitation, he lowered his head and moved out of my path. I marched up to the front door, reaching for the brass knocker when the door slid open.

"Baldassare," I said. "It's a pleasure." I gave a curt nod of my head and tilted it to the side, exposing my neck, a show of submission when entering a more powerful Vampire's lair.

Baldassare was in charge of the northern parts of the land, dealing with those fae pricks who lived there. It suited Baldassare perfectly, since his veins were made of ice.

He studied me with narrowed eyes at first, then huffed a

strange half laugh. "Oh, nice of you to drop in," he snarled. "But where are my manners? Come in." He stepped aside and drew the door open wider.

I stepped over the threshold without a second thought, my gaze lifting in that fleeting moment, scanning the foyer made of black marble, the portraits with golden frames lining the walls, warriors, Lords, anyone they thought worthy.

But we were alone in the room.

A frantic buzz washed over me, my muscles flexing, and I barely held myself back from running through the temple, calling for Asena. I had to find her. It killed me not knowing if she was safe.

Opening my mind, I reached out as far as I could for any trace of her, when the same faint trickle of energy lifted the hairs on my arms.

Was she here? I couldn't fucking tell.

My hands clenched.

She was mine. And I'd find her no matter how long it took.

"Let me take your coat," Baldassare said, already pulling at the collar, and I shrugged the coat down my arms.

"We have matters to discuss with you," he announced. "So, this may be an opportune time."

His words worried me. Of course, they wouldn't let the whole war thing go, I knew that coming here. But I needed to somehow search the temple without them knowing, so until then, I'd play the game of not revealing the truth to save Asena's head. *That* was my priority.

Baldassare stepped alongside me, wearing a frilly shirt the color of a stormy sky, high collar, long, loose sleeves, and black gloves matching his leather pants. He always dressed elaborately.

"Join us in the main room."

I followed without a word but studied the hallway we walked along, the set of stone stairs heading up to one of the towers, and the dark hall leading toward the stairs to the basement. Could she be up there? I clenched my jaw to hold back from darting up there. Not yet. Not yet.

"You have Wolves on your doorstep," I murmured.

"Oh, we know. Those mongrels are closing in, but they won't make a move. Not until the leaders' gathering coming up. One last, great talk." He snorted, clearly not believing in keeping peace. "Martel refuses to listen to reason and eliminate them all. Element of surprise worked for us many times, do you remember?"

He stared at me with excitement in those green eyes., with hunger for the old days when blood seeped into the soil daily.

"That was a long time ago."

He'd fought alongside me in countless wars, ruthless and bloody, though it was never enough for him until we'd demolished everyone. But back then, I wasn't any better. I wanted status and recognition. I got it, but at what price? I shook those thoughts aside. They were done. Only now counted.

He remembered war, while I remembered Asena's whispers, the softness of her skin, the delicious moans on my lips. My chest squeezed, and if I'd had a beating heart, it would be shattered now that I'd lost her.

Pushing open the door, we strolled inside the main room of the tower, which had a lofty ceiling and everything painted black for effect. An enormous fireplace roared to life in the corner, tossing light over the paintings on the walls and the empty thrones.

Master Martel was there, his back to us, his long white hair draped over his shoulders. He cleared his throat and abruptly turned to us, wiping the blood from his mouth. At his feet, a shadow shifted, and a young girl rose in front of him. Maybe fifteen or sixteen, she wore a simple white gown, blood dripping from her neck, three perfect dots staining the material over her small chest. It reminded me of stained snow, of a time when we'd fought the Wolves in a surprise attack many decades ago. When we'd wiped out an entire pack on a cold winter's night as a warning. That was one of many instigators that'd triggered this war, and one of the reasons I unfortunately agreed with Baldassare that peace talks wouldn't work. Too much blood had been spilled on all sides to forgive and forget.

The young girl turned and rushed barefoot across the room, then slid into a side door, vanishing.

"Sorry for the interruption," I said, tipping my head back, exposing my neck, showing him I offered myself, as was the custom. If he so chose, he could bite into my throat, take as he pleased without a whimper from me. As the master, he carried that privilege.

"You've come to join my war, correct?" he asked, expressionless. His gaze flickered to my face, my chest, my hands. Was he searching for signs of battle? For a weapon?

"As I said to Corvina, I won't be involved."

Fury twisted his face and his lips warped into a deadly grin filled with menace. "You think you have a choice? I sent Corvina as a courtesy, not as an option." His voice boomed in the lofty room, his words echoing around us.

I prepared for battle, because it was coming to me whether I liked it or not, but it wasn't the same war Martel was waging. I planned to save Asena and bring her back to me. That was the only fight I cared for.

I stood tall, holding his stare, my anger ablaze in my chest. "That was the reason for my visit." My words were clipped and short. "She left in a hurry. I wanted to make sure she was home safe. We had unfinished business. So I'm here to check with her. Is she around?" I glanced around the room as if showing I expected her to walk in at any moment and join us.

Baldassare was a blank slate again, offering nothing but a confused look. "We haven't seen her." He stepped closer, arms stiff by his sides, the black cape he wore dragging behind him on the wooden floor. "Viktor is beside himself with worry for her. He's out in the woods searching." A bemused smile split his mouth, fangs slipping out and over his lower lip. "Anything you can enlighten us with to aid in our search?" The muscles in his jaw tensed.

I swallowed thickly and cocked a brow at his question.

He knew I lied, knew Viktor wouldn't find Corvina, but we played these dancing games because the truth came with consequences. With repercussions that couldn't be taken back.

The master Vampire clapped a hand to my shoulder. "Be a good boy, won't you. Tell me what I want to hear. Join my army, and we will no longer speak of Corvina."

Ice filled me. He so quickly dismissed one of his own to get what he wanted. It had always been that way with Martel.

My lip curled upward and I looked away. "Leave it with me a while longer."

Martel snatched my arm, iron fingers locked around me. "Don't think too long. My patience is wearing thin. You've gone against us once before, I'm sure you remember well." His sneer of cynicism came out as a snarl.

Fury roared through me that he'd remind me... the prick always did that.

I lifted my gaze to meet the fierceness behind his. And he fucking knew... of course he knew Corvina would never run.

Baldassare chortled as he stalked around me. "We might have ourselves an old-fashioned hunt. Oh, Viktor will be happy." He beamed only the way a monster could when the promise of bloodshed and death was offered.

I scowled at the threat. I'd come to them for an answer, but all I did was invite the devil closer.

But Asena was all I had left, all I fought for, the only thing worth living for. I wouldn't lose her again, so I'd do what was needed.

Neither said a word, but they studied me, watched me with intensity. My muscles twitched as a desperate urgency to put them in their place crashed through me, throttled me.

I imagined lashing out, claws and fangs ripping their throats out, watching them extinguish. One I could destroy, but I doubted two. They were older than me, more powerful, so I held the promise of what I'd do to them inside for now. But their time would come, and I'd never stop fighting, because the moment I did was the moment I'd die.

Neither could be trusted, so I lowered my head as a sign of respect I didn't hold. "I have taken enough of your time. I shall see myself out." Not waiting for their response, I turned and walked out.

"I hope you reconsider the proposal, Arkyn," Martel called out after me.

I gave a nod of my head and shut the door to the main room.

Then I ran faster than possible, lunging up the steps and heading to the top room where Martel would keep prisoners years ago. The slivers of moonlight from the narrow windows was enough light for me to see the rooms were nothing but cobwebs and wooden boxes, stinking of rotten garbage and freshly turned soil.

Fucking nothing.

Asena! This was once used as a dungeon to host enemies and victims. The last time I was at the temple, I'd come up here to select a meal, a young villager they'd caught wandering the woods. But those were memories from ancient times.

The sound of creaking wooden beams came from below. My skin prickled, and I sprinted back downstairs, terrified I'd see Martel and Baldassare waiting for me in the foyer, but they hadn't emerged.

Glancing toward the stairs to the basement, I'd stepped in that direction when the door to the main room creaked open.

Anger crashed into me that I had to run and hide. I darted to the door and snatched my coat from the hook, pulling it on.

I glanced over my shoulder as I reached for the handle, to see Baldassare with his back to me, talking to Martel in the room.

"I'll arrange that at once," he murmured.

I rushed outside where the bitter cold wrapped around me, closing the door to the temple. Rage burned through me, and I clenched my fists, hating that I'd skirted around the main issue.

Are you in the temple, Asena?

No response, and I trembled with fury. I still heard her voice from before and pictured her with me, remembered her curves beneath the candlelight, and my cock hardened at the image of her naked, wanting me, giving herself to me. Images of me slamming into her haunted me, desire to have her quivering against me drove me to insanity.

Take care with her, Cassian would tell me. But she was stronger than anyone realized. She'd endured so much loss, and still she fought. She'd keep fighting and I'd find her before she finally broke. I couldn't lose again.

A guard emerged from the nearby woods and greeted me with darkened eyes. "Leaving so soon?"

"Yes," I responded and approached my black stallion. His head raised up and down with a snort, hot air streaming from his nostrils.

"Home, my friend." I grabbed the pommel and stepped into the stirrup, then I threw myself up and onto the horse's back. We left in haste.

The night closed in around me, and my chest tightened, racked with utter sorrow and heartbreak. All I could think was that I had to find Asena before the bigger war arrived and I lost her forever.

6

ASENA

"*The Wolves are howling.*"

I lifted my head and cracked open my eyes, to find the young maid standing outside my cell. Fragments of memories flooded in. I knew her...somehow. My thoughts were slow, filled with fog and memories that were not my own. "What did you say?"

"The Wolves." She stepped closer and held out a bowl of steaming stew. "I heard whispers. The Vampires say they'll attack."

I sucked in a breath and pushed up on trembling arms before a cry tore from my lips. Agony drove through my foot and tore all the way up my leg.

"Looks infected," she said and lifted a careful gaze to mine, then looked away. "If they attack, we're all done for anyway."

What did that mean? The throb in my leg intensified until I moaned and gripped my knee. The pain was deeper now, gnawing bone, poisoning my blood. I closed my eyes for a moment and tried to gather my strength.

"It's okay," she whispered. "It doesn't matter anymore."

The stew splashed against the sides of the bowl, some of the liquid spilled over. I stared at my food slowly dribbling down the outside, only to fall to the floor. Hunger raged to the surface, pushing the throb of my foot down to second place.

I shot forward, swallowing the cry of agony, as I shoved my hand through the bars and reached for the bowl.

"You do realize what's out there, don't you?" she murmured, her boots splashing through the puddles of water to hold out the stew. "Monsters, terrifying monsters who'll tear you apart."

"No different to the monsters in here, for me anyway." My hands trembled when I gripped the bowl.

My whole world became that food. Not one drop crested the rim. Not one morsel dropped to the floor. I didn't even care about the spoon. I was far beyond that now, riddled with rage and hunger. I carefully worked the bowl between the gaps in the bars and lifted it to my lips.

Warmth filled my mouth and slid down the back of my throat. I closed my eyes and swayed with the pleasure.

"I think it had a little too much salt," she murmured as I opened my eyes and lifted the bowl once more.

I'd never felt hunger before, not real hunger that twisted your insides and turned you into a ravenous beast. I yanked the bowl to my mouth and gulped greedily.

My belly let out a snarl and a stab of pain. I didn't care at that moment, didn't care about anything other than sating that wild need. I chewed, savoring the hunks of meat and bits of potato, until the bowl was empty.

"More," I gasped, and dragged the back of my hand across my lips. "I need more."

"I'll see if there is—" She started until a howl ripped through the air. She jerked her gaze to the window high above and took a step backwards. "No... not, not yet. They can't come yet. We've not packed...we're not..."

I shoved the bowl through the gap in the bars. "More, please."

But there was no reaching her now. Her boots splashed through the puddles, and the bottom of her dress soaked through. She turned on her heel in an instant and lunged for the stairs.

"Hey!" Desperation drove me forward. I grabbed the bars. "I need more food!"

The panicked sound of her steps echoed through the cellar like the hooves of a galloping horse. Not once did she slow, not once did she look back at me. She just climbed stair after stair, leaving me standing with an empty bowl in my outstretched hand.

"I need more." Hopelessness hit me like a wave. "More food."

I dragged my hand back inside and stared at the grainy remnants on the side of the bowl. I licked the mess, sliding my tongue around until the wooden bowl was clean.

Still my belly rumbled and snarled, and the agony in my foot drove to the surface of my attention. I hobbled, gripping the bowl with one hand and my knee with the other, I made my way to the rusted carcass of the bed once more.

The muscles in my back howled with agony as I crawled onto the hard base. Tears welled in my eyes. There was nowhere to move, nowhere to walk or sit that wasn't infested with rats or their feces. The rancid air burned as I inhaled. I pulled the collar of Cassian's shirt higher.

It smelled of him, that primal, masculine smell. I inhaled and lowered myself down. If I closed my eyes, I could see him, standing in the darkness as he had that first night I saw him in the forest.

He was savage and ferocious, dark eyes glittering as he narrowed in on me.

Did he know me then?

Did he know I was the one?

You're delirious, the words drifted through the darkness of my mind as the throbbing ache of my foot speared a fresh wave of agony into my leg.

I curled my arms around the empty bowl and hugged it tight. I focused on the bowl, like it was the only lifeline I had left. Warm stew sloshed in my belly, making me drowsy. I closed my eyes, letting myself drift away once more.

Sleep came for me...and with it, came my Vampires.

Only they weren't the Vampires I knew...

They were younger, different somehow.

Seductively Sinful, eyes alight with purpose.

Through the wonder of slumber, Arkyn smiled, looking up at me. *"Aelin..."* he whispered and grasped my chin in his long, perfect fingers, lifting my gaze to his. I saw him then, really saw him. He was different, younger. His eyes had a spark I didn't know.

A spark of happiness. A spark of love.

"Aelin," he repeated, and brushed his thumb across my cheek as I bent down to him. There was a carafe in my hand. Blood red wine spilled from the mouth to splash in the belly of a golden chalice.

I waited for the flinch of a name so foreign. But there was none, just warmth that floated through me, warmth and a fleeting sense of familiarity. Everything was familiar. Me. Them. *Us.*

"You serve us so well." Cassian leaned backwards across the table and plonked his boots on the corner of the table, legs crossed at the ankles "And as succulent as this red wine is, you are even more so."

Laughter spilled from my lips with a shake of my head. "Flattery will get you everywhere, won't it, Cassian?"

He grinned in response. "I goddamn hope so."

Heat flushed in my cheeks as images were conjured. Bare flesh, caught breaths, him naked and perfect above me, his body moving inside mine. We'd lain together more times than I could count and still I couldn't get enough of him. I wanted those wild eyes fixed on mine. I wanted those perfect muscles clenching as he worked my body.

"Aelin, are you okay?"

My breath caught at the third voice. I already knew who I'd find on the other side, across from Cassian. "Yes...Lorcan," I answered and met the dark eyes of my lover. "Perfectly fine."

Arkyn, sitting at the head of the table, reached for my hand. "You seem...distracted."

"With the three of you sitting in front of me, no wonder I'm a little *preoccupied*," I forced a smile and tried to hold onto my thoughts.

This was a dream...nothing more than a dream.

No, not a dream, but a memory. The words drifted across my mind and raced through the threads of time. I was both me and her...both entwined, both occupying the one body.

I stepped forward and lowered the carafe to the table as Arkyn's fingers entwined with mine. "Talk to me."

I glanced around the room like it was all brand new, but I knew this room, just like I knew that name. "I feel...strange. Like I'm not quite myself."

Concern flared in Arkyn's gaze. He gently pulled me closer, catching me in his arms like I weighed nothing at all. His dark eyes bored into mine, searching. "Are you ill?"

I shook my head. "No, I have no fever, no aches. I just," I glanced around the room. But it wasn't the room I cared about.

It was them.

My Vampires.

"Maybe you need a rest?" Cassian slid his feet from the table and rose. "I could take you to bed?"

The thought of that made my pulse race. My Vampires' nostrils flared as desire swept through me like a hot July wind. Maybe this was all nothing? Maybe fear ruled my thoughts. God knows war took a toll on all of us...

War...

I turned my gaze to Arkyn and my breath caught in my chest. *War.* I saw him now, saw the intensity...the unmatched power hovering under the surface. He was feared...more feared than anyone else I'd ever known. Even his own kind trembled at the sound of his name, and yet here he was, staring into my eyes, desperate for me. I wanted to hold onto him. No, I *needed* to hold onto him. Our hold on this world was fragile. If I lost him...

A tremor tore through my body. "Take me to bed," I whispered. "All of you...take me to bed and hold onto me tight."

His brows furrowed for a second. The look of confusion was swept aside as he rose without a sound, like the predator he was, and swept me from my feet.

Chairs scraped against the stone floor. I wanted to turn my head and take in these faintly familiar surroundings. But I was captivated by his gaze, held hostage by his arms. I was tethered to him in ways I couldn't fathom, like a woven set of strands, the four of us became the fabric of our destinies.

"Don't leave me." I wound my fingers through the thick curls of his hair. "Don't ever leave me."

"Never." The word was instant, like a reflex, like it came from the heart and not the head. So unlike him. Arkyn was calculating and savage--to everyone else but me.

Why? Why me?

I tried to search for the answer in his gaze, just as I'd tried a thousand times.

But there was nothing more than the reflection of my gaze staring into his.

Dark, *unfathomable* eyes. He was a mystery, a terrifying mystery.

Footsteps echoed behind us as Arkyn carried me into our room. Thick animal hides were piled on the floor in front of the fire, soft underneath me as Arkyn lowered me. I sank into the

Wolves' thick winter coats as Lorcan piled more wood in the hearth's belly.

"Tell me how you don't feel yourself," Arkyn demanded. He moved with slow precision, gently tugging the tie at the top of my dress, unraveling the bonds with agonizing precision, and all the while he held my gaze, and stared into the abyss that was my soul. "Tell me everything you feel."

"Scared." The word was a whisper. "I feel scared, like a wave is rushing toward me. A wave I don't see. But I can *feel* it. I can feel it coming."

His fingers froze for a frantic heartbeat. Something crossed his eyes, some fleeting panic that welled in the depths. "Cassian," he commanded, "Aelin here is in need of your skills."

I swallowed a flinch as he eased backwards on the thick hides.

"I am *always* happy to oblige," Cassian murmured as he knelt at my feet.

He removed my shoes and then delved under the hemline of my dress. Cool fingers raced against my warm skin. I tried to focus on the sensation, tried to tear my gaze away from Arkyn as he stretched out in front of the fire and watched us.

But there was something he wasn't saying, something in the flicker of terror in his eyes. Lips pressed against my knee, then moved to the inside of my thigh. Cassian reached up and bared my breast.

Arkyn's gaze lowered as my nipples hardened in response. I opened my legs wider, letting Cassian kiss where he wanted to kiss. Lorcan sank to the thick hide beside me, his fingers making short work of the last ties on my bodice, and pulled the dress higher.

I sank my hands into the fur and lifted my hips. The skirt slid upwards underneath me, leaving me bare for my Vampires.

"My God, you are beautiful." Cassian breathed the words between kisses as he gently eased my knees apart.

An arch of my spine, and I was completely bare. I looked down the length of my body as Cassian moved between my thighs. He lifted his gaze as he kissed me, opening his mouth and gently licking the top of my slit.

I trembled with the sensation. My breath caught as I shifted my gaze to Arkyn. Still he watched me, drinking in every shudder as Cassian sank lower on the hide. His tongue slipped inside me, gentle and teasing. My pulse sped as Lorcan's finger brushed the length of my cheek and turned my gaze toward him.

I loved them all in equal measure. All three of my Vampires filled a void inside me, but it was that void that spoke to me now...that void where tendrils of another's life mingled with mine.

Aelin.

Asena.

A gasp tore from my lips as Cassian kissed me deeper, *hungrily.* Lorcan swallowed my cry, his tongue licking my lower lip before he claimed my mouth with his own.

Tender flesh was scraped by pointed fangs, both in my mouth and between my legs. Cassian clenched his grip around my button, grinding my core against his mouth as he swallowed my desire. Lorcan's fingers brushed the peaks of my breasts, moving from one to the other, kneading and tantalizing, delving his tongue deeper into my mouth at the same time Cassian speared into my body.

That wave was coming, bearing down on me, dark and brooding. It was a wave of danger...a tsunami of terror under a stormy gray sky. I arched my back and lowered my hands. Muscles quivered as I lifted my head, taking Lorcan's kiss with me. I needed more.

More. I needed more.

I opened my eyes and kissed Lorcan. But it was Arkyn I sought with a ravenous gaze, and the warrior watched me, his own eyes filled with predatory hunger. I raked my fingers into Cassian's long hair and gripped him as that wave bore down on me.

"I love you, Asena," Arkyn whispered. *"I've always loved you."*

The end came like an explosion. I cried out and pressed Cassian's lips to my core, jerking and shuddering.

"I'm here, Asena," Arkyn whispered through my mind. *"I'm right here..."*

7

My skin prickled with a familiarity. A sensation that clawed over my chest.

I jerked upright in bed, ripped from the most incredible dream, holding onto that sizzling feeling. The more I held onto it, the stronger it grew, the more it made me feel like I wasn't alone.

I'd felt this sensation before, each time the three Sinful reached out for me. It was here, in my mind and in my veins, a knowing they were near.

Scrambling to my feet, I cringed as my wounded foot hit the damp floor of my prison cell, the foot swollen and red and so infected that it drained me of energy. But adrenaline pushed me to limp to the metal bars. I grabbed them, icy to the touch, and yelled, "Help, I'm down here! Arkyn, Cassian, Lorcan! Please!"

I gripped the bars with all my strength, screaming. "I'm in the basement." The words streamed over my raw throat as I kept shouting until I felt nothing but sorrow spearing a hole through my chest.

I couldn't stop shaking and my whole body was racked with

anxiety, with the fear that they were near and had no clue I was so close.

Shouting over and over, I called for them.

Please hear me.

Please.

When no one came, I backed away, tears streaming down my cheeks. I couldn't reach my Sinful, and I'd be stuck here until I died. I felt numb all over and my body seemed to beg me to collapse, to get back into bed, to stop the agony shooting up my leg, to give in.

But I wouldn't give up, wouldn't allow pain to stop me from fighting. My jaw clenched, and I turned to the small window high up on the wall. Hobbling to the bed, I put all my weight into the effort and pushed the metal contraption. Its feet scraped the floor with a screech that rose the hairs on my arms.

I shoved the bed with all my might, ignoring the flaring ache pulsing up my leg. With the bed under the window, I scrambled up on the worn framework and reached up. My fingers caught the ledge of the window, and I held on as I stepped up on the metal bar at the end of the bed with my good foot and pushed myself higher to peer outside.

Winds lashed the night, trees swaying, the shrubs bowing back and forth.

But beyond that, shadows moved. I squinted for a better look, to see someone tall marching toward a...I stared closer...toward a horse.

The stranger threw himself onto the animal's back. Dressed in black, he melted against the night's backdrop. He took one last look toward the building.

Arkyn! Dark and furious, his hair fluttered in the wind.

My heart clenched.

A scream rose through me, and it burst from my lips. I yelled and yelled, slammed my fist into the window.

"Arkyn, I'm here. Arkyn, please. Look this way." I never stopped, just bellowed my cries for help.

But he was gone in a flash, riding into the night, and my hopes dashed with him, ripped to shreds, and now they floated through me like ash.

Only my sobs echoed off the walls, and I collapsed back onto the bed and lay there, curling in on myself, drowning in a black pit.

Arkyn. His name swirled in my mind, spiraling endlessly. I'd been so close. He was here… in this temple. I could almost reach out and touch him, but it hadn't been close enough.

The tears kept falling and I cried into my hands, exhausted, aching, and terrified. I was always a fighter, and I'd ended up in Nightingale Manor to get revenge for my parents' deaths. But I wasn't meant to end up here, to die here, when there was so much for me to still uncover. Mysteries that didn't make sense, things that revolved around me.

My throat felt thick and raw each time I swallowed.

Lying there filled me with a sense of hopelessness, like the room closed in around me. I was taken back to years ago, to when I'd found my parents slaughtered in the house, to when I'd wanted nothing more than to join them in death.

And now…now I fought for my life, grasping to keep breathing and hold my head above the surface of the cesspool of evil surrounding me.

I closed my eyes, pretending for those few moments that I wasn't in a prison with an infected foot, that I might die at the hands of those sadistic Vampires, that somehow Arkyn would ride back on his horse and save me.

"Where are we going?" my words seemed to slur, or maybe they only sounded that way in my head. Sleep still clung to my mind and body, so the guard carried me in his arms from my cell when his patience wore too thin from waiting for me to get up. Now we climbed the stairs and he marched right into a room with a long cherrywood table sitting across the middle. Elaborate black candelabras and gold-rimmed plates were set up for dinner, but the only food on the table was a bowls of fruit. My mouth salivated. The flames from the candles flickered in the air, releasing wisps of black. The burning scent clogged my nostrils. Everything seemed too sensitive to me today.

The guard placed me on my feet near the fireplace, and I appreciated his care. He must have felt my freezing skin and taken pity.

I didn't move from the spot, warming myself, feeling like I floated on air to have heat finally spreading over me, chasing away the permanent cold in my bones. My throat choked up at how much I needed this. A bit of sympathy from the guard meant the world to me, and I blinked away the tears that wanted to fall.

The room seemed to swirl around me, and when I stared at the grand portraits on the walls, I could have sworn the Vampires in the pictures moved. I shook my head, rubbed my eyes, trying to see straight.

The guard had walked out and closed the door, leaving me completely on my own. Was this a test? I kept staring at the corners, expecting someone to step out. I even peeked under the table, but it was just me. Then my eyes settled on the bowls of fruit. My stomach stung so hard from starvation, so I limped closer, keeping an eye on the door, my ears pricked.

With no one in sight, I reached out hungrily to the closest bowl and snatched a handful of green grapes, then pushed them into my mouth. They burst on my tongue, sweetness spreading through my mouth, and they were the best things I'd tasted in my whole life. My cheeks were full, but I crammed more into my mouth, unable to eat quickly enough.

Tears fell from the corners of my eyes to finally be able to eat more than small bowls of soup here and there. Next, I grabbed a plum and devoured it in no time. With the seed, I pushed it into the pocket of my dress, to not leave any evidence.

I shuffled the fruit in the bowl so they looked untouched and moved to the second one along the table. With a mouthful of grapes, the creak of floorboards sounded behind me.

My stomach dropped to my feet. I dropped the fruit back into the bowl, swallowed, and spun, to see the door opening. With my heart pounding hard in my chest, I barely stood upright, between the dizziness and my blurry vision.

The white-haired Vampire strolled inside, meeting my gaze, revealing nothing in his stoic expression. The long silk coat he wore was buttoned from knees to throat, collar upright, white hair striking against the midnight fabric.

The tap, tap, tap of footsteps followed him into the room, and someone stepped out from behind him. Someone I recognized.

Windblown, deep brown hair pushed off her face.

Excited pale eyes.

Dressed in a gorgeous garnet gown with a plunging neckline and belt cinching in her waist, she held grapes from the vine in one hand and a crystal glass of white wine in the other, smiling like she was at a fair and the world was all rainbows and flowers.

"Chaska!" I screamed her name with excitement and hobbled toward her as fast as I could.

He eyes were on me, widening as I crashed into her, hugging her so tightly. Tears streamed down my cheeks. Something about not being alone, about having an ally, about not doing this on my own eased the dread swallowing me.

"I can't believe you're here," I whispered, knowing the Vampire watched. But I was too shaken, too excited, too emotional, to try to make sense of why my friend had turned up. "Did they take you, too?"

But the tension in her body never softened, and she didn't return my embrace. I pulled back, studying her face for an expression to understand what was going on.

Her hand came up to her mouth and she popped a grape into it, chewing and staring at me with a smug look that made no sense to me.

Alarms went off in my mind that something was wrong. "What's going on, Chaska?" I breathed the barely audible words.

She eyed me up and down, her nose scrunching in disdain. I felt her judgment burning through me.

Behind me, the Vampire sat in a chair near the table, legs crossed, watching us with amusement.

I sucked in shaky breaths, one after the other, my brain too lethargic to make even a guess at what I'd missed.

"You thought you were perfect," she snapped. "You thought you were the one. There's more than the Sinful, Asena." Her eyes narrowed at me, looking like she was so proud of herself.

My lower lip wobbled at her words, my mind trying to decipher what she'd just said. But my hands were clenching and unclenching as anger surged through me. She wasn't here to save me… or even to join me.

Blinking away the frenzy in my head, I murmured, "What are you doing, Chaska?"

Tears clouded my vision. The damn things kept coming and coming tonight, and I was barely holding it together, barely able to string two thoughts together, but I'd never expected this.

Her gaze skipped over my shoulder toward the Vampire, and I stepped aside to look his way, too, to wait for the explanation.

"Tell me, dear," he cooed, his deep voice and authoritative, his gaze settled on Chaska. "Tell me the truth now. Tell me what happened to Corvina."

Rocking on my heels, I barely stood upright, and hearing his question told me exactly what was going on. I couldn't stop shaking and my every fear was coming to life.

These Vampires only kept me alive until they heard the truth about Corvina, until they heard the words they sought.

"Chaska," I blurted, my voice tightening "Please." I grasped her wrist, staring at her, pleading.

She stared at me with disgust that I'd touch her. Since when had she become this person?

"Why are you acting like this? We shared a room together, we helped each other. I thought we were friends." I urged.

She scoffed. "Is that what you called it? Friends. We were in a competition, and we all did what we could to survive. We'd keep doing what we could to survive," she sneered.

Her words were a slap to my face, a punch to the gut. Had I been so blind to not see through her lies, to miss the clues that she'd misled me this whole time? I wasn't sure what hurt worse in that moment… her betrayal or knowing exactly what she planned to tell the vicious Vampire.

I balled my hands into fists so hard my knuckles turned white, and I wanted to use them on Chaska, to shut her up, to make her see that she'd be sending me to my death. Except, she already knew that, didn't she?

"You don't need to do this," I pleaded in soft words, terror lashing over my chest.

"This is my choice, Asena. I can't return home, ever. I'd rather die than let my father lay another hand, another whip on me." She ripped free from my grip and drank the rest of the wine in one gulp, the glass shaking in her hand.

Fury and vulnerability trembled beneath her words, and I saw the terror in her eyes, saw that she'd do anything to find herself a place amid these monsters than return to the one back home. But at what expense? At my expense?

"Are you sure you want to do this? You won't find the salvation you seek... not within these walls," I warned. "Look at me, look what they've done. Do you really think you're safe here?"

What would she do? Drag Polaris into this, as she was the one who'd killed the Vampire? Chaska also had a hand to play in Corvina's demise.

The Vampire behind me cleared his throat, signifying an urgency, an impatience.

Chaska's jaw tightened, and she didn't answer my question. She turned to face the Vampire. "She killed Corvina. All because she wanted Arkyn to herself. She wanted all three Sinful, not prepared to share."

"She's lying!" I spun toward the Vampire. "I didn't kill Corvina. I wouldn't."

My heart struck my ribcage so hard, it was going to burst free. Dread closed in around me, the edges of my vision already feathering in darkness.

The paintings around me seemed to be dancing across the wall, the fire coming to life in the hearth. Someone was laughing in my ear. I kept blinking, trying to clear my mind as my feet slipped backward until I hit the wall, my pulse thundering with panic. I braced my hands against the wall holding me up, too scared to move, too scared to breathe.

My gaze fell on the Vampire, expecting him to lunge, to tear me apart.

A jagged sob escaped my throat. And I was scared, more than I'd been in my entire life.

Peeking up through lashes, I saw the Vampire rising to his feet, tall and ominous, and coming my way.

"Please, no," I mumbled, and everything became too much,

the darkness cinched in around me so fast, I fell into its grasp and welcomed the escape.

When I opened my eyes, I forced myself to sit up, to push through the sharp aches in my body. I sat on the filthy, wet floor of my prison cell, dingy, moldy, reeking, and with a rat scurrying across the room, passing right in front of my feet.

I wasn't dead. Patting my body and looking down, I was still in my clothes, and I found no puncture wounds on my neck or arms from bites.

Wait, was this a trick? Another fucking game?

My head hurt so much that I couldn't even tell what was real or possibly a hallucination anymore. Maybe my mind was playing tricks. I rubbed the tears from my eyes, tired of feeling my mind fuzzing in and out of reality.

Had I dreamed the whole thing with the Vampire and Chaska?

I was losing my mind, but relief rattled through me that it had been a nightmare. Chaska wouldn't betray me, we'd been through so much. She was involved in Corvina's death, too.

Shoving myself to my feet, I wobbled, stilling for a moment until my head settled. When the food came, I'd feel better again. I always did after eating something to give me a little strength.

I turned toward my bed, but the shadow in the corner shifted.

Frozen, I didn't move. "Who's there?"

Chaska stepped out of the corner, hair messed up, pretty dress torn, and blood dripping from her split lip. Tears drenched her cheeks as she looked at me with utter and complete hopelessness and sorrow.

"No, no, no! You can't be real. That didn't happen. It's in my head." I smacked my palm against my forehead, retreating. "You wouldn't betray me, *you wouldn't!*" I bellowed.

Chaska stepped closer, real as life.

A snigger slithered from her lips. Pain flared through my chest as I stared at her. This wasn't a nightmare. She had really turned against me...all for what? For pretty clothes and her own Vampires to seduce her.

Tears slipped down my cheeks. I shook my head and lifted my gaze to her. "What have you done, Chaska? *What have you done?*"

8

Arkyn

The howls of Wolves cut through the air all around me. I hunkered under the cover of a thick fir tree and scanned the darkness. There were too many...too many to kill all on my own--tonight at least.

A flash of movement came at my right, and the thunderous sound of paws of a beast in full flight beat the ground. I gripped the hilt of my blade and watched as the beast launched into the air and leaped over a fallen tree.

Danger danced along my spine as I lifted my gaze to the decrepit mansion on the hill. This wasn't right. Wolves didn't outright attack, not like this...not unless they were provoked.

I glanced behind me and thought of my horse. I had set it free. One slap on the rump and the stallion had taken off, leaving me alone, surrounded by my mortal enemy.

I shoved forward, masked by the trail of the Wolf, I hurried forward. War was not unknown to me, bloodshed a way of life. But it didn't need to be *her* life.

That silent pit in my chest shuddered with agony. I drove my boots into the forest floor and pushed ahead. A blur of movement came from my left. Thick midnight fur shone in the moonlight as the beast ran.

I'd hidden in the darkness under the reaching arms of a towering pine and buried myself in the pine needles and earth like a goddamn corpse. The shit itched, falling under my shirt as I ran, but I was past caring now.

Asena was the only thing I cared about. Her pain...her pleasure. *Her life.* That was the only thing that drove me. The *only* thing that made me run with Wolves.

I slowed at the edge of a clearing and scanned the trees. The pack was thunder without rain, galloping...*hunting.* Something was driving it, some kind of call to arms I couldn't sense.

A lone howl ripped through the air in front of me. Goosebumps raced up my arms with the call, snatching my breath. I scanned the treeline once more and drove forward, stepped out into the moonlight and raced across the plain. But the moment I hit midway, I knew this had been a mistake.

I caught the flash of movement behind me before I drove my boots into the earth and speared forwards. The beast's paws cracked the earth like boulders as it came after me with predatory precision.

Outnumbered and barely armed, all I had was a thousand years of war as a weapon. And as I hit the treeline on the other side and turned to face the gigantic beast...I knew I'd need not my skills of warfare--but a miracle.

The beast was bigger than I'd ever seen before. Silver eyes tracked me in the darkness. I gripped the hilt as a guttural snarl echoed around me. Thick rust-colored fur looked like blood in the moonlight.

His shoulders reached my waist, and the beast far outweighed me. White fangs shone as he stepped from the clearing and into the trees. I gripped the knife and stepped backwards. "I didn't come here for you," I warned and lifted my hand. "So if you make this about us, you're going to lose."

A sickening snarl vibrated the air all around me. I took a step backwards, driving deeper into the gloom as the howls of its pack turned insistent. They were at the mansion...about to attack.

Asena...I stole a breath and stopped moving.

The beast slunk closer, its massive paws sinking into the dirt.

"Looks like it's time for war," I murmured.

The beast stilled, hunkered back on its massive hind legs, and then *lunged.*

Asena

I stared at Chaska, who still hadn't said a word, but seemed to curl in on herself across the prison cell from me. Shadows shifted across her face, and my blood was boiling that she'd told the Vampires I killed Corvina. She had to that see no matter what she told them, she would end up here.

Fog stained my thoughts, but I had no doubt what she did last night was no hallucination.

"Asena," she murmured, her voice broken, her pain clear.

But I couldn't do this, not after she'd betrayed me once before, and now again. I saw exactly who she was, the type of person she was, and I didn't need her in my life. I turned my back to her, silence falling, and all I could do was stand there, trying to sort out my own confusion, not worry about hers.

I just wanted her to leave me alone from now on.

A loud howl rang through the night, and I flinched at the piercing sound, like it came from right outside the window.

I swallowed thickly, glancing up at the small window, wondering what was going on out there.

"Do you think the Wolves are planning to attack?" Chaska asked in a trembling voice. "Remember how close they were to Nightingale Manor?"

I turned my head in her direction. "Don't, just don't talk to me or pretend we're anything."

Her mouth dropped open, shocked by my words, and it stunned me that she'd think what she'd done was alright, that I'd forgive and forget so easily.

Deep breath. Deep breath. Deep breath.

The pounding of footsteps thumped, and I glanced up to see a shadow racing down the stairs.

An enormous guard with large ears and his shirt pulled taut across his chest fumbled with the cell door lock. He pushed the door open. "You," he growled and pointed at Chaska, "with me."

Chaska let out a whimper and recoiled.

With a scoff, the guard marched inside after her.

I trembled, frozen on the spot.

He snatched her by the arm and hauled her along. She stumbled after him, crying out, "I don't want to go, please don't."

My heart splintered, but what could I do? He locked the door, and Chaska's gaze swung toward me one last time with a devastating look like she knew they were taking her to her death.

"I'm sorry," was all she cried, and then she was gone

I was shaking fiercely, tears pricking my eyes. I hated this place, loathed it.

A blinding flash came from outside.

Boom! Boom!

The explosions reverberated around me, the walls and floor shaking so violently, I could barely stand. I threw myself toward the bed, my hands lashing out to grab the bedframe, grasping it for dear life.

I cast a glance around. What the hell was going on?

Another howl, followed by more. Wolves! What were they doing?

Boom!

I lurched on the bed.

The glass from the window shattered and the ground was quivering. Dust and tiny stones fell from overhead, hitting my head and shoulders.

Shock riveted me to the spot. Was the whole temple coming down, with me buried underneath it?

I had to get out of here.

A large hunk of stone broke away from the ceiling and came crashing down just as a rat scrambled across the room. Thud, and a small squeak sounded. I cringed and looked away.

Recoiling, I hit the wall with my back and couldn't stop trembling.

I couldn't stay here. I pushed off the wall and staggered to the metal bars, gripping them, strangling them.

"Let me out! I'm still down here. Someone, please!"

Screams bellowed from upstairs, the crash of something falling, more yelling.

I shrink back, hugging myself, barely able to breathe from fear.

Arkyn… had he returned? But the Wolves, they'd come, too.

Fuck!

Arkyn

The beast lunged through the air and hit me like a boulder. I took the impact hard and crashed to the ground. But years of combat experience made me roll from the strike. I pushed up from the ground, the knife still in my hand.

"I don't want to do this," I warned, then lifted my gaze to the towers of the temple poking above the pine trees. "But you stand between me and the woman I love, so choose, Wolf...and choose carefully."

The black animal climbed to its feet and shook its body, its scraggly fur. Hard breaths were a gust of air. It turned its head and glanced through the spindled branches to the towering black mansion in the distance. A growl vibrated through its body, tearing from its chest as it swung its mammoth head toward me, took one slow step, and pawed the ground with unmerciful claws.

"Have it your way, then."

Boom! The explosion rocked the air, followed by another just as deafening.

I threw out a hand as the ground trembled. Through the trees I caught sight as the first tower of the temple fell, and that black pit inside my chest throbbed with pain. "What the hell?"

Savage breaths tore my gaze from the sight. The Wolf stalked closer, its silver eyes trained on me. That was what the beast wanted, that was what it had come for. I settled my gaze on the monstrosity. "Who are you attacking? The Vampires...or the mortal woman?"

The beast never answered, just raked its fucking claws through the dirt, leaving gashes in the earth. I hadn't come here to hurt the beast. But now it'd come to that.

Strangely, I felt comfort with that. I wore a monster's skin more easily than I did my own. I gripped the blade and followed the Wolf's movements. With a thick barrel chest and a long lean flank, all brawn, let's hope there wasn't much brain. I took a step but, instead of moving toward the fur-wearing beast, I stepped backwards and then lunged into the trees.

I moved fast, tearing in and out of the trees until I came around to the rear of the beast.

Wolves were inherently lazy, none more than a brute like this one.

I cut through the trees behind it and lunged at its back. Wolves tracked heartbeats, it was lucky for me I had none. I jumped on the beast's back as it swung its massive head my way. Two slashes with the blade and I'd sliced through the tendons of its back legs.

It dropped to the ground with a piercing howl. I dragged the back of my hand across my mouth. I was alone out here, and far from where I lived. But my home was trapped in that mansion and, as the third explosion rocked the air, I knew time for her had run out.

"It's run out for you, too, my friend."

The beast tried to lunge, dragging its useless legs behind it. But it hadn't the strength to balance on one paw and come after me. I'd been counting on that. "I love her," I flanked the Wolf as it stumbled and fell. "I've killed to keep her safe...and I'll do it again."

I moved fast, dodging its movement, to straddle its body. I climbed the beast, feeling the desperation shiver through its body, until my blade plunged deep.

Blood gushed from the wound at its neck. Warmth spluttered onto the earth it'd raked only moments before. I rolled as it hit the ground, then pushed to my feet. I didn't wait for the beast to die. Instead, I turned to the plumes of black smoke as it billowed from the castle, and ran as fast as I could.

She was in there, calling me...screaming my name.

I'm coming for you, Asena...I'm coming.

Asena

Smoke slipped into the cells from the shattered window, curling around the room like a black serpent of death. I sucked in the bitter stench and coughed.

The choking burning kept coming, tearing fire from my lungs to scorch my throat. Parts of the temple were burning. I could smell the soot and the metal, it burned my eyes, leaving them to weep dirty tears.

Unmerciful howls sliced through the night sky. I swiped a filthy sleeve across my face and lifted my gaze to the shattered window high above. I wound my hands around the bars, and clenched them tightly, rattling the damn cage until my bones shook. My escape was up there, a bit tight, but if I could somehow climb that high…

Arkyn.

I closed my eyes and swayed with exhaustion. He will come back for me. He *will* come back.

For him, for Cassian, for Lorcan, I'd find a way to get out before it was too late.

Screams cut through the air upstairs, piercing and howling, filled with terror and pain. Chaska? Was she hurt?

The creak of the door hinges sounded, and I flinched around.

Someone cloaked in black stumbled down the stairs, his face concealed by a hood, but his eyes… they were pale, glistening with savagery. "You're all alone now," he growled.

I shuddered at the sound of his voice and felt my blood run cold.

My abductor stumbled when he moved, weaving in a drunken fog. Coins jangled in his pockets, money and gold. He took what he wanted. *Wasn't that what he said?* He took the Vampires' wealth, and now he was here for me.

My heart hammered in my chest, and I recoiled.

I glanced around the cell through the haze of smoke for a

weapon and found nothing more than chunks of rock fallen from above.

Panic raged through that unseen connection. I waited for the blinding lash of pain to follow. Only this time it didn't come. This time, there was nothing but freedom...pure, desperate freedom. *Arkyn...Arkyn!*

My pig of an abductor drew nearer. His thick, glistening lips curling at the corners, he stared at me. But under the collar of his shirt, there was fresh blood. I stared at the splatter as he moved, fang marks sank deep...*but were they Vampire...or were they Wolf?*

Arkyn?

"I'm going to fuck you," he grinned. "And then I'm going to kill you slowly...*Vampire...who*—" he never finished the word.

A massive hunk of stone carved through the billowing, thick smoke and hit him in the back of the head.

A cough tore from my lips as the sickening *crunch* followed. He stumbled forward, his eyes glazing as he toppled to the ground and landed in a puddle of shit and filth. I sucked in the smoke, unable to tear my gaze from the sight of his lifeless eyes. Acid rose in the back of my throat. I coughed and swallowed, convinced I was going to throw up.

Out of the haze he came, a silhouette striding forward, tall and powerful. My heart gave a stutter as a voice pierced the bitter fog. "I told you these Vampires would be the death of you, Asena. Maybe now you'll listen."

And as the smoke cleared a bit and the outline coming closer sharpened, my knees gave way.

"Jacob?"

9

"No," I whispered and stumbled backwards. "It can't be."

"Oh, but it can," he growled, and fixed those brown eyes on me.

Brown eyes I once knew better than I knew my own. But I didn't know this man...who walked around in familiar skin. No, I didn't know him at all.

He bent down to the sickening slug of a man who lay dead on the floor in front of the cells and grabbed the keys from his grasp. "You want out, don't you?" Silver glinted as he looked at me.

Silver...

Silver...

And outside the howl of a Wolf tore through the air. *Snap,* the lock gave way and the cell door swung open with a howl of the hinge.

"You want to stay here? The others will come soon enough, they've already breached the place upstairs and killed everyone who wasn't dead before. Your choice, stay and die...or," he lifted his hand.

I stared at his open hand, and the lines across his palm. I'd traced those lines, lying in the sun. I'd spoken of a future...a future where we were just friends. But as I met his gaze now, I could see that'd changed.

A crash tore through the rooms above. Screams followed. A woman's screams. *Chaska?* I winced and swallowed a cry as I took a step, but the second I put weight on my foot, my leg gave way.

Strong hands grabbed me before I hit the floor. He lifted me like I weighed nothing at all and cradled me against his chest. "You stink like Wolf," I muttered.

"And you reek of Vampire," he retorted. "Only, I have a reason to smell like a Wolf. Tell me, Asena. Have you drunk from them? Have you tasted Vampire blood?"

I flinched at the thought as he carried me from that cell and out through the cellar. Choking smoke burned my eyes and seared my nose. I winced at the acrid sting and even though I hated myself for it, I turned my head and buried my face into Jacob's chest.

His strong, lithe body flexed as he moved. He'd grown bigger in the months since I'd seen him, stronger, too. A wave of fresh air hit me as the pain in my leg reached higher, carving an unseen blade from my foot into my thigh.

I ground my teeth and swallowed my cry as Jacob lifted my legs, his nostrils flaring slowly...in fact the whole world was slow, everything but the agony in my leg as it inched higher and higher, stabbing and twisting, cutting deep. Tendrils of smoke wafted around us, turning from black to gray...

The night was gray...his face was gray.

"You're going to pass out," he murmured, his words warped and slow.

My head rolled backward on his arm, and my mouth fell open. I tried to hold on to the world around me, tried to focus on the jolt of his strides and not the shadows of his face.

His familiar face.

"You've changed." The words were a slur as he scanned the darkness and focused on something in the distance.

"So, have you, Asena? So... have you?"

Branches swallowed the stars above me. But the darkness wasn't done, moving in to clutch me in its grasp.

"Sleep, Asena...when you wake up, we'll be far from here, and you'll be safe...with me."

I didn't want to sleep. I wanted to shake my head and shove him away. I wanted to fall to the ground and crawl on hands and knees if I had to. My Vampires were out here somewhere...my *Ark—*

Thunder filled my dreams.

Thunder and darkness, rain clouds racing the wind.

It was all I could see, all I could feel. I stood in a void of darkness, of nothing, and nothing was all I felt.

Aelin...

I swiveled in that emptiness, watching the storm rage all around me. The bolts of lightning were blinding.

Aelin...where are you?

"Arkyn?" I scanned the violence, searching for his face.

He was there, on the horizon, pale and unmoving, like a ghost in a dream.

"Aelin, come to me." Arkyn called and lifted his hand toward me.

I tried to move from the emptiness, but my feet were stuck, no, actually it was just the one. I looked down to see my foot stuck in the darkness, and the black, inky void spewed its poison through my veins, crawling up past my knee and into my thigh.

"Easy now," a male growled.

I knew that voice. *I knew that voice.* I cracked open my eyes to the same darkness and stole a breath. Embers billowed into the dark sky.

"You're awake."

I turned my head as fire burned through me. I was the cause of the embers. I was the one on fire. A moan ripped free, low and savage, tearing blood from the back of my throat to dance across my tongue.

"Easy there, Asena. You're sick."

He stepped from the darkness, the orange caressing his face. Brown eyes sparkling with hunger.

"Jacob?" I whispered as a shiver tore along my spine.

The sounds of the forest moved around us. Sticks snapped, the call of an owl soared, and above me through the canopy of trees, stars glinted like heavenly diamonds.

There was no throb of my foot anymore. Just agony that reached higher and higher, until I felt the poison in my chest. I moaned and rolled forward to grasp my knee.

"It's too deep now." Jacob sat beside me.

There was a hardness in his gaze, a cold, savage resignation. One I wasn't going to like.

"Would you stay with me?" he asked and stared at the ground. "If you had a choice...would you stay by my side and never leave?"

The answer mingled with a groan. I rocked with the agony, piercing my nails into my knee. "Please, Jacob. The pain...*the pain.*"

Still he sat there, oblivious to my cries. Uncaring...*unreachable* in that moment.

"Answer me," he snarled and finally turned to meet my gaze. "Would you stay with me?"

I shook my head as Arkyn, Cassian, and Lorcan filled my mind. "No...no, I wouldn't stay."

A hardness settled in his gaze as he gave me a nod of his head. "That's what I figured."

He lifted his hand and pressed his wrist against his mouth as he parted his lips and bit down on the flesh. Blood ran in rivulets down the inside of his arm.

I didn't have time to react. Swallowed by the agony in my leg, I was helpless when he settled those dark, unfathomable eyes on me and then lifted his hand toward me. "I figured you'd say that."

Panic surged through me at the sight of his blood. I jerked my gaze to his. "No...no, Jacob...*Jacob, NO!*"

Warmth pressed against my mouth and then drove harder. With a snarl of rage, he smeared his blood all over me, my lips, inside my mouth. And as the metallic taste of blood bloomed in my mouth, he let out a savage roar filled with depravity and rage.

I lashed out with a weak fist and beat his chest, panic and rage mingling into a dangerous cocktail. I kicked and clawed, fighting him with everything I had.

"Shhh." He gripped the back of my neck with one hand and held his wrist to my mouth.

My muffled screams were useless. Still, I kicked and clawed, beating his body with weak blows. But I may as well have been beating a tornado. He took what he wanted anyway. Until, in an instant...he just let me go.

I drove my foot against the ground, dragging my infected leg. I managed to get off the ground and scurried away. Tears came so fast they took me by surprise. I swiped my mouth with the back of my hand, still I tasted blood. "What did you do, Jacob...*what did you do!*"

He just stared at me, like he was a stranger...like he was a *beast.*

"I saved you."

They were the only words he muttered. The *only* words I heard as fire tore along my throat and plunged into my belly. I doubled over with pain, grabbing my middle. The fire blurred, embers turned to black.

"It'll be all over soon." Jacob pushed off the ground, rising like a mountain in the distance.

I jerked my gaze upwards and stumbled backwards as he came striding toward me, long, sure, powerful strides eating the distance between us.

"You'll thank me when it's done."

My knees gave way, sending me crashing down. But this time, his arms didn't save me, this time I hit the forest floor with a savage *thud*. Pain tore through my leg and into my hip. My scream shattered the air, driving away the stars above me until blackness reached out with a consuming fist and snatched me back.

I became aware of movement, of his steps as they crunched the dried pine needles on the forest floor and his hands as he slid one under my back and the other under my knees before he lifted me once more.

I floated in the emptiness, caught between slumber and being awake. My body shuddered, but the pain was dull here, dull and...gnawing. Jacob said nothing, there were no words of comfort, or to explain what he'd done, and as the fire of his blood moved through my body and spread outwards, it met that savage black hunger.

Pain met pain.

And the result was catastrophic.

A sickening growl echoed in the vast emptiness of my mind, and for a moment, I didn't realize the sound was mine.

***

His steps swayed me. My arm fell backwards over my head, fingers reaching for the ground. *Thud...thud...thud...*I jolted with every step, head snapping backwards as his boots impacted with the ground. In the distance, a Wolf howled, the sound long and sorrowful.

Jacob shoved, taking one massive stride, but this time there was no bounce of my head, no snatch and jerk of my spine. There was only the sound of rocks clattering beneath us.

Rocks...

Jacob gripped me in his strong arms and stepped again, and again, moving faster with every stride. Air buffeted my face like a cold, bitter slap. My eyes fluttered open with the sensation and sunlight stabbed in.

The mountain jerked and rose above me. I stared at the sheer cliff face and tried to piece together what had happened.

"Don't move...I don't want to drop you," Jacob growled, and reached higher.

Strong arms flexed as his fingers found a hold in the huge slabs of stone. He gave a grunt and then lifted. I caught the tremble of his muscles, the power and the strength all around me, and I turned my head.

There was nothing but the drop...and the ground far below us. Rocks fell in our wake as Jacob climbed once more, using only one hand to balance both our weights. I watched that rock as it tumbled and bounced off the stone wall, to freefall until the faint *smack* came seconds later.

Seconds.

That's how you worked out how deep the well was...seconds...I closed my eyes and tried not to move as the ground slipped further and further away.

There was no running up here, no fighting, no... *Sinful.*

Pain roared through my chest, and a muffled sound escaped my lips. Wetness spilled at the corner of my eye. I was lost to them now...completely and utterly lost. The sun beat down on me, scattering white sparks behind my eyes.

I'd hardly felt the warmth of the sun, but I felt it now. It beat off the smooth rocks behind me, and burned the back of my arm as it grazed along the cliff. Still we climbed higher...and higher...*and higher.*

"You going to open your eyes now?"

I focused on my breaths and the dullness in my body. Shivers wracked my belly, spidering pain swallowing every inch of me. I did what he demanded, cracked open my eyes, to find cool gloom. My cracked lips burned, stinging as a bead of sweat raced along the flesh and slipped inside my mouth. "Where are we?"

"Don't worry, we're safe."

Wasn't the answer I wanted. My body jerked and shuddered, muscles wound tight until my spine bowed and my legs started to shudder.

"You have a fever," he murmured and came closer.

There was the trickling sound of water as it splashed into a bowl. He set it next to where I lay and eased down next to me. A fire crackled and snapped, faint puffs of smoke drifted higher and were swept away.

I closed my eyes once more and rolled on my side. My body jerked and shuddered, and sweat stuck Cassian's white shirt against my back.

"Easy now." Jacob reached into the bowl and grasped a sodden rag.

Drops felt like heaven as they hit my skin. He dipped the rag back into the bowl and ran the cloth over my forehead. His brow furrowed the longer he stared at me, squeezing the cloth until the drops gathered substance and raced along my forehead.

I closed my eyes and moaned with the sensation.

His thumb skimmed my lips, and a drop of cool fresh water slipped in. I moaned and opened my mouth, and his thumb slipped in. "Fuck, you're beautiful, Asena." His tone was dark and dangerous.

Monsters used that tone.

Beasts waiting in the dark.

I sucked the last trace of water from his thumb before he slid it from my mouth and dipped back into the bowl. Drop by drop he fed me, letting the crisp seduction slide over the back of my tongue.

I swallowed, taking as much as I could as my body jerked and shuddered. He pulled his hand free and grasped the cloth once more. Fabric slid against my fevered skin. He dragged the washcloth down the long line of my throat as my spine arched and I pressed my body into the coolness.

Jagged breaths filled my ears. The cool slipped lower, drops splattered the open neckline of Cassian's shirt, then grazed my breasts.

I opened my eyes to watch him. Shudders tore through my limbs. "More...please, more water."

He reached his hand into the bowl and trickled drops over my breasts once more. In his eyes, I saw myself. Cassian's white cotton shirt was now wet and stuck against my breasts. Danger dwelled in his eyes...unhinged with longing.

I'd seen that look before.

I'd felt that hunger.

It was one that took what it wanted without care, and as my nipples hardened from the cool fabric against my skin, I knew there was no escaping him...the man I'd thought of as a friend was now my enemy.

10

I didn't dare move.

Jacob was the epitome of a warrior. Powerful, battled-hardened expression, heaving for breath, and hunger growing in those piercing eyes. Except, it wasn't war he craved.

His starved gaze lowered from my face.

His attention lingered on the thin white shirt Cassian had given me to wear. A shirt that was now wet and clinging to me, sticking to my breasts. My nipples pinched tighter, pushing against the fabric.

Was he going to take what he craved without permission? A savagery lashed his face, tormented and fragile. I'd seen men go mad with lust like that. But would Jacob? Would he take me against my will, gag my screams, and take what he wanted, over and over?

Fear grew inside me, promising darkness if I didn't escape, didn't fight.

Except everything still hurt. My body was exhausted. He'd overpower me in no time.

But Jacob had been my friend once.

The man I considered a brother.

Yet, I'd had no clue he was a Wolf.

A goddamn Wolf like the ones that we'd feared, who stole people from our village. Did he know? Was he involved?

"Why didn't you tell me?" I whispered.

I caught the glint of silver eyes as he lifted his gaze, then looked away.

My flesh prickled and sweat collected across my nape. It dripped down my back like the slow, savage drag of a finger.

Every time I looked at him, all I saw was Wolf. And I was torn on the inside that I'd been so oblivious. Had I missed the clues that he wasn't a human like me?

I might have once called him my friend, but now... Now I wasn't sure what we were. Or who exactly this man was, besides dangerous. I couldn't afford to show him my fear until I better understood his intentions.

My fingers flexed over the coat on my lap, and I dragged it to my throat.

"How are you feeling?" he asked instead of answering my damn question, reaching over, wetting my forehead with the cool rag. "The worst part of the infection is over."

"Fine," I muttered. *But you still haven't answered my damn question, have you?*

"I'm always here for you, Asena. I've told you before you could rely on me." His words darkened like I'd let him down. I remembered his anger when I'd left for the Sinful selection. His fury that I wouldn't stay with him. And his last words haunted me still.

Are you that blinded by your own need to get away from this town...or is it me you're running from?

He had kissed me.

He'd taken my mouth like the act would change everything between us.

But it hadn't. Not for me...

My heart didn't spark for him as it did for my Sinful, the three Vampires who'd dragged me into their world, ripped my life away, made me see there was so much more to them than what I'd originally thought. Our flawed happily-ever-after was all I grasped onto now, all I desired, despite the chaos and turmoil it brought. I couldn't picture another ending for us, no matter how broken it left me.

Instead of fearing the monsters, I now yearned for them. Maybe I was one of them to let myself fall so heavily.

When I didn't respond, the corded muscles in Jacob's strong arms and neck tensed, expecting more from me than I could give.

I broke my gaze from him and cast a glance at the sparking fire that lit up the large cave, the layers of fur blankets I lay on, the wind howling outside, the opening of the cave cloaked in darkness.

I filled my voice with a bravado I wasn't feeling right now, but Jacob didn't need to know how much I shook on the inside that the friend I'd thought I once had now lied to me. The betrayal hung over me like a noose, but maybe I was wrong. Maybe he had enough reason for hiding this from me.

"This whole time, and you couldn't tell me?" My words wouldn't come out right, they trembled too hard as my brain tried to catch up.

"I couldn't," he muttered, and reached out to touch my hand, but I pulled away from him.

"God, Jacob. I told you everything. And you…" my voice faded. I swallowed thickly. "When did that happen to you?"

"It's not a curse," he spat, like I'd just slapped him across the face. "You look at me like I'm diseased. You pull away like I'll hurt you. The abominations are the *Vampires*, the walking dead. I have a beating heart, a soul, just like you." His face tightened with fury, hand clenching the blanket over me.

"But you had to be turned. All Wolves are turned with a bite," I insisted, needing to know, to understand.

He eased back and settled on his heels, raking a hand through his hair.

"You want to know? *You really want to know?*" He shoved up from the blanket and paced the floor of the cavern. "I was just a kid, Asena. Just a stupid goddamn kid, playing on a swing in my backyard. I didn't even see the beast come for me. The coward attacked from behind." Jacob peeled back the collar of his coat, showing me the deep claw and teeth marks over his collarbone. Now healed, the skin that had grown over the wounds was bumpy and slightly pinker than the rest of his skin, a constant reminder of what had been done to him.

"I'm sorry." I reached for his hand as he neared. Warm fingers entwined with mine. Whatever this was...whatever he'd done to save me, he was still a friend to me. I held onto that, held onto the memories of all the days and nights we'd spent together after my parents were murdered. "You're lucky you survived."

"Lucky?" he growled, and stared at my fingers within his. "Luck had nothing to do with it. It was fate, Asena. Fate that turned me into something that can kill Vampires. Fate that has led me to you again."

His voice turned dark and dangerous. He lifted those dark eyes to mine.

"I survived." His head jerked upward, fierceness returning to his expression. "I lied to my adopted parents and I hid the wound. And at the next full moon, I turned. I'd do it all again...every terrifying, agonizing minute. I'd do it all again for you..."

My fingers slipped from his.

You're leaving me...for what? Hate and bloodshed?

"Fate came for me years later, when I got my revenge, too,"

That spark in his eyes dulled. Danger slipped into the room, stealthy and brutal. He admitted proudly, the emotions on his face sliding away, replaced by the warrior once more. He was changing the topic.

"Revenge?"

"I tracked down the beast who'd turned me. He never saw it coming, just like I hadn't." He smirked with such evil that it made me uncomfortable.

"He used to live in these very woods, you know." His smile was vile, and he must have seen me grimace. "Eye for an eye, Asena. That's the world we live in. Isn't that why you went with the Sinful? To drive your blade into their icy hearts?"

His mouth pursed. "This is who I am, Asena. A product of a horrible attack, and I've made the most of what I have. What are you doing?"

What was I doing?

For so long I'd been living in a dream, one so focused on getting revenge, I lost sight of myself. In truth, I hadn't cared about myself for too long, but looking back, I saw how blinded I'd become to my anger.

But without that path set in motion, I would never have met the Sinful, never had my life rekindled again or given me purpose beyond revenge.

"Don't look at me that way," Jacob snapped. "I saved you, saved you from that prison, saved you from..." the words raged in his eyes, still they never slipped from his lips. "You look at me with those same judging eyes."

He said those words again, the ones that reminded me that I owed him, that he'd done me a favor which needed a form of payment. And I hated him for it.

"I'm not judging you," I said. But my mind was swirling with everything he'd told me.

"You want to know what life is," he continued. Before I could respond, he kept talking, pacing around in the cave, the fire tossing his shadow across the walls. His shadow almost seemed to take on the form of a Wolf.

"Life is when a bunch of things happen to you, things you have no control over. Life is survival with what is handed to us and what we do with that information."

I tilted my head back, meeting his gaze, finding strong words that pummeled the back of my mind. "And is part of the survival attacking humans? Or were you protecting the villagers who were stolen and killed by Wolf attacks?" I wanted it to be the latter so insanely, to believe my friend was still inside this Wolf.

He halted with his back to the opening of the cave, where a silhouette darted past, then vanished. I wanted to say something, but his words distracted me.

"Innocent lives were lost, but it wasn't all our doing."

All *our* doing? "You weren't alone in the village, were you?" He couldn't have been, and I recalled all the times he'd gone into the woods to hunt alone, never worried, but always came back at night with several rabbits or a boar. He said he was the perfect hunter, but he was keeping things from me then, just like he was now. I felt it in my clenching gut.

A snapping twig sounded outside, and another dark figure rushed past like a specter of shadows, so fast I couldn't work out what it was.

I flinched backward, the hairs on my arms lifting.

Jacob glanced back over his shoulder to the outside, but he didn't seem worried.

I closed my eyes for a moment to calm my racing thoughts, my hammering heart, to ground myself, because everything was becoming too much, way too much.

"You need to trust me, Asena. I'll keep you safe, protect you with my life."

Trust?

How could I trust someone I feared? Someone who lied.

When I opened my eyes, Jacob was there, standing so very close, his head tilted to the side, studying me like a predator studies its prey.

Was I prey to him?

Someone meek and mild, someone who didn't have her own thoughts and needs.

The fire behind him seemed to glow around him, shadows slicing harshly over his face. He offered me a faint quirk of a grin. "Rest a while longer. Your body needs it." He stalked across the cave and crouched down against the wall across from me, knees bent, arms draped over them, eyes on me.

I couldn't decipher his look, but I knew without a shadow of a doubt that he wasn't going to let me walk out of there and back to Nightingale Manor.

Curling to my side, I slid further under the blankets, covering half my face so I didn't see him, and shut my eyes. An ache washed over me, followed by exhaustion. It wasn't long before sleep took me.

"*Aelin,*" Arkyn's distraught voice called me again.

My heart soared, and I whirled on my feet to face him, standing on a balcony, overlooking a great expanse of land. The sun dipped over the horizon, reds and purples streaking the sky like claw marks streaking flesh, looking ominously beautiful, but on the inside, I was torn and shattered.

"I have to go," he said, his lashes half obscuring those sorrowful blue eyes. And my heart was beating so hard, so heavily, I wanted to die.

"No, please don't leave." At my pleading words, he tilted his head high, and I saw the torturous agony in his gaze, the glistening terror of what was coming. He knew this might be the end. "I had a dream last night," I explained. "A dream of your fall."

A cry escaped my lips, my breaths coming too fast, my

shoulders shuddering as my tears fell at the memory of him taken from me.

I knew it deep in my soul, saw it come from miles away, yet I stood there helplessly, not sure how to stop the storm encroaching.

I took hurried steps to Arkyn and leaned against him, my arms folded around him. I pressed my cheek to his chest, savoring the feel of him, how perfectly we fit together. No heart beat in his chest, but he had more soul than most of those monsters who wanted us dead. I etched him onto my mind, his musky scent, the hard muscles rippling under my hands, every curve and dip, everything about him I wanted to remember, to keep tucked into my mind, to never forget.

"Aelin, you make it sound like I'm going to my death." His thumb and index finger captured my chin and lifted my head back as he gazed down at me. He tilted his head closer, his words a whispering breath on my face, "If I ever lost you, I'd rip apart the world, the universe, the underworld to find you again. I give you my word, being called to lead the Vampire army to war isn't going to take me from you."

Tears streamed down my cheeks. There were so many words I wanted to tell him, but instead, I drowned in the fear of losing him, feeling like I skated on ice without knowing how thin it was beneath me.

The faintest of caresses brushed my lips, like he tried to imprint himself on me… tried to remember how I tasted to take with him. I closed my eyes, letting myself fall and believe this moment would never cease.

The smell of burning wood and meat roasting teased my nostrils, and I opened my eyes. Arkyn was gone, and only shadows danced across the cave's walls. I tried to make sense of my dream. It felt so real, so fucking real that my heart was pounding in my ears, sweat dripped down my face, and I felt sick to my stomach with sorrow. Was I missing him so much that I dreamed about losing him forever?

Footsteps scuffed the stone floor, and I pushed myself to a sitting position, rubbing my eyes.

Jacob was sitting in front of the fire, head low, and outside, another silhouette flitted across the opening... a silhouette in the form a Wolf.

11

Jacob had stopped talking to me and glancing my way. He just poked the fattest rabbit I'd ever seen, roasting over the fire. I stole a breath and dragged in the delicious scent before pushing further upright with a trembling arm on the makeshift bed.

"That smells delicious."

But he never glanced my way, just sat with his back to me and stared into the flames. I hadn't heard him leave, hadn't realized he'd hunted and returned. I hadn't heard him move at all. The thought of that wore at me for some strange reason.

"You were fast," I prodded. "And that rabbit looks fat."

He shoved forward and added another stick to the fire before jerking his head toward the cup beside me. "There's water beside you. Take it slow, your body's still fatigued from the fever."

My hands shook as I reached for the wooden cup and lifted it to my lips. Cold water slipped along the back of my throat and hit my belly.

I moaned and gulped, taking long swallows before the cup was yanked from my greedy lips.

"I *said* take it slow," he growled and settled those enigmatic eyes on me.

My stomach tightened, howling and slashing agony through my middle. I clutched my belly and doubled over, closing my eyes. My breaths were carried on a moan as I rocked.

"Your body needs time, sip the water next time and you won't suffer."

But that was just it, wasn't it? I *was* suffering. I *was* in pain. I opened my eyes and jerked my gaze to his, meeting the hellfire in his with my own. "What are we doing here, Jacob? What's the plan?"

He turned away, leaving my questions unanswered...*again.*

"You must have some kind of plan, right? I mean, take a look at this place." Agony turned into fury, and I used that cold steel of rage to push myself off the blankets, and attempted to stand.

My knees trembled, and so did my voice.

But it didn't matter. I was here, and so was he...and it was about time we had this out in the open. "What...is...the...fucking...plan, Jacob?"

"Don't talk like that," he snapped. "You don't have to be like that, not anymore, not when you're with me."

I sucked in a shuddering breath and felt the water sloshing in my belly like a weight. "Like what? What am I like, I really want to know."

He just glowered at the fire, stabbing it with a pointed stick. Was it me he was poking at? Me he was driving the sharp end of the stick into? I forced a step and shifted my gaze to the blackened skin of the rabbit, sizzling and hissing.

"You've changed."

The words seemed to roll from what whatever black pit of rage he held inside, spewing like rancid smoke into the air.

"Changed? You're one to fucking talk. At least I didn't lie. You knew who I was, every step of the goddamn way."

"Who you *were*," he growled, and jerked his deadly gaze to

me. "Past tense. I don't know the person standing in front of me now."

Something had changed in the few minutes I'd been asleep. Some kind of shift that I hadn't been aware of. But I was aware of it now--*blindingly aware.*

I held his gaze, then looked around the cavern. There were hides piled in the corner, thick hides. The short brown hair of bison covered most of them, the ends reaching over the side, hiding some of the others. But the splash of orange from a fox lay underneath the plush white of a winter rabbit's hide. More lay on the floor underneath me, thick, suffocating, the stench cloying and heavy.

Hides like that you didn't just get from a season...you collected them over a year, a year of hunting in the spring and stalking in the snow. But it hadn't been a year, had it?

Which meant it wasn't his cavern...

My breath caught. If not his cavern, then whose was it?

I lifted my gaze from the stack of furs and glanced into the belly of the mountain. Strands of my hair ruffled with a gust of wind, wind that came from somewhere. I was willing to bet this tight crevice led to somewhere else, through the mountain and out the other side.

"I saw the bite marks."

I stilled as a slither of ice ran down my spine.

"The ones on your thigh. You let them do that to you? What kind of sick woman are you?"

I spun at the callous, menacing words. "You did *what?*"

He lifted his gaze to me then, and the flames of the fire danced in his eyes. One shove from the floor and he rose to his full height. "You let those *disgusting, filthy, fucking beasts between your legs?* You really are what he called you back in that cell, aren't you? You are a *whore.*"

My voice shook in a mixture of fear and rage as I took a step and stabbed the air, "Don't you *fucking dare judge me!*" I was unraveling, spooling out from the middle of a pit of slavery the kind I'd never met before.

And so was Jacob.

He closed the space between us in an instant, barreling toward me like a beast out of control. *"You let them bite you!"* he roared, demented eyes dangerous and wild. "Did you let them fuck you, too?"

He grabbed my arm, hard fingers bruising as he clenched tight. I saw the beast he'd become then...maybe he'd been a beast all along and I hadn't known it, a Wolf in a friend's clothing.

"What the fuck?"

We jerked our gazes toward the sound as a shadow filled the cavern's opening. Shadows splashed across his face, but I didn't have to see the silver sheen in his eyes to know he was a Wolf. I could smell his stench from here.

"What the hell is going on?" the stranger growled, and stepped closer.

And as the shadows softened across his face and his features sharpened, I saw the markings across his skin, ancient markings of a Wolf pack I'd seen once before, on the night they'd taken a boy from our hometown.

Black markings wrapped around his thick, muscular arms and reached upwards, circling his throat with intricate letters in words I didn't know. He settled those barbaric eyes on me and my skin crawled. His predator's voice was a throbbing growl. "You told us the mortal was dead."

There was a flinch from Jacob, a tiny pulse at his temple I'd seen before when we'd been cornered by one of the guys from town, a guy who thought because I was alone, that I was fair game.

I'd had my knife then, and had practiced throwing it with precision until I hit the mark time and time again. I could've taken him. I could've unleashed the steel with a flick of my wrist and sent him screaming back to mommy with a blade hilt-deep in his shoulder.

But I didn't have the chance to. Jacob had stepped forward, and the same twitch happened then as happened now. Blood had followed in that quiet laneway back home, blood and screaming and rage.

But as this Wolf stalked forward, casting me a careful glance as he stepped further into the cavern, I knew this was no kid from the streets.

He moved like a predator, thick rolling muscles and battle-worn body. Scars raked along his side, thick silver claw marks that'd healed some time ago. Like Jacob's, they were born of violence, clawed and beaten and left behind to die. Those who made it became ruthless and unmerciful, warriors who lived and died by their teeth.

"What did you think you were going to do with her, Jacob? Did you think the rest of the pack wouldn't find out?"

"You didn't." Jacob held the male's deadly gaze.

"You have a responsibility to the pack...and that," he cast me a glare, "that spells trouble. She needs to leave, Jacob. Now, before the others find out."

My pulse surged with the words. I took a slow step to the side, skirting Jacob, as he stood on one side of the fire and the older Wolf stood on the other.

"No." Jacob answered. "She stays."

The Wolf's lips curled as he bared his teeth. "You'll take a woman's side over the pack?" He came forward, stepping all the way up to the flames.

The rabbit still hissed and sizzled, some of the flesh turning black.

Jacob never answered, just stared the older Wolf down. I didn't understand what was happening. There was no command given to Jacob. No power in the strength of the hierarchy. Jacob should've cowered in the presence of this male, not meet his stare with utter defiance. Not like an *Alpha...*

An Alpha?

I jerked my gaze to Jacob. No...no, he can't be.

"They'll come for her after nightfall. Is that what you want? You're prepared to send your pack to die for a bloodsucking harlot like that?"

"I'm getting real fucking sick of being called names," I growled.

But they never glanced my way, never acknowledged they heard me at all. I kept my gaze down and took another step toward the mouth of the cavern, wanting to stay away from both of them, until, in a blinding blur...the older Wolf leaped.

He moved fast, on the cusp of a kill, only this time the kill was me.

I was grabbed by the arm and jerked from my feet. Blinding sun beat down into my eyes as he shoved me from the cavern and out onto the rocky ledge. The ground was blurred so far down. I stared at the tops of giant trees as a cold-blooded roar swept around me.

Rocks scattered, plunging through the air as they fell. I was wrenched backwards and my heart slammed against the confines of my chest as I windmilled my arms and stumbled back into the cavern.

My weak knees gave way and I fell, hitting the ground hard. Pain screamed in my knees as the two Wolves slammed each other to the dirt floor. Embers sparked in the cavern and flew through the air. I slapped at them as they burned right through my shirt and seared my skin.

But there was no time to care about being burned, as the two powerful men landed blow after brutal blow. Blood flew through the air with the nauseating sounds of fists on flesh. I scrambled out of their way as the rabbit toppled into the flames, and the sickening growls of two fully grown predators going head to head filled the air.

The sounds rebounded, guttural and dangerous. I scurried out of their way, shoving my back against the wall as they rolled around the fire toward me. Jacob was on top, wrenching his fist backwards before unleashing deadly blows. I'd never seen him like this, never so sickening...never so *animalistic.*

I lifted my gaze to the world outside. I could take my chance...try not to fall to my death. *Crack!* My stomach rolled with the sound. I jerked my gaze to where the older Wolf lay, dazed.

Blood trickled from the corners of his mouth. His lips were split, eyes rolled upwards until all I saw were the whites.

Jacob's sawing breaths filled my ears. He stumbled, shoved up, and fell on top of the beta before trying again. Only this time, when he achieved a stand, he grabbed the older Wolf's shirt and heaved his torso from the ground.

The Wolf's feet dragged behind him as Jacob grunted and jerked his body from the cavern and out to the ledge. My stomach tightened, heartbeat pulsing in the back of my throat, as Jacob glanced over his shoulder and those dark, merciless eyes pinned me where I stood. Then, with a terrifying shove, he pushed the male Wolf over the ledge.

12

"**No!**"

I lunged forward as the Wolf slipped over the edge of the landing and bounced off a stone ledge below the mouth of the cavern. My fingers were trembling, still I reached into the air, my arm dangling over the side.

Panic blurred that moment. The whole world seemed to stop, before the sickening *thud* seconds later. Jacob slowly rose, like he had all the time in the world...like he hadn't just thrown a man to his death. My breaths were all I had, all I felt, the only way I knew I was still alive.

"What?" he growled, staring out at the faint pinks and purples of an oncoming sunset. "Don't tell me you haven't seen two men fight to the death before."

To the death?

I'd seen death--the horrific image of my own parents filled my mind, their necks torn open and bleeding. I'd seen revenge. I'd seen desperation--but this...this wasn't any of those kinds of fights. No... this *was a silencing.*

A sinister lick of chilling cold crept along my spine.

The Jacob I knew once had cared for others. But he was not that person anymore. He was a murderer...and a captor. He was dangerous...especially to me. I pushed myself backwards from the precarious edge. Maybe I was next, if I didn't give him what he wanted.

And what was that? What *did* he want, exactly?

He didn't bother to contain his sneer when he turned in my direction, glaring at me through narrowed eyes, blood splashed over his cheek.

He considered me for a heartbeat. "You look surprised. Do the Sinful not kill people without mercy? They leave massacres in their wake, yet you look at me like I'm the monster." His voice reverberated off the stone walls.

"He was one of you," I protested as I stepped backwards, sinking into the shadows of the cave once more. "And you..."

"One of me? You can't even say it, can you?" He turned on me, stalking forward, pushing me until I tripped and hit the cavern wall. "*Wolf,* Asena. I'm a fucking Wolf. I've always *been* a Wolf, even before I was bitten."

I flinched at the words.

"I love this...this savagery." He stared down at his hands as though he expected to see blood. "This kill-or-be-killed fight for survival. They made me Alpha for a reason."

Because they were scared of him. Because this monster in front of me had enough hate inside him to kill the world. I didn't know how I hadn't seen this before.

How long had I been oblivious to the real Jacob? How many times had he hidden the lies in his eyes?

"Can you say the same about yourself?" he continued. "Living with shame and pretense while you whore yourself with Vampires. They are the enemies, Asena. They'll rip your throat out when you least expect it and they'll drain your body, leaving nothing behind but neat puncture wounds, just like the ones inside your thigh."

The words stuck inside my head.

Neat puncture wounds.

But I didn't have time to dwell on the image. Rage flashed inside me. "And you think I'm safer with you?"

His hand lashed out and snatched my wrist, fingers coiled so tightly, it stopped the blood circulation. Pain bloomed, crushing and grinding. But I refused to show him the agony. Fury warped his expression as he stared at me, eyebrows pulled together, nose wrinkled, the corners of his lips curling upward over sharpened canines. Except, looking at them more closely, I saw they weren't normal teeth, but jagged on the sides, with dozens of smaller sharp edges. Easier to tear flesh with when he attacked his victims, I guessed. One bite was all it'd take for him to rip through skin, to tear my throat out.

"Are you going to hurl me over the cliff, too?" I stood up to him, shaking nonetheless, but I held my head high.

That was when I knew that no amount of convincing or anything I said or did would ever change him from what he'd become.

His twisted features hardened and I braced myself, readied to fight him to the end.

Instead, he slowly unfurled his fingers from around my wrist and released me, the pressure easing. I stepped away from him at once as he looked confused for a moment.

He turned away and sauntered toward the fire. "I'll never hurt you, Asena. I told you that. I was protecting you."

I pressed my lips together. "You could have let me go...you could've left with me if that was the only thing you cared about. Instead, you decided to silence him...forever."

He didn't say a word, but crouched by the flames, replacing the half-cooked rabbit over the flames like nothing had happened.

Innocent lives, isn't that what he'd said?

Innocent lives were lost, but it wasn't all our doing.

Neat little puncture wounds.

Innocent lives lost.

The words clashed and clanged inside my head, like pieces of a jigsaw trying to fit.

He had killed some of the townsfolk and seemed perfectly alright with tearing apart families, leaving nothing but heartbreak and grief behind. This whole time, he'd pretended to care, to be one of us, but *he* was the real monster.

"Wolves and Vampires have always been mortal enemies, they've always hated each other. That's why, when those Wolf attacks happened in town, you never seemed distraught, but any mention of Vampires, and you became enraged. But this is more than that, isn't it? This is more than one breed against the other, more than the taking of sides." I accused.

He looked over his shoulder at me, those Wolf eyes darkening. "You have no idea how many Wolves I fought to protect the town. How long I'd defended *everyone...*" brown eyes darkened to almost black, the color of dirt, cold, packed, grave-dirt.

"But not everyone, though," the words slipped free. "You didn't protect everyone, not from other Wolves and not from the Vampires."

"We can fix this, Asena. I found you, saved you, and now we can rule together. You can rule by my side. And no one will ever touch you."

Rule?

My stomach churned, and the cruelness in his words terrified me.

"A mortal can't rule a Wolf pack, Jacob, even I know that." I met his savage gaze with my own.

"No, they can't."

I stiffened at the words and slowly risked glancing toward the ledge outside the cave. Was that why he'd silenced the older

Wolf? Was that why he'd hidden me here, away from the rest of his pack?

Would the Wolves come now?

Would they come for me?

Arkyn. Cassian. Lorcan.

My heart beat for my Vampires, calling with a constant pulse, an aching, hollow thing, always wanting, always needing, but never having. Pain webbed through my body, sharp and haunting. It seemed I was always trying to find my way back to them, only to be snatched away once more.

I stumbled on my feet, clenching my jaw to ride the agony.

A dull drum of pain beat in the back of my head. I swallowed the pain and tried again...*Arkyn, can you hear me?*

Blinding agony swept through me once more. Whatever curse the Vampires had on me still lingered, fainter than before, but it was still there, still flaring deep with the thought of them.

I cast an eye over to the cave opening, and then the room that offered no weapon but fur blankets, wooden cups, burning logs. In slow motion, I took sidesteps along the wall toward the opening.

"I've learned something since you left me." He rose to his feet, turning to face me.

My heart slammed into my ribcage, and I froze on the spot, my voice quivering. "What's that?"

"That if I wanted anything in life, waiting for it to happen was a fucking mistake. I had to take it with my hands and teeth." His hands balled into fists. "Just like I took this pack."

Anger exploded inside me. "With fear," I snapped. "Those Wolves leaving you gifts outside the cave, they were too terrified to come near you. That's not how you command a family."

"Family?" he scoffed. "Please. I've been your only family since you lost your parents, and look how you treated me. My own parents abandoned me as a child, and then so did you. But we

can still make this work, Asena. If you stay here long enough, their power over you will fade away."

"Power?" I whispered.

My heart boomed. *Love, that's what he meant. My love for them will fade away.*

I trembled with the deafening thunder in my chest. My fingers danced, twitching and curling, as the cave seemed to fade away. "Is that what you think? That they've somehow put a spell on me?"

"It's what I *choose* to believe," he forced the words through clenched teeth.

I stood at a crossroads; one road led to survival, and a lie, the other, to truth and maybe my own fall from the ledge of this cave.

But *both* led to freedom.

Freedom from him.

Lie to him, that voice inside my head whispered, and for a second I thought it was Arkyn's voice I heard...that my Sinful had found a way inside my head. *Lie to him and live. We will find you.*

"Things are going to change," Jacob continued, oblivious to the war inside my head. "You will learn to obey me. You will learn that there is only the way of the Wolf. It's for your own good, Asena. There's a war building out there, Wolves, and Dragons, and darker things...beasts that bring the blackest night. Beasts that snatched women from their beds while they slept and did unspeakable things to them. Things your depravity has never known. You won't go outside this cave unless I'm with you, Asena. You'll stay here until you can be trusted, and until the pack accepts you as their own."

"Stay here..." the words spilled from my lips.

Just another cell...just another captor. Another Corvina and Chaska. Betrayer. *Beast.* "You will lie with me. I'll mark you as mine. You'll be safe then," his voice was softer now, *huskier,* filled with years of longing. "It's for the best."

He came closer, pushing me against jagged edges of rock, like the open jaws of the cavern. "Mark me?"

"My teeth," he whispered, and fire danced in his eyes. "My body. I'm a strong lover, Asena...a *thorough* lover." He licked his lips, his eyes flicking to the open neckline of my shirt, and then to my breasts.

I knew what was in his head, knew the image he conjured, the image of me racked with fever, of the white cotton shirt Cassian had given me still soaked to my skin and sticking to my breasts, of my hardened nipples peaked under that fabric, just waiting for his fingers.

Did he ache to touch me? Did he see himself reaching out to brush a thumb across a tight nub? *I saw the bite marks,* his own words filled me. "Did you touch me while I was asleep, Jacob?"

He flinched and jerked his gaze to my eyes. Panic filled me, blinding, screaming panic. I could hardly hear through the howls of rage in my head.

"Well, did you? Did you push my skirt high? Did you part my thighs? Did you touch the place that torments you?" My own fingers trembled...but blind panic had a way of showing the captive the path to freedom. "The place of both your nightmares and your dreams?"

And sometimes the tormentor needed a little torment of their own. My fingers reached for the top button of my shirt. "Do you want to know what they did to me...in the dark...in the bloodlust? Do you want to know how they dressed me in a pretty dress and made me dance in a room filled with strangers? How they made me seduce a man I didn't even know, how they made me parade my body like it was his for the taking?"

A guttural, raw sound echoed in his chest and spilled from his lips.

"And how they ripped me from that dance floor and carried

me to a darkened room...where they tore that pretty dress from my body? How they kissed me, and not on my mouth?"

Jacob went still. Cold, unfathomable rage danced in his eyes. I knew then...knew as the pieces of the puzzle slipped into place.

Neat little puncture wounds.

Innocent lives were lost.

"It was *you* who killed my parents, wasn't it, Jacob? You who tore their throats out. You who left them bleeding on the floor."

"Yes." The word spilled from his lips.

One brow rose as though he didn't realize he'd spoken the truth. "They were going to take you from me. Going to send you back to your real parents. I was never going to see you again. I couldn't have that."

My lips trembled with the words. Deep down, I'd known all along they weren't blood of my blood. But I'd loved them...I loved them and he took them from me.

In an instant, my lip stopped quivering. I sank into that icy pit of rage, plunged into the depths without even taking a breath. My parents...pain slashed through me. I couldn't think about them now, couldn't let myself be consumed by their loss.

All these years, I'd hated the wrong beasts. All these years, I'd blamed the Sinful, and the murderer had been right in front of my nose. I swallowed that pain, used it as a steel to sharpen my blade.

"They fucked me...they *all* fucked me. They rode my body with their tongues and their cocks, and I liked it...*no*, not liked-- *I loved it.*"

His chest rose in savage breaths as my fingers worked the buttons, opening my shirt until the cool cavern air reached in with greedy fingers and I shoved the shirt aside. My breasts bounced, laid bare to his gaze.

I hardened, pulse racing, stomach in knots.

"Love?" He stared at my body like it was his for the taking. "Is that what you feel for those savages?" He jerked his gaze to mine. "You've allowed those filthy Sinful to get into your head and between your legs, to taint your skin with their touches, with their fangs." A heavy growl rumbled in his chest. "I'm going to murder them for ever touching you, Asena. You'll forget them, I promise you, and if you don't, well...I don't really care. I'll fuck the Sinful from your body *and* your mind if I have to. You won't even remember them when my cock stretches you wide."

He moved closer, his massive hand cupping my breast. Warmth pressed against me, where my body ached for cold.

Fear punched through me. I wanted to laugh at him. To make him feel like the miserable, scared little boy he'd always been as he kneaded my body and skimmed his thumb across my nipple. But I swallowed that urge. I clamped down on the insides of my cheeks until I tasted blood.

He stared at me like a starved, forgotten Wolf, a predator who was insatiable--only this barbarian wanted my body and not my blood. Holding my breath, I took a reckless step backwards. The rabbit still hissed over the fire. I did the only thing I knew to do. I met his stare, parted my lips, and uttered the words I never expected to hear. "Take off your clothes, Jacob. I want to see what I'm getting in return."

He grew silent, searching my eyes for a hint of a lie.

"You want me to spell it out for you? You saw me...and I'm betting you touched me, too."

A hint of blush rose in his cheeks. I swallowed the flinch of disgust and rage at the brutality and what he'd done to me and, instead, I forced a breathless whisper. "Take off your clothes and let's get this over with."

The corners of his lip curled. "Get this over with? Fine. You want me to fuck you, then I'll fuck you. I'll fuck you until that Sinful heart of yours starts beating real blood and then I'll make love to you. I'll use you as a whore until you become my wife, *if that's what it takes.*"

He lowered his hand and took half a step backwards, his hands dropping to the ties at the front of his trousers. He was already hard under the fabric, already thick and long, curving against his thigh. I swallowed hard and tried to fight the panic.

One tie after another, he opened his pants and then slid his thumbs under the waistline before shoving them to his feet. He was hard alright. His heavily veined shaft pulsed all the way from his balls to the tip. My mind raced, returning to Arkyn as he'd pressed me against the wall and buried himself between my thighs.

"Now what do you want, Asena?" Jacob purred, his eyes riveted on my gaze. "Now tell me what you want."

"Lie down," I commanded and gripped the sides of my skirt, hiking them up until I grasped my panties.

His breath caught as I slid the fabric down and stepped out of them. There was a brief flash of my slit, enough to make him sink to his knees. "You're going to ride me? Is that what's going to happen here? You going to climb on top of me and ride me like a beast?"

"Shut up," I snapped, my panties fisted in my hand as I stepped forward.

My knees shook, my will was trembling. I'd do anything to get back to them.

I'd do anything.

Jacob sank back on his haunches and then shoved his legs out as I stepped over him. I fisted my panties and snatched the length of my skirt upwards once more. "Lie back."

He did as I commanded. There was no fight in Jacob anymore, only lust, as his eyes traveled upwards while my rising skirt revealed my bare legs and inched toward my thighs.

Terror was rising in me with the surge of his breath. I lowered my gaze to his ready cock. A dip, of my knees and it'd all be over. I'd impale my body with his. He'd fuck me, just as he'd said he would, the truth raged in his eyes as I slowly sank downwards and my thighs parted.

"Close your eyes," I whispered. "Just for the first time, close your eyes." I lifted my dress higher, letting him see what he wanted to see.

Me, open for him.

Me, ready for him.

"Jesus fucking Christ," Jacob growled before he did as I'd commanded and his lids sank.

In the corner of my eye, the pink sky had darkened to deep purple. Night was coming...and with it...*the race of my life.* I dropped my skirt and reached outwards, my panties wadded in my grasp.

The hot stone still burned through to my fingers as I gripped the rock from the fire pit in my hand. But I'd bear the pain...for *freedom.*

I shoved the rock below his waiting cock, ramming it into his balls with everything I had, and then I shoved upwards, using what little strength my fever-ridden body had left.

And I ran.

Darkness was falling outside, but inside the cavern, Jacob's screams were deafening. I spun and lunged, not for the gaping mouth to the world outside, but to the darkness, to the night, and I scurried past the thick mountain of animal hides to the thin opening barely big enough for me.

Rocks scraped my skin. I gripped my seared panties and turned sideways. Jagged edges tore my flesh, stinging as I slipped through. Jacob's screams reached for me, spearing through the thin crack as I slipped deeper into the mountain and raced for the other side.

Emptiness swallowed me, there was no trace of light here. I hurried and stumbled, as Jacob's howls of pain and rage grew fainter.

The night was here...and so were the beasts who lived within it.

"I'm coming, Arkyn!" I screamed. "Do you hear me? *I'm coming!*"

And I will find you, his voice was as clear as it had ever been.

Like he ran beside me.

Like he held out his hand and led me through the cavern.

Asena, Arkyn growled...*Run...*

BOOK FIVE

1

ARKYN

Run to me, Asena. I drove the thought through my mind and out into the darkness as I speared into the darkened forest.

The vibrant red glow of the sun cut through the canopy overhead. Panic reared as I lunged between thick tree trunks on every side of me. I slammed my boots to the ground, holding onto that connection between us like my life depended on it.

In a way it did.

Asena was my life.

She was my constant driving force, my neverending battle to keep her heart beating, *and her life in this world.*

Desperation surged through me. I would not let her down, *not this time.* Fists curled, pumping through the air, I raced the fading light.

The hiss of my skin was instant. Faint light washed over my arm, burning and singing with its deadly touch.

Pain followed, tearing my mind from the faint connection we shared. I bared my teeth, and swallowed the growl of agony. Faint traces of red spilled between outstretched branches. I hugged the shadows, shoving the agony aside, before I scanned the growing darkness and ran faster.

Arkyn! she screamed, her desperation cleaving my mind.

I will find you, I shoved the desperate thought into the inky void. *Run to me, Asena, and I will find you.*

Desperation clawed along my throat, until I couldn't feel anything else. I jerked my gaze to the canopy as the last traces of red sunlight slipped away and shadows moved in.

I unleashed a roar, my battle cry tearing through the forest as I shot forward. She was still out of reach. High up, hiding in the darkness. I lifted my gaze to the faint feel of her. She was terrified, running...*through a mountain,* the words came to me.

Her terror filled me, her pulse like thunder in my ears.

I'd tear this world apart to get to her.

And I wasn't the only one...

Trees blurred all around me. Cassian and Lorcan were behind me somewhere, still held hostage by the threat in the sky.

Hurry, I sent a command to them. *She's running out of time.*

I didn't wait for a response, never slowed, just hurtled my body over a fallen tree and kept running. Darkness swallowed me, the crunch of the forest floor under my boots the only sounds I left behind.

I could feel her pain as she shoved against the sharp rock walls, her desperation, her rage. She was a shooting star up close, blindingly carving through my cold, dead, midnight world. Her dull and lifeless emotions were sharpening now, becoming clearer every minute she was alive. Whatever blanket of magic they used to cover her was now slipping. Our connection roared through, her panic, her terror, as she raced through the mountain.

I'd felt the moment she'd grabbed the rock from the fire. The screams in her head had filled mine. *That's the way,* I guided her with my own desperation. *Run to me, Asena.*

My boots slipped against slick leaves as I raced the incline of a hill and crested the rise. Faint white wisps of smoke drifted from a house in the distance. Night moved in faster now, somehow linked to my fight, *urging me to hurry.*

I did hurry, my focus not just on the trees ahead, but on every step Asena took as she tripped, fell, and shoved to her feet once more.

A dark blur whipped through the trees to my right. A midnight beast raced the sun. But that was no Wolf...*and no Vampire.*

I let out a savage snarl as I raced past the first house on the crest of the hill and scurried down the other side. More houses dotted the landscape in the valley. Worn reds and browns blending into rotting leaves.

Outlaws.

I'd seen communities like this, those who lived apart from the towns, who preferred to take their chances with the fur-cloaked beasts, *outside* our protection. As I raced through the middle of those ramshackle buildings, a different kind of beast exited a house, carrying a young woman over his shoulder.

Darkness spilled out around him. Shadows didn't just fall at his feet, but cloaked him instead, like a shroud, like he was the void itself.

Fae.

I clenched my jaw and slowed my steps. Of all the fucking monsters to run into...*why this one?* The creature was big. Bigger than the Wolves who hunted in the forest and, as he turned and lifted those infernal obsidian eyes to mine, hate mingled with surprise...a dangerous cocktail.

I glanced to my right as another Unseelie stepped out from amongst the trees and turned his attention on me.

"Going somewhere, *Vampire?*" the beast at my right growled.

I sucked in a breath and lifted my gaze, glancing at the woman over his shoulder and the savage glint in his eyes. *Asena,* she was all I cared about...all I needed. I shook my head, and lifted my hands. "This is not my fight."

Slow movements, *careful movements.* The wicked midnight creatures were dangerous enough on their own--but two of them? Two was suicide...even for a Vampire.

The woman over his shoulder gave a jolt, and then a moan, coming to in a rush. "What is this?" she moaned. "Where..."

She jerked her gaze to me and stiffened, head down, long black hair cascading like a waterfall until the tips brushed the back of the Fae's massive thighs.

The Unseelie turned a mammoth head, long dark hair falling down his shoulders. "Sleep," he commanded the woman.

Her gaze connected with mine, and I knew she was past the point of succumbing to his command. Her scream was like shattering glass, cutting the air with jagged edges, making me wince with the sound. Legs and arms flailed as she beat her fists against the Unseelie's head. But she may as well have been beating the night.

Small, feeble blows were useless against a monster like that.

Just like they'd be useless against someone like me.

The beast just gripped her thighs with a monstrous hand and took a step toward me. "She is ours," he warned.

Lights came on inside the other derelict houses, doors opened and men came out.

"Not my fight," I growled as the second Fae flanked my side. "I have no interest in the mortal woman." *Not* that *mortal woman, anyway...*

"Sleep," the second midnight beast commanded the mortals as they spilled from their homes to find immortal beasts in a stand-off.

"If you're not here for the woman, then why are you here, *Vampire?*" the beast snarled.

Arkyn! Asena cried out inside my head as she scrambled out of the mountain cavern and into the night.

"I'm coming," I answered.

"Coming?" The scouting Fae turned and stepped into my path.

"Let me pass, Unseelie," I threatened. "I have no fight with you."

"See, that's the problem." He took a step closer. "Can't let you pass now, Vampire, can we? For all we know, you'll be back with your brood and hunt our asses down."

I understood now, resigned to the cold, hard truth right in front of me. The didn't just see a Vampire...*they saw a commander.*

The beast wrestled the woman, shaking her on his shoulder as she kicked and wailed like a Banshee. I jerked my gaze from the Unseelie to what was obviously his commander. This Fae was small, more brains and not as much brawn, still he was a sizable opponent--if I wasn't desperate to get away. "I have no interest in your mortal woman, nor will I return. My fight is with the Wolves."

Red lips peeled back from glinting white teeth as the leader took a step closer. Black eyes glinted like the stars. "Now why is it that I don't believe you?"

"Believe what you want," I warned as a tightness cut across my chest.

*Tear them apart...*the need rose swiftly. *Kill them all if you have to*--I lifted my head and stared into the distance. *Whatever it takes.*

I clenched my fists and settled my gaze on the closest. "I'm giving you a chance now. Let me pass unharmed and I will forget I saw you."

The smaller Fae stepped closer as the big brute made for the trees. They cared about two things; getting the mortal woman they wanted and silencing those left behind.

"Let me down now!" the woman howled with rage and terror and went for the beast's eyes with her nails.

She fought that one, still he never hit her, never hurt her. Just grasped her with those massive hands as her nightdress rode higher up her legs. "What do you want with them?" I turned back to the one in charge and dropped my hand to the knife at my waist. "You don't bleed them, don't eat them, as far as I know."

The Unseelie just grinned and took a step forward, closing the distance. "Wouldn't you like to know, Vampire."

The towering beast of a Fae was gone in an instant, leaving behind the booming thunder of his steps, and the screams of his victim. There was no way out of this for me now.

Resignation settled in my bones as I palmed the hilt of my blade and settled into the fighting stance. They were savage warriors, cruel and unpredictable. Unmerciful. I'd heard the horror stories...and clashed with them twice before.

But never on my own.

"I'm gonna tear you apart, Vampire," the warrior said and came closer.

Dark eyes sparkled with the truth. But it wasn't *my* truth. And with a primal snarl, I shot forward faster than he expected.

The big beast's eyes widened as he lifted his hand to meet my blow. I showed him why he wasn't the only beast feared. My blade sank deep in his thick body, slashing across his chest...leaving a trail of red blood behind. "If it can bleed," I smiled "then I can kill it."

He stumbled backwards and lifted his arm, swiping a massive hand across his chest to stare at the smear of blood.

His lips curled, and a guttural rumble echoed in the back of his throat, spilling out into the night. Harsh breaths filled the night as he settled those infernal eyes on me, and then he lunged.

He hit me like a boulder, taking me down to the ground. He was heavy, crushing me with his weight, drawing me in close...I settled my gaze on the thick vein at his neck, and then wrapped my arms around him and struck, my fangs sinking into his flesh.

Warmth filled me, and the power of his line followed. Soul-destroying malice swept through me like a storm. I held on, swallowing until I could take no more. I did it for Asena...*all for Asena.* I tore away from his neck, taking a hunk of flesh and tendon with me.

He roared above me, driving out with a fist that connected with my cheek. My head snapped to the side, tearing me from underneath the Unseelie Fae.

He stumbled, slamming his hand over the gaping hole in the side of his neck. "What the fuck?"

I smiled and lifted my hand, swiping the mess from my mouth. "Like I said...*if it bleeds.*" With Asena's cries tearing through my mind, I lunged, driving my boots into the ground and lifted the blade into the air.

Hate mingled with savagery. Lorcan and Cassian's energy coursed through my veins. They were close...and gaining ground every second. I slashed the knife down at the same time the Unseelie lifted his hand, protecting the wound at his neck.

With a desperate roar, he shoved me backwards, driving the blade into his own flesh. I flew through the air and hit the ground, the knife slipping from my grasp as I rolled. He was on me in an instant, blood flying from his arm and his neck to splatter on my cheek.

His hands were around my throat, long, savage fangs coming for my own vein. Stars sparked in my eyes as I did the only thing I could from this position and drove my knee into his groin.

The beast's eyes widened. There was an *oof* before his hold around my neck eased. I shoved the commander, driving my hips off the ground and thrust him free.

"Goddamn sonofabitch," he snarled.

I wasn't above fighting dirty, not where Asena was concerned.

There was no escaping the end, not the one I wanted…but the one I was forced into and, as the rush of my bloodline swept through me and Lorcan appeared at my side, he threw his own dagger through the air toward me.

Cassian on one side, and Lorcan on the other, I gripped the blade and set to finish this once and for all. The Unseelie stumbled backwards, his wide eyes tearing from me to find my two warriors at my side.

"You should've let him go when you had the chance." Lorcan neared. "And now you never will."

The beast never trembled, never showed an ounce of fear. Not that I expected him to. Instead, he lifted his hands and clenched his fists, blood flowing in rivulets down his arms.

In another time and place, I might've allowed myself to respect the beast.

But Asena was running now, scrambling down the last of the cliff face to lunge for the trees. The Wolf was on her, filled with rage and pain. She'd never survive him.

I raced forward, driving the blade into the middle of the Unseelie before he had a chance to strike. He gasped, his eyes widening. I grabbed him around the neck, drawing him into the weapon, and then yanked the blade high.

Flesh and bone.

Sinew and sin.

It was all the same to me. Same death. Same desperation.

"Arkyn," my second called and took a step, his focus drawn to the darkness in the distance.

I pulled away, taking the knife with me and watched the dark Fae fall to his knees.

I didn't wait for the thud, never waited for that spark in his eyes to dull. The blow was a mortal wound, even for an Unseelie like him. I looked down at Lorcan's blade, the iron was dull, smeared with Unseelie blood.

It was the only blade my second-in-command carried, and the only blade that was deadly to the Fae. The only one he'd never see the end of. I cast the knife through the air, twirling end over end, until Lorcan caught it.

The Unseelie let out a gasp as I plucked my own knife from amongst the fallen leaves. "I truly am sorry," I murmured and lifted my gaze.

Cassian took a step, and then another, followed by Lorcan as they raced ahead. As I strode forward and then lengthened my strides, I knew in my heart I'd spill more blood before this night was done.

Run to me Asena, I urged. *We are almost there.*

2

Wolves howled in the distance, and I grimaced, throwing a gaze over my shoulder. The settling night choked the forest, chasing away the remaining pockets of light.

Arkyn, I reached for him in my mind, and thin weblike threads of our connection moved over my brain, filling my body with warmth.

Keep running and don't stop. Don't ever stop. I'm coming. We're coming.

His words drove me, my steps pounding the forest floor, and I sucked sharp, ragged breaths into my lungs. The breeze was cold tonight and it tugged on my clothes and hair.

But I winced and clamped my jaw each time I stepped onto a sharp rock. Burning pain shot up my leg from my injured foot. The fever may have passed, but the wound hadn't healed. But stopping wasn't an option.

If Jacob caught me, he'd hurt me in the most vicious way. My freedom had been stolen from me, but I'd die before letting that monster claim me.

My breaths hiccuped from everything that had happened

too fast, and tears blurred my vision. The bastard killed my parents just so they wouldn't take me away from him! He was so fucking young when he did that, what atrocities was he capable of now?

Son of a bitch. He deserved so much worse than a rock to this dick. He didn't deserve to live. Grief surged with each expelled breath as I pictured my parents on the kitchen floor, bloody, with throats torn, their bodies covered in bite marks.

Vampires, Jacob had insisted at the time. *The Vampires did this.* He'd forced those thoughts into my head, and I was too broken, sinking too deep, to make sense of anything logically. I cried for weeks and couldn't understand why anyone would murder my parents.

I was just a freaking child, terrified and left alone in this world.

Vampires, he pressed the issue, telling everyone he'd seen one in town that same day of my parents' death, and even convinced the village elders.

So I believed Jacob. I grasped onto anything he said. Even if he was only a few years older than me, I looked up to him and took the helping hand he offered. He was all I had left, and I fucking believed him.

My insides were alight at what he'd done, everything he'd taken from me.

My foot caught on a tree root and I stumbled over a shrub, lurching forward in a wild pinwheel of my arms, my heart hammering. Stumbling, I caught myself before I fell over.

That was so close. "Just calm down," I mumbled to myself.

Strange sounds growled behind me.

Panic raked through me, shuddering at the core, my lungs straining to keep up.

The growls continued, and I jerked around, a whimper on my lips. I stared into the forest, holding my breath. I gazed up at the mountain where Jacob's den stood. The memory brought back agony and heartache. I'd always trusted him, always believed he was there for me. Lies, everything was a lie.

And he wouldn't be far behind me, he'd chase me to the farthest reaches of the world and kill me before letting me escape. He'd rather see me dead than end up with the Vampires.

Gulping mouthfuls of air, I turned and ran again. Every step seemed to be miles away from reaching the Sinful, and I was now running full tilt, ducking under lower branches and leaping over dead logs.

I was determined to survive, to prove Jacob wrong, to show him that despite manipulating my earlier years, he wouldn't win. He wouldn't control me ever again.

Paws hitting the ground carried faintly on the wind. My heart pounded in my rib cage, and I jerked my gaze behind me, seeing movement between the trees closer to the mountain. They were coming. Jacob and his pack were coming.

I whimpered with terror and pushed myself faster, harder. I blinked back the tears, hissing each time I stepped on a stone, but never stopped.

Asena, I will find you, just never stop.

The Wolves are coming for me. I reached a rock wall, connected to the mountain. I winced as I frantically looked from side to side, to see how far it stretched outward. Spinning around, the shadows in the distance moved closer, fast, huge, and vicious.

Run!

And I did. I took the only path away from the mountain, away from the stone wall. My feet punched the ground, arms swinging, and my breaths raced as I came out to an ocean of pines.

Never stop.

Never stop.

Never stop.

The land sloped downward, my feet slipping over the dried leaves and twigs and I almost tripped over. I grasped the branches and oversized shrubs to stop myself from falling head over heels.

A great roar sounded overhead, followed by a blinding snap of light. The heavens came to life in the blink of an eye.

Fire licked the sky like hell had cracked open the heavens and was descending upon us.

Ferocious.

Terrifying.

I screamed and flinched toward an enormous tree, hiding beneath its heavily laden branches.

Gripping the trunk with trembling hands, I glanced up through the gaps of the branches. I was too scared to make a sound.

Two winged beasts speared through the darkening sky. Wings spanned out, barbed tails lashing left and right, and fire spewed from their gaping mouths.

Dragons! Oh, fuck!

The enormous monsters soared high above in our land. They rarely traveled to these parts of the territories and stayed closer to their mountains. So why were they here?

The dreadful screeching sound came again, piercing my ears. The world trembled beneath my feet. If Dragons were attacking, we were as good as dead.

Overhead, the sky was on fire each time a Dragon unleashed a breathful of flames. The stench of burning wood reached me. Far behind me, an explosion of flames hit the woods, orange flames devouring everything it touched. In the blink of light, the shadows following me splayed out in every direction. The pack. They were scattering, and I had to get out of this hellish place. I ran.

But...Abruptly, I halted. My heart beat furiously as I teetered on my feet, concealed by the shadows of lofty trees. The heavy stench of burning flooded the air, the sudden sharp blast of winds buffeting against me.

My nerves were stretched taut, and the urge to run jarred through me. But my feet were glued to the ground, my mouth hanging open. My fear tripled at seeing a monster coming right in my direction.

A Dragon descended toward me from high above, its scales glistening a russet color. Wings folded tight against its body, it skimmed over the tops of the forest. Its eyes gleamed red, like fire burned behind them. Dagger-like horns ran from the top of its head and down to the back of its neck. Smoke wafted from flaring nostrils, and it was enormous. It'd devour me in one bite.

The scent of fire wafted as it swooshed low overhead, passing me, sending the trees into a wild sway, the gust of wind crashing against me. Desperately, I held onto the tree.

I whipped my head around to follow it, as my heart nearly stopped beating.

When it roared, fire shot from its mouth, singeing the branches in its path, leaving behind a fiery glow.

It unleashed a world-shattering screech as its enormous wings snapped wide and beat, taking it higher, clearing the trees. It rose so fast, it vanished from my sight in mere moments.

Intense heat lashed over my body from the burning forest, and I backpedaled, covering my face and eyes from the inferno. The Dragons were attacking the woods, marketing their territory, making their presence known.

I stared out after it, unable to believe what I'd just seen, trying to get my mind around what happened. Dragons were feared, but rarely seen, and that was the first time I'd seen such a beast.

Something wasn't right. Why were they here?

If, by some miracle, I escaped the Wolves, I didn't want to end up a victim of the Dragons.

Keep running. Arkyn's voice came again. *The sun is almost gone.*

I groaned from the fiery blaze of the burning trees and turned to my right, then ran faster than I thought possible. I'd heard stories about Dragons who held no control over their beast sides, who attacked the moment they were angered. And they always showed their dominance by burning down enemy lands. Many said they hid treasure in the mountains. Piles and piles of gold and jewels, though no one had ever seen the treasure. I wasn't sure if I believed that tale, but the myth that worried most girls was that they could smell someone's blood and tell if they were a virgin. And that was how they determined which females they kidnapped from villages. That story I believed, since so many humans went missing in those villages near the Dragons' mountains. Though I never understood why eating a virgin tasted better than others.

A single howl from somewhere behind me rent the air, and I drove myself harder. One leg after the other, I rushed down the hill, the rustling of foliage under my feet stolen by the wind whipping the branches around me. I prayed it would also disperse my scent from the Wolves.

The snap of a twig sounded.

I flinched around with dread, my chest locking up, and my legs tangled underneath me. My feet suddenly slipped out from under me. I fell on my ass and slid down the steep hill, my stomach lurching to the back of my throat.

I screamed as I moved faster and faster, now rolling out of control, the world rushing past in a blur, my head spinning. My breaths grew ragged and harsh, and I was terrified. I knew the pain was coming, and I tensed, waiting to hit something, to fall off a cliff, something to stop my momentum.

Everything darkened around me, engulfing me and swallowing my vision. The air shoved against me, and I shut my eyes, waiting, screaming for the inevitable.

The ground was solid, the shrubs I crushed were pins

stabbing into my flesh and ripping my hair out. I felt my bones move and ache, almost jangling inside me.

One moment I was rolling, the next thing I was airborne, and my eyes shot open, my arms and legs flinging outward. But I fell too fast to see anything and hit a pool of icy water, dragged underneath, the air stolen from my lungs. I hit a pebbly river floor, my skin grazed and cut.

I cried, dread strangling me. I couldn't die here, not after everything.

Asena, cross the river. Cassian and Lorcan called me in unison, and I reached for them in my mind, desperately needing them. Their voices were a lifeline I clung to... for them, I'd keep fighting.

Still, fear ripped through me as I wildly thrashed and kicked to reach the surface. The gushing water pushed and pushed me, dragging me like a wild stampede.

I kept paddling when I fell into the river. My head broke the surface, and I gasped for air. But the raging current washed over me, dragging me under once more, its frozen claws driving icy cold into my flesh.

Beating my legs and arms against the current, swallowing the icy water, I fought with everything I had. I no longer felt my body. Adrenaline had taken over, consumed me, as I fought for my life.

I'd survive. I had to. I didn't go through everything to drown in a damn river.

Popping back to the surface, I gasped for air, and fought to stay afloat.

I passed a boulder in the river and I frantically reached out for it, fingers grappling over the wet surface, fingernails digging in, finding purchase. I held on as the water shoved me around the stone. I latched onto it with both arms and stayed there, clinging to it, drawing in fast breaths. Tears fell endlessly.

I'm so scared.

We're close, Asena. You've come so far, Lorcan answered that time.

My teeth were chattering, and I held still, terrified.

You fall down ten times, you get up eleven times, my beautiful baby, Arkyn whispered. *Please, keep going. For me, for us.*

The river rushed past me, and at first, I didn't move, but trembled from the cold, from the terror throttling me. My body ached and everything seemed too hard. I choked on my cries, so tired of running.

Looking back up the river, I eyed the small cliff I must have tumbled off. I had no idea how I'd survived that, but somehow, I had.

Arkyn was right. Sitting here made me an easy target. I had to move, had to keep going. They'd be here soon, they had to. The red from the sky was vanishing, and night would be here in a heartbeat.

Casting a glance around, I spotted several large rocks sticking out of the river like the one I clung onto. With the next stone a bit further down from me, I pushed myself off my rock and paddled wildly to cross the rapids as it carried me down. I threw myself at the next stop, breathing insanely hard, and holding on for a few moments before I moved from one stone to the next. No thinking, or I'd freeze with fear. When I finally moved closer to the other side of the river and my feet touched the pebbled bottom, I flung myself toward the shore.

Dragging myself out of the freezing river, I groaned against the pain. My whole body shuddered with agony, my muscles trembling. I stared down at my torn clothes, ripped and reddened skin, my knees grazed but not bleeding. Everything ached and burned.

When the wind came again, it carried with it an iciness I'd never felt before, and I shivered, rubbing my arms.

Cross the water and run. Move fast. Arkyn's voice streamed through my mind.

A guttural growl came from the woods at my back. I paused only long enough to notice black shapes emerging from the woods across the river.

A shiver ran through me at how fast the Wolves moved, how quickly they'd tracked me. All I pictured was the fury on Jacob's face back in the cave, the rage in his voice, how his jaw clenched like he was ready to strike. And now… after what I'd done, he'd carry no mercy for me. He'd murder me, just as he had my parents.

I whipped out of there, bursting into the woods, running for my life again.

3

Wolves bayed all around me. They were getting closer, gaining with every beat of my heart.

So are we, Lorcan growled inside my mind.

I raced amongst the trees, my soaked dress slapped around my legs, sticking and tangling, making me stumble. I shoved out a hand, slamming it against the trunk of a tree. My legs shook, my breaths were like fire in my chest. I shook my head, chasing the blur from my eyes. "I can't do this…"

Can and will *do it,* Arkyn's demanding voice cut through my mind. I pushed against the tree, listening to the savage sounds of them charging through the water behind me.

There was no way I could outrun them, no way I'd survive this night.

You only have to get to us, my Vampire growled. I closed my eyes for a second, and like a lightning strike, he filled my mind. *I will get to you, Asena. Keep running, my love…keep running.*

I took his strength, used it in place of my own, and shoved away from the tree. My steps were slow at first, sticks stabbed and cut as I began to race forward. Barking followed behind me, howls that sent shivers along my arms. A cry slipped from my lips as I shoved forward. I ran blindly, everywhere I looked there were trees and more trees.

I could be running in circles for all I knew. Slick leaves stuck to my feet as I scrambled over a fallen tree and raced around a thicket of thorny brambles.

I had to keep going...keep pushing forward, no matter what.

A blur came from my right, and the pounding of paws followed. They were trying to race ahead, cutting me off. I scanned the darkness and drove forward. There was a steep drop to one side...the bottom filled with darkness.

I jerked my gaze behind me and then hurried ahead, dropping to my hands and feet to scramble down the steep drop. My feet slipped from under me just as my dress caught on a snapped root sticking out of the ground.

The sound of tearing fabric filled my ears before the rush of air followed. I fell, hitting the ground with a brutal thud. Air rushed from my lips. Pain followed as I tried to breathe, and an unseen band around my chest cinched tighter.

Hurry...Lorcan's voice tore through my mind. *You can do this, Asena...hurry.*

I closed my eyes for a panicked heartbeat and then shoved forward. The trees were thicker down here, clumped tighter like a blanket all around me. Short, panting breaths were all I had. I used them, timing my steps, and made it to the first group of trees and stilled.

My breaths deepened, the strap around my chest loosening with every second. I shoved from the trunk and hurried forward, but movement came from my right...like a flash in the darkness.

"I'm going to fucking kill you...you goddamn *bitch!*" Jacob roared.

I froze, fear slicing through me like an icy blade.

He was up there, hunting...*hurting.*

I shoved forward, stumbling to the next stand of trees and

reached out, leaning on smooth, tall trunks. I did that. I tried not to think about the moment I'd shoved that rock into him, but the second I pushed the image away, it came roaring back.

I could still feel his thick body between my thighs, see the need raging in his eyes, still smell that heady, cloaking scent of his hunger. Even now, my fingers stung, burned from my grip on that stone. The hiss of his flesh haunted me.

I hurried forward, racing the call of Wolves above me, and shoved out from a clump of fir trees, heading to the next. But the moment I stepped out into the small clearing, I felt it.

A Wolf...waiting for me.

"Going somewhere?" the male growled as he strode out into the opening.

I flinched, my heart hammering, and scanned the forest behind him.

"Don't worry." He headed for me with long, powerful strides. "We're all alone down here...*for now.*"

I shook my head and stumbled backwards, shoving out my hand behind me. "Stay away from me."

"You almost killed our Alpha," he snarled, closing the distance between us. He had thick, strong, bulging muscles under tanned skin, too big for me to fight, even if I'd had the element of surprise.

I said nothing, just risked a glance behind me and kept moving backwards. The ground dropped away again far off in the distance, like we were racing along a ledge.

"There's nowhere to run," he came for me, darkness and danger in his eyes.

I whipped my body around in that moment, my heart lunging as I raced forward.

"I always like it when they run," the Wolf growled behind me.

I did run, stumbling and lunging. My vision blurred at the edges, narrowing down to the cluster of trees in front of me.

Sickening snarls spilled out around me, punctured with a sadistic chuckle. I was a toy to him...a *plaything.* In that moment, I knew how a mouse felt under the watchful eyes of the cat.

No, Asena, Arkyn's growl pierced the terror inside my head. *You are far from a mouse. You are a lion. You are stronger than you think. Run, my love...run, we are almost there.*

I shoved forward, clutching hold of Arkyn's words, using them as a crutch to keep going forward. Darkness was all around me. My breaths turned white in front of me as the cold, bitter night air swept in. Still I hurried forward, reaching out to snap a thick branch as I stumbled.

"Come now, Mortal," the Wolf sighed.

"Stay away from me," I wielded the shattered branch like a club, swinging it through the air behind me. "Don't make me hurt you."

Hurt him, Cassian urged. *Tear the beast apart...or I'll gladly do it for you.*

But the Wolf just chuckled and kept striding forward with massive, ground-eating strides.

My heel caught on something, pitching me backwards. I threw out my hand and the branch tore free, hitting the ground. I risked a glance at the branch and then at the Wolf once more.

"You were saying?" One brow rose as he grinned. He was ugly when he smiled, cruel and sadistic...I'd seen a smile like that before.

...mortal whore! My captor's words tore through me.

But there were no Vampires to save me here, no secrets I could bargain with. There was nothing but the endless forest and the desperate baying of the pack as they searched for me.

"No one but us, sweetheart," the Wolf smiled, baring long, wicked fangs.

My heart leaping at the sight, I spun and lunged, but not for the trees...I'd find no safety there. I had only one hope...one reckless fight for survival.

I headed for the ledge...for that sheer drop into the unknown. *Please don't die...please don't die...*my own thoughts pleaded, consuming me as I raced for that edge. A tree had fallen, hanging into the dark void. I raced for that tree, hurtling my body through the air, with the pounding sounds of the Wolf on my heels.

"No!" he roared.

I reached for the edge, driving my heels into the soft forest ground and lunged, until I was hit from the side.

I slammed onto the ground, stars dancing behind my eyes, as the Wolf reared over me. "Going somewhere?" His words blasted my face with his heavy breath.

I turned away from his gaze and stared at the edge, inches away. "Get the *fuck* off me!"

"Or what?" he chided, his heavy body crushing mine while he forced my knees to part and slid between my thighs. "What are you going to do, *Vampire bitch?*"

"I'm so fucking sick to death of people degrading me." Cold, hard rage slipped into my tone as I turned to face him once more. "You small-minded, pathetic piece of shit."

But my insults made no impact, instead he ground his body against mine, thrusting his hips. He was already hard...already hungry.

A savage to the core.

My blood ran cold with the feel of him. Terror welled inside my stomach. "You'll die." I met the silver shine in his eyes. "A most horrible death."

He just sniggered. "I don't see your Vampires around here, *Vampire whore.*"

My gaze trembled, drawn to the movement at his back. But I kept my focus on the sparkle of delight in his eyes. "No," I whispered at the glint of a blade, "she will."

The sudden jerk of the blade against his throat made me scream. Hard, feral eyes met mine as blood splashed against my chest. The Wolf behind him rose and wrenched my attacker's head backwards, opening the slash even more.

"This was your last victim, Lette." The female snarled, and dragged his body from mine. I pushed my feet against the ground and shoved backwards.

She just stared at me with a mixture of sympathy and disgust, her fingers entwined in the male's long hair. He jerked and bucked, reaching up to grasp her wrist.

But there was no escaping what was coming for him...*death*. I tore my gaze from her to the dying Wolf and, even though I hated it, a surge of satisfaction swept through me.

"Run." The female commanded. "My fight was with this one, not the others."

I gave a nod, fully understanding now. I was on my own from this moment forward.

Me against a pack of hungry, terrifying Wolves.

I shoved up from the ground and stumbled forward as the sickening, hacking sounds of a knife came once more. Silence followed, a chilling silence that swallowed me whole.

I made for the steep decline once more, only this time, it was no plunge to my death. I reached out and grasped a branch of the fallen tree, using it as a rope to slide down to the bottom.

Howls turned faint above me, moving further away. But they'd be after me again soon enough. I needed to hurry. I raced forward, the warm blood on my chest cooling fast. Maybe the scent would protect me...*and maybe my Vampires would think I was a threat?*

Arkyn! I roared. *I'm covered in Wolf's blood.*

The savage roar of his delight filled me. *That's my warrior,* he growled.

Just know it's me, I pleaded.

Asena, Lorcan's voice was as clear through my mind as the cold, night air. *I'd know you if you wore his pelt and howled at the damn moon. We are close, my love. Keep running.*

Hope surged inside me as I pushed forward, grabbing handfuls of dead grass for traction, and scurrying up the incline of the gully. I was going to make it...I was--the sharp, warning growl cut through the trees on my right.

My heart nearly stopped at the sound as I jerked my gaze toward the darkness. A flash of white was followed by the rush of a thick sable coat. Wolves ran in their animal form, driving long, lean bodies through the forest toward me.

Asena! Arkyn roared.

A heavy *thud* echoed behind me. I spun, looking into the silver eyes of the biggest Wolf I'd ever seen. I knew who it was, even as it limped toward me, black lips curling to reveal its teeth.

"Jacob," his name spilled from my lips.

I shook my head and took a step backwards.

"No," I cried, thrusting out my hands. "Don't do this."

Still he came closer, slick trails of saliva dripping from his lips, until he stopped. In a heartbeat, bones snapped, driving his thick body down to the ground. Muscles rolled, tendons stretched, and the thick coat of fur was gone, his body drew it inside, leaving pink skin in its wake.

"I'm going to fucking kill you," the guttural words raked over my soul as he rose. "Starting with your fucking tongue."

There was no compassion in his eyes now, no hope of a love rekindled, even if it was only one-sided. There was only the monster laid bare, the beast he'd always been.

"I never wanted to hurt you." I shook my head. "But you gave me no choice."

"I gave you no choice!" he roared, standing to his full height. "Look what you did to me!" He opened his arms and spread his legs, giving me a full view of blackened skin and charred flesh.

I didn't want to lower my gaze...didn't want to see what I'd done.

His cock was red, raw, and blistered, bits of flesh flaking off to fall onto the ground. It seemed like shifting into his beast hadn't healed him.

"I can't wait to hear you scream. I can't wait to see the moment where you know death has come for you...it could've been different, Asena. If only you loved me."

He strode forward.

More Wolves came out from the trees. I counted three...four, and stopped counting, and then stopped moving. My legs trembled as I held my ground, as the towering Alpha stared me down.

There was no point in running. My legs trembled, knees locking and unlocking, barely able to hold my weight. I sucked in hard breaths as Jacob lowered his gaze to his warrior's blood across my chest.

A Wolf lunged at my side, jaws snapping, teeth gnashing the air. I whimpered, and closed my eyes. This was it...*the end.*

Arkyn. Cassian...Lorcan. I whispered their names, one...last...time...

But there was no answer. No blinding flare of hope, no desperate words to keep me fighting. There was just silence...*just empty silence.*

This was death.

True death.

I opened my eyes, seeing my fate in the savage, glinting eyes of the Wolf as Jacob opened his jaws, ready to strike.

Until, out of the consuming darkness, came a roar like I'd never heard before. A blood-curdling, chilling roar...*no, a battle cry!*

Jacob lifted his massive head as a blur cut across me. Strands of my hair lashed my forehead with the blast as Jacob was hit and thrown through the air.

I cried out at the sight as Arkyn landed on his feet in front of me, dishevelled, desperate, and very...*very* pissed off. Another gust of wind, one at my right...and then another at my left.

Cassian...and Lorcan, sucking in heavy breaths, eyeing the Wolves around us.

"You," Arkyn lifted his hand, the tip of his knife pointed at Jacob. "You, I will slaughter."

My heart lunged as my Vampire turned his head and met my gaze, then finished, "But I have no fight with the rest of your pack."

Jacob shoved his heels against the ground and scurried to stand like the rodent he was. "Fucking bitch!"

His anger raged at me. Arkyn stood in front, shielding me with his body.

He was so much bigger and more powerful than I remembered him. A shiver traveled through me at the sight. He was a god... a battle god. I remembered the paintings in the manor, in the temple, of him in armor, of the slain behind him. He was in his element. I saw it in the rigid way he held himself, in how his gaze was everywhere at once, aware where every one of his enemies remained.

Jacob turned his head at the howl of wolves and stepped backwards. Cassian and Lorcan took a step, standing side by side with their commander, sentinels, warriors. I almost choked on my tears at seeing them. It was all too much, too much running, too much hate and war.

Tears slid down my cheeks before I could stop them.

Arkyn marched toward me, and I crashed against him. My arms snapped around him as I molded my body against his, feeling familiar and comforted, like I'd been in his arms hundreds of times before.

Tears fell, and I cried from all the terror, from almost dying, from missing the Sinful. In that moment, I would do anything he asked, anything he wanted, because I trusted him with my life. My breaths still came too fast as I tried to calm my racing heart.

It was a weird thing to have wanted to run from them for so long, to want to get revenge for my parents' deaths, but I'd been wrong. I'd been so *fucking* wrong about so much. Now, I craved to be with the Sinful with a hunger I'd never experienced before.

Arkyn kissed the top of my head, and for those few stolen moments, he held me tight, arms around me trembling like losing me would tear him apart. I looked up at the Vampire through tear-blurred eyes, at the perfect full lips, sharp cheekbones, and those intoxicating blue eyes that offered me solace and love.

"I thought I'd never see any of you again," I admitted, but those words weren't even close to how I felt inside, how my heart trembled at the thought of losing them, how everything between us seemed so familiar but just out of my grasp, almost like I'd been here before. Regardless, through all the chaos of my mind and life, I had no doubt that I was meant to be with them. I knew that now, more than I ever had.

"He'll never touch you again," Arkyn growled.

"His pack rules these woods. They're everywhere," I warned.

Cassian and Lorcan stepped closer, their faces taut and battle-ready, but when they met my gaze, a softness swept over their expressions. They carried a need just like the one clutching my heart.

I clung onto Arkyn. "I wish we could just fly out of here, leave all this death behind. I don't want anything to happen to any of you."

His gaze turned to the shadows coming in front around us, the four-legged predators hunting, trapping their prey.

He swiveled back to me. "*We* are the ones who won't let anything happen to *you*."

And I believed every word, believed they'd lay their lives on the line for mine.

He leaned down and kissed me quickly, the tenderest of touches, flooding me with warmth. I held onto him for dear life, kissing him back like somehow this might be our last time. I hated thinking that way, but the strangest déjà vu streamed over my mind.

Growls and roars echoed from within the woods around us, and I flinched. Arkyn held me close to him, a protective arm around my back.

Cassian darted to the right, Lorcan left, gone in a heartbeat.

Arkyn pulled back from me too soon… it would always be too soon, but this wasn't the place to get caught up in being sentimental.

Shadows closed in from further ahead, and my pulse drummed through my veins.

"Stay low and out of sight. Let us handle the Wolves. This is long overdue," he growled.

He walked me hastily to an oversized pine. "Sit here, and if anything comes near you, you scream for me. Understand?" His hand cupped my face, and the fury behind his eyes was terrifying. It wasn't for me, but those who'd hurt me.

I fell to my knees and sat on my heels, my back to the tree. I couldn't stop shaking, and my instinct had me wanting to keep running. But there was nowhere to go. The Wolves would keep coming and coming.

"I'd die to keep you safe," Arkyn whispered. Then he whipped around and lunged for the two Wolves racing up behind him. They all moved so fast and clashed, the sound thunderous, dust from the ground billowing around them.

He'd die for me? His words whirled in my mind over and over. There was something between the four of us, something I felt I ought to know, but didn't. I felt the shattered pieces of my heart each time they touched me, but none of it made sense to me. The only thing I understood was that I needed them to not die and stay near me..

I couldn't move as I watched in terror the sheer strength of Arkyn ripping one Wolf off him while pummeling a fist into another's head. But they kept coming, more and more.

I inched forward, needing to help him. My throat thickened with the thought of him hurt. Where were Cassian and Lorcan? I scanned the woods, but only night filled my vision in every direction.

The silvery hue of the moon only revealed the monsters fighting in the small clearing they'd stumbled into, filled with arms and legs and fur and snarls.

Explosive growls, the breaking of branches, the familiar sound of fights came from all around me.

One of the Wolves battling Arkyn flew across from the battleground and slammed into a tree, a second one was sent in the opposite direction. My Vampire was left standing with two more Wolves lying unmoving at his feet, blood seeping from wounds on their flanks and necks.

Arkyn stepped over the dead, having no thought for the Wolves now.

A beast flung itself at him.

"Arkyn," I bellowed, reaching out for him.

Pivoting, he turned to the attacker and snatched the beast by the jaw while still swinging the wolf around from the momentum. He grasped the top and bottom jaws and ripped them apart with his bare hands.

I cringed when I heard the snap of bones, a whimper, and then his body discarded to the ground. Swallowing hard, I stilled, sucking in ragged breaths.

Arkyn's clothes were torn and hanging off his strong body. Blood was splattered over his face, a heavy flow of blood dripping down his arm, but it wasn't his. He moved with too much stealth, showing no response to pain. He was everything I'd seen in those paintings of him as a warrior. That was who stood in front of me now. The epitome of danger, and it was wrong for me to think it, but I loved him this way. My body reacted in a way I never expected when seeing someone so powerful and splattered in blood. I'd feared Vampires my entire life, loathed them. But now...now there was something primal and raw about Arkyn and the others, and I'd give myself to him this very moment if he asked, strip naked and let him take me. My heart beat for him, for Cassian, for Lorcan. All three were mine, that I knew now, and I belonged to them.

My stomach dropped when two more Wolves charged and Arkyn lunged for them with a ferocity I'd never seen before.

He'd fight the devil himself if he appeared, and I was so glad to have Arkyn on my side.

More of the creatures rushed forward, shadows shifting all around us. The foliage behind me snapped. Panic lashed through my chest, and I grabbed a stick from the ground and turned to face the threat.

A figure stepped forward on two feet.

I held my breath, raising the weapon.

Cassian emerged from the dark, dropping a Wolf's head from his grip. Blood dripped from his fingers, and more smeared the side of his face.

My heart soared at seeing him. "Cassian, are you hurt?" I gasped. "Where's Lorcan?"

"He's close, just finishing off some mutts." He smiled, still devilishly handsome, even with death all around us. "Are you alright, beautiful?"

I nodded fast when a rumble of thunder roared overhead, and I jumped. The Dragons were in our land, the woodland burned, and Wolves and Vampires were at war. The world felt like it was coming to an end.

An explosion of growls erupted from all around. Enormous teeth glinted from the woods to my right, glowing silver eyes flashed, and then a monstrous Wolf stepped forward, larger than the others. Black with thick shaggy fur around pointy ears, haunches that seesawed with each step, lips peeled back over long fangs promised death. And I knew at once who it was.

Jacob.

He lingered at the side of the open area where we fought, watching us, meeting my gaze.

I trembled from the fury behind his gaze, at the way his hackles bristled behind his neck as he leaned down in an attack posture. I gripped the stick tighter until my knuckles turned white.

Lorcan emerged from the trees, a scratch down the front of his chest, but it didn't seem to bother him. He was all warrior, shoulders broad, his mouth pulled into a grin, hands balled.

Wolves emerged from all around us, and Cassian snatched my hand, hauling me with him. I stumbled after him, a cry grazing my throat, my gaze never leaving Jacob as he stayed there, watching as his pack came for us.

I was surrounded by the three Vampires.

The Wolves attacked, and the bloody war began again.

Grunts and snarls, blood and limbs were tossed everywhere, the Vampires fighting endlessly, not letting one wolf get near me. They took down beast after beast, punching and breaking bones.

My fingers flexed around the branch, and when Lorcan turned his back with the swarm of beasts, I whacked the stick into a Wolf reaching out to bite him.

A brown beast lunged toward me, muscles rippling beneath its fur. It rushed past them as Lorcan and Cassian battled their own monsters, and I groaned, swinging my branch up and smashing it down over its head.

The weight of it slammed into my side, its sharp teeth latching onto my dress and dragging me. My knees buckled and I staggered as I swung the branch into its side. The damn thing snapped.

But he'd hauled me from the clearing as I thrashed to rip out of his grasp.

He dumped me near the woods, and I scrambled back across the ground until my back hit a tree. The Wolf stretched his spine, amber eyes glowing, a growl rumbling in his chest. Then in a flash, he leapt back into the fight.

Leaving me alone.

Panic caught in my lungs when movement caught my attention from the left of the battleground.

Jacob rose out of the shadows, the sliver of moonlight hitting the side of his face revealing the silver glint of his gaze. Cold. Savage. Ominous. His lips curled upward, baring his teeth.

I trembled, our gazes locked for those few moments. His words from the cave came streaming back to me.

You've allowed those filthy Sinful to get into your head and between your legs, to taint your skin with their touches, with their fangs. I'm going to murder them for ever touching you, Asena. You'll forget them, I promise you.

Retribution flooded his gaze, and I knew one of us wouldn't live through the night. He intended to kill anyone who stood in his way... including me.

Growls and the thump of bodies hitting the ground sounded around us. Except Jacob didn't care. His Wolf eyes stayed on me. Always on me.

Terrifying.

I gritted my teeth, my hand patting the ground around me.

Jacob rushed to me in a few long strides, taking the form of a human, lifting himself, drawing back into his flesh, bones stretching, skin popping as it spread on his naked form.

I scrambled to my feet, my heart in my throat, and I snatched the first thing my hand touched, a broken branch.

He grabbed me by the neck, and I swung the weapon in my hand at his head. The wood just crumbled in my grip.

The bastard smirked.

I was choking, and raised my hands to his iron fingers that were squeezing my windpipe. Digging at his hand, I raked my nails over his flesh, wincing, tears streaming from my eyes as my lungs screamed for air.

He slapped my hands away. "Doesn't feel good, does it, bitch. I offered you everything, a spot by my side, but you chose a walking corpse to fuck you, didn't you?"

I kicked his legs, clawing at his arm to release me, but he didn't budge. My chest burned from the lack of oxygen, the edges of my vision already blurring and darkening.

Behind him, the Wolves piled onto the Vampires, keeping them occupied while he held me.

"Asena, I hate what you're making me do."

Every fiber of my being was yelling for air. I fought and thrashed, but my head felt like it was about to explode.

I *had* to take a breath.

Arkyn, I screamed in my mind. *Arkyn!*

My mind was blaring with the drumming of my heartbeat, with panic that Jacob would kill me.

He growled, fury rolling from his gaze, his fingers squeezing so hard now, the world around me faded in and out. In and out.

Suddenly, Jacob was ripped from me, a blur tearing him from my throat.

I fell to the ground, coughing, trying desperately to fill my lungs. Dragging huge mouthfuls of air into my body, I was shaking at how close to death I'd come.

Goosebumps prickled my arms as I looked up to see Arkyn

and Jacob fighting. The world tilted around me and I struggled to stay upright. Lorcan and Cassian rose up from the massacre of bodies around them. They were bloodied, clothes ripped, but stared over at their commander fighting the pack Alpha, waiting.

Jacob lunged for Arkyn's throat, teeth bared, claws extended.

But Arkyn was too fast on his feet. He sidestepped in the blink of an eye, making it look so easy, but it wouldn't have been for a mortal. In that same moment, he slammed a clawed hand into the Wolf's chest... breaking through flesh and bones... and ripped out Jacob's beating heart.

I gasped at the sight.

Blood poured from the gaping hole in Jacob's chest. He stood there for those few miniscule moments, stunned. When he looked at me, I met the face of my friend who'd I'd grown up with, not the monster he'd concealed. For him I'd grieve, for the fake person I thought cared for me.

Not the monster who fell to his knees then smacked the ground with his face.

Arkyn dropped the heart next to his body and rushed over to me, scanning me head to toe, his clean hand cupping my face. "Did he hurt you?" he asked.

But my response was stolen by a tremendous howl echoing from the woods in the direction I'd run from.

All four of us turned in that direction.

An explosion of shadows raced out from the forest, an army of Wolves, coming right for us.

Darkness crashed over me and a chill of fear ripped down my spine.

"Fuck!" Lorcan murmured.

He snatched my arm and we raced into the woods. We ran for our lives.

5

"Asena," Arkyn called me. *"My love."*

I tried to fight the darkness, but the Wolves surrounded me, blurred beasts, cloaked in midnight, hidden amongst the trees.

"Wake up, Asena," Cassian called. "We're almost there."

I cracked open my eyes and felt the weight of exhaustion in an instant. But I didn't need to worry...the weight wasn't mine to carry alone.

Arkyn looked down, giving me a perfect smile. A smile I never thought I'd see again. I reached up as a tear slid from the corner of my eye. "Is it really you?"

"It's really me." He cradled me against his chest. "You're safe now."

I stole a breath and let his words sink in. "I thought I was dreaming, thought it was all..."

"Not a dream." Lorcan's hand rested on my own, fingers skimming my arm before he gripped my hand and moved forward half a step to lift my fingers to his lips, keeping up with us as Arkyn carried me. "You're with us now...and not even a goddamn war will tear us apart again."

With his words, the past came crashing forward in my mind.

The Vampires.

The Wolves...

Jacob.

I swallowed as acid rose in the back of my throat. Lorcan's gaze bored into my own. "Leave him behind us," he urged. "In the past, where he belongs."

Mystery etched deep in his words. But there were no secrets among us...*any of us.* The mind-connection was stronger than ever before. So strong, I felt every surge of desire that was usually hidden behind a stony gaze.

Lorcan lowered my hand with a seductive smile. "You're ours now. We are your present and your future. We've searched for you for an eternity," he murmured. "And we'll be with you until the end of time."

There was a tremble in his words, a *fragility,* almost like he didn't believe them. But he turned, lowering my hand with such gentleness it took my breath away. Arkyn's arms tightened around me as I scanned the edge of the forest around us.

If I didn't see another damn fir tree for the rest of my life, it'd be too soon. "I can walk." I lifted my gaze to Arkyn's.

There was a flare of concern in his eyes. "Not on that foot, you can't."

Desperation raged. I didn't want to be weak, not now. "At least let me try."

A battle raged inside him, until finally he gave a slow nod and then stopped to lower my feet to the ground. An ache carved deep as my bare feet hit the ground.

"Keep to the grass," he murmured and brushed his thumb along my cheek. "It'll be softer."

I gave a weak smile and took his hand when his touch fell from my face. Arkyn was on one side and Cassian on the other, with Lorcan leading the way. My heart gave a flutter, still I swallowed the feeling and lifted my gaze to the towering mountain in the distance.

A mountain that looked vaguely familiar.

My steps slowed as my breath caught. I jerked my gaze to Arkyn. "You led me here?"

There was a hint of a grin. "We need somewhere to rest and tend to your wounds. What better way than to meet an old friend?"

I glanced at the faint sparkle of lights high up and felt myself drawn closer. This wasn't just an old friend...this was a catalyst. "Domina," I whispered. "You brought me to Domina?"

"Yes." Arkyn surged forward as Lorcan raced ahead, tearing through the night in a blur. "She's long been an ally. A light in the dark, none more so than tonight."

Even though the old woman from the mountain had betrayed me to the Sinful, the pain I still felt was now also mingled with excitement. I turned my head, finding the tiny glitter of my hometown in the distance. I wanted to see her, to find out all she knew. To finally uncover the truth about me...and my past.

"Come on," Arkyn urged. "She's waiting."

I lengthened my stride, swallowing the ache as my bare feet hit the soft grass until the grass ended, leaving way for the hard incline of the mountain.

"My turn," Cassian growled as he opened his arms and reached for me.

I let him pick me up, wrapping my arms around his neck and holding on tight. His long dark hair skimmed my arms. I closed my eyes and buried my face in his neck, taking a moment to let his presence soothe me.

I'd take it all; every caress, every kiss...every glance, and I'd never take it for granted again. Cassian smiled at me when I finally pulled away, his dark eyes glinting in the moonlight.

"I'd carry you for the rest of your life if I could," he murmured, his lips curled seductively.

"I might just let you," I answered, leaning in.

The brush of his lips was perfect, soft and trembling. So much power and need, all hovering under the surface--*just waiting.*

I opened my mouth, taking his lips, and slid my fingers through his hair. I wanted him...I wanted all of them, wanted them to wash the horror from my mind. It was so hard to breathe, so hard to not be terrified.

Sadness echoed in his eyes, an emptiness so deep it threatened to draw me in, like it was a black hole, like *he* was a black hole.

"I must stink like a sewer," I said, and pulled away.

He gave a small chuckle and shook his head. "Even if you did, there's no way any of us would notice. We have you safe and sound, that's all that matters."

He carried me over sharp sticks and hard rocks as we climbed the mountain. The faint feeling of the familiar woven amongst the birth of our love. I stood with one foot in my past and the other in my future, lost to the feel of him, to that dark, sensual scent of seduction. He was the first of the Sinful I'd seen, the first who snatched my attention with his cruel tone and demanding eyes.

He was the first one I'd kissed, the first one I'd wanted...but now, with my arms wrapped around his neck, I couldn't imagine my life not having all three of them.

"Everything okay?" Arkyn moved forward, meeting Lorcan as he stepped out of the shadows.

"She's ready." He glanced my way before slipping his gaze to Arkyn.

With a nod, the Vampire leader took me from Cassian's arms. "You have to walk on your own from here into the house, can you do that?"

My body ached with exhaustion, my muscles trembled, my feet pulsed with agony, but I nodded.

"Her power will find you," he explained.

Cassian's gaze met my own, his dark eyes glittering with desperation and hunger. "I'm okay," I answered. "I can do this."

Surprise. Love. *Devotion.* They echoed from those endless dark depths at my words. With Cassian's nod, Arkyn lowered my feet to the ground. I swallowed the wince and forced my trembling legs to stand strong. "I'm good, see?" I forced the words and took a step.

The sky lightened in the distance, revealing the tops of towering mountains on the horizon. Instead of relief, the sight brought fear. I jerked my gaze toward Arkyn.

There was strain on his face, a tension that hadn't been there before. I surged forward, forcing myself up the mountain. Power rippled through me with every step, meeting my bare feet with a coldness I'd never felt before.

That bitter sting swept along my legs as I stepped into the trees. They followed, not rushing me, not saying a word as I found the familiar path through the trees. That dark energy swept through my middle and raced toward my chest, leaving me breathless.

With every stride, I was drawn deeper into the old woman's power. I knew the second she stepped out of the house carved into the side of the mountain, knew with every ounce of ache left in my body, and as that cold, savage power raced through my chest and along my neck, I strode out from the trees and lifted my gaze to her.

The old woman waited for me, standing outside her house...and for a second, I felt a dance of something else through me, a kind of familiarity I hadn't experienced before. *Déjà vu.*

She smiled and held out her arms as I neared. "Asena, my child."

"Domina." I closed the distance as that sweeping energy swallowed my mind.

She wrapped frail arms around me, drawing me close. Blue eyes sparkled with affection and love as she pulled away and then lifted her gaze to the sky. "Come...hurry all of you, inside, the sun is rising."

Footsteps echoed like a thunderous beat inside me as I followed her into the house. It felt strange coming back here, haunting almost. So many lies and truths lay between us, a chasm of difference. I wasn't the same naive young woman who'd sought her out for information about my parents' murderers anymore. I was someone who held the truth...well, most of it.

Arkyn, Cassian, and Lorcan stepped inside and then closed the door.

"Inside?" The old woman met their gazes. "You'll be safe in there."

Inside? I looked around the neat little cottage built from the rock of the mountain.

"Yes, thank you," Arkyn murmured before he met my gaze and held out his hand. "You're safe here."

"You all are," Domina said and hurried us toward the end of her little home with a wave of her hand.

Lorcan was first, shoving the far wall until it gave a *click* and pushed inwards with a scrape of stone. Darkness waited for us, until Lorcan turned and took a torch from Domina.

Then we were inside the mountain, stepping into the darkness once more. Terror reached out for me, gripping me in its grasp. In a heartbeat, I was back there in the cavern, with Jacob's screams all around me. I stilled, my heart hammering, fear palpable and real, just like Jacob was right here once more-- wanting me...killing me.

"Asena?" Arkyn called my name. But he sounded so far away from me. His cool touch on my arm made me flinch.

Panic flared in his gaze. "What is it?"

My throat tightened. How could I tell him about the terror inside my mind? It wasn't just Jacob. It was the woman in my head...the woman whose memories of Arkyn, Cassian, and Lorcan I saw. Memories I'd lived.

Memories I'd loved.

Memories that haunted me.

"It's okay," Domina grasped my hand and ran her gnarled old fingers along my knuckles. "You see her, don't you?"

Arkyn stiffened. "The other woman, she has memories of the Vampires, no?"

My breath caught as I jerked my gaze toward her. "You know that?"

She just smiled and stepped forward, leading me deeper into the mountain. I followed her, my gaze fixed on the soft amber light illuminating her round, wrinkled face. A face that looked a little familiar.

"We have a lot to talk about, Asena...and the Sinful need to rest." She glanced toward Arkyn and nodded. "I'll take care of her, Vampire. You have nothing to fear."

Domina released my hand as Arkyn took me in his arms. "Come find me soon, okay?" Flames echoed in his eyes, the kind that burned me from the inside.

His hands slid around my waist, fingers splayed wide against the curve of my ass, driving my body against his. Need glinted in his eyes, the kind I could melt into. His lips were made of promises, his smile wicked and enticing. But there was a tiredness, too, an exhaustion that came with the brightening sun.

"Sleep," I whispered as I brushed my lips against his. "And then I'm all yours."

His deep, sensuous chuckle did all kinds of dangerous things to my body. "Asena, my love. You have *always* been mine." He pulled away an inch to glance toward the old woman. "It's about time you learned the truth of that."

With a nod, he stepped back, sliding his hands from around my waist before he turned away. Cassian smiled, and Lorcan looked at me with longing before he, too, slipped into the darkness, leaving me alone with Domina.

"They'll be fine," she murmured and bent to light another torch. "There's beds and pillows back there. We have coffee...coffee, and things to discuss."

This was no simple cavern. As the torchlight grew stronger, more of the old woman's hidden home was revealed.

"I didn't know this was here." I glanced around at a table and chairs, at thick, woven rugs of bright burgundy reds and deep royal blues. The intricate markings and plush fabric drew me closer. "These are beautiful."

"Turkish," she answered, "just like you."

I flinched at the words. "What?"

She just smiled a sad, soft smile. "Sit, Asena. Let me make us some nice strong coffee and I'll tell you all you want to know."

She motioned toward the wooden chairs and thick, heavy throws while she fiddled about in a small makeshift kitchen. Pots and pans hung from hooks embedded in the cavern wall. Filled glass canisters lined the shelves. A flint was struck, kindling set alight. I watched her as she went to work building a fire and setting a pot over the hungry flames.

"That man who came to see you, Emin. He is your real father, Asena. Someone I'd hoped you'd never know."

I clutched the warm throw against me as the cold mountain air settled against my skin. *My father? My real...father?* My head spun with her words. This was a woman who betrayed me as soon as I'd had my back turned. She was the one who wrote to the Sinful when I came to her in confidence, determined to avenge my parents' killers.

So consumed by rage, I'd failed to see the real killer right in front of me.

I closed my eyes as the scent of strong coffee wafted through the cavern. Jacob had killed my parents in a blinding fit of rage. He was a liar and a murderer, playing to my weaknesses...keeping me at his side all that time.

I looked away from her as the first tear fell. Guilt swallowed me, taking me down that long, lonely road of despair.

"I guess we should start this the right way," Domina murmured, her focus on the two cups in front of her as she poured coffee into each one. "With introductions."

She set the coffee pot down, grasped both cups, and walked toward me, her eyes shining with secrets untold.

"I guess this is where you tell me who you really are." I held her gaze, even as she handed me a cup. "And how you've been working with the Vampires all this time."

She just smiled and shook her head. "No, Asena. I meant to introduce you...to yourself, my child...or I should say, *Your Highness.*"

I stiffened with the words, the coffee cup hot in my grasp, but still, I couldn't feel a thing. "What did you say?"

"Your father? Lord Emin is actually the direct descendant of Ottoman, the Sultan of Turkey...and you, being his only daughter, means you are, by right, a princess."

The ground seemed to drop out from under me. Darkness swirled in my mind, and in that emptiness, I saw the faces of my parents, and the ramshackle, fallen-down home I grew up in. "You're wrong." I lifted my gaze. "That's not me."

"And yet you've always known there was something different about you, didn't you? Some underlying current that set you apart from all those around you."

"Like I was on the outside of my life looking in," I whispered.

She nodded and sipped her coffee. "And now you know why. The Sultan was a great man, but a cruel and terrible man. He commanded legions of warriors against the Vampire uprising. You were his pride and joy, Asena. The only hope an unforgiving man like him has."

The way she talked about me and the Sultan's daughter was like we were one and the same. My breath caught. "The woman in my dreams…"

Domina sipped her steaming coffee. "She is you and you are her."

I turned my head and stared into the darkness. "Aelin?"

"Princess Aelin."

"She loved the Sinful?"

"The same way as you love them."

My heart thundered as the pieces slipped into place. This was why they felt so familiar, why I was inexplicably drawn to them. I had her memories of her love…and of her death. That dark pit filled with the squeal of rats filled my mind.

The past reached out, but if she'd died…then did that mean I was destined to die in the darkness, too?

"The answers are at Nightingale," Domina answered. "There, you'll be able to close the circle. There, you can find your future, whatever that might be."

Nightingale. *Home.* A tremor cut through my chest.

I wanted to finish this. I wanted to know everything. I wanted to finally be chosen and sit with my Sinful. I sipped my coffee…waiting for my lovers to rest. I paced the floor, then dozed in the chair, and when I couldn't wait a second longer, I turned toward the darkness.

"I'll be outside," Domina murmured. "They'll know when to leave."

I stepped deeper into the darkness as she left. The icy cavern air danced along my skin, stealing my breath. Fear moved in as I stepped into the darkness and searched for movement.

"Over here, my love." Arkyn murmured, his voice husky, filled with sleep.

I stumbled, kicking stones out of my way, as I headed for the sound of his voice.

"Hold out your hand," Arkyn commanded.

Any other time, I might've been in fear for my life with those words, but not with him, *never* with him. I reached out, fingers delving into the inky void, and met his touch.

"I'm here," he murmured and grasped my fingers. "But it's too early."

He guided me down to the bed he slept on, pressed against the carved-out cavern wall.The mattress gave a *clunk* under my weight. "I'm sorry, I just—"

"Never be sorry for wanting to be with me," he murmured, and drew me closer. "I'd fight the sun itself just to be with you."

I molded my body against his, turning to run my hands along his bare chest. He'd removed his shirt...*what about his pants?*

A low, erotic chuckle rumbled in the back of his throat. "Go ahead," he urged, his voice no longer thick with sleep. "Check if you must."

I flinched, and jerked my eyes to his.

"I read your thoughts like I read your heart, Asena," he murmured, and closed his eyes.

Leaving me lying there...wondering what I'd find in the dark. My heart hammered as I lifted my hand, my fingers skimming his arm. He never moved, never even flinched. I turned my head and looked to the others.

"They won't rouse for at least another hour...it looks like we have time to fill in... *somehow.*"

There was that chuckle again. That low, wicked rumbled that did unspeakable things to me. Heat flared through my core. I clamped my thighs together and trailed my fingers over his hand as it lay against his waist.

My heart was thundering, pulse quickening, as I skimmed along the hard muscles of his chest. I knew what I wanted, what

I *needed.* In my head, it played out...me pinned under the weight of his body, his hands all over me, fangs scraping my neck.

In a bold move, I leaned closer, lowering my hand to exactly where I wanted it to be.

Fingers curled around his hard cock.

He was ready...*so very ready.*

"Careful there," he growled, his voice husky and dangerous.

And it turned me on. "Why?" I slid my grip along his length from tip to base. "I think I like dangerous."

With a guttural snarl, he surged forward, pushing me backwards until my spine pressed into the mattress.

"Is this what you want?' he asked, and shoved my knees apart, driving his body between my thighs.

I was wet in an instant. "Ask...*ask me like that again,*" I gasped.

That dangerous, seductive growling chuckle echoed once more. "Why?" He thrust his hips forward and yanked up my dress. Skin to skin, sex to sex, his hard length pressed between us. "Does this turn you on, Asena?"

My body quivered with anticipation. Just the sound of that terrifying deliciousness made me wetter.

"How about this?" He lowered his head to the side of my neck and kissed my skin before pressing the points of his fangs over my vein. "I want you so bad I can barely think. I can't sleep...I can't do anything but see you with him...*with that Wolf,* knowing what you had to do to save yourself. Did he look at this body?"

He splayed out his hand and cupped my breast, kneading, *claiming.* I arched my back, driving my head into the pillow.

"This body that belongs to me?" Arkyn warned. "Did he touch what didn't belong to him? Did he touch what is *mine?*"

With an infernal snarl, he pushed his hips forward, thrusting against my core, then slipped inside. My seared panties had been long discarded, leaving me naked down there. I splayed my thighs wider as he surged inside me.

Filling me. Claiming me.

Making me his.

"Mine," he warned. "I will fight death itself to have you."

My climax came, bearing down like a violent summer squall. *This* was what I needed, what I wanted. Arkyn's touch was seared into my memory as he thrust deeper inside me, bringing me closer to the brink as he whispered against my neck. "I would die a thousand deaths to have you like this...one last time."

And with a roar, he struck, piercing my neck with his fangs and my body with his desire. I cried out, wrapping my legs around his waist and clawing his back, pulling him into me.

This was my Sinful. This was my future.

This was where I was meant to be. With my Vampires.

For eternity.

6

Never in a million years did I think I'd ever be happy to return to Nightingale Manor. I remembered my first time arriving here, the fear, the hatred, the Sinful greeting us as we climbed out of the carriage, then the girls and I were taken to our rooms. I hated the Sinful so violently then, and now I might shatter into a thousand pieces if they died. My arrival here felt like a lifetime away, like I'd dealt with different Vampires than the ones who'd rescued me, who'd fought to keep me alive.

The old woman's words still hadn't sunk in, that I came from the Sultan's line, that I had royal blood, and that was how I was somehow connected to that other woman's memories. I had so many questions as the thoughts revolved around and around in my mind.

I glanced up at the enormous manor made of black brick. It towered over us, throwing shadows across the woods. I still struggled to believe I'd survived and somehow made it back here. I glanced behind, to see Lorcan at my back, staying close like Cassian and Arkyn were doing. They weren't letting me out of their sights, and I couldn't deny that having these powerful

Vampires being so protective over me had my heart beating hard in the best possible way.

Cassian slid a large palm across my lower back, flooding me with warmth. I looked up at him, at the red splatter of dried blood across his brow, at the way he smiled when he met my gaze.

"Thank you." I couldn't say the words enough times.

"For you, I would tear the world apart. We all would," he said, and I didn't doubt him for a moment.

"Nothing was keeping us from you, Asena," Lorcan added.

When I glanced over at Arkyn, he had the same strong glint in his gaze, the admiration, the fear of what they'd almost lost, and something I was becoming familiar with seeing in their expressions…sympathy and warmth.

These tough, ruthless Sinful showed me a side of themselves they kept hidden from others. I had so many questions, but right now I was ready to head inside and get out of the woods.

Arkyn pushed open the metal-studded front door.

We stepped into the foyer where the entryway to the ballroom lay wide open, and there was definitely a strangeness to returning here. Before I was ripped out of here by those other Vampires, I'd seen the manor as my prison, somewhere I stayed under the watchful eye of the Sinful, but now something felt different.

We stepped into the empty room, and memories flooded me, from the dance with the stranger, to the storm, and Corvina's arrival. So many recollections of times that had made no sense back then… there was still a lot I didn't understand, but I planned on finding out exactly what was going on.

I trailed after Arkyn, who took the lead and left the ballroom behind, marching into the hall. My bare feet padded on the cold stone floor in our marched walk. I glanced around, hoping to see the other girls, or even the servants, but it was quiet, not a soul in sight.

"Do you think the girls returned home?" I asked, my thoughts going to Polaris, seeing her run from the manor before chaos broke out. I hoped she'd arrived home in one piece.

"Perhaps," Lorcan answered.

When we turned toward the study, Arkyn pushed the two doors open and swept inside.

A small group of girls flinched and scrambled to their feet, huddled together as if expecting a monster to descend upon them. I couldn't blame them. Anyone who'd stayed here would forever question what lurked in the shadows.

There were five girls waiting, including Nilsine and Aislinn. No sight of Devika or Sarai, so I assumed they must have snuck out and run away.

Arkyn held himself tall, his chin high, and stared at the girls with the same stubborn expression he'd always carried.

"You are no longer required to remain in Nightingale Manor," he announced. "You are free to leave whenever you want, but I must warn you that a war is raging outside these walls."

No one said a word. He was letting them go after everything. They barely blinked, and stared at Arkyn like they might have misheard him. Nilsine's eyes seemed to almost glint with curiosity, like a cat focused on its prey.

"You expect us to just walk out now? Will carriages be provided for a safe journey home?"

"At this moment, I can't guarantee safety in the woods. You can stay and you will have a roof and food until the battle settles down."

"Unless they came to your door?" she snapped, bravery crossing her face.

"Be very careful, Nilsine." His voice was sharp and bitter, having zero patience for her, then he turned away.

"My lord," a deep voice interrupted.

I swung around, to find a guard approaching Arkyn, whispering something in his ear.

He met my gaze. "We'll be right back."

I nodded and he left, with Cassian and Lorcan on his heels.

When I turned to Nilsine, her face had tightened, her hands resting on her hips. "So, it's official then," she said. "You're the chosen."

I squared my shoulders and tilted my head back. I'd faced monsters that would leave her quaking in her boots, so her words didn't frighten me. "That's none of your business."

She arched a brow at my tone.

Aislinn shoved past her friend, smiling widely, and stepped closer. "What was out there? Tell us everything." The three other girls joined her, and I ignored that Nilsine stayed back. That was probably better.

"The world outside these walls is in chaos," I started. "Wolves are attacking Vampires. Vampires are fighting Vampires. And the Dragons are here."

They gasped, one girl clutching a hand to her chest. "Are you sure? I've heard if they attack, we're already dead."

"The fire-breathing monster who flew inches over my head was definitely a Dragon. They're huge and I would never want to face one. But he wasn't attacking me, it almost looked like he might be targeting the Wolves."

"Polaris had fought Dragons," Nilsin called out with her smug voice, and I nodded, remembering her stories. There was a reason she wasn't scared of much, why she was the one who'd ended up driving the blade into Corvina's heart. She'd lived with terrifying beasts on her doorstep.

"Tell us more," a red-haired girl asked me, so I talked about how large the Wolves were, how they worked in a pack. I couldn't bring myself to explain the whole incident with Jacob. I wanted that buried and long forgotten, just like his life. I mourned my parents long ago and grieved. The hole in my heart would never heal for them, but I refused to give the monster who'd taken them from me any space in my mind.

"Asena," Lorcan called from the doorway, and I turned to see him leaning against the door, his eyes smiling, calling me to him. And I went to him instantly, my legs shuffling over the stone floor until he took my hand.

I glanced over my shoulders at the five remaining girls, unsure if they'd stay or leave. I wished them no harm, not even Nilsine, so I said over my shoulder, "I'd suggest staying here until the woods are safe again."

Before being whisked away, I caught Nilsine's sneer, and I knew she'd do the opposite. That was her choice.

"Where are we going?" I asked, staring up at Lorcan, whose fingers intertwined with mine.

There was excitement crossing his face. "You'll see. We have something to show you." With my hand in his, we descended and followed halls I hadn't visited before. The walls glimmered like they were studded with diamonds and I felt like I was outside rather than underground. Even the heavy smell of soil wasn't present. The flickering torches on the walls lit our path, the stone floor icy under my feet, my skin prickling with cold. I rubbed my arms.

Lorcan halted and swept me off my feet into his arms. I pressed myself against his chest, an arm around his neck, and up so close, I couldn't help but admire how incredibly handsome he was. Those sharp cheekbones, strong jaw, hypnotizing eyes. But his lips caught my attention, and he noticed me staring. I reached up and wiped some of the blood from his brow with my thumb.

He kissed my forearm, sending the flutter of butterflies in my stomach into a frenzy, batting their wings hard. I stared into those deep eyes, desperate to lose myself and forget all the horrible fighting outside these walls.

When someone cleared their throat, I pulled back, my

breaths racing, and I looked over my shoulder. Cassian stood in an open doorway farther down the hall. His smile was one of urgency, and when we reached him, Lorcan set me back on my feet. It was Cassian who now collected my hand and drew me inside quickly.

"This way."

Velvet and gold were everywhere I looked. Garnet red fabric with golden trimmings hung on the huge king-sized bed that could easily sleep ten people. A black chandelier dripping with crystals illuminated golden-framed paintings that resembled windows overlooking glorious landscapes, and did not feel like we were underground at all. Golden sconces with flaming torches lit up each corner. A dresser against the back wall was filled with boxes of jewelry spilling out, a closet with one door open revealed gowns in every color, in silk, chiffon, and lace.

Deep plush rugs ran the length of the stone floor of the enormous room, and I walked toward one, my feet sinking into the lushness, my toes wiggling.

"This is the most beautiful room I've ever seen."

"And it's yours," Arkyn answered.

I turned around as he stepped out from an adjoining door, his clothes already changed from the torn, bloody ones from the battle. He wore simple black pants and a long-sleeved V-neck shirt that made him look taller. The scratch across his collarbone already looked closed over. It wouldn't be long before it was healed and all traces gone.

"What do you mean, mine?"

"This is your room and ours," Cassian answered, his lips quirking like he might break out into a huge smile. "We'll all occupy this room together."

I searched their eyes for laughter or something about mocking me. "Why? I mean... why?"

"You don't want to share with us?" Lorcan asked, his head

tilted to the side, his lips twitching like they were fighting a grin.

"Yes, I'd love to," the response flew out of my mouth. "But you all want to share with me?"

Arkyn laughed, the most incredible sound I'd ever heard, and he closed the distance between us. My heart constricted at watching him stride close, at the joy in his gaze. He meant every word.

His fingers brushed over my cheek before pushing them through my hair, cradling the back of my head. "There are things you still need to understand, and we're going to explain everything to you." The faintest of smiles played on his lips like he was bursting to tell me now.

I nodded, but instead, he turned me around by my shoulders and walked me to the door he'd emerged from.

"First, there's a hot bath waiting for you, then we'll serve a feast."

I twisted around to face him as the shadows cut sharply over his full lips and handsome face. He looked like a prince who'd just stepped out of my dreams. He had the fierceness of a warrior, but the body of a god. And when he touched me, he knew exactly how to seduce.

"Go in now, and we'll be waiting." He offered me a faint quirk of a smile.

So I stepped into the room, which had a large golden bathtub waiting for me. Steam wafted from the water's surface. The black slatted floor and walls glinted from the fiery torches on the walls. Near the tub was a small table with a bowl of fresh blueberries and strawberries, along with a crystal glass of juice. On the other side was another table with several soaps.

A pulsing excitement built inside me. I looked over at Arkyn, leaning a shoulder against the doorframe, his arms folded casually over his chest. My heart was racing, my mind flooded with all kinds of delicious images that involved me, the Sinful, and the bathtub.

His dark lashes obscured his eyes, but it was clear he wasn't planning on leaving, so I turned from him and peeled off my torn, filthy clothes. They fell at my feet in a heap, and I stepped into the bath, the hot water stinging my cuts. This was exactly what I needed. I crouched down and released a long exhale, loving the warmth's embrace. Stretching out my legs, I lay back, watching small soap bubbles slide to the surface.

Everything felt surreal. Yesterday I was trapped, facing my own death, terrified... now I lounged in a golden bathtub, waiting on my every wish to be fulfilled.

Arkyn watched me with those intense eyes, his gaze dipping down to my chest, to the peaks of my nipples poking out of the soapy water.

It didn't take long before he stepped into the room and knelt alongside the tub. He pushed the sleeves of his shirt up before reaching for a bar of soap.

"May I wash you?" he asked in a voice that left me trembling with need.

I nodded. How could I ever say no to such a request? He dipped his arm in the water up to his elbow, and we stared at each other. When he took my arm and started lathering me, gently scrubbing the dirt from my flesh, it was me who broke away first and lowered my gaze. When I glanced back up, a smile was dawning on his lips.

"You're so beautiful when you're shy." His gaze swept over my body in the water, at the curves of my breasts teasing the surface of the water, before he reached over and took my other arm to wash.

"Do you think we're safe here?" I asked, hating that I brought up the topic to something miserable, but it kept preying on my mind.

"Is any place really safe?" he asked as he dropped the soap

into the tub and rubbed his hands together, lathering them. "But with us, you will be safe. That I can promise. Sit up for me."

I did as he asked, and I noticed the warmth spreading through his gaze. His hand gingerly touched my shoulders, my neck, working the lather over my skin, his touch covering me in goosebumps. His hand glided over the tops of my breasts.

My whole body tingled, my mind focused on every point he touched, how my nipples hardened in anticipation.

"I like this," he murmured. "Like that we've finally found you and you're ours now. You don't need to be afraid of anything." His fingers lingered lower over my breast, and my breath hitched.

I arched against his touch and couldn't help but feel a bit smug that I got to share a bedroom with them.

My pulse was racing. "It's not that I'm scared." The words fell from my lips. Words that made no sense when I couldn't concentrate on anything but his large hand slipping over my breast, his fingers sweeping underneath. Squeezing my thighs tighter heightened the pulsing between my legs.

He ran his hand upward along my neck and over my cheek, smirking.

I splashed him.

He laughed, reaching in with both hands and clasping the sides of my head. My mouth opened for him before my mind even caught up with what he was doing. He kissed me hard, like nothing in the world could tear us part. His wicked tongue pressed into my mouth and I drew him in, tasting him. I ran my hands through his hair, drawing him closer, needing him.

A hand feathered down the valley of my breasts and over my stomach, leaving me trembling.

"Open," he gave a simple, harsh command, and I obeyed, widening my thighs.

He reached down, finding the fiery heat he ignited within

me, and his deft fingers stroked me before pressing two fingers inside. My skin was on fire with lust.

I arched and moaned, my body shuddering rapidly with arousal. I'd missed him so incredibly much.

"Make that sound again," he whispered, his voice dripping with desire. He lowered himself over me, taking a hardened nipple between his teeth, gnawing ever so lightly. His tongue lashed out and flicked me, and I was pretty sure I was in love with that devious tongue.

His fingers never stopped, his thumb on my clit, and everything fell from my mind. My body floated on a cloud of euphoria, carrying me away from everything.

My pleasure spiraled higher and higher. I gripped the edges of the tub. Lost in the haze of the climax crashing through me, my toes curled. I shuddered, letting the climax work me, and I rode the orgasm that ripped through me so fast, so deliciously fast. Finally, I let my body slump in the tub, a grin spreading my lips as I looked up at Arkyn.

He sat back on his heels, admiring me. "I adore the way your cheeks glow after you orgasm."

"And I adore everything about you." I reached up and grasped his wrist. "I want to know more about you, about Cassian and Lorcan."

He studied me with his head tilting forward, eyes scrutinizing me like he was trying to read my thoughts. "How much more?"

"Everything," I smirked.

"It might take some time."

"I have all the time in the world."

He climbed to his feet, and I couldn't ignore the bulge in his pants, couldn't stop my mind from going to where he climbed into the tub with me and took me over and over. "When you're finished, I will tell you anything you want."

"Thank you." I watched him saunter out of there. I chewed

on my lower lip, still on a high from the climax, and I intended to make sure he kept his word.

By the time I'd washed myself, my fingers resembled dried prunes, so I climbed out and grabbed the folded towel near the tub.

Once dried and my hair wrapped up in the towel, I walked, barefoot and naked, into the bedroom. A quick look showed the main door was closed, with no Sinful in sight, so I moved to the closet and dug through the dozens of dresses that had me heady with excitement. Never in my life had I seen so many glorious clothes, never mind all in one place.

Finally, I settled on the simplest of the gowns and put it on.

The midnight-dark silk dress fell to my ankles, the fabric clinging to me like a lover's touch. Across my chest and down the long sleeves, tiny twinkling diamonds covered the fabric.

Glancing down at myself, I loved the way I looked, the fabric following every curve. Finding a pair of black shoes with no heels, I fastened the straps around my ankles and made my way upstairs.

Arkyn had mentioned something about food, so I followed the path we'd traveled down here until I reached the dining room. A light breeze brushed past me, pushing against my dress like invisible fingers caressing me.

The doors to the dining room stood wide open and inside, the other girls were already at the table, and the food was being brought out. Platters of carved roasts, fresh bread, churned butter, vegetables. My stomach growled at the sight.

Arkyn was sitting at the table, his attention on me, and the butterflies in my stomach fluttered at the glint in his widening eyes.

"Wow," Cassian said, drawing everyone's attention. "You are...*breathtaking.*"

Nilsine groaned under her breath, but I refused to pay her any attention.

My mouth opened with words, but they were stolen by the harsh shuffle of feet coming from behind me.

Arkyn's demeanor changed in a heartbeat, to one with a callous, vicious expression as his attention flipped to the doorway.

I turned to see what was going on.

A huge guard was dragging a girl into the room and shoved her forward. She fell to her knees before us and looked up at all of us with a smirk.

"Chaska?" I gasped.

7

jerked my gaze to Arkyn, but he didn't look surprised at all. Actually, none of my Vampires did. "What's going on?"

Arkyn just dabbed the corner of his mouth with a napkin and slowly placed it beside him on the table.

"Get the fuck off me!" Chaska roared as she jerked and thrashed, trying desperately to tear her arm from the guard's hold.

"You wanted answers, Asena." Arkyn rose carefully, drawing Chaska's gaze. "I think it's time you understood the depths someone will go to to destroy those you love, all in the name of hatred and jealousy. Don't you...*Chaska?*"

My heart was stuck in the back of my throat. The world seemed to fade away in that moment. There was nothing but us...nothing but this moment.

"I said, *get the fuck off me!*" Chaska howled, and fought like a feral cat, hissing and spitting.

"Chaska?" I murmured. "What is Arkyn talking about?"

She refused to look at me...refused to even acknowledge I'd

spoken. I found myself rising to stand next to Arkyn. My Sinful warrior just glared at Chaska.

"Are you going to tell her, or shall I?" Darkness spilled into Arkyn's words, darkness and danger...*and death.*

"Tell her *what?*" Chaska spat. Her eyes were wide, her hair disheveled. She was filthy, her dress caked with mud and smeared with soot. I remembered her betrayal, her cruel, sadistic laughter as she lied to Corvina's lovers.

"Reveal yourself...your true face, not this face of a liar." Arkyn stepped closer. "You hide yourself behind magic and hate, but no more..."

Chaska just curled her lip, baring her teeth. "You'd like that, wouldn't you? Like to see me reduced to nothing so I can grovel at your feet."

If she hid another face, she didn't reveal it to me.

"Why, Chaska?" I stepped a bit behind Arkyn.

Cassian and Lorcan rose to their feet and stepped toward us. They were my protectors, my warriors...they were my lovers and more than that...they were there.

Always there.

Always searching.

Always telling me the truth...

Truth was a beast in the room now, a hulking, savage thing that grew more and more desperate to evade me. I saw it in her eyes...saw it in the way she twitched and refused to meet my gaze.

A sickening sound slithered out of Chaska's lips, silencing the muffled whispers and gasps of shocked surprise from the others around the table.

"It was *always* you, wasn't it?" Chaska hissed to the floor.

Her dirty, mud-crusted hair hid her eyes, but I didn't need to look into those depths to see her rage...I heard it in her words.

"Perfect Aelin, just like perfect Asena. I hated you then almost as much as I hate you now."

"You hate me?" I whispered, trying to understand. "Why?"

"This was supposed to be mine." Her grimy hair parted as she lifted her gaze.

I stiffened as her dark eyes met mine. Gone was the friend I'd thought I knew...the one who I shared not just a room with, but my hopes and dreams...and my life.

The past rose up inside me. I saw her in the echo, in another time, and through another's eyes. She stood before Aelin, just as she stood before me now, and my heart stuttered a beat.

"You were there," I stepped toward her. "In Aelin's memories."

"Did you think you were the only one fucking special?" she snarled. "That you were somehow *blessed* to suffer again and again over endless lifetimes and endless *deaths*."

Fear plunged deep, cold and cruel, cutting through me like a blade.

Chaska stepped closer, pulling against the guard's hold until Arkyn gave a small nod and moved closer. There was no way she was getting to me, not now, not here. Chairs scraped next to the table, someone climbed to their feet and backed away from the terror in front of us.

"*I* was the one to be married. *I was the one to be chosen!*" Chaska jerked her arm free. "But because of you, I was the one rejected...*by them, and then my own flesh and blood.*"

"You loved them?" The words hurt as they slipped free.

In my head, I saw her with them, kissing...touching...naked and alive.

"Love? You really are stupid, aren't you? It was all about *power*," she answered stepping toward us. "Power that was supposed to be mine."

"Chaska?" Aislinn called her name.

But she never looked her way, she was locked in the past, and the longer I stood there, the clearer I saw the truth.

They don't love you. "They don't love you." The same words echoed from my past as they slipped from my lips.

In that moment, Aelin and I were more than just shared memories...it was almost as though we were one and the same. The same body, the same mind...the same heart.

"I was the one who was supposed to rule. *I* was the one supposed to sit on that throne. But you...you had to go and take it from me, didn't you? You had to tear my future apart with a simple fucking kiss, a kiss that started all this." She gave a snort and jerked her gaze to Arkyn. "He fell head over heels in love. They all did."

My heart was thundering, one pulse trapped in the past and the other in the present.

"So on the night they sent their refusal of my hand in marriage, I took the one thing they wanted most of all."

A growl echoed in Arkyn's chest, low and threatening. In that moment, he was a beast...a killer...*a Vampire.*

"I took you," she continued, looking at me. "And I've been taking you from them in every lifetime since."

"Every lifetime?" I glanced at Arkyn.

"I gave them every opportunity to love me...for them to choose me. Still they prefer pain and death over my hand in marriage."

"We were *never* going to take your hand in marriage, Chaska," Arkyn answered, his tone icy. "Not now...and not then."

*Every lifetime...*the words resounded in my mind. "Every lifetime." I lifted my gaze, but it wasn't to Chaska...it was to Arkyn.

Pain roared in the perfect depths of his gaze. Pain and suffering, the kind carried across a lifetime...*an immortal lifetime.* "I'm her, aren't I?"

"Yes." He answered, so neat...so simple.

I closed my eyes for a heartbeat.

"You aren't just the direct descendant, Asena." His fingers ran along my arm, and a shiver raced along my spine.

In *her* memories, his touch was just the same, so riveting, like nothing in the world existed but them...*my Sinful.*

"You *are* her," he finished.

"No," I whispered, and opened my eyes. "I can't be."

Grief swallowed me. I wasn't that stranger inside my head. I was me...I was real, not fragments of terror trapped in a dark well filled with rats. Tears slipped down my cheeks. I had memories, real memories.

Of my mother...

And my father.

My world shook, a world built on lies. A world that was so fragile it was like sand falling through the cracks of Aelin's world.

You are her...

If I am her, then why can't I remember? If I'm her, then why can't I change any of this? My past...my future...my *life?*

*You are her...*Arkyn's words echoed.

I opened my eyes and met the three Sinful's gazes. Concern flared deep and blinding as the past reached for them, and I slipped, falling through the cracks that divided me from her...

And I was lost in the past once more...

8

I remember...

Crackling energy surged through me like a tremendous wave, crashing into me over and over. My vision shimmied, blurring and coming back into view slowly, along with a strong smell of fire. The snapping and spitting embers had me turning to the marble fireplace with a columned mantel and an arched opening.

Cobblestone walls surrounded me, while I sat on the edge of my bed, staring around the bedroom, trying to bring my thoughts into focus.

I'd been here before, a room pulsing with longing, arousal, love... but those memories were like spiderwebs, sticking to my mind, but too far to clearly reach.

Up on my feet, I moved to the door and emerged into a dark hallway with only torches sticking out from the walls for light. No windows, and the place carried a faint waft of lavender and sage. Enormous tapestries hung from the walls between the fiery torches, elaborate rugs with fiery orange and red hues ran the length of the hall. There were shadows everywhere.

The flutter of my long gown against my legs drew my

attention. A dress the color of the deepest seas cascaded to my ankles in light waves, the corset pulled tight around my chest, embroidered with white swirls. Flowing sleeves made of the thinnest chiffon material cinched in at my wrists with tiny black buttons.

Dark hair tumbled over my shoulders in soft curls flowing over my chest.

With fast steps, I moved toward an open door at the end of the hall, where the bitter wind howled. I stepped out onto an enormous stone bridge that connected two buildings, grand castles with pointed roofs that reached for the starry sky.

I'd walked this passage hundreds of times before, but tonight, my flesh shivered with an unknown, an unseen danger.

Crenellations flanked either side of me on the stone bridge, and I peered over the edge. The dizzying height had me grasping onto the bridge as my world swayed. Down, down, down below was the gate to the castle and beyond lay an open land swallowed by the night.

Voices from the other building drew my attention, familiar male voices.

Arkyn. Cassian. Lorcan. My heart fluttered with anticipation, and I didn't remember moving, but I had already crossed the wide bridge and pushed through the open door to the throne room.

Marble floors, golden columns, And black drapes framing the windows. Only three thrones filled the large room, a place for visitors and meetings of the leaders.

Arkyn sat stiffly on a dark stone throne, his white shirt gaping open at his throat, deep brown hair falling around his ears. Cassian wore a cape, standing with his back to me, staring out the window, while Lorcan turned in my direction with a smile. The fire in his amber eyes was ablaze today, worry thinning his lips. His black hair fell in waves over his shoulders, and my fingers tingled with memory of running them through his hair, fisting it while he kissed me, claiming my body as his. But today, the fire in his gaze burned with fury and something I hadn't seen behind his gaze before... fear.

"This isn't a good time, Aelin," he whispered to me.

But my attention fell on a girl who stood before Arkyn in a beautiful dress made of black fabric that glinted in the flames from the torches in the room. Tight around her chest, the tops of her breasts were pushed high, her shoulders bare, the skirt made of several layers of silk. Brown locks sat on her shoulders.

Chaska. The name floated in my mind.

"Is this her?" the brunette demanded, her gaze swinging toward me, filled with hatred. "Is this the princess you chose over me?"

Her words shuddered through me like shattering glass. Chose?

"What's going on?" I asked, staring from one Sinful to the next.

"Aelin, please leave," Arkyn's command was fierce, but a tremor wove under his voice. Something terrified him.

"No, let her stay." Chaska jutted out an arm in my direction and, behind me, the heavy door shut with a loud clap of its own accord.

I flinched and met her narrowed, pale eyes. Magic. She was a witch. My father, the Sultan who ruled the lands beyond the Black Sea, hired witches, worked with curses. But only the elite were ever permitted to interact with those involved in witchcraft...more specifically, only the males of higher standing, never the females. We were simply kept for marriages, so leaving him one night without anyone knowing hadn't been a hard decision for me.

He'd often said I was his favorite, but he also intended to marry me to the most important family for a perfect union to strengthen his war against the Vampires.

Against my Sinful. We were meant to be enemies, but I couldn't control this damn heart in my chest.

Lorcan was at my side in flash, Cassian moved closer, his cape sweeping the floor behind him.

Arkyn shoved to his feet, glaring at the witch. "That's enough, Csilla."

Csilla, that was her name, not Chaska. Why had I thought Chaska?

"Lorcan?" I sucked in a deep breath and glanced up at him. "What's going on?"

"You, my princess," Csilla began with a shrill voice, "stole these lords from me, stole my throne."

"Enough lies." Arkyn turned to me.

"Then tell her the truth," Csilla insisted.

"Yes, please tell me," I pleaded, not wanting to believe the men I'd given my heart to, who I'd left my family for, were hiding a terrible secret. I held myself stiffly erect, waiting for the words.

Arkyn sighed heavily, his jaw set firmly, then glanced at me. "Plans were set in motion for me to wed Csilla before my visit to your country over the Black Sea. Together with Cassian and Lorcan, we were there for peace talks, but you stole our hearts the moment we saw you in the field. From our first kiss, I knew we were meant to be. A kiss that stayed with me whenever we were apart. We all knew then there was no one else for us. And you felt the connection, too, I saw it in your eyes. Those weeks we spent together confirmed it for us, confirmed there was no one else for us, and we were prepared to share you to ensure we got to keep you all for ourselves. When we returned home, I called off the wedding. It's you we intend to spend our lives with, not Csilla."

A growl-type sound erupted from the girl, who glared at me. "Fucking whore. You slept with them, didn't you, spread those thighs to steal them from me."

"I-I didn't know any of this." My feet slipped backward, my heart pounding in my ears.

"We've spoken with your father," Cassian growled at Csilla. "The marriage has been cancelled."

"Yes, because *she* stole you from me." Csilla's nostrils flared as she took a long breath of air. "Did you know your rejection put shame on my family, and my father has tossed me onto the streets? All because of her," she bellowed, pointing at me. Her words trembled with rage, the room seeming to vibrate around us, dust falling from the ceiling.

Terror lashed over my chest at the power dancing on my skin. I shifted on my feet, my mind whirling to come up with something to say to put her at ease, to make her understand I knew nothing of this.

"I'm sorry," I said. "What I feel for--"

"You don't need to apologize." Arkyn cut me off and stepped down from his throne approaching the girl who had to be about my age, eighteen. Heartache pummeled me to hear the agony in her voice, to hear she was homeless.

She stared up at Arkyn like she might start crying in his presence, beg him to take her. She naturally seemed to lean forward, ready for him to take her into his arms, but he did not. And that was when I saw this was so much more than her family ostracizing her.

She loved Arkyn. Loved him to the point where it had driven her insane to see him with another...with me.

And it hurt to see her in such pain.

The energy in the air changed, the hairs on my arms lifted. Csilla breathed faster, her hands curled into fists.

I stepped forward. "Please, we can help you," I implored.

She turned toward me, mumbling words under her breath, and then all hell broke loose.

Arkyn lunged for her, as did Cassian.

Lorcan snatched my arm and violently dragged me toward the door.

"Wait." My heart hammered in my chest, and I shook uncontrollably. I could fix this if I could just speak with her, make her understand.

I glanced back to see both Sinful thrown off their feet and into the air, held several feet off the floor while blood dripped from their mouths, eyes, ears.

Fear clung to my ribs, choking the breath out of me, squeezing me until I was afraid I might pass out.

"Stop!" I ripped free from Lorcan, my gaze meeting Csilla's, searching for any morsel of sympathy, for something to grasp onto. But all I saw was raw fury and a desperation for revenge.

"Don't hurt them," I pleaded. "Please."

Csilla's nose scrunched up in response. "They hurt me and they'll hurt you, too. They don't love you."

Lorcan grabbed me, hands tight on my waist, and he hauled me backward with force.

But he was ripped from me in seconds.

I stumbled and spun to see him also thrust into the air, bleeding, his limbs kicking, no words coming from his gaping mouth.

A scream fell past my lips. I couldn't think straight and rushed for Csilla, crashing into her, taking her off her feet. We both tumbled to the floor.

"What do you want? You can have anything, just leave me with them." I hated how weak I sounded, it cut me to pieces to see the Sinful slowly being killed.

Unease pricked the back of my neck when, with a flick of her hand, I flew across the room and slammed into the wall. I slumped like a sack of potatoes, the air knocked out of my lungs. I gasped for each breath, all the while searching for a weapon, then saw the glint of metal in Arkyn's boot as he was suspended in the air several feet away, the blade he always carried with him.

My stomach flipped as Csilla rose to her feet as if strings pulled her up and off the floor.

Power slid over me like a slithering snake coiling around me.

Always strike when the opponent isn't expecting it, the words tumbled into my mind.

I scrambled forward and snatched the blade from Arkyn's boot, then hurled it at Csilla's chest, just as I'd trained. All those years of sneaking at the back of the palace with the guards to train pushed me to fight, not crumble and cry. The opposite of what Father had always expected of me.

The blade stopped midflight, inches from Csilla's face, then dropped, clattering as it hit the stone floor.

My mouth fell open and panic throttled through me. I slid my gaze to my men, who remained suspended, blood dripping to the floor beneath them. My hands clenched while my skin crawled.

"Don't do this," I demanded. "Do you want to be with a man who doesn't love you?" My words rolled out so fast, I wasn't sure what, if any, of them made sense. But I'd die before I'd let her take them from me.

She scoffed. "I pity you," she said. "You are caught in their deceit. They will suffer for eternity for what they did to me. They will learn to understand what losing a loved one feels like, over and over and over." She shot her gaze up to the Sinful. They thrust against the invisible hold, their voices just mumbling sounds.

My heart clenched, and a cry pushed past my throat.

"How many times do you think you can lose a loved one before it completely breaks you?" Csilla asked Arkyn. "How many times can you watch her die?"

Her words weren't making sense, but they terrified me.

When she lowered her eyes to me, I slipped back. The

monster behind those eyes had no remorse and I was just a means to make the Sinful suffer. I saw my death in her eyes.

The walls around me trembled, the curtains fluttered with an invisible wind, and she jutted an arm in my direction.

Invisible hands grabbed me and shoved me into the air, squeezing the life out of me. Suspended like my lovers, I could barely see them from the corner of my eye. I thrashed and thrashed, but it was useless. I could barely move, hardly breathe.

Panic sliced through me, and I screamed.

Csilla spoke words I didn't comprehend, her voice rising.

Magic prickled down my arms, and darkness crowded at the edges of my vision. Tears stung my eyes.

"Don't do this. Please, I'll do anything you want, just let us go."

But she didn't acknowledge me, not a word.

My skin itched, and the heat of energy punched through me, spreading through my veins, claiming me all over. Intensity shook me, and I screamed with the terror of death coming for me... that was all I saw as I glared down at Csilla. She was casting a spell on us, cursing us, and I was terrified out of my mind. I was going to die here... Just as I'd found my true loves, I'd die.

A figure rushed into the room behind Csilla, a woman fisting her long skirt to move with haste. The rippling power over me changed to one that swayed between scorching lava to the that of icy coldness.

Csilla twisted around with a sneer.

"What have you done?" the older woman I recognized said. She had long hair just like Csilla and the brightest eyes. Domina, her name came to me. I'd met her once at the local market here where we spoke about the best herbs for healing.

"Help," I screamed but she didn't seem to notice. Her attention was only on Csilla.

She backed away from the woman.

The air in the room thickened so heavily, I could barely draw a breath.

Domina hurled an arm out toward her daughter, sparks of energy crackling over her fingers.

"Aelin," the woman yelled out. "Blood of my blood...heart of your heart. Only one can be saved, Aelin."

My head spun with confusion.

But Csilla moved too fast, turning to me with the blackest of eyes and hurling a bolt of white light toward me.

It struck like lightning into my chest, and I convulsed, my whole body shuddering. I was tossed across the room so fast my world spun, and smashed through the window. Glass splintered into thousands of shards, then I was released from her hold.

Csilla's laughter boomed in the night, menacing and vile.

I plummeted through the night from the highest tower. My screams rang out and I flailed for purchase, for something, but nothing would help me now. Nothing. Death was coming for me.

All I could see was her rage-filled face and those black eyes.

And then I hit the ground.

9

"*A sena!*" Arkyn's roar cut through the past.

My head hit the floor and bounced. Pain followed, spearing through my head like a shard of glass, jagged and vicious. I blinked and tried to open my eyes.

"What the fuck did *you do?*" Cassian was a blur against the flicker of a candle's light as he grabbed Chaska and hauled her to her feet.

But the past was reaching for me, determined to suck me back down.

"Asena, can you hear me?" Arkyn brushed his finger against my cheek. "I can't lose you...not again...not this time."

His voice grew colder, inhuman...*threatening.* I tried to hold onto the present, tried to feel his touch more than I felt Aelin's world as he gently lowered my head to the floor once more and rose to stand. "Break the spell, Chaska. Break the spell, and do it now."

Her laughter rebounded from the castle walls, guttural and haunting. I closed my eyes, listening to the same sickening echo in my head. She'd laughed at Aelin when she pushed Aelin from the tower, laughed and laughed and *laughed.*

Just like she laughed now.

"No," I growled and shoved myself from the floor. "You're not winning. Not anymore."

"Break the spell, Chaska," Arkyn growled and closed the distance.

There was no more asking in his tone, no more pleading. There was just *telling.* He grabbed her from Lorcan and yanked her close.

Gone was the gentle man who'd carried me like I was made of the finest crystal. Gone was the man who'd brushed hair from my eyes and pulled the covers higher to keep me warm. Gone was the man who'd risked it all to save me--*to protect me.* In his place was the Vampire I'd seen in the forest, the one who'd lunged from the darkness to tear apart the Wolves.

The warrior...

The slayer.

"I might not be able to kill you, but I *will* make the rest of your natural life a living hell." He gripped her head and twisted, exposing her neck. Still she laughed, jerking and shuddering with howls of laughter.

With a savage roar, Arkyn opened his mouth wide, exposing his wicked fangs, and struck. Blood spurted from the bite marks on her neck. The stream was almost neon red in my grayed-out world as Arkyn shoved her backwards in one cruel move and then turned his head and spat.

Rivulets ran down her neck and stained her filthy dress as Arkyn swiped a hand across his mouth.

Chaska hit the floor on hands and knees, then stilled, her head lowered, blood draining down her pale skin. "What?" She reached up and pressed a hand across the puncture wounds. "Don't like the taste of my blood, *Arkyn?*"

He looked down at her with a mixture of pity and rage.

"You liked it good enough when we were fucking."

He stilled. Cold, merciless rage spilled into the room.

The air turned bitter, sending goosebumps along my skin.

"What did you say?" he snarled.

Careful words. Chilling words. I shoved against the floor /and stumbled to my feet. But those around the table were riveted by Chaska as she turned to face him.

"You heard me," she snarled as blood ran through the gaps of her fingers.

A tortured noise wrenched from the back of my throat. Arkyn flinched at the sound.

No matter how hard I tried to push the image from my mind, all I saw was them...*together.* His naked body on top of hers...her nails raking the skin of his back, her ravishing sighs echoing in my head.

I turned away, unable to look at him, or her, as Arkyn's voice filled the room. "I *never* touched you, Chaska. You sicken me."

"I *sicken you?*" she snapped. "I FUCKING sicken *you?*"

Something unseen brushed me. I braced against the blow, but Aislinn stumbled backwards.

"You're the one who sickens *me!*" Chaska screamed.

That blast of air came once more, casting my hair from my face...ruffling the skirt of my dress, and I wasn't the only one who felt it.

Lorcan turned his head and looked at me, confusion darkening his eyes. He stepped backwards, and then behind Arkyn. He fell into position like a soldier does meeting the enemy, only, as he stepped again, I realized he wasn't protecting Arkyn...*he was protecting me.*

"You took everything from me!" Chaska roared, tearing her gaze from Arkyn to find me. "My life...*my future!*"

I shook my head and took a step forward. "No, *I* made the mistake of trusting you, of being your friend. And you betrayed me now just as you did then."

"Break the spell, Chaska." Cassian stepped closer. "Break it now, or so help me Hell..."

"You'll what, Cassian? You'll destroy me?" She dropped her hand from her neck, to show the blood coursing from the bite wounds. "I'm already destroyed, thanks to perfect little Princess Aelin."

"Do you really hate me that much?" The pain in her voice drew me closer. I wanted to feel that burning sting of rage, but all I felt was sadness. "You are my friend...I care about you."

She bared her teeth and whipped her gaze to mine. The air trembled as she lifted her hand. "And that's why I'll never break it, why you'll die over and over again. Each time, they'll suffer. Each time, they'll stand there and watch you die."

Arkyn was a blur of movement, lunging across the space to grab her by the arm and yank her backwards. "I'll kill you...right here, right now."

She stumbled with his grasp, her face contorting with pain. "Do it," she cried. "She'll die just the same. Nothing can save her...not you...not me dying. You get what you deserve."

With a savage roar, he shoved her across the room. Her arms flew backwards, palms out...but she didn't fall. She barely even stumbled. Instead, the air grew heavier, charged with some kind of energy. Chaska shoved her hands outwards, pushing the air.

With it came a pulse, like the air suddenly came alive and shoved back.

I stumbled with the blow, as a snarl came from one of the other women. "You pushed me?"

There was a mumble of a response, something snide and snapping before a shove followed. In a heartbeat, there was more shoving, more pushing, more cruel words slung from one to another.

In the middle of the room, Chaska smiled her sadistic smile. "You want hate? I'll give you fucking hate." She spread her arms open wider and closed her eyes, and that same electric pulse boomed through the room once more.

Paintings crashed to the floor, the heavy wooden table moved three inches.

"What the fuck are you doing?" Arkyn roared, fighting the blast of power.

Chaska opened her eyes, and sparks danced as she screamed. "I'm giving you what you want, *aren't I?* Someone to hate...someone to hurt?"

Books tumbled from the falling bookshelves, plates fell from the table to smash against the floor. Screams filled the room, but they weren't screams of surprise or terror, they were filled with hate. The other women around the table turned on each other, lunging across toppled chairs to pull each other's hair and claw and kick.

"Fucking bitch!" Nilsine roared, and spun on Aislinn.

The two women grappled, yanking fistfuls of long hair as they drove each other into the edge of the table. But pain alone didn't stop the fight.

"Enough!" Arkyn bellowed.

But this time, not even the threat of the Sinful stopped them. The walls trembled and cracks raced as another boom shattered the air.

Chaska laughed, throwing back her head and howling until the pulse was tainted with her callous glee.

"Stop this!" Cassian yanked Chaska forward until she slammed against his hard chest. *"Stop this now!"*

But there was no end to this...not now and not from the past. Aelin reached through the echo of time to pull me into her. Memories collided, mine...*hers.* But they were *all* mine, weren't they?

"End the spell, Chaska, I'm begging you," Cassian hissed.

I stilled with the words. Pain and desperation cut deep. My breaths paused, chaos still reigned in the room, but in that moment ,there was nothing but him...my beautiful, powerful *Vampire.*

"You want me to suffer?" He shook his head. "I suffer, we *all* do. Every time we've lost her...and every time we find her. You can't know what that feels like, to live for eternity watching your entire world slip away over and over again. So I'm asking you...*no, I'm begging* you, break the spell, end this once and for all. Tell me what it will take? Money...lands? You can have it all. They mean nothing to me--*to any of us.* Just give her to us," he turned to find me. "She is all we ever need."

My heart pounded, clenching and trembling, the sound deafening in my ears as Arkyn turned to find me...and then Lorcan. I stumbled forward, reaching out my hand. "Chaska, please, I know there's goodness in you. I've seen it...*I've felt it.* End this misery. Break the spell and we can *all* be free."

"Free?" Chaska winced at the word. "I'll never be free, Aelin...so why should you?"

Happiness waited for me here, happiness and truth and love. I met Arkyn's gaze and then Lorcan's, and Cassian's. "You can be happy. There is someone out there waiting for you. I just know it. I can help you. Let me help you."

No, she answered in the past and it resounded in the present. "No."

Blood of my blood...heart of your heart. Only one can be saved, Aelin. The words slipped into my mind. Memories crowded in as another boom tore through the air. Glass shattered and Cassian stumbled backwards.

I fell and hit the floor hard. Shards of glass cut my palm, and the sting swallowed me whole.

Chaska was the epicenter, the eye of the storm, and the more enraged she became, the more powerful each blast of hatred was as it tore through the air.

Through the windows, a fireball burst above the trees and into the sky.

Dragons...

Energy slipped from me, bleeding away like the cut on my

hand. I slumped to the floor as the screams of the others filled the room, the sickening sound of fists on flesh following, hatred mingled with howls of terror.

All the women beat at each other with bloodied fists and hurled insults. But this wasn't them...none of this was.

"Asena!" Lorcan raced toward me as I lifted my gaze to Chaska.

This was all her...

The end.

The darkness...

Fate.

"Chaska."

I sucked in a hard breath and turned my head. Lorcan pulled me into his arms as Domina stepped into the swirling, energy-filled anarchy. The old woman stumbled and grasped the corner of the table, then set her sights on the cause of this terror.

"Momma?" Chaska murmured.

The sonic blasts seemed to die away as Domina stepped forward. "Chaska, my daughter. I'm here."

Shock registered on Chaska's face. There was a flinch, and then a slow exhale. "I thought you were dead?"

"Not dead...*waiting.*" Arkyn glanced toward the old woman as she continued. "It's time for this to end, my sweet girl. Time to cast away the power and the spells. Show yourself to me now. Show me the daughter I loved."

"The one you cast aside, you mean?"

Domina shook her head. "I never cast you aside, Chaska. Not my own flesh and blood. You were the one who left us. Don't you remember? You left us that night, ran out in the thunderstorm, and we never saw you again."

"He never told you, did he?"

"Told me?" Domina whispered.

"How Daddy threw me out of the house, how he said I was a

failure of a daughter, how he wished I'd been born a son, then he might've had use of me."

"No," the old woman pressed a hand to her chest. "He never..."

"But you didn't look for me, did you?" It was the voice of a child who answered, a small, helpless, hurting child and not the cruel woman she'd become. "You lived all these years, Momma. Did you ever once wonder where I was? How much I was hurting, or how much I needed you?"

"In a way, I searched for you." The old woman gave a nod and stepped closer, but she cast a careful gaze at Arkyn. "I knew where you were. I knew what you were doing, and I tried to end it then, just as I'm trying to end it now."

The movement wasn't lost on Chaska as she glared at the Vampire. "Them? You chose *them?*"

"I chose the right side, the *honest* side. Can't you see that?" The old woman held her hands out in front of her, pleading. "There is only loss this way, only pain and suffering."

"So it was *you?*" Chaska murmured. "You trying to break my spell. You trying to sabotage me every step of the way? You the Vampires used to find her."

A chasm of emptiness lingered in her stare as she turned toward me. The air seemed to ripple around her. Her features shifted slightly, and gone were the almond-shaped dark eyes, gone was the splattering of freckles across her pale skin.

What was left was ugly.

Gray pock-marked skin, soft and sagging, sparse tufts of long gray hair.

"Oh, Chaska," Domina cried and stumbled forward. "My daughter...my sweet, sweet daughter."

Domina wrapped her arms around the old decrepit woman. I could only stare as Chaska held my gaze. But the hate was still the same, consuming and controlling, still a well of poison inside her. Poison that spilled out through her words. "I hate you. I wish you were dead."

As she whispered those words to me, I felt the cold brush of death. In the blur of the past, Chaska's mask slipped back into place. The liar. The deceiver. The *murderer....*

Then she lunged.

10

Chaska flew at me, her face twisted, darkening eyes erupting with rage.

My heart barely worked and all logical thoughts rushed from my mind. I threw myself out of her path, into a roll and scrambled back to my feet, pivoting around.

I swallowed hard, fear wedged in my throat.

"Chaska, don't do this." I raised my palms in some sort of peace offering, but she was seething, and I was her target.

In that sliver of a heartbeat, everything around me came sharply into focus. Even with the past weighing heavily on me... Chaska's betrayal, her revenge, her curse, my eyes were wide open. Her throwing me out the window to my death sealed my fate, as it had every lifetime afterwards.

The memories tore at my insides like broken shards of glass.

God knew how many times I'd died and come back! How many times the Sinful watched me perish, grieved, and, by some miracle, found a way to keep going. They held onto the hope of finding me again. That was why they ran the choosings, why they had those lists of girls' names in the books. All those years, all those lifetimes, they'd searched for me over and over, hoping one of the times I returned, they'd hold onto me forever.

But Chaska was never going to allow that to happen, was she?

Fury lashed violently over my chest that she'd taken so much from us, made us all suffer for so long.

The sounds of the other girls fighting viciously fell into the background, as did the Sinful, the Vampires who had always held a piece of my heart even if I didn't know it, but it was Domina who spoke and grabbed my attention.

"Chaska, this won't end well. I tried to make you admit your obsession is wrong. Come with me and we can make this better."

"Fuck off with your reason, Momma," she snarled, glaring at Domina. "You're with them, aren't you? And all of you hate me. But it doesn't matter. Everything will work out now. Everything will be fine as soon as she's out of my way." Her eyes landed on me, seeming to pierce through my soul.

Domina didn't react. She didn't expect anything less from her daughter, it seemed, but she tried to help her. Just like when she'd put a spell on her as I was thrown out the window, a spell that must have brought her along on this insane revolving curse Chaska had dragged us all into.

My gaze dropped to Chaska's fisted hands, at the fiery energy sparking off her skin. Her stiff shoulders rose, her body trembling with rage. A gut-wrenching snarl escaped her lips instead of words.

"Chaska." Domina stepped closer, her head tilted back, her expression stern. "This is enough. Release them, and I'll help you. Come with me."

Chaska's mouth twitched and she was shaking her head. "Stop it, just fucking stop pretending to care. You didn't then and you don't now."

I itched to move, to do something, but the air crackled with energy between the two witches.

Swiftly, Domina raised her arms, and a tremendous gust of wind rushed into the dining room, buffeting us. It ripped at my hair and clothes, the intensity growing, circling Chaska. I stumbled backward a few steps, everyone else frozen and watching.

I couldn't look away, praying with everything I had that Domina could finish this, end her daughter's reign.

Brutal power rushed down my arms, sharp like hundreds of needles scraping over my skin. These witches were powerful, so damn strong that it felt like this manor might come apart at the seams.

An image flashed behind my eyes in a heartbeat.

Me, clasping my throat as acid prickled over my tongue... poisonous and bitter. The glass of water in my grasp dropped and shattered at my feet as I staggered, feeling wrong all over, like my insides were twisting in on themselves.

"What did you do?" My words gargled toward the servant with brown curls who had handed me the glass. The woman who resembled Chaska...who had *been* Chaska. She backed away, her lips slyly crawling into a menacing grin, satisfaction glowing in her eyes.

Arkyn grabbed me into his arms, tears pooling in his eyes at knowing what was coming for me. Agony ripped across his expression, his fingers digging into my arms, trying to hold me for as long as possible before I slipped away.

A heartbreaking cry fell from his lips, a sound filled with drowning sorrow, with a lifetime of misery, and tears fell from his eyes. "Not yet, it's too soon this time."

His agony shattered me, and I reached for his face, shaking, drawing him closer, needing him.

But the darkness came too fast and stole me from his embrace.

Slowly, I was back in Nightingale Manor, my chest splintering, my eyes watering. I tried to shake the feeling, the past that clung to my mind.

Power kept dancing around me, the energy from Domina racing around Chaska's, encasing her.

The air ripped past me, back and forth. I staggered until my back hit a wall, my gaze finding Lorcan stumbling, as well, Cassian on his knees, and Arkyn grabbing onto the throne for stability.

Domina held her daughter in the vortex that tore at the dining room, while the other girls screamed as they dove for cover. Vases toppled, curtains fluttered like flags on a battleground. Chaska was yelling words I couldn't hear above the roaring growls of the storm bursting to life inside the room.

My vision flicked and another image flashed over me like a wild rapid.

Me, inside a cage, starved, filthy, barely able to move. I'd been starved for weeks. The musty smell of a cave flooded my nostrils. I'd been there for so long, forgotten. Life barely clinging to me, but I fought, waiting for my men to find me, to rescue me.

Until Lorcan arrived with the fury of the world. He ripped the metal door off its hinges and scooped me into his arms.

Except it was a little too late. I felt the energy in me fading like a loose thread pulled from my life, unraveling into nothing.

"Aeiln, I traveled the world to find you." His strong voice trembled, his arms tight as he pressed me to his chest, his mouth finding mine. And his cries broke me as I slipped away.

Driven back to reality in Nightingale Manor, I rocked on my feet, tears drenching my cheeks, my chest feeling like it had been cleaved in half.

The Sinful were blurs beyond my watery eyes, cries falling from my mouth at the endless torture, the pain we'd endured. My whole body felt like it had been lit on fire. And all I wanted was to take them into my arms, to take away their heartbreak. To tell them my love was endless and I would fight for them...for us, and I wasn't going anywhere this time.

I pushed myself upright. This was my opportunity to change the past, to end this maddening vortex of horror.

The neverending wind from Domina's power shoved me back to the wall, but I lunged for the dining table, to where the cutlery and plates had tumbled to the floor. Diving to my hands and knees, I snatched a sharp, serrated steak knife, catching the eye of Nilsine, who crouched under the table, her face blanched, terror leaving her whimpering.

We were all pawns, just pieces in this insanity that had to end.

Clasping the handle of the knife tightly, I whipped back around just as another flash collided into me, taking me back into the past.

"Chain her up," a woman in a black cape demanded, her hand clutching a whip. It was Chaska...always Chaska. She stared at me with a smirk as two guards dragged me through a dungeon and shackled me to a wall.

My screams went unheard, pleas wasted on the encroaching monster. She raised her whip, and the leather came down with fury, biting into the flesh over my shoulder and chest. I screamed, my body convulsing, each blow deeper, faster, and all I heard was her vile laughter. The cackle that imprinted itself onto my mind with each slash and flinch of agony.

I couldn't remember how much time had passed, but when someone touched me, I flinched, then whimpered as everything hurt too much. I broke into a cough, my body convulsing with sharpening pain, and my hand came away from my mouth with blood.

"Aelin," Cassian's voice called, and I lifted my head to him. He kneeled in front of me as I lay on the dirty dungeon floor.

He lifted me up as gingerly as he could, while I cried with agony.

"I love you. I will always love you," was all he whispered in my ear. No words of healing or making it through, because he knew how badly injured I was. He'd seen it too many times to believe otherwise.

I stared into those green eyes that always made me forget myself and the world around me, and again, they brought me comfort as I drew my last breath.

Thrown back to the real world, a loathing come over me so abrupt and raw, my insides were boiling.

I hated Chaska more than I could hate anything in this world, more than death itself.

Chaska pushed herself out of the cyclonic wind, her hair wild, eyes black, wearing her haggard appearance.

I trembled with rage, my knuckles white against the blade's handle.

Murderer.

She'd killed me so many times, enjoying every blow, and now I saw the truth. She might have cursed me because of love at first, but that had morphed into hunger for power. She enjoyed torturing me, killing me in every filthy way possible, all for her satisfaction because she couldn't get what she wanted. So, while she said she wanted power, that had changed now, too... she'd now become the darkest of monsters who wanted nothing more than to make us suffer.

Chaska's face reddened, and she turned on her mother. Without pause, she screamed so loudly that my ears felt pierced. I slammed my hands over them.

Domina cried out and collapsed onto her knees, blood seeping from her nose and eyes, then fell to the ground with a thud of finality.

She'd killed her?

"Domina!" I lunged for her, but Chaska stepped into my path, giving me a grim smile.

Shivers wracked my body, because she wouldn't give up, not now or ever.

With her snarl, a sudden explosion of burning energy raked down my flesh. Piercing. Cutting. Stabbing into me.

Rage coiled inside me, dark and violent. The urgency to defeat her pounded through me, to do what it took to finish this.

Movement blurred around me.

Then she charged toward me, the glint of a blade in her hand.

My heart pounded in my chest. I swung my knife out, muscles tensed.

I'd fight her.

Fight to the end.

She thrust her blade toward my heart.

I leaped out of the way and spun on my heels, weapon poised, except she wasn't going for me.

Chaska slammed into Arkyn, who'd been at my back this whole time. She stumbled from him, laughing that sound that reminded me of everything she'd done to me.

Arkyn dropped to his knees, and my eyes fell to the knife plunged into his chest, right over his heart.

My world died in those few moments of frozen time when everything I'd been through slammed into me, the past lives, the Sinful's fight to find me, the horrendous splinter of my heart shattering into thousands of pieces that would never fit back together again.

Rage flooded me so fast, and I threw myself at Chaska's back without thinking. Both of us tumbled to the floor, me on top of her. Only anger consumed me, had me burning up.

Screaming, I drove my knife into her back, over and over. Blood splashed my face, coated my arms, but fury turned me into a maniac. I wanted her to suffer for everything she'd done and ripped from me. To feel every stab, to beg for mercy as I had done so many times. To cry all the tears my Sinful had shed.

"I hate you, I fucking hate you!" I roared, feeling like I'd floated out of my body, staring down at myself...driven to madness.

"Asena," Lorcan murmured, and someone placed a hand on my shoulder.

I paused, my heart beating frantically. Blood covered everything. I gasped for breath and stared down at the mess, the unmoving body, my shaking hand. The knife fell from my grip and clattered to the floor near Chaska.

The darkness clouding my mind dissipated, but fear rushed quickly to take its place.

"He's dead," Cassian said.

I jerked my head up, eyes locked on Arkyn, who had fallen onto his back, red staining his shirt. My stomach clenched, and I scrambled over to him. Falling to my knees, fear was an endless scream inside me, dragging me under with its icy claws.

"Arkyn," I cried, my voice shuddering.

Those blue eyes had lost their brightness, their evanescence. My gut went cold.

He cocked his head to the side to look at me. A paleness crept over his flesh. His hand reached for mine.

Cassian and Lorcan were there, their expressions torn with gravity, with the same distraught feeling breaking me.

I reached for the knife in his chest, but Cassian placed a hand on mine. "It won't make a difference." His words were barely audible.

The tears were endless and nothing but whimpering sounds fell from my throat. I leaned over Arkyn, closer to his face. I remembered all the times he'd whispered in my ear, the goosebumps he left from the lightest touch. The memories of our time together across all the lifetimes bubbling up inside me. "Don't leave me, alright? We can fix this somehow, please."

I kissed his lips.

Faint words escaped his mouth. "I will always love you." His grip slackened and fell away from my hand.

He went silent after that, and I remained so still, it felt like I had thrown myself off the edge of a cliff. I shook with cries, tasting the sorrow, swallowed by its darkness.

There were no words, no anger, no regret, no apologies. Nothing but silence.

I stared over at the pool of blood around Chaska's dead body and thought of what she'd taken from me. Her death wasn't punishment enough. Domina's body lay close by. So much death.

Blood of my blood...heart of your heart. Only one can be saved, Aelin. Her words hummed through my mind, her warning when Chaska had first placed a spell on me.

I didn't think beyond the desperation choking me.

Blood of my blood...heart of your heart.

Domina had given me the answer.

With revived hope, I reached for the blade in Arkyn's chest and wrenched it free, making a sickening sound.

"Asena?" Cassian called me with fear in his voice.

I couldn't concentrate on anything else. I buzzed with adrenaline, and without a single thought, I turned the blade toward me and plunged it into my heart.

Lorcan dove for me, saying words I couldn't completely hear.

Ripples of agonizing pain tore through me, shredding my heart...my flesh and blood, as I lifted a shaking hand, swiped the blood that spilled from the wound, and held it out to my Vampire... Arkyn, *my Sinful,* and smeared it across his lips.

11

"*She's awake!*"

Lorcan's cry called me to the surface. I opened my eyes and blinked into the blur. White blended into gray and then slowly sharpened.

"There she is." Cassian's face sharpened as he leaned closer, dark hair and darker eyes were all I saw.

Blood of my blood...heart of your heart. The words resounded inside my head. A flare of pain followed, carving through my chest, hard at first, catching my breath. What...*what happened?* I tried to remember...

The knife...

My heart...

Arkyn.

I sucked in a hard breath and the faces sharpened around me. Familiar faces, *perfect faces.* I looked to Cassian, and then Lorcan, searching the room. *Where was Arkyn?*

"Arkyn," my voice came out hoarse and raw. I licked my lips and tried again. "Arkyn...where is he?"

"Asena," Cassian started, but the lie slipped from his

560

eyes...that pretense of happiness *cracked,* and what lay behind it chilled me to the core. He gave a shake of his head.

Pain turned savage and biting, like fangs in my heart. An image rose to the surface. Arkyn's pale, lifeless face, his hand so cold to my touch. I closed my eyes and shoved the image aside, but it rose once more, filling the darkness, swallowing me whole.

My Arkyn...was dea—

"Asena."

I wrenched my eyes open at the sound of Arkyn's voice. I didn't care about the pain. I lifted my head, and there he was, standing in the doorway, but there was no smile for me...no rush of love.

There was *nothing but agony,* agony that carved lines into his perfect face, agony that made him take a slow step toward me.

I held my breath, braced myself for pain, and shoved against the bed. Memories returned with a rush. The knife plunging fast, faster than I expected, taking me by surprise. The way my hands shook, fingers trembling, as I swiped my blood on Arkyn's lips.

Blood of my blood...heart of your heart.

Those words raged louder now than ever before as I shoved against the bed and lowered my feet to the floor. No one moved toward me, they barely said a word. Just stared at me like I was the one hovering at death's door.

"You scared us." Cassian smiled and stepped closer, reaching out a hand.

His touch was perfect, strong and gentle as he stepped toward me. I glanced around the darkened room. "This isn't the dining room...where are we?"

"In our dark room." Cassian was the one who answered as he lifted a hand and brushed some strands of my hair from my cheek.

My dress pulled tight as I rose. I lowered my head to the soft blue dress...the same one I'd worn at the seduction dance all those months ago. God, that seemed like a lifetime away. I looked to Cassian, concern flaring deep.

"We had to change your dress," he murmured, searching my eyes.

Lorcan cleared his throat, but he made no move toward me.

"Do you remember why?" Cassian prompted.

My fingers trembled as I lifted them and pressed against my chest. My breath caught as the sudden realization dawned on me. "I died."

Agony ravaged Cassian's eyes for a second.

I died.

That's why the dark room.

That's why he felt so different.

I lowered my gaze to my hand. *That's why I felt different.*

Panic raced, tearing through my body as I shook my head. But as the terror gathered like a building storm my, own voice slipped into my head...*I knew this would happen. I knew the moment I left my home it would come to this.*

"You died for me," brittle words slipped from Arkyn's lips. "Do you realize that?"

He choked on the words, forcing them out like they were shards of glass cutting him from the inside.

I jerked my gaze to his. My own terror raged in his eyes as he came closer. "All the years I fought for you, all the years I searched for you, all the years I prayed to never find you, somehow hoping I might spare you all of this...*of us.*"

Agony carried me away as something slick fell from the corner of my eye. I reached up and swiped the tear as Arkyn jerked his gaze to my hand. A tortured sound escaped from the back of his throat as he grasped my wrist.

A drop of blood was smeared across my fingertip. My tears now ran red. Cassian let out a groan filled with pain as Lorcan just turned away.

"This was *never* meant to happen," Arkyn whispered and gently lifted my fingers to his lips. "But you left me no choice. It was either watch you die once more, or give you…"

He opened his mouth, taking my finger inside. *Give me?* My body trembled…I knew. I knew what he'd given me…the blood of a Vampire.

His blood.

I wanted to scream, to rage and curse. I wanted to unleash the trembling of horror inside me, but I was swept away with a different kind of need.

One that had no bounds. One that tore through my midnight world as blinding as the sun. One that had driven that knife into my heart. One that had risked it all to save him and, as Arkyn licked the drop of blood from my finger, I whispered, "This was always my future. The one I believed in… *the one I wanted.* To be with you. *All* of you. For eternity."

Lorcan spun, eyes riveted to mine.

"This is my destiny," I whispered as that storm raged inside me with conviction. "You fought for me…you killed for me. All those years, all those lifetimes."

Arkyn pulled my finger from his lips and pressed my hand to his chest. "For this moment…I would suffer more."

A different kind of heartbeat filled me. A booming so loud it was almost deafening as I answered, "I know you would." Hunger raged as a flare of pain tore through my mouth.

I winced with the sting and opened my mouth, my tongue skimming across needle-sharp points of fangs.

My fangs.

A guttural groan of desire echoed in the back of his throat as I slipped my hand from his and pressed my finger against the wicked points. A hiss filled the room, one consumed with hunger and need. *Not one of blood.*

My body reacted more keenly and sharply than anything I'd ever experienced before. I closed my eyes and pressed my finger against the pointed ends. "Lorcan," I whispered as hunger raged, "do that again."

The sinister, violent hiss filled the room. I was swept away in its desperation, in its need. *In their need,* and a rumbling growl of ravenous hunger tore through my body. I opened my eyes as Lorcan and Cassian came closer.

Savagery lingered in the dark depths. Lorcan licked his lips as his own fangs grew long.

"Asena," Arkyn growled as he swept his gaze down my body. "We can't wait any longer."

These were the monsters I'd come to claim.

The *beasts* I'd despised.

The *creatures* I'd thought had killed my parents.

Instead, they'd found me...they'd *saved me.*

They *loved* me.

I slipped my finger from my lip and cocked my head to the side, running a line down my vein with my finger.

"Jesus Christ," Lorcan growled, and wrenched those ravenous eyes to mine.

Arkyn chuckled, the sound dangerous and deadly before, in a nonexistent heartbeat, he stepped forward and swept my feet from the floor. "You are a temptress, aren't you?"

"There's no tempting with me." Cassian reached for the buttons of his shirt. "I'm all in." He tried his best, fumbling while unable to take his eyes from me, and then, with a snarl, he ripped the shirt in two.

Buttons flew through the air, but I lost sight of them, hearing them ping against the walls as Arkyn eased me onto the bed once more. Softness swallowed me, chiffon and lace and the touch of Arkyn's hand over the place that once held a beating heart.

"This." He splayed his fingers wide, "is ours...just as ours are yours."

My heart. My body. My mind. *My soul...*I pressed my head

back into the pillow, arching my spine to meet his touch, and reached for the tie of my dress.

"Leave it on," Lorcan growled and worked the buttons of his black shirt nice and slow. "For the beginning, at least."

They wanted me in this dress...the same dress I'd worn on my first trial. The dress I'd used to seduce a man and, as I stared into the hunger in their eyes, I knew I'd seduced a monster instead.

No, not a monster. A Vampire.

Three of them, actually.

Arkyn slid his hand lower until his little finger skimmed the swell of my breast. My nipple tightened and my breath caught. I stared into his eyes, and the smoldering heat there.

"Don't plan on leaving this bed anytime soon," Arkyn snarled.

"For at least the next ten years." Lorcan dropped his shirt to the floor.

"Let's make it a hundred." Cassian shoved his pants to the floor.

His cock sprang free, hard and ready. Heat flared through me like an inferno. The bedsprings howled under our weight and, for some strange reason, that was the most delicious sound in the world.

Echoes of the past surfaced, memories that were not mine and yet they somehow were. It was Aelin who sighed as Cassian delved under her dress and lifted her leg, Aelin who felt the tremors as he kissed the inside of her ankle...but it was me who reached for him, me who parted her thighs...*me* who felt the weight of his body against mine.

Me who kissed him...

I cupped his face, his beautiful, exotic face and stared into Cassian's eyes. "I love you."

He froze, brow furrowing for a second before his eyes widened. I turned to Arkyn and held out my hand. "I love you...I love all three of you. You are my past, my present, and my future."

Arkyn was the first to smile, his lips curling just enough to reveal the points of his fangs. My heart fluttered, even dead and unbeating in my chest, for those few moments.

"You have no idea how good that sounds," Arkyn murmured, lowering his head.

His lips touched my neck, kissing the skin over my vein. "I'd like to say we love you, too...but we prefer our actions to speak instead of our words."

"Damn right," Lorcan agreed.

I shuddered with Arkyn's lips at my neck and Cassian's on the inside of my knee. A moan tore free as the realization dawned. They weren't cold...not their mouths, not their touches. They were perfect...utterly perfect. My dress was shoved higher, making way for desire as Cassian pressed his lips to the insides of my thighs.

"Hell, you're beautiful," Lorcan whispered.

He traced his finger down my cheek and then along the edge of my jaw as Arkyn pushed the cup of my dress aside and slipped agile fingers inside. His mouth followed, taking the tight nipple into his mouth.

Hunger raged in Lorcan's eyes, the kind that stole my breath and nailed me to the bed. I ran my hand over his tight shoulders and speared my fingers into his hair as Cassian parted my thighs.

Lorcan swallowed my cry as Cassian licked along my crease. Heat flared, burning me from the inside. Arkyn grazed the sharp points of his fangs along my nipple as Cassian drew the tiny nub at the top of my crease into his mouth.

The sensation was too much, swallowing and consuming me like a tornado. Hunger raged to the surface, punching out my fangs. Lorcan flinched as he kissed me, pulling away to lick the cut on his lips. The sweet taste of his blood bloomed like a deadly flower in my mouth.

"I'm sorry," I whispered as he smiled.

"Sorry?" he murmured, lowering his mouth once more. His thumb curled around the point of my chin and eased down, opening my mouth as his gaze went to my fangs. "I've never seen something so perfect in all my life. You're perfect, Asena, just as you are."

His own fangs slipped over his blood red lips. Cassian echoed that by slipping a finger down my crease and then inside.

I arched my back with the sensation and that aching hunger roared to the surface.

"You are a *force*," Arkyn snarled, giving my nipple one last lick before lifting his head.

Cassian kissed inside my thigh again before sliding his finger deeper inside me and then out.

Both Cassian and Lorcan gave way for their Alpha as Arkyn settled his body between my thighs.

"And just in case you forget." He shoved the opening of his pants aside, releasing his ready cock. A perfect tear glistened at the tip. The sight drove that need deeper inside me, until it was all I could feel. I opened my thighs wider, my body quaking as Arkyn surged forward, those dark eyes fixed on mine as he roared, "I'll remind you."

Pressure built at my entrance before he slid inside. I punched my hands into the mattress, the sheet balled in my fists as my Vampire let out an inhuman growl and plunged deeper.

He was mine in that moment. *They all were.* Lorcan kissed me, taking my tongue into his mouth, and licked the points of my fangs.

Until the pressure built inside.

Dark rose inside me.

Like a storm desperate to break.

"That's it," Arkyn urged as his body surged into mine.

He was drawing me closer, to something more than a climax, to something hungrier...something more *savage*.

Lorcan broke the kiss and pulled away as Arkyn thrust harder.

I was breathtakingly aware of his power...aware of his strength...aware of the blood that flowed through his veins. The blood of my lover. The blood of my Alpha.

The blood of my *Sire*.

With a ravenous snarl, I reached up, grabbed his waist with one hand and the nape of his neck with the other, meeting the thrust of his hips with my own.

A grunt tore free from him as I flipped us over and slammed his spine against the mattress. But there was no look of surprise from my lover, no panic in his eyes, just pure satisfaction.

"That's it," he urged, lowering his hands to my hips and rocking me forward, finding a new rhythm. He turned his head slightly, exposing his neck.

As if he knew exactly what I needed.

He rocked me harder, driving his cock deeper until, with a grunt, he stilled. In that moment, clarity found me. I struck hard, driving my fangs into his neck. Blood rushed to fill my mouth and slid down my neck.

Arkyn groaned, the sound vibrating in the back of my throat as he slid his arms around me, trapping me to him.

"That's it," he growled. "Take me."

My climax hit me like a blow, tearing through my body and my mind as I swallowed.

I knew what that dangerous need was now, knew the beast that lingered in my hunger and, as I swallowed Arkyn's blood, I knew so much more.

Every battle he'd fought in my name.

Every time he'd found me...and lost me once more.

I saw his memories, the hate, and the hurt.

I saw him...all of him.

His wants and desires and, as the image of my own face filled me, I shuddered my release.

I pulled away from him, releasing my fangs from his vein, and licked the wound, just as he'd done for me so many times before.

"Do you see now?" he whispered. "Do you see who you are to me?"

My heart was full to bursting...filled with his love.

"Me next," Cassian urged.

His body and his vein, ready for me. Arkyn lowered his hands from my waist and nodded. "Go to him, Asena. Take from us all you need. Let us sate your hunger."

Cassian tugged at the binding of my dress, sliding it from my body as I climbed from Arkyn to straddle Cassian's thighs.

"Ride me," he moaned. "Ride me and bite deep, my love."

I did, taking his body into mine, and when my fangs pierced his veins, I was filled with more than just his blood. I was filled with his desperation and loyalty. I was filled with the first moment he saw me in the forest all those months ago.

I felt the surge of excitement as our gazes connected. Excitement he'd swallowed, and the memory of his voice filled my head.... *don't be scared of me, Asena...for I have waited a lifetime to find you.*

I saw the rage in my eyes, the determination and desperation to avenge my parents' murder...how wrong I'd been. I pulled away, licking the wounds I'd left behind as Cassian thrust deep inside me.

Love. That's what I felt from both of them...and that's what waited for me in Lorcan's eyes. My sweet, beautiful Lorcan. He leaned forward, kissing my neck as Cassian gave a shudder and stilled, hard breaths making his chest rise and then fall.

Lorcan kissed the nape of my neck and ran his finger along

my spine as he reached around and cupped my breast. "See me," he urged. "See all of me."

I turned my head as Cassian rose and lifted me gently.

I took my time with Lorcan, biting deep, letting him take me away into the past where he'd searched for me...desperate to find me once more.

Until he did.

He stood in the shadows outside my home with the letter in his hand. *The letter from Domina.* He watched me, aching with desire to break down my door and take me into his arms.

As I swallowed his blood, I knew it all.

And was filled with not just his love...*with all their love.*

12

$\mathcal{A}$rkyn stared at me with captivating blue eyes, holding lifetimes of memories behind them. "The world is still at war, it always has been, but together, nothing can stand in our way. An eternity waits for us to make up for everything we lost. And I mean *everything!*"

A laugh spilled from my lips as a strange feeling of freedom and excitement bloomed in my chest. I'd always thought becoming a Vampire was a life sentence, a prison to my hunger, but in truth, it was no different than normal life where, if I fed regularly, the starvation never set in. Now I had unimaginable strength and endurance and I could live forever. Best of all, I had three Vampires to help me. There was something almost satisfying about knowing death was so far from me...after all the recent deaths, I welcomed the change, embraced it, loved it.

Arkyn's hands tightened around my waist. I reached up and traced my fingers across the beautiful planes of his face, the sharpness of his cheekbones, the fullness of his lips. Lips I lifted myself toward and kissed. Sparks erupted through me like they did every time I kissed my Sinful, and I softened against Arkyn, pressing myself against his muscled chest.

"You are mine now, and no one will take you from us ever again," he breathed the words. "Now it's time to live like you've never done before." He pressed a hand to the side of my neck, his touch light yet dominating.

"Yes." I giggled, unable to stop the fluttering in my chest.

"We will give you anything you desire. Any wish."

"Wish?"

"I will give you the world, have it kneel at my feet, if that's your desire. For you, nothing is too much."

I adored when he stared at me like only I existed, and couldn't help but love that he promised so much.

"I think," Cassian said from behind me, his hands sliding around my hips, his chest pressed to my back. "That it's time we show her." He placed small kisses on my shoulder, bare from the strapless gown I wore.

Breaking free from Arkyn, I turned toward Cassian, pinned between the two Sinful, and looked up at the incredibly handsome Vampire, the devious grin pulling the corners of his lips upward, inviting me, calling me.

"Show me what?" I asked, smiling widely, adoring everything about Cassian's playfulness, how his fingers traced down my arms, how I couldn't stop imagining him lifting me off my feet and making love to me against the wall.

His hand found the side of my face before his fingers speared through my hair, drawing me toward him. Our mouths clashed in an explosive fire of desire, teeth, and tongues, and I gave myself to him, took what I wanted, and together, we were perfect.

"Agree, it's about time," Lorcan added.

Breathless from the wanton desires swelling inside me, I turned to find him standing in the doorway of our shared bedroom, and my stomach burst with butterflies, with an eagerness to reach for him. As if an invisible cord wrapped itself around my waist, drawing me to him, I moved toward him eagerly, and took his hand in mine. I couldn't imagine my life without my Sinful.

"Let me show you." His eyes twinkled as he took me by the hand out of the room and upstairs, my chiffon dress caressing my legs in our hurried walk.

We crossed the courtyard where the night shone brilliantly with stars and the heavy moon hung low, casting the land in a silvery hue.

Footsteps closed in behind us with the other two following. I had been fighting for so long, thinking for years my purpose was only revenge … and now it seemed like my life was the beginning of a fairy tale, the girl who found she'd lived life after life under a curse, only to be rescued by love. And to discover she had already gained the hearts of three Vampires all along but just needed to open her eyes.

It sounded almost poetic, if I hadn't experienced the horrendous near-death experiences and excruciating pain to get here.

Lorcan gestured toward the ballroom. When I stepped forward, my mouth dropped open at the elaborate decorations. There were crystal chandeliers, curtains the color of the darkest midnight, the faintest music from a small band in the far corner, which grew louder as we entered. The room was completely clean after the storm that had torn through here. No other guests were there, just us.

Arkyn gave a slight bow in front of me and offered me his hand in a formal offering that left me giddy. He watched me with that perfect face. He was glorious, made of pure muscle that filled the black suit, resembling a god.

I sucked in a breath and accepted his hand. These Vampires were gods, *my* gods.

He drew me deeper into the ballroom and spun me toward him so fast, I burst out laughing before crashing against his chest, hands splayed over his hard pecs.

"Oh, I didn't expect that," I chuckled.

"Then be prepared for lots of surprises."

The music's beat picked up, the sound twirling around us as Arkyn swept me into his arms and moved with me in a gracious dance of spins and pivots, a dance that came to me from another life when I'd practiced, and now it felt natural. We flowed in graceful arcs, the whole time Arkyn's gaze never leaving me. His smile was hypnotic, intoxicating.

His fingers lowered, circling over the curve of my ass, leaving me gasping. Not a word, but the smirk on his face told me of a hundred and one ways he'd fuck me. And I craved them all, still remembering the four of us together in a moment of complete bliss and tangled arms and legs. I wanted that every night, me and my Vampires.

In a swift move and a wink of an eye, Arkyn sent me into a twirl on my feet, and it was Cassian who caught me, then carried me into a dance of our own.

"I never expected this," I murmured.

"Of course you didn't, but you will find living with us will open a whole new world for you, things you never could have imagined in your wildest dreams."

I couldn't control the effect he had on me, how my stomach fluttered. "You better keep your word," I teased as he spun me right toward Lorcan.

Tall, dark, and handsome, he collected me in his embrace and drew me into a sweeping backward bend, his lips on mine so smoothly, and I kissed him back with eagerness. Then we moved together like ribbons in the wind. Weightless in their arms, I floated on air, unable to remember the last time I beamed with such joy and love and laughter.

His gaze devoured me, lingering on my throat, then the tops of my breasts bounced, and I hummed under his gaze.

"The things I want to do to you," he whispered as he raised me off my feet by my waist then lowered me, our bodies coming together as I slid back to my feet, and the hardness in his pants nestled against my stomach.

But we kept dancing, taking turn after turn with the Sinful, until my feet ached in the heels. When we finally came to a pause, it was still a strange sensation to not be breathless, not have a racing heart in my chest. Something I'd get used to with time, I was sure.

Arkyn, Cassian, and Lorcn stood in front of me, staring at me with a strange look in their eyes.

"What's going on?" I asked.

They each dropped to one knee before me.

For a few moments, I was convinced I was seeing wrong. I blinked back the tears in my eyes, swallowed past my thickening throat, my thoughts tumbling too fast to make sense of this.

"Will you choose us?" Arkyn asked, words so simple, yet they raced in my mind, and it took me a bit to make sense of what he was asking.

"Choose you?"

"Us finding you all this time wasn't about us choosing you, Asena," Lorcan explained.

"It was you accepting us, choosing us to be with you," Cassian added with the sexiest grin.

Their words worked over my mind. This whole time, I'd assumed the Sinful were selecting a girl to be by their side, but I'd had it wrong, so very wrong.

Emotions were a mess inside me, and a tear slipping free from my eye.

"I sure hope that's a tear of happiness," Cassian muttered.

I couldn't stop smiling. "Yes." The word slipped past my lips. "Yes, I choose you three as mine. For this life and every other, for eternity. I choose each of you to be mine."

Reaching down with shaky arms, I accepted each of their hands, then Lorcan dragged me closer and they embraced me, taking me in the middle of them, lips and hands all over me.

I'd always felt I didn't belong, felt different. For the longest time, I'd lived with one mission on my mind, never letting anyone get close, and I'd forgotten how incredible it was to be really loved. I hated crying so much lately, but this time they were tears of happiness and the overwhelming realization that I would never be alone again.

"Come, we have so much more to show you," Cassian grabbed my hand and drew me away in a fast walk, sounding quite excited.

We stepped inside the first room we'd entered after arriving at Nightingale Manor, but the room looked new and redecorated. The chandelier burned brightly with dozens of candles, woven tapestries of orange and red sunsets draped the walls, there were framed paintings of various maps of the world. Four thrones stood toward the back wall. There were three black ones, and between them stood a golden one, crested with diamonds. It stood slightly taller than the rest, elegantly carved with roses on the arms and legs. It was beyond impressive and, for the briefest moment, I thought about how simple my life had become before I came here. Now... I could barely find the words to express how perfect my life had become.

Three Sinful stared at me, waiting for a response.

"Looks to me like you three are needing yourselves a Vampire Queen." I raised a playful eyebrow, before Lorcan chuckled and made that gorgeous sound that completely undid me.

He rushed over and lifted me into his arms. I leaned down and caught his mouth with mine, letting myself drown in his love.

He carried me over to the wall and held me as we faced a gorgeous painting of the map of our land, villages across the sea, and mountains depicted with tiny houses. It was an enormous landscape and there were so many places I wanted to visit one day, like the water renowned for giving you youthful looks, the Dead-Man's Cliff that overlooked the Black Sea in the far distance, and The Weeping Woods, said to be so haunted it left everyone touched.

"All of this land," Cassian said as the other two joined us, "is our territory. Mine. Arkyn's. Lorcan's. And now yours."

Those words affected me more than I thought...me, the girl who was lost most of her life was not part of something so beyond my imagination.

"So we own all this land?"

"Not just own, gorgeous," Arkyn added, his hand on my arm, and I slid out of Lorcan's embrace. "But these are lands and farms and mountains we defend to keep everyone living here safe."

I blinked hard, remembering all the tales back in my home of villagers who pledged their loyalty to the Sinful. That whole time, I'd questioned if they did keep us safe, and they had been true to their word. Our village was vulnerable because of Jacob.

"I want to help you keep people safe," I said.

"And you will soon," Cassian answered.

I strolled over to the thrones, my stomach doing a funny giddy thing where I still couldn't believe I had my own *throne*. I flopped down into my gold seat, crossed my legs, and lay my hands on the arms. With a raised chin, practicing my grace, I asked my three Sinful, "So, what happens now?"

"Now," Arkyn replied, strolling toward me with unimaginable sexiness in his walk, then collecting my hand in his and raising it to his mouth, "now, my Vampire Queen, we begin our lives."

They're made of fire...and hunger. Three Dragon Lords hunting for an ancient bloodline...They came for my sister. But they left with me.

Click here to keep reading with **Chosen by the Dragon Book 1**

Stay up to date with my releases - **click here to join my mail list.**

WHO IS ATLAS?

Dark Forbidden Romance author who loves anything dark. For exclusives and discounts on my online store go to https://atlasrosedarkromance.com/